BLOOD SPORT

CHLOE HIGGINS

ISBN: 978-0-9756171-0-6
Editing by Anisa Worthington
Proofread by Haley Thompson
Cover design and formatting by Melissa Cunningham at Book Love Designs
Interior images: Kellie Armitt
All Right Reserved

PLAYLIST

RUNRUNRUN - Dutch Melrose
THE DEATH OF PEACE OF MIND - Bad Omens
Hot - Avril Lavigne
Demons - Imagine Dragons
The Sound - The 1975
Just Pretend - Bad Omens
Lovely Liar - Stevie Howie
Nameless - Stevie Howie
American Horror Show - Snow Wife
Dicked Down in Dallas - Trey Lewis
I Don't Give A - Missio feat. Zeale
Dirty Thoughts - Chloe Adams feat. Nation Haven
Psycho - "THA REMIX" - Pertinence feat. TEHYA
Dreams - Fleetwood Mac
Iris - The Goo Goo Dolls
Yes or No - Jung Kook
Have You Ever Needed Someone So Bad - Def Leppard
Morally Grey - April Jai feat. Nation Haven

This is for all the girlies who want a vampire book boyfriend who is possessive, has tattoos and piercings, is the best hand necklace, and isn't afraid to pull on a mask and take you whenever, wherever. The blood-sucking is just a bonus.

CHAPTER I

EVIE

Blood spills down the staircase in waves, each drop hitting the next wooden step with a deafening thud. The sound rings out in my ears as I watch the dark red liquid seep into the wood, staining it. The sharp smell of metallic hits my nostrils, almost making me gag.

My heart is in my throat as I stare at the scene, too afraid to lift my eyes to what I know is likely lying at the top of the staircase. This is my house. The home I share with my parents. In what world would this be anyone else's blood but theirs? Still, I'm hopeful that my initial instincts are wrong, and that the waterfall of blood belongs to someone else. Anyone else.

Inhaling sharply, needing as much air in my lungs as possible, I slowly lift my eyes up the staircase, past the pouring blood, until I spot a hand hanging just off the top step. The first thing I notice is the large diamond on the dainty finger. It's enough for my stomach to twist in pain.

No, it can't be. I refuse to believe it is her hand.

But it doesn't take long for my brain to catch up with the reality of what I'm seeing. Not only does the hand belong to my mother, but I see my father's arm resting over her stomach as she lay on her back, her soulless eyes staring straight ahead at the ceiling. Drops of blood land on her pale face, falling from the splatter on the roof, but of course, she doesn't flinch.

My heart lurches into my throat as I stare at the horror scene before me. My school bag drops to the floor beside me as my knees hit the hardwood floor, blood soaking through my leggings. From the floor, I can see how blood-soaked my parent's clothes are and even the deep gashes slashed across their chests. My brain is trying to comprehend the scene, and I can't help but wonder if I'm dreaming or if this is my reality.

What the hell happened while I was at school?

Who would do such a thing to my parents and leave them like this for me to find? The thought only makes my stomach twist with nausea, and I have to fight back the bile threatening to make its way up my throat.

Clutching at my stomach, I lift my eyes to where my parents lay motionless. The whispers of the wind, the pelting of the rain on the roof, and my harsh breathing as I struggle to fill my lungs are the only sounds in the house right now. I want to scream and cry and demand to know what happened to them, but I don't do either of those things. Instead, I burst into tears, cover my face as wetness streaks down my cheeks, and fall to the floor, not caring that I'm covered in blood. *Their* blood.

I feel helpless at this moment, not knowing what to do. I know I should call the police, but my body is frozen in fear and my mind is blank. All I can do is cry and cry. Cry for my parents and what has happened to them. Cry for me because I don't know what my future is going to look like moving forward, and cry because I'm so fucking lost and confused.

Evie.

My head snaps up at the sound of my name. Did I just hear my mom's voice? Surely not.

Evie.

The voice is louder this time as if it's coming from right beside me. I turn in the direction it came from, and all I see is the empty kitchen where plates of food are laid out on the dining table as if my parents were just getting ready to sit down for lunch before they were attacked.

Evie.

I frown, looking around the room. Why does the voice sound like it's coming from inside of my head?

Evie!

My vision blurs at the edges, changing the scenery from the nightmare of that night to the brightly lit room I share with my best friend. My heart is hammering in my chest as I blink rapidly, making sure that this is my reality and not the terrible memory I had to relive in my nightmare.

"Are you okay, Evie? You were groaning in your sleep."

I focus on Rylee who is sitting on her bed against the opposite wall. Her long blonde hair is styled in a light wave over her right shoulder, and her pale gray eyes bore into mine. I can see concern and worry hidden in the depths of her irises, but that's nothing new. Rylee has witnessed multiple nightmares of mine that always end with me waking up to her calling my name. It's something I appreciate greatly.

A sigh escapes my lips as I rub at my tired eyes, shaking my head softly. "I'm okay. Thank you for waking me."

A small smile touches her lips as she readjusts the white and pink summer dress pooling around her thighs. "Was it another dream of the night your parents died?"

I swallow hard and nod, unable to meet her eyes. "Yeah. They have become a lot more... intense these past few weeks. The images have become more vivid. I remember everything so clearly even though the incident happened twelve years ago."

"Maybe your body is trying to tell you something," Rylee says with a shrug, fiddling with the ring on her middle finger.

I raise a brow at her. "And what is it trying to tell me? That I need to figure out who killed them. Rylee, I've been trying to do that for years now and nothing has changed in terms of information. Not even Miles has been able to find anything useful. That I know of."

Rylee sighs, chewing on her bottom lip. "I know. I'm sorry, Evie."

I run a frustrated hand over my face. I'm not mad at Rylee, I'm just exhausted. These dreams—rather, nightmares—are so exhausting that it's hard to focus on much else, let alone control my attitude and feelings. Rylee means well, I know she does, which is why I hate being short with her when she doesn't deserve it. Rylee has been there for me and Miles since the day I found them murdered. I have always thought of her as a sister, ever since I was five years old, and I know my parents felt the same. Growing up, she was always over at our house for dinner, a sleepover, or even just to play in our pool. She is such a large part of my life and I know I wouldn't be where I am without the unconditional support and love she shows me, even when I feel as though I don't deserve it.

She has been there for me through every shit thing that has happened in my life, so I'm sure she understands when my emotions are all over the place. She's amazing like that.

"No, I'm sorry for my attitude," I say softly, offering her a small smile. "You're just trying to help, and I appreciate that."

"You know I'll always have your back," Rylee says. She turns to look at the alarm clock on her bedside table, her eyes widening slightly. "And having your back means I must tell you you're running late for class."

My eyes widen when I see the time on my phone. 9:45 a.m. Shit, my class starts in fifteen minutes and the building I'm in is a good twenty-minute walk from the sorority house. Without wasting any time, I jump out of bed and rush toward my chest of drawers next to Rylee's and pull out a pair of black linen shorts and a white tank top. I may be in a rush, but the weather outside is no joke. If I'm going to be running to class in this heat, I need to make sure I'm dressed appropriately.

Rylee watches from her bed as I quickly get dressed, throw my long hair into a bun on the top of my head, slip on my Nike shoes, and rush out the door with my tote bag flying behind me. I don't stop to say hello to the girls I pass on the staircase for fear that it'll only make me later for class, but I'll be sure to tell them the reason when I get home tonight. They've seen me do this enough times that I'm sure they don't even bat an eye now. It's just part of living in a sorority house.

Once on the sidewalk, running as fast as my tired legs will allow me, I make my way toward the science buildings. The sun is beaming down on my skin, the heat reminding me that I forgot to apply sunscreen before running out the front door like a bat out of hell. Sweat is already pouring down my temples and the back of my neck, sliding down my back.

I'm not one to normally sleep past my alarm, but the nightmares take a lot of my energy and somehow cause me to sleep through the multiple alarms I set on my phone.

Those damn nightmares.

With the science buildings in sight, I can breathe a sigh of relief. As I slow to a walk out the front of the building where my lecture is being held, I glance down at my phone. 10:01 a.m.

Oh, thank God. I'm not as late as I thought I was going to be.

Cool air blasts against my skin when I enter the building, instantly cooling me down as I rush to class which is thankfully being held on the first floor. I don't think I would have the energy to climb multiple staircases in my condition of no breakfast and no coffee. Waiting for the elevator would take too much time.

Yeah, I'm a mess.

Thankfully, I manage to slip into the room without anyone noticing me just as the professor starts the lecture. I snag a seat in the back row, sink low into it, and open my laptop. My energy battery is low for both my laptop and my body. I'm not surprised by that in the slightest. I tend to always forget to put my laptop on charge before crashing for the night. It's a habit I'm trying hard to break.

As the professor begins discussing the topic for the weak, I ignore the low battery symbol flashing on the screen, open the folder titled 'physical health', and pull up a blank page, ready to take notes. Although I don't know how much I'll be able to retain without coffee coursing through my body, my mind is still focused on the nightmare I had.

My education is important to me, but all I can think about is who killed my parents and why the person—or people—responsible were never caught.

A sigh of relief escapes my lips when the professor announces the end of the lecture and I'm able to leave and rush down the street to my favorite coffee shop—Bluebird Co. Now that I'm not in a rush as I was this morning, I'm able to enjoy the sunshine on my skin as I walk among other students heading to their classes or getting food like I am.

The University of Washington campus is stunning. Everywhere I look there are lush trees and an abundance of flowers in the multiple garden beds in front of the sandstone buildings. What drew me to this campus was the main courtyard at the center of the campus which is lined by what feels like endless rows of cherry blossom trees. The few weeks in March and April they're in season make attending WSU worth it.

I don't waste any time grabbing an iced vanilla latte and a slice of smashed avocado on toast before leaving the shop. Not wanting to feel cooped up in a small space, I decided to find a shady spot to sit on one of the many lawns across campus. Thankfully, there are many trees around, so it doesn't take me long to find one with no one under it, sit down to drink my coffee, and finally get some food in me after a two-hour lecture.

The first sip of coffee is enough to instantly wake me up, putting me in a much better mood. It's almost as if I can feel the caffeine coursing through my veins. I lean against the thick base of the tree, pull my phone out of my pocket to scroll through my messages, and take a bite of the avocado toast. I click on the first unread message, which happens to be from my brother.

Miles: Sis, are you going to be home tonight?

I want to stop by and check in on you. Feels like forever since I've seen you.

Evie: I saw you three days ago whenI went to one of your games.

But, yes, I'll be home tonight. I'll see you then.

Biting into the toast, I continue to scroll through my phone, enjoying the quiet time to myself. My college classes have been ramping up lately with the content and assessments, so that has been time-consuming and hurts my brain. On top of that, I have to deal with my over-protective brother, who I swear is always keeping tabs on me no matter what I'm doing. But I still love him despite this and understand his concerns.

All of this is enough to make me want to scream into a pillow, so I cherish these moments when I don't have to think too much or worry. It's just me and Mother Nature co-existing quietly.

Unfortunately, the peace doesn't last long.

A twig snapping nearby forces my eyes away from my phone to see where the noise came from. When I see the person walking toward me, I can't help but audibly groan and roll my eyes. I should've fucking known he would find me here.

"Evie, what a pleasure to see you on this fine day," Roman greets, flashing a smile.

I roll my eyes and put down the half-eaten slice of toast. "I wish I could say the same, but you just ruined my day, so thanks for that."

Roman's brows turn down into a frown as he stands over me. His height should make him appear intimidating, but all I feel is annoyed by his unwanted presence. Ever since we broke up a few weeks ago, this man has been on a war path to win me back, but he doesn't know how to take no for an answer.

"Evie, your words wound me," he says, clutching at his heart as if it were really wounded. "But that's okay, I forgive you. I'm just glad to see you."

"Roman, you've been stalking me for weeks now, so I'm not at all surprised that you found me here," I say, gesturing around at the open lawn space where other students are relaxing in the shade as a reprieve from the blistering sun. "If you're going to stalk me, at least be more subtle about it."

"There's no need for the attitude," Roman grumbles, shoving his hands into the pockets of his jean shorts. I want to gag at the sight. No man should be wearing shorts like *that*, especially not fucking white jorts.

I stare at his face, looking at him dead in his chocolate brown eyes. His hair is shorter today as if he had taken a shaver to it recently, cropping the hair close to the scalp. When we first started dating a year ago, his blonde hair was longer, but in the last few months, he had decided that he no longer liked it long and wanted to keep it cropped.

Each to their own, I guess.

"I don't have time for this, Roman, or you," I grumble and stand to my feet, collecting my belongings, wanting to be anywhere but here with my ex-boyfriend. "I broke up with you for a reason, and you need to accept that and move on."

"I don't want to move on, Evie," he pleads, following close behind as I begin walking away from the tree with no real destination in mind. "I can't live without you."

"You cheated on me," I remind him flatly. "Maybe you should've thought about the repercussions of me finding out before you stuck your dick in that girl at the frat party. Or were you just hoping I wouldn't find out?"

That is enough to shut him up for a minute while I gather myself. A few months ago, my friend, Jaycee, who had been at the fraternity party that night, kept an eye on Roman for me because I couldn't attend since I had a lot of schoolwork to do at the time. It wasn't that I didn't trust Roman, but I thought an extra pair of eyes on him wouldn't hurt. He had a habit of... being flirty with other girls when I wasn't around.

Turns out, I couldn't trust him despite how long we had been together. My friend saw him walk upstairs with a random girl and they returned ten minutes later looking disheveled, the girl fixing her hair and make-up and Roman appearing smug. I don't know why he was acting smug when he was only able to last less than ten minutes, but I digress.

Jaycee told me she overheard the girl bragging about sleeping with him and even hoped that I would find out.

What a waste of a fucking year.

"Evie, I—"

"I don't want to fucking hear it," I snap, whirling around to face him. His eyes widen as he stares down at me, stopping dead in his tracks. "Stop stalking me and move on. I've been trying to play nice when you don't deserve it, but I'm at my breaking point. If you don't fucking stop this, I'll have no choice but to tell my brother."

That threat is enough to make him take a step back.

"You wouldn't."

"Oh, I would," I say, raising a brow as if to challenge him. "He knows we broke up but doesn't know the real reason. If you want to stay on the soccer team, it's in your best interest to leave me the hell alone."

Roman frowns, his unkept eyebrows pulling together. "Now that's just fucking cruel, Ev. There is no need for that."

I raise a brow at him as if encouraging him to challenge me. "Then don't fuck with me anymore."

He scoffs and shakes his head. The evil glimmer in his dark eyes is disturbing, to say the least. "You don't know what I'm capable of, Evie. But you'll soon find out."

I wave off his threat, not believing a single word he says. "Okay, whatever. Just get the fuck out of my face."

Roman stares me down for a moment, his eyes unblinking, before he turns and walks away.

That is all I need for me to turn on my heels and begin walking back to the sorority house, my half-eaten avocado toast in my hand, and my iced coffee in the other. I'm in desperate need of a nap before my online class later this afternoon.

I have barely taken a few steps when I feel an intense gaze on the side of my face, rooting me to the floor. I know it's not Roman because he has already walked away.

No, this is a different gaze entirely, one that has kept me awake multiple nights.

I turn to my right and instantly lock eyes with baby-blue irises that are partially hidden behind locks of curly brown hair. Despite this, their intensity is just as strong as his eyes bore into mine. I swallow hard, unable to tear my gaze away from him.

Holy fuck, this man really is something.

I manage to take in the rest of him as he leans against the side of a nearby building, biting into a bright red apple. His free hand is shoved into the pocket of his black jeans as he chews on the contents of the apple, the veins in his right arm popping under the ink swirling across his skin. The metal ring in his lip catches the sunlight just as the corner of his mouth turns up into a smirk.

The sight alone is enough to make my thighs clench together, my core tightening.

I don't know how, but I manage to tear my eyes away from him—despite how desperately I wanted to continue watching him eat that apple, making the simple action appear sexier than it should—and continue to walk back to the sorority house.

My heart is pounding in my throat and my thighs are slick just by being in his mere presence. Shit, I don't know how he can make me as weak in the knees as he does, but I'm not complaining. Sometimes, I wonder if he can feel the energy pulsating between us, but then I'm reminded of who he is and have no choice but to give up on the idea.

Because not only is he the captain of the soccer team, but he's my brother's best friend.

This means Jaylen Black is completely off-limits and it fucking sucks. He's the forbidden apple that I so desperately want to take a bite from but know I'll be poisoned if I do.

CHAPTER 2
EVIE

I desperately need a shower when I return home from the showdown with Roman. Sweat is slick across my skin, making my clothes feel heavy on my body. I just feel... gross and want nothing more than to rinse off under the spray of the showerhead. Maybe even a cold shower might do me some good.

Especially after seeing Jaylen.

Fucking *Jaylen*.

God the man is the most attractive human being I've ever laid eyes on, and I'm not being dramatic. He's every girl's wet dream. Not only is he insanely handsome and easy on the eyes, but he's so damn charming that it makes my heart pulse so hard in my chest that I'm afraid it's going to crack a rib. Something about him makes me want to rip his clothes off and be taken by him in such a primal way that it makes my cheeks flush and my core ache.

Not only is he good-looking, but he's smart, too. He's studying engineering at WSU with Miles. When I was in high school, Jaylen would talk about his interest in the structure of high-rise buildings and the way they're designed. I often found myself intrigued listening to him talk about buildings he wanted to design in the future, even though at my young age I had no clue what he was talking about. But it was the way his face would light up with joy when speaking about it that would make me smile. It only made me like him more.

The only problem is, he's my brother's fucking best friend.

Miles would blow his top if he knew I had the hots for his best friend. The same person we've known since we were kids and used to come by the house almost every afternoon to play with us. Well, mostly Miles, but I always liked to jump in, especially if Rylee wasn't around.

When we were younger, we were like three peas in a pod. We were always together, and when we weren't, Miles and I would talk about how excited we were to see Jaylen the next day at school. Thankfully, Miles was cool with me tagging along in their friendship. Most big brothers would find it annoying, but not Miles. He always found a way to make sure I was included and never felt left out, which is something I have always appreciated.

As we got older and Miles and Jaylen started to get into playing soccer, to the point where they were on track to get a college scholarship, that's when Miles began to become more... aware of me and Jaylen. It wasn't until I was sixteen that Miles made the point that Jaylen was off-limits to date because he didn't want me to get hurt. At the time, I didn't know what he meant by that and was pissed that he was trying to control who I dated. But when I got to college, I finally understood Miles's warning.

Jaylen is the biggest playboy in all of Washington State University.

It wasn't until I went to my first fraternity party that I understood just how much Jaylen had grown into himself over the years and how much women loved him. At that party, it was clear that multiple women were ready to drop their panties for him in the blink of an eye if he asked them to, and he loved the attention. I mean, you would have to be blind to not be hypnotized by his charm.

From then on, I realized that it was okay for me to be attracted to him, but maybe Miles was right about not dating him. With the way that man smiles and makes my knees weak, I just know he would break my heart if given the chance, and I don't know if that's something I would be able to handle.

When I walk through the front door, Rylee is sitting in the living room with two other girls who live down the hallway from our room. They are watching the news like little old women. The headline reads, 'Another body found in Pullman, bringing the victim count to five.'

Jaycee smiles at me from her spot next to Candie. "Evie, were you able to make it to class on time? I saw you flying down the stairs this morning like a bat out of hell."

I plop on the couch opposite them, right next to Rylee. "I made it just on time, thank God. If it wasn't for Rylee, I would've been much later than I was."

Rylee nudges me with her elbow, and I look over at her. "Aren't you glad to have me as a friend?"

I smile, knowing I'm more than grateful to have her as my friend. I would be fucking lost without her. "Absolutely."

Jaycee's short black hair swishes across the top of her shoulders as she looks at us, her eyes wide with excitement. "It's Friday night, so how does everyone feel about going out tonight? I was told about this new hot club downtown called *Black Rose*. It's supposed to have great vibes and even nicer cocktails. Who's in?"

"Me!" Candie squeals, her brown curls bouncing around in small waves with the movement of her body. Her pale blue eyes are wide with excitement. "I've also heard about that place. Everyone is saying it's going to be the hottest club in Pullman soon."

I raise a brow at her. "Who has said that? I've never heard of this club."

"It's meant to be exclusive," Jaycee explains, her eyes almost black. "You can only get in by invite, and thankfully, I know a guy from my class who was able to get us on the list for tonight."

"Really?" Rylee says, looking between me and the girls. "Well, if we're already on the list I don't see why we shouldn't go. Right, Evie?"

I sigh. I love a good night out hitting the town with my friends as much as the next college student, but I'm exhausted after the horrendous nightmare I experienced and the bad mood seeing Roman put me in. My mind is telling me to decline and stay in for the night with a good book, but my heart is telling me that I should enjoy this night out because I won't be in college forever with these girls, so I should enjoy moments like these when they arise.

"Fuck it," I say with a smile, which makes Candie squeal with excitement. "Let's do it. But I have to shower first and attend my online class, but afterward, I'll be ready for a drink."

"That's the spirit," Rylee cheers, her smile wide. "This will be a night I'm sure we won't forget."

It is almost 9 p.m. when I slip on a pair of ankle boots to pair with the black skater dress I picked out. Rylee wanted me to wear something fancier, but I pointed out that we don't know the vibe of this club, so it's better to play it safe with a more casual outfit to avoid standing out. There is nothing worse than walking into a new establishment you've never been to and having all eyes on you. It makes me uncomfortable, so it's always safer to dress casually than to stand out in the crowd.

I turn to Rylee who is sitting on her bed scrolling through her phone, already dressed and ready to leave in a bright orange romper and black high heels. She looks stunning, as usual.

"I'm ready," I announce, slipping my phone into the small side bag I bring with me on nights out. "Are Jaycee and Candie ready, too?"

"They're already downstairs waiting for us," Rylee says as she stands, slipping her phone into her pocket. "Oh, they said Miles is here to see you. Something about him having already texted you earlier today to say he was dropping by."

I facepalm myself and shake my head. With everything that had happened today, I forgot that he had texted me to say he would be stopping by to check in on me, something he likes to do every week when he gets the chance.

"Right, I forgot about that," I murmur as I leave the bedroom with Rylee hot on my heels.

As we make our way down the staircase, I spot Jaycee and Candie standing by the front door with Miles. He's smiling as the two women talk over the top of each other, clearly excited to see him.

Miles is a familiar face in the sorority house. When I got accepted to live here after all the other accommodations had been filled, Miles and my Aunt Jas—who took us in after our parents' death—helped me move in. He made a point to get to know all the girls who lived in the house. Something about wanting to make sure I don't live with any weird people. Because of this, and the fact that he's on the school soccer team, whenever he drops by, he's flocked by a swarm of women who want to talk to him. I find it amusing because he always looks overwhelmed, his eyes begging me to help him, but I know he loves the attention all the same.

When I reach the bottom of the staircase, Miles's eyes lock with mine, emerald with blue flecks, and his brown hair a mess around his ears. It's like looking in the mirror. He's wearing his training jersey that is covered in grass stains. He smiles, ignoring what Candie is saying as he watches me walk toward them.

Candie stops speaking when I join the small circle they had formed around Miles, her cheeks turning a soft pink as she stares at the floor. I know she has the biggest crush on my brother. It's so obvious how shy she gets around him. He hasn't noticed—at least, I think he hasn't—but I think it's very sweet.

"Thank you for keeping my brother company," I say to the girls with a smile. "I'll only be a moment. I'll join you in the taxi in a bit."

The three girls head out the front door, but not before waving goodbye to Miles, to which he happily returns. When it's just the two of us, I raise a brow at him. "You don't need to check in on me so much. You know I'm more than capable of looking after myself."

"I know," he says with a nod, but I know he doesn't believe what he just said. "Anyway, where are you going tonight? The outfit paired with the ice blonde section in your hair is giving Y2K."

"Hey, I think it pairs well together." I roll my eyes playfully. Two-toned hair is the trend right now, so I don't regret dying a section at the front blonde. "But the girls and I are going out for some drinks downtown." I won't mention the name of the bar because I do not doubt that Miles would find a way to keep a close eye on me, whether it be by going to the club himself or finding out if someone he knows is there and asking them to keep tabs on me. I wouldn't put it past him. Either way, it's not something I want to deal with.

Miles lowers his eyes at me, shifting slightly on the spot. "Be careful, Evie. Make sure you keep a watchful eye on your surroundings. There are a lot of weird people in Pullman."

I laugh, shaking my head. "You're so dramatic, Miles. I'll be fine, I promise. I don't think I'll need to worry about ending up on a true crime podcast when I know I can call you for help if I need it."

Miles nods but doesn't say anything as he stares at me. My brother has always been intense, but lately, he seems... on edge when it comes to my safety. I just thought it was trauma from what happened to our parents, but now I'm starting to think it's more than that.

But I don't have any reason to believe it is anything other than him just being overprotective.

"There have been a few murders around the city, so please just be careful, Ev," he finally says, a lingering double meaning to his words that I can't quite understand. I'm not even going to try. Miles has always been one to talk in riddles at times.

"Of course," I agree, eyeing him carefully, trying to see beyond the wall he has put up between us.

"Okay, you've checked in with me and see that I'm alive, so can I go now, Mr. Intense? I'm sorry I can't stay to talk longer."

That brings a smile to his face, washing away the intense gaze his eyes held moments ago.

"Yes, you can go. But make sure to call me if you need anything, okay?"

I chuckle and lean in to hug him goodbye. "Yes, I will."

As I'm walking out the front door, one of my housemates, Amara, walks past the foyer with a cup of instant noodles in her hand, the steam blowing across her smooth skin. Her pale blue eyes are intense as they stare me down, offering a dirty look as she passes by and heads upstairs, flicking her blonde hair over her shoulder.

I don't know what it is about Amara, but I simply do not like her. She gives me a weird vibe. Apparently, the feeling is mutual.

When I join the girls in the waiting taxi in the driveway, the driver turns up the loud pop music at Jaycee's request, and we all wave goodbye to Miles as he gets into his car. The drive to *Black Rose* is short, but that could be because I was distracted by Jaycee passing around her flask filled with Tequilla, offering everyone shots. I was not about to say no to a cheeky shot before going to the bar.

The driver drops us off at the front of the building, and I'm surprised to see that the line of people waiting to get in is wrapped around the building. Candie wasn't kidding when she said that this place is building its way up to be the hottest bar in downtown Pullman.

Thankfully, Jaycee's source for getting us on the invited list works and we're able to bypass the line of unhappy people waiting in the humid summer air. Rylee holds my hand as we enter the dark venue, the only source of light being the strobe lights from above the DJ deck that is set up in the right corner of the room and the display wall of alcohol bottles behind the bar. The décor certainly fits the name of the venue. The bar top is sleek black wood, red tablecloths cover the black tables scattered around the room, and the walls are red brick, giving the room a gothic feel to it. My shoes stick to the black linoleum floor as we push past large groups of people. I don't even want to know what I'm stepping in right now.

The area may be small, but there is a lot of energy floating around this room as the rhythmic base of the music rattles my heart. The smell of cheap cologne invades my senses as we make our way toward the bar. A couple grinds on each other, giving a clear *fuck me* look with their eyes, and multiple groups of girls dance together on the dancefloor, their hands in the air as the liquid in their glasses splashes over the side with the movement. I almost roll my eyes when I see a guy wearing a thick gold chain around his neck with chunky rings on his sausage fingers, his eyes watching said group of girls with a creepy smile on his lips.

While the girls rush to the bar to order a drink, my eyes drift to the staircase next to the DJ deck that leads to a second floor. What is that floor used for? I can't see much because of the dark lighting, but it looks like there might be more rooms located up there. What could they possibly be used for?

"Evie! What do you want?" Candie calls out to me over the music.

"Just order me whatever you're—" My eyes lock with a familiar pair of ocean eyes watching me from across the room. A shiver races down my spine at the familiar feeling of being watched.

I watch as Jaylen walks up the mysterious staircase with a beautiful woman hanging off his arm, excitement clear in her eyes as she looks at him. But he's looking at me, and I'm enraptured by him. He's dressed in a black long-sleeved shirt with the button undone at the top to reveal enough of his chest that it has my mouth slightly watering, and long black chinos. I've never seen him wear anything with color, but I think it suits him. Dark and mysterious.

His tongue darts out to lick his lips before a smirk tugs at the corner of his mouth. I swallow hard at the sight.

Jaylen and the girl walk around the corner when they reach the top, disappearing into the darkness of the second floor. When I can no longer see him, I inhale sharply, wondering what the hell he is doing here and where he just took that girl.

Is this some kind of weird sex club that allows patrons to get a private room?

Whatever the case, I'm determined to know what is on the second floor. Why? I have no idea. The rational part of my mind is telling me to ignore it and him, but the other more unhinged part is screaming at me to see what is upstairs, and I'm going to listen to it. But first, I need a few drinks in me as liquid courage.

As I turn to walk toward the girls standing at the bar waiting for our drinks, I feel my phone vibrate in my side bag. Pulling it out, I see it's a text message from Roman. I roll my eyes. Why have I not blocked this motherfucker's number yet?

> Roman: If you don't get back together with me, you're going to regret it.
>
> *I'm done playing these games, Evie.*
>
> Evie: Stop texting me, weirdo. I'll block your number.
>
> Roman: If you do, then you won't be around to witness the show.

I swallow hard. What the fuck does he mean by that?

CHAPTER 3
EVIE

The five cocktails—or was it six?—running through my veins make my head feel light and airy, the room slightly spinning as I look across the table at my friends. Jaycee and Rylee are laughing at something Candie said, but their laughter sounds like I'm floating underwater.

I didn't intend to get this tipsy, but after seeing Jaylen and telling myself I would go upstairs to investigate, I needed to make sure I had some liquid courage coursing through my veins. I was going to stop after the third one, but I got carried away with the conversation of our group.

As bustling bodies dance and move around us, all I can focus on is what is upstairs and why Jaylen and that woman haven't returned. I don't know how much time has passed since we locked eyes, but I know it's been at least an hour or two if I had to guess.

What the hell are they doing up there?

In the back of my mind, I have a feeling I know what they're doing.

But why am I so curious to find out the answer? I don't know.

"I still can't believe you hooked up with that guy, Candie," Rylee giggles, her cheeks slightly red from the alcohol.

Candie shrugs, sipping on her fruity cocktail. "It was a dare. Who am I to say no?"

I was too preoccupied thinking about that random text message Roman sent earlier in the night to witness Candie making good on the dare she was given by Jaycee. From what I've heard the girls say, she just walked up to a guy sitting at a table nearby, ignoring his group of friends, and kissed him without warning. Of course, he was more than into it, but Candie made sure to stop after a few seconds, leaving the guy wanting more. Now, he can't stop looking in our direction.

"Yeah, funny," I murmur, not paying the conversation any mind as I stare across the room at the staircase, my fingers itching to go see what is up there.

And that text message... What did Roman mean about watching a show? I'm sure this is just his way of trying to draw me back in, but it's not going to work. I would rather individually pluck out each of my eyelashes than ever consider getting back together with him.

"Are you even paying any attention?" Jaycee asks with a raised brow. Her jet-black hair is pin-straight, resting just above her shoulders. The smoky eye look she went for enhances how dark and intense her irises are and complements her high cheekbones.

"Not really," I admit, refocusing my attention on my friend. "Sorry, I'm just a little distracted."

"Well, we all know why," Rylee grins, sharing a knowing look with Jaycee and Candie.

I sit up a little straighter, cupping the cool glass of the cocktail in front of me. "Why?" The girls giggle, making me frown. "Just tell me."

"We all saw Jaylen walk in with that girl," Jaycee says,

tilting her head to the side. "And we all know your history with him."

I snort, shaking my head. "We don't have a history, Jay. He's my brother's best friend, and we grew up together, that's it."

"Yeah, that's what I call history," she counters with a grin. "I get it, okay? Jaylen is the hottest guy on campus, we all know that. You would be stupid not to find him attractive."

"It's not just that." I sigh, chewing on my bottom lip. "You know Miles would kill me if I acted on my attraction for Jaylen. Besides, I think Jaylen has enough women to worry about besides his friend's sister. We all know what he's like."

The girls nod in agreement, and Rylee leans over to bump her shoulder against mine. "He's a playboy, Ev, so maybe it is a good idea to steer clear of him, for the safety of your heart. But that doesn't mean you can't fantasize about him."

I chuckle. "Oh, that happens more often than you might think."

We all giggle and fall into comfortable small talk, trying to raise our voices above the booming music blasting from the DJ deck behind us. Jaycee is studying to become a veterinarian, Candie is studying business, and Rylee is studying visual arts. We may all be in different degrees and have different interests, but we're still the best of friends and know how to have a good time.

When we all moved in and learned we would be living down the hall from each other, it was the start of a blossoming friendship. When living in a sorority house, it feels impossible to befriend every single girl because there are a lot of house-mates, and not everyone is destined to be friends with differing personalities, so I'm glad that Jaycee and Candie are so easy to be around. We have shared many enjoyable and unforgettable nights out, including this one, and I know how this is going to end. Before leaving, we'll walk until we find a fast food restaurant, order the greasiest food, and then head back to the house to sleep well into the next afternoon, riding out our hangovers.

Could I ask for a better night?

"What's up with Amara?" I randomly ask, my words slurring slightly as my vision becomes a little more blurred from the alcohol. I need to cut myself off after this cocktail, otherwise, I won't be able to leave the club on my own two feet. "I think she hates me."

Candie waves me off with her perfectly manicured hand and flips a lock of brown hair over her shoulder. "I'm sure she doesn't hate you, Ev. She probably just doesn't know you very well."

"We've lived in the same house for nearly three years. You'd think we'd know each other pretty well by now," I deadpan.

"Maybe she's jealous of you," Jaycee offers with a shrug. "From what I know about Amara, she feels threatened by anyone who is on her level, whether that is looks or intelligence. I think you fit into that category."

I laugh and shake my head at the ridiculousness of that statement. "There is no way any of that is true."

"Who knows?" Jaycee says with a knowing smile. "Or maybe Amara just doesn't like anyone, so it's not something you need to stress yourself out over."

I hum, chewing on my bottom lip. Ever since my first day in the house with the new girls who arrived at the same time as me, Amara being one of them, we have never been able to get on with each other. Every time I try to start a conversation or be nice, Amara will always shoot me a dirty look and leave immediately. At first, it didn't get on my nerves, but now it does.

Why doesn't she like me? That's all I want to know.

26

"You're right," I say with a sharp exhale. "Fuck her."

The girls laugh in unison as Candie says, "Yeah, fuck her!"

A moment later, I excuse myself to go to the bathroom, making sure to take my side bag with me. Jaycee does the same, saying that she is going to meet up with the mystery guy who got us into the bar. I manage to find the bathroom down a small corridor near our table, being met by many drunk girls. Some are sharing a cubical, laughing or gagging, and others are standing at the sinks crying and holding each other. It made for great entertainment while I did my business and washed my hands.

I leave the bathroom, stand in the corridor, and watch my friends, smiling at the sight of seeing them so happy. But then my attention drifts back to Jaylen and the gnawing curiosity that has been pushed to the back of my mind for the past couple of hours. Maybe this is the perfect opportunity for me to slip away from the group and see what is going on upstairs. Since I saw Jaylen go up there, I have spotted multiple people also going up there.

I need to know what is on that floor, and I need to know now.

I round the corridor and slip into the throng of people nearby so as not to be spotted by my friends. The last thing I need is for them to want to follow me or talk me out of following Jaylen. It's not what I want to hear right now.

Once through the crowd of people, I reach the wooden staircase leading to the second floor. With my hand on the railing and one foot on the first step, I look up, having a flash-back of the night my parents died before quickly shaking it off and walking up the steps, hoping and praying none of my friends spot me.

When I reach the top, I'm met with a long hallway with multiple doors on each side. The walls are black to match the theme downstairs, and it feels eery and quiet, despite how many people I saw walk up here. As I walk further down the hallway, the quietness shifts and I'm met with loud moaning. My eyes widen as my steps falter.

Okay, maybe this place is a weird sex club that only some people are privy to knowing.

I hold my breath as I continue to walk, not knowing what to do from here. As I pass by the doors, the windows that accompany them are covered by thick black drapes, blocking me from viewing what is happening inside. As curious as I am about what is going on up here and possibly finding where Jaylen went, it would be rude of me to peek inside if given the chance. This seems like a private area, so I'm sure the people inside don't want a peeping Tom looking through the window.

I wonder which room Jaylen is in and if the soft moans filtering through my ears are coming from the woman he brought up here. My cheeks flare at the thought.

Not now, Evie, I scold myself.

As I near the end of the hallway, the room on the right surprisingly has the drapes open. I can see into the room from where I am, a red glow against the black wall. I inhale sharply, not wanting to be seen or heard because I have a feeling I'm not meant to be up here unless I use one of the rooms.

With my heart in my throat, I walk up to the window and peer inside, expecting to see strangers. However, what I witness is much more shocking. Not only do I find Jaylen on a large bed with black bedding, but I found him with the woman he brought up here riding his cock hard and fast, her large breasts bouncing wildly with the movement. The woman has her mouth open wide, groaning as she grips Jaylen's thighs for support.

But that isn't the shocking part.

No, the shocking part that has my mouth hanging open

and my eyes wide with fear is the fact that Jaylen has his face buried in the woman's neck, blood pouring down her sternum and onto his bare chest, mixing with the light sheen of sweat on both of their skin.

What the *fuck*?

A sharp gasp leaves my throat, my hand flying up to keep it in my mouth, but I'm too slow. Somehow, Jaylen hears the noise because his head turns in my direction, his curly hair falling over his eyes, damp with sweat, and crimson blood smeared across his cheeks. But I see them... his *eyes*.

They're fucking *red*.

And not only that, but he has razor-sharp fangs that are dripping with blood—the blood of that woman—while she rides him like he's a fucking mechanical bull, not taking notice of my presence, her eyes focused on him while he watches me intently.

"Holy shit," I breathe, staggering backward.

CHAPTER 4

EVIE

I don't think I've ever known fear quite like this.

Yes, I saw the murdered bodies of my parents which still haunts me to this day, but I have never seen anything like *this*.

It doesn't feel like I'm in my body as Jaylen and I stare at each other, the air around us tense and frigid. I want to scream or yell for help, but it feels as if my lips are glued together, unable to make even the smallest sound. And by the look of horror on Jaylen's face, I can tell he feels the same way.

I don't even know what to think or feel about what I just witnessed, but I do know one thing—I thought sucking people's blood and being undead only existed in the movies. But is he really what I think he is? Or is he just into some weird shit? I'm hoping it's the latter because I don't know what I will do if it is the former.

There is no way in *hell* that my brother's best friend is a *vampire*.

I refuse to believe it, even if the evidence is staring me right in the face.

I take another shaky step back, my heart ready to beat out of my chest. This makes something click within Jaylen because, in the blink of an eye, he is standing in front of me, somehow wearing pants.

How the fuck did he move so quickly?

Blood streaks stain his sweaty chest, but that's not what I'm focused on. All I can do is stare Jaylen in the eye, his irises now back to the normal shade of baby blue I'm used to seeing. His chest is heaving as he inhales sharply, staring down at me, using his 6'4 height to his advantage.

After what I just witnessed, I should feel more intimidated, but not with Jaylen. I've known this man for most of my life, and even though he's covered in blood, I don't feel scared to be in his presence. I don't know how to explain it, but even after witnessing him suck the blood of a random girl, I'm not afraid of him. If anything, I'm confused as fuck.

"Evie," he drawls, his voice raspy and filled with remaining lust. The red light above the bed that illuminates the room makes him appear menacing. Darker. "What the hell are you doing here?"

I swallow hard, peering past him into the room. The girl is just sitting on the bed, staring down at her pink nails, acting as if she wasn't just riding Jaylen and letting him suck on her neck. The thought sends a shiver down my spine.

"I-I," I stammer, trying to find my voice. "I was looking for the bathroom." There is no way in hell I came up here in search of him, only to find him in *that* position.

Jaylen doesn't say anything, he just stares down at me through the curls hanging over his eyes. I have so many questions I want to ask him, but my head is fuzzy from the alcohol and trying to come to terms with what just happened.

Knowing Jaylen for as long as I have, how did I not know about this part of his life?

I suppose, why would he tell *me* about what he likes to do

in the bedroom and with whom? It's none of my business, and yet, I'm curious as hell.

"Well, you need to leave. Now," he says, his eyes boring into mine. I can feel something—words—pulsing at my temples as he says, "You didn't see any of this, okay? What you just saw didn't happen."

I frown. "Jaylen, what the fuck are you saying? I know what I saw was real. I may be tipsy, but you sucking that girl's blood was as clear as day."

His eyes widen as he takes a step back. "What the..."

I use the brief moment of shock as my getaway car from the situation. Being in Jaylen's presence is suffocating and tense, especially when he looks like this—bloody, sweating, and still somehow stunning—and images of him drinking blood flash in my mind, the memory of his sharp fangs, that are now seemingly gone, a reminder of the gravity of the situation at hand.

"You're right, I need to leave," I say quickly, my head swarming with too much information for my tipsy ass to handle.

As swiftly as I can, I turn on my heels and begin running down the long hallway until I reach the top of the staircase. I don't hear Jaylen's footsteps behind me or hear his voice telling me to stop, so I continue down the staircase and rush to the front door. I can't face my friends after what just happened, so the easiest thing for me to do is get the hell out of here and explain everything later.

Once I'm out on the sidewalk, the warm air sticking to my skin, I pull out my phone to send a text message to Rylee.

> Evie: I had to leave because I'm not feeling well, but I'll see you at home.

Shoving my phone back into my side bag, I swing it over my shoulder and begin the walk home. I could use the fresh air on my face, despite how humid it is, and allow it to clear my head because God knows I have too many thoughts swirling around up there.

As I walk with my arms wrapped around my waist, all I can think about is Jaylen and what the fuck just happened back there. When Jaycee said this club was exclusive, I now know why. It's potentially a place for... *vampires* to feed off humans. And if that's not the case and I'm wrong, then it's just a club that allows people with a blood kink to let off some steam.

Growing up, I used to read about vampires in novels that my mom would buy for Miles and me; although, I was more into it than he was. I learned all the myths and lore that there was to know, and even read *Dracula* by Bram Stoker too many times to count. But that's where it ended. I never thought that they existed in the real world, much less know someone who might be one.

I pinch myself to make sure that this isn't another one of the many fucked nightmares I'm used to having.

A hiss leaves my lips at the sharp pain caused by the pinch, my skin slightly torn from my nails.

Yep. This is fucking *real*.

I kick at a rock on the sidewalk, watching as it rolls along the cement before rolling off into the gutter. Does Miles know about Jaylen and what he likes to get up to at *Black Rose*? I don't want to outright call him a vampire if this is something else entirely, but that's essentially what I saw.

If I were to let Miles in on Jaylen's secret, I just know he would grill me about why I was even searching for Jaylen in the first place, and how I stumbled upon the incident. I would rather not have to explain to my brother that I was looking for his best friend because something deep within me was too curious not to know what he was doing.

And that's not a conversation I want to have with him.

Okay, so maybe keeping Miles in the dark might be my only option while I figure out what is going on myself. Do I even want to know more about this? My head is screaming no and telling me to run as far away from Jaylen as I can, whereas my heart—and lower regions—know I can't stay away from him. I hate to admit it but seeing him like that with that girl made my core tingle more than it should've.

What the *fuck* is wrong with me?

I exhale sharply and shake my head, wrapping my arms tighter around my waist. The rest of the walk is silent, both around me and inside my head. I want to think about what to do next from here, but my mind is blank as I stare at the ground. Maybe it's better if I keep my thoughts to a minimum so as not to overwhelm myself.

By the time the sorority house comes into view, I've probably been walking for about thirty minutes, but it doesn't feel like it. I could've kept walking, getting lost in the nothingness, but my legs are beginning to grow tired, and my skin is slick with sweat. All I want is to have a warm shower, crawl into bed, and forget that tonight ever happened.

Only I can't forget when Jaylen is sitting on the front porch, his eyes trained on me.

I stop in my tracks and pinch the bridge of my nose. "For fucks sake."

Jaylen takes this as his opportunity to walk down the stairs and meet me halfway down the driveway. He pulls his lip ring between his teeth and folds his arms over his chest, the ink embedded in his skin straining against the slick fabric of the buttoned-down shirt, the sleeves rolled up to his elbows. Specks of blood stain the edges of the collar and the base of his throat.

I lick my lips at the sight of him but try to stay focused because he's standing here, right in front of me, and seems to have been waiting for my return.

Now that's not something that was on my bingo card for tonight.

"Evie," he says lowly, his eyes never leaving mine. They're intense, and thankfully, not red.

I sigh at the way he says my name, purposely pronouncing each syllable slowly and deliberately. It makes my heart race. "Jaylen, what are you doing here?"

"To see you, of course," he answers, shoving his hands into the pockets of his chinos. "I need to talk to you about what happened tonight, and what you... saw."

"What is there to talk about?" I ask, tilting my head to the side. "You told me to leave and pretend I didn't see what I did, so that's what I'm doing."

"But you *didn't* forget, and that's the problem." He shakes his head, running a hand through his tousled hair. The muscles in his arm ripple with the movement, making it hard for me to focus on his face.

I quirk a brow, wanting to ask what he meant by that, but decide not to push it. There are more pressing questions I want to ask him.

"What are you?" I ask lowly. "And answer me truthfully."

Jaylen tilts his head to the side, his eyes boring into mine. "I think you already know."

I swallow past the lump in my throat. "You're a vampire, right?"

"If I told you I am, would you believe me?"

I want to say no because I'd rather not believe that his being a vampire is a reality. *My* reality. It would be easier to pretend that he has a blood kink and likes to drink people's blood, but I know that's not the truth. I know Jaylen well enough to know when he's lying because his eyes twitch slightly to the right, unable to hold eye contact.

But right now, his eyes are locked on mine, not twitching in the slightest. Instead, they're hard, and holding my gaze so intensely that I'm the one unable to look him in the eye.

Shit.

I blow out a short breath, shaking my head. "I want to say no, but I would be lying to myself."

Jaylen stands a little straighter, his tongue darting out to lick his bottom lip, tugging the lip ring between his teeth. "Then I think you have yourself the answer, little angel."

CHAPTER 5
EVIE

I shake my head, not wanting to believe that what Jaylen is saying is true. There is no way in fucking *hell* that this man is a vampire. This same kid who scraped his knees so badly on our driveway after tripping over while chasing my brother that my mom had to patch him up before driving him home. The same kid who used to tease me in elementary school for wearing my hair in two pigtails because he said I looked dorky, pegging me with the nickname *Piggy*.

There is no way that this same kid—rather, man—is a *vampire*.

And how did I go so many years not knowing?

I want to ask him when he called me little angel, but my mind is still stuck on the fact that he's a fucking blood-sucking creature that needs blood to survive. The nickname is the least of my concerns.

"Having a hard time believing me?"

Jaylen's raspy voice snaps me out of my thoughts. He is still standing in front of me with his hands in his pockets and his eyes moving across my face, acting so nonchalant about the whole thing.

Why is he not freaking out about me knowing his deepest,

darkest secret? Because as far as I know, vampires aren't known to humans. Well, in my case, I only found out less than an hour ago, but the point still stands.

So, why is he acting so... casual?

"Yes," I say slowly. "Maybe. I don't know."

"I have more proof if you want me to show you," he offers with a shrug, his eyes never leaving my face.

The image of his fangs digging into that girl's neck, blood pouring down the sharp edges onto his chest, is still vivid behind my eyes. I shake my head. "No, I think I'm good. But thanks, though. I know what I saw back at the club and surprisingly... I believe you."

Jaylen quirks a brow, an amused smirk tugging at the corner of his mouth. "You do? Well, that was a lot easier than I thought it was going to be. You had me worried for a second there."

I raise a brow at him. "What did you expect I would do? Run away screaming that you're a vampire at the top of my lungs? I'm not an idiot, Jaylen. I know what would happen if I were to do that."

His eyes narrow slightly, the blue in his irises darkening ever so slightly. "And what would happen to you?"

"You'd probably rip my throat out, or worse, the world would know about you and your... *kind*." Although, I don't think that he actually would hurt me.

His tongue darts out to lick his lower lip. The action has me enraptured. "Well, you're right about one of those things. Vampires are still... in the closet, as we like to say."

"*We?*" I say, raising a brow at him. "Do you have other vampire friends I don't know about?"

Jaylen bites back an amused smile. "Maybe. But I do have my connections outside of Pullman. We prefer to have our real identities hidden from the public, presenting how we want in

40

order to avoid detection. Let's just say that it wouldn't be *good* if society were to find out that we exist."

I fold my arms over my chest. "How can you hide what you truly are? Wait... don't vampires burn under direct sunlight?"

I may have read a lot about vampires growing up, but how much of what I know is factual and not just myths? There are so many questions circling my brain that I want to ask Jaylen, but I'm still coming to terms with the bombshell he just dropped on me, so maybe I need to approach this more delicately. Besides, I don't want to overwhelm him.

Jaylen chuckles. "Oh, sweet little angel, you're so cute. I don't know if you've noticed, but I walk around in the daytime just fine."

My cheeks flush at the stupidity of my question, all logic going out the window now that I know this secret, and the fact that he called me cute. And his *little angel*. That's not a sentence I've heard from his mouth before. I like it.

"I have so many questions to ask but don't know where to start," I admit, letting my arms fall to hang loosely by my side.

"I figured as much," Jaylen says with a shrug. "But there is plenty of time for you to ask your questions, and I promise I'll answer them in due time." His eyes darken further as he steps toward me, invading my space with his large mass and height.

My breath hitches in my throat at the proximity, my lungs gasping for air as if his mere presence sucked me dry. Being this close to Jaylen is like standing too close to a bonfire, the flames licking at your side, just inches away from burning you as embers float around your head. And for whatever reason, I'd let this man fucking burn me if given the chance.

"There is a more pressing matter at hand." His breath is warm against my lips as he stares deep into my soul, holding me hostage where I stand. I swallow hard. "I want to know why it didn't work."

"Why what didn't work?"

Jaylen inhales sharply, his eyes once again searching my features as if waiting to find something he couldn't before. "When I compelled you," he explained. "I want to know why it *didn't* work."

I frown, trying to understand what he's referring to when the realization suddenly hits me. After I caught Jaylen with that girl, witnessing him drinking her blood, he cornered me in front of the room, and I remember *something* pushing against my brain but didn't know what it was. The sensation was odd, but I brushed it away because I was too in shock by what I had just seen. Now, I'm starting to realize what Jaylen was doing to me.

"You were trying to push words into my mind," I say softly, chewing on my bottom lip.

Jaylen's eyes dip to my lips for a second before he shuts his eyes and groans. "You have to stop doing that, Ev. It drives me crazy."

My eyes widen, my bottom lip falling from my teeth. What the—

His eyes snap back open, and for a split second, I see part of his eyes are red before they turn back to their normal ocean color. "And yes, I was trying to push words into your mind. I was trying to compel you to not remember a thing of what you just saw, and yet, for some reason, it didn't work. That has never happened to me before."

I frown. "Have you ever tried to compel me or Miles in the past?" The thought that Jaylen could just compel Miles—and not me, apparently—to do anything is slightly terrifying.

He shakes his head. "Never."

"How many people have you had to compel to forget what you are?" I question, wrapping my arms around my waist.

Jaylen smirks and my heart begins to race at how stunning

this man is. "Let's just say I've had to do it my fair share of times, especially at the club."

I blush as images of Jaylen and that girl at the *Black Rose* once again flash in my mind. Now more than ever I'm curious to know more about that bar. Is it a place for vampires to go and feed on willing humans, but compel them to forget what happened? What happens if the human doesn't give consent? I have so many questions and not enough answers.

"What is so special about you, Evie?" Jaylen says slowly, licking his lips. "Why can't I compel you? To make matters worse, you don't *smell* like us. You smell... normal. Human. But that doesn't make sense."

I inhale sharply, unable to get air into my lungs when all I can smell is the scent of Jaylen's sandalwood cologne as it invades my nostrils and consumes my senses. I want to take a step back to breathe fresh air, but he has me pinned to the ground just by looking into my eyes.

All I can do is shrug. I didn't know vampires existed until tonight, which means I didn't know I couldn't be compelled by one either. Which, in hindsight, is nice to know in case I am to encounter a vampire who isn't Jaylen in the future.

"Interesting," he breathes. "Do I scare you, Ev?"

The rhythmic beating of my heart can be felt in my ears as I stare at Jaylen, his question closing around my heart. At first, I was scared of him, especially when I saw blood dripping from razor-sharp fangs. But now that I'm standing here in front of him, his ocean eyes boring into mine, filled with such intensity that it's hard for me to breathe, I realize that I'm not afraid of him.

Call me stupid, but I'm not afraid of this man now that I know he's a vampire. Maybe I like the thrill of danger that I feel when I'm with him or maybe it's because I can still see the Jaylen that I grew up with despite this new identity.

Whatever the case may be, I only find him more attractive now and that's probably very fucked up to say, but I don't care.

If he wanted to kill me, no matter how long he has been this way, he would've done so by now. But he hasn't, and that has to mean something. Right?

I shake my head. "No. I'm not afraid of you."

Jaylen grins before taking a step back, putting some space between us. I gasp for air as the burning sensation I felt from being so close to him finally subsides. Holy shit this man is intense.

"Does Miles know what you are?" I ask, my heart racing in my chest.

Jaylen shakes his head, those soft curls bouncing with the movement. "No, he doesn't, and it's going to stay that way, okay? I may not be able to compel you, but I can sure as hell convince you from saying anything."

"I promise I won't say anything." If Miles knew the truth about Jaylen, it would only cause trouble between them, and I don't want to see that happen.

Jaylen nods and looks over my shoulder. Frowning, I spin to see what he's looking at when, after a moment, I hear the sound of a car driving down the road before pulling into the driveway. It's a taxi.

I turn to face Jaylen. "Could you hear the car coming?"

He nods, a smile tugging at the corner of his mouth. "Let's just say there is still a lot for you to learn about me, little angel."

The sound of high-pitched laughter causes me to turn back to the taxi to see Rylee, Candie, and Jaycee exiting, holding each other up by the waist so as not to fall. I smile, glad they managed to get home safely. They all say goodnight to the driver before walking toward me and Jaylen. They're so consumed in their giggling that they don't notice us until the very last second.

Rylee is the first to notice me, her eyes going wide. "You're home," she smiles, her eyes moving to look at Jaylen. "And you have a guest."

I roll my eyes at the knowing look she gives me. God, I hope Jaylen didn't see it, too. "Jaylen just wanted to make sure I got home safe since I wasn't feeling well."

"How kind of him," Candie giggles, holding onto Jaycee's shoulders. They both decided to wear dresses tonight which probably wasn't the smartest decision given the state they've ended up in. Jaycee grunts, trying to hold Candie's weight so they both don't go toppling over.

"I'm just glad you're home safe," Jaycee says, tugging on Candie. "Come on, let's get inside and go to bed."

"Jaycee went upstairs at the club with the guy who got us on the list," Candie says, wiggling her brows at Jaycee, who rolls her eyes.

The girls walk past me, waving goodbye to Jaylen as they go. He simply nods in response, his eyes never leaving mine. As they pass by, I look at Jaycee and notice two small puncture marks on the side of her neck. My eyes widen as a small gasp leaves my lips.

"What the—"

"She'll be okay," Jaylen interjects, somehow knowing exactly what I was going to say. "She won't remember a thing about him being a vampire."

I turn to look at him. "So, she was compelled to forget he is a vampire, but she remembers everything else?"

He nods, shoving his hands into the pocket of his chinos. "That's how it works at the *Black Rose*. Before she was compelled, whoever the guy was would've told her what he was and got consent to feed from her. To avoid society finding out about us, all willing human participants are compelled to forget that we're vampires, and that's it."

"And if she didn't give consent?"

"Then she would've been compelled to forget she was even asked the question," he says with a shrug.

I hum in acknowledgment, mulling over the information in my head. I just hope that whoever this guy is that Jaycee slept with treated her right and didn't take advantage of her. I'll have to try and find a time to ask her about it.

"I'll let you go," Jaylen says after a moment. "But I'm sure I'll see you around."

I watch in stunned silence as he walks past me and disappears down the empty street, blending in with the darkness. There is more I want to say to him or ask, but my brain is overloaded with information that I can't seem to organize my thoughts coherently enough to get the words out.

But Jaylen is right. I will be seeing him around because now that I know what he is, I'm determined to learn more about him. The only thing is, I can't let my brother find out.

JAYLEN

I watch my little angel's eyes move across the darkness of the street, unable to see me lurking in the shadows, using nearby parked cars as a shield. After a moment, she sighs and turns to follow her friends inside the house. I can hear the rhythmic thumping of her heart as she disappears behind the closed front door.

It's now my new favorite sound.

Evie finding out I'm a vampire was not something I thought would happen tonight.

Yes, I like to let her know that I'm watching her. Always watching. Even when she doesn't know it. But when I walked upstairs with... fuck, I can't remember her name, I hadn't anticipated that she would follow me. I can only guess curiosity got the best of her, and I'm not mad about it.

Keeping this secret from Evie and Miles for the past four years has been harder than I thought it would be. Having to hide the deep thirst that often consumes me when I haven't fed and my heightened senses in public spaces hasn't been easy. But somehow, I made it work. Miles doesn't know a thing —that I know of—and I was hoping it would stay that way with Evie, but... my little angel is a curious girl.

She is a smart woman, I know this. When we were kids, she would spend a lot of her time reading whatever book she could get her hands on. Genre wasn't an issue for her because all she wanted was to further her knowledge—fiction and non-fiction. It's one of the things I like most about her. Not only is she intelligent, but insanely beautiful with her amazonite eyes and a smile that could light up an entire city if it were to lose power. I find myself having to resist the urge to run my knuckles across her high cheekbones and count every freckle on her cheeks and nose.

It pains me that I have had to keep her at arm's length because of Miles. I've had to repress these feelings over the years because there was never a right time to take the next step. What if I made a move and she rejected me? It would fucking kill me. I don't think I would ever recover. And I don't want to go against my best friend's wishes of dating his sister, but it's so fucking hard to resist her. There is only so much I can take.

After tonight, I no longer have to question her feelings. I

could see the excitement mixed with fear in her eyes when she looked at me. And the way her heart beat fast when I was inches away from her body. It is clear, to me, at least, that she is attracted to me. If anything, it's the green light I've been waiting five years for.

I smile. "You'll be mine soon, little angel."

CHAPTER 6
EVIE

Monday morning classes are always the hardest. Not only do I have the Monday blues, but I'm not at all focused or interested in being in class. In fact, I think I'd prefer to watch paint dry than listen to my professor discuss all the different reasons why sleep is important for our body and overall health.

Funny, since I didn't get much sleep this weekend because all I could think about is fucking Jaylen Black.

Thoughts of him have been consuming my mind since the moment he left the sorority house, leaving me speechless in the driveway. There are so many more questions I want to ask him about what it's like to be a vampire and *how* he became one. Because surely he wasn't a vampire when we were kids, right?

This is why I need to talk to him, to learn more about what he is, but I can't get close enough to him for that to happen. Not when my brother is always with him and has warned me away from Jaylen multiple times. At first, I was willing to listen to his warnings, but now all logic has gone out the window because I don't want to stay away from him even though I know I should. Knowing what he is should scare the shit out of me and have me running for the hills, but instead, it has only made me more curious about him.

And *that's* what scares me.

I shouldn't still be attracted to Jaylen knowing that he needs to drink human blood to survive and frequents a bar that allows vampires to sleep with humans and drink their blood at the same time. But for some reason, I *am* still attracted to him, despite all of that.

What the fuck is wrong with me?

I shake the thought from my head just as the professor is wrapping up the class. *Thank God*. Wanting to be anywhere else but here, I pack away my things and follow the throng of students out of the room and into the fresh, humid, Pullman air. I can't wait for it to be Fall already so I don't have to deal with this heat anymore.

As I'm walking to Bluebird Co., my phone vibrates in my pocket.

> Miles: Sis, can you please grab me some lunch? I'm at practice.
>
> I'll owe you one!

I roll my eyes and type my response.

> Evie: Sure, just let me know what you want.

While I'm standing in line at the coffee shop, listening to the conversations happening around me—especially the one the two girls are having in front of me about one of their boyfriends cheating on them, and knowing that feeling all too well—Miles finally texts back with his lunch order.

Once I have my coffee and bag of sandwiches in my hand, I make my way across campus, passing students heading to class and sitting out in the sun on the lawn, to one of the many sports stadiums WSU has to offer. With the sun beaming down on my skin, I can feel sweat pooling in my pores. I don't know how Miles can train in this kind of weather. I would be convinced that I'd get heat stroke and die, which may seem a little dramatic, but true.

Instant relief washes over me when I step through the entrance of the stadium and make my way down a few long hallways until I see the opening to the pitch. The grass is blinding under the sunlight, so I slip my sunglasses on, gazing at the men running around until I spot a familiar head of brown hair.

Miles spots me almost at the same time, jogging over to meet me in the shade. His tanned skin is glistening with sweat and small blades of grass litter his neck. I want to tell him to wipe it off, but I don't get the chance before he's grabbing at the bag in my hand.

"Hold your horses, cowboy," I say as I switch my iced coffee to my other hand, allowing him to fully open the paper bag. "There is one in there for me, so don't even think about snatching it up."

Miles rolls his eyes as he takes his two turkey, cheese, and salad sandwiches out of the bag. "I wouldn't dream of it. But thank you for doing this. I was an idiot and left my apartment before I could grab something for lunch."

I raise a brow at him. "Let me guess, you slept through your alarm again?"

He nods, taking a bite out of one of the sandwiches. "I had a late night, can you blame me?"

"I would say that sounds like a *you* problem."

Again, Miles rolls his eyes and continues to eat his sandwich. "Anyway, did you have a good night on Friday? I wanted to text you, but didn't want to seem..."

"Overbearing," I finish for him with a smile. "And don't worry, I had a good night." *Yeah, I saw your best friend drinking the blood of a woman while she rode his cock,* I want to say, but for obvious reasons keep that thought to myself. "We went to the *Black Rose.*"

Miles stops chewing, his eyes boring into mine. He swallows hard, licking his lips. "The *Black Rose*? How did you get in there?"

I shrug, looking past him in search of a head of messy curls and stunning baby-blue eyes, but come up short. "Jaycee knows a guy who got us on the list. It was a very nice bar, so I understand why it's so exclusive."

Roman is running around behind Miles, kicking the ball between him and two other guys while they train. Thankfully, he hasn't spotted me, but that doesn't mean he won't soon. Somehow, he can always feel my presence no matter where I am. It's disturbing, really.

"Be careful at the *Black Rose,*" Miles warns, his eyes darkening slightly, breaking through my thoughts.

I frown. "Why? Have you been there before?" I know why *I* should be cautious at the *Black Rose*, but does Miles know, too?

He shrugs, the darkness in his eyes evaporating like it was never there. "I've just heard some things about it is all. Just... be careful, okay? I don't want you getting hurt, especially not after what happened—"

"—to our parents. Yes, I know, Miles," I interject with a smile. "I'm twenty-one now, so I know how to take care of myself."

Miles smiles, shaking his head. He reaches up and rubs his hand on the top of my head, messing up the perfectly styled ponytail that took me what felt like forever to do this morning. "I know. I'm just a worry wart, you know that."

"Hey!" I protest, trying to flatten the flyaway hairs. "Learn to put some trust in me, okay?"

"Okay, sis. I'll try."

I point a finger toward the pitch. "How's practice going? When is the next game?"

"This Saturday," he says, halfway through the first sandwich. "You're coming to watch, right?"

I smile. "I wouldn't miss it for the world."

Miles has been a massive soccer fan for as long as I can remember. He would always come into my room and talk about his favorite team—from memory, I think it's a team called Inter Miami, but I could be wrong—and gush about his favorite player. It always made me smile. My favorite moments from summer vacation would be watching Miles and Jaylen kick a soccer ball around the backyard and doing a funny dance whenever they scored a goal. It's a core memory I'll never forget, which is why I'm my brother's number one fan.

It's only right to return the support when he does so much for me. The least I can do is support him in doing what he loves the most.

I can see Miles's mouth moving, but I can't hear what he's saying because I finally spot the one person who has been on my mind since Friday night.

Jaylen.

He's standing among a group of members of the team talking, but his eyes are focused on me. The sweat is glistening off his strong, toned arms, making the muscles more defined under the black shirt he's wearing. I can't take my eyes off the ink covering his entire right arm. I remember when he got most of those tattoos, wanting to fill his arm with images of fantasy creatures from myths. Now I know *why*.

Jaylen captures his lip ring between his teeth, shooting a smirk my way.

If it was possible to melt into a puddle, I would be sliding over the concrete and into the grass right now.

Miles clears his throat, forcing me to tear my eyes away from Jaylen and refocus on him. He's frowning at me. *Shit, did he catch me checking out his best friend?*

"Ev, were you even listening to me?"

I lick my bottom lip. "Sorry, I was, uh... getting lost in my thoughts. What were you saying?"

"I was saying that you'll need to come over one night soon so we can watch a movie together," Miles repeats. "Just like old times."

I smile, ignoring the way my heart is pounding in my chest because I can still feel Jaylen watching me. "Yeah, sure, that sounds great. Just the two of us?"

Miles shrugs, scrunching up the wrapper of the sandwich he just finished, his mouth full. "Maybe Jaylen, Ethan, and Preston too, but we'll see."

My heart stills in my chest. "Jaylen?"

"Yeah. Is that going to be a problem?"

I swallow hard and shake my head. "Nope. Not a problem at all."

Besides the fact that your best friend is a fucking vampire and I want to rip off his clothes and feel his hard, toned body beneath me even though I shouldn't. There is no problem at all, brother.

54

"Night, Ry," I say, turning to my best friend. She has her comforter pulled up to her chin as the ceiling fan spins on high in an attempt to cool the room down. "You don't mind if I keep my lamp on, do you?"

Rylee shakes her head, flipping onto her side to face the wall. "I don't mind. Just don't be up too late, okay? You have an early class."

"As long as I don't have another nightmare, I should be fine," I tease, although I'm deadly serious. If I can sleep through the night, I will likely wake before the alarm I set.

"Goodnight," she says softly, reaching over to switch her lamp off.

I sigh, settling into the soft sheets, and pull my comforter up to my chin as the air from the ceiling fan above begins to grow cold. It's almost 11 p.m. and I'm not as tired as I should be after a long day of classes. Normally, it would annoy me to no end, but it's a blessing in disguise because it means I get to read the book I started last week in peace without someone in the house looking to interrupt me.

Opening the book to the bookmark I left on page 102, I begin reading from where I left off. It's a typical romance novel that makes you smile like an idiot at 2D words and swoon like a lovesick high school student. It's cheesy, cliché, and over-done, but God do I fucking love it. It's a guilty pleasure of mine.

As I get to the end of the page, waiting for the main characters to kiss, my phone vibrates on the bedside table. Groaning, I lay the book down on my chest. Whoever this is better be worth my time because I was just about to get to the juicy part of the book.

It's an unread message from Roman. I roll my eyes and move to delete the message without reading it, not in the mood for his shit, but a photo attached to the message is what catches my eye.

What the fuck is that?

Clicking into it, my eyes widen at what he said.

> Roman: You should've taken me seriously, Evie. If you don't want this photo to get out, you'll reconsider getting back together with me.

I stare at the image attached—it's a photo of me lying in bed wearing black lacy lingerie with a duvet resting on my exposed stomach. My eyes are closed, so it's clear I'm sleeping.

Did this fucking psycho take pictures of me while I was asleep?

Anger begins to brew in my veins as I type back a response. I'm not going to stoop to this motherfucker's level. He is the creep for taking photos of me while I was sleeping, regardless of whether we were together or not. It's weird, and I'm not going to let him use it against me.

> Evie: You're a fucking psycho. If you don't leave me alone I'm going to call the cops.

> Roman: There is more than just this photo. More explicit ones. Do you really want to take the chance?

My eyes widen. Does he really have more photos of me? How long was he taking photos of me without my knowledge or consent? A shiver races down my spine at the thought. This man is more unhinged than I had thought. And he's doing all of this to get me back? Well, he's going about it the wrong way.

I refuse to let him manipulate me like this.

> Evie: Fuck you. I'm not playing these stupid games with you. Delete my number.

My eyes flick to the unread text message that just came in, only to see it's from Jaylen. My eyes widen as I push myself up, closing the book on my lap. What the hell is he doing messaging me? I must admit, it's a nice change in pace from my conversation with Roman.

> Jaylen: Little angel.

I frown at the text message. What the hell is he doing texting me this late at night? Scrolling back through our past messages, our conversations have only ever consisted of him asking me if I know where Miles is or if I can grab them something to eat and drink while at practice. Getting a message like this from him is something new to me.

> Jaylen: I know you're awake.

57

Now that grabs my attention.

> Evie: How do you know that for sure?

> Jaylen: Because I know you.
>
> And also... I can see your bedroom light is on.

My eyes widen as my head snaps to look at the window beside my bed with the curtains drawn back. What the actual fuck?

With my heart in my throat, I quietly slip out of bed, so as not to disturb Rylee, and peek out the window. To my surprise, Jaylen is leaning against the large tree just outside of our window dressed in black sweatpants and a tight black shirt, his eyes peering up at me. A grin splits across his face as he shakes his phone, the screen lighting up.

The cheeky motherfu—

Huffing, I lift my phone from my side and type my response.

> Evie: What the hell are you doing here?

Jaylen: I was out on a little... adventure and thought I would stop by since I was in the area.

Evie: You stopped by to see me?

Jaylen: Is it such a crime to want to see you?

I don't know how to respond to that because I can't figure out his motives. Out of all the things he could be doing with his time, and it being this late at night, why would he choose to come and see me? I'm just his best friend's little sister. Surely, I don't mean that much to him to warrant a drop-in like this.

Unless he's only doing it to keep an eye on me, making sure I haven't told anyone about his little secret.

Evie: If you're worried that I've told someone what you are, you don't need to be.

Jaylen: That's not why I'm here.

I look out the window, my heart thrumming in my throat. When I catch Jaylen's eye, he waves for me to come downstairs. Feeling like I don't have much of a choice, I place my phone on the bedside table, switch off my lamp, and make my way out of the room.

Thankfully, all the girls in the house are asleep, so I can slip out the back door undetected. The humid air instantly makes my skin feel sticky as I walk across the damp grass to the tree Jaylen is still leaning against. When he sees me approaching, he pushes the curls away from his face and smiles.

"Well, don't you look cute, little angel?"

I look down at the tiny black pajama shorts and cream camisole I decided to put on after my shower earlier. Hearing Jaylen's compliment, I suddenly feel self-conscious under his intense gaze.

Instead of commenting that he called me cute again, I say, "What brings you here this lovely evening, Jaylen?"

He pulls his lip ring between his teeth, a habit I'm slowly starting to pick up on the more we interact. Of course, we would speak every so often since he is my brother's best friend, but ever since that night at the *Black Rose*, something has shifted between us, bringing us closer than we once were.

"I just wanted to say thank you," he finally says.

I fold my arms over my chest and quirk a brow. "And this isn't something you could say over text?"

He shrugs, a cheeky grin pulling at the corner of his mouth. "I could have, but I prefer doing it the old-fashioned way. Besides, talking through text doesn't allow me to see the way your cheeks flush when I'm around."

My eyes widen. "What! They don't..."

"Save it," Jaylen interjects, tilting his head to the side. "You can't hide it from me."

I huff, hating that he knows just how much he affects me.

Maybe he's always known, but now he can use it to his advantage. Damn him.

"Anyway," he continues, "I just wanted to thank you for keeping my secret, especially from Miles. I know how close you two are, so I know it must've been hard."

Not really, I want to tell him, *because I know the consequences if I do*, but instead, I say, "You two are just as close. Why haven't you told him what you are?"

He sighs, shaking his head. "It's a little more complicated than that."

"Why?" I question. "He's your best friend. I'm sure he would understand."

"I just... can't," he breathes. "With all the murders happening in the area, it's best that no one else knows what I am."

"Murders," I say slowly, connecting the dots in my head, noting the concern in his voice. "So, the murders are related to vampires? You're not the one killing these people, are you?"

Jaylen shakes his head. The moonlight shining through the leaves cast a soft glow over his features. He looks ethereal. "I'm not, but there is someone out there killing these people and making it look almost satanic. The victims are drained of their blood with two puncture marks to their throat."

I mull over what he's saying for a moment, chewing on my bottom lip. "So, someone out there is staging these murders to look like a vampire did it?"

"Yes and no," Jaylen answers. "I know it's a vampire hunter who is killing these vampires, but why they are staging the scene to make it appear like it was done by a satanic cult is what I don't understand."

My eyes widen. "Vampires? How do you know the victims are vampires?"

Jaylen's eyes bore into mine, the baby blue partially

obscured by the shadows across his face. "I have my sources, which is why I need to be careful and keep a low profile. If this hunter catches wind of me somehow, I'm toast. I'll end up just like the others and that's not what I want. That's why I came here to thank you, Ev."

I swallow hard. I had no idea that the murders happening in the area were the work of a vampire hunter. To me, it just seemed like some sicko on the loose that couldn't be captured or found. The last thing I was expecting the case to be was a hunter tracking down vampires and taking them out.

It didn't even cross my mind that vampire hunters exist along with vampires. The whole thing is still a new concept to me, so it's not something that would have crossed my mind. I want to ask him more about the hunter and if he has any suspicions of who it may be, but I keep the thought to myself. If he's this worried about being found out, it seems likely that he has no clue who this madman is.

There is still so much more I need to learn about Jaylen and the world of vampires, but it's too much for my brain to comprehend right now.

"That's okay," is all I manage to say. "Just... be careful."

Jaylen takes a step forward, our bodies inches apart. My breath hitches in my throat at the sudden proximity, and I'm reminded of how divine he smells and how his body can make mine submit to him.

"I should probably tell you the same," he murmurs, his eyes intense as they stare into mine. "The last thing you want is for your brother to know how much you want me. I can smell it all over you."

My heart just about stops beating in my chest, and I open my mouth to respond, to tell him that he's fucking dreaming but in the blink of an eye, Jaylen is gone. I whirl around trying to find him, but all I'm met with is darkness, aside from the moonlight shining through the treetop.

I exhale sharply, trying to calm my racing heart as I stand alone in the backyard.

I want to curse Jaylen out for his words, but the thing is... he's absolutely right. Miles can't know about the attraction I feel toward Jaylen because if he does, I'll be the one that's toast.

CHAPTER 7

EVIE

I don't know how I was roped into a girl's day with Jaycee, Candie, and Rylee, yet here I am with my feet plunged into a round tub of warm water while a woman with the quiet nature of a mouse shapes my fingernails. My nails had chipped black nail polish on them that I painted nearly a month ago, with some of it refusing to come off no matter how long I picked at it.

The poor woman has her work cut out for her.

My ears buzz with the sound of the girl's voice talking beside me, but all I can focus on is the water bubbling around my ankles and the way the nail file brushes against the skin under my nails.

Ever since my conversation with Miles about the *Black Rose* on Monday, it's all I've been able to think about, the topic consuming my thoughts and leaving me distracted and confused. Why did Miles warn me to be careful about attending the *Black Rose*? I mean, I know *why*, but I want to know what he meant by it.

Does he know that the *Black Rose* is a feeding ground for vampires to indulge and get their fix safely? I mean, it's the only explanation I can think of because, besides that detail, the bar is just like every other one in Pullman. There is nothing sketchy or wary about it. It's just a... normal bar, besides the blood-sucking vampires lurking upstairs.

It seems Miles knows more about this than he's letting on, but I can't complain because I do, too.

But my question is *how*? How does he know about the truth behind *Black Rose* and what is he not telling me?

"Earth to Evie."

Rylee's voice breaks me out of my thoughts, forcing me to turn to look at her. She's sitting in the chair next to me, her eyes locked on mine as she waits for me to say something. Jaycee and Candie are doing the same from their seats.

I clear my throat and smile. "Sorry, I was lost in thought again. What were we talking about?"

"You seem to have been doing that a lot lately," Jaycee comments, eyeing me. "Is everything all right?"

I glance at her neck where the two puncture marks from last weekend are barely yellow bruises, fading in with her tan skin. The next morning when we were all sitting on the couch in the living room hungover with coffees in our hands, Candie noticed the marks on Jaycee's neck. Of course, after being compelled by the mystery vampire who took her upstairs, she doesn't remember a thing—blaming the lack of memory on being drunk—and thinks that maybe he had given her a hickey, but she doesn't remember/

Good, I'm glad she doesn't remember. It's better that way.

"Yeah, I just... have a lot on my mind, but it's nothing, I promise," I reassure with a small smile. "Anyway, what were you guys talking about?"

"Just what has been happening in Pullman recently," Candie answers.

I frown, looking between the girls. "What's been going on?"

"The murders, duh." Candie looks down at the nail tech working on her nails, watching as she swipes on a coat of baby pink polish. "You've heard about them, right?"

I nod, leaning back in my seat. I'm reminded of my conversation with Jaylen where he revealed the truth about the murders. But, of course, I can't tell the girls what I know, so I decide to play dumb. "Miles mentioned it before we went to the *Black Rose*, but I didn't think much about it."

"They have found several people murdered in the area, drained of their blood," Rylee provides, her love for true crime shining through her eyes. "They found another one last night, their body lying in the park just down the road from our place."

"From what I've heard," Jaycee says, "they are connecting all the murders and saying there is a serial killer on the loose. Something about a satanic cult, too."

"In Pullman?" Candie gasps, her eyes wide. "That's so scary. I don't want to leave the house now."

"You'll be fine," Rylee reassures with a small smile. "Just don't go anywhere alone, okay? We all need to stick together, especially in a time like this. Being in a group or a pair is much better than being alone."

"I agree," I say with a nod. Although none of them are vampires so they likely won't be a target, it doesn't hurt to be cautious of other dangers. "No one goes out by themselves, okay?"

The girls agree in unison, and I go back to getting lost in my thoughts, because what's new?

Pullman isn't known for having many violent crimes, but that's not to say that crime doesn't exist here at all. So, the fact that all these murders are happening in the area has citizens on edge and invested in the story.

When I see Jaylen, I'll have to ask him more questions about the murders and vampires in general.

When I see him.

The thought of seeing Jaylen has my skin tingling with excitement. It's wrong for me to still find him attractive after finding out the truth about him, but I just can't help it. My heart races wildly whenever he's around, which hasn't changed since finding out he's a vampire. I *should* be afraid of him, but I'm not, and that's a problem.

We finish up at the nail salon, leaving with freshly painted toes and fingernails, before making our way to the food court to grab something for lunch. My stomach is all but growling at me by the time we find a table and sit down with our sushi. For it being a Friday afternoon, the tables are mostly filled with shoppers—kids hanging out with their friends after school, workers on their lunch breaks, or couples and families sitting together.

I listen as Rylee tells us about the latest romance book she's reading, and Candie explains how she's already falling behind on notes for her classes. I listen quietly, trying to appear interested, but all I can think about is who the vampire hunter may be and if they're lurking among us, blending in with the crowd while they stalk their prey.

I've never thought about the fact that vampires could be walking among us undetected, blending in effortlessly. If Jaylen is anything to go by, they are no different than humans in appearance, and that makes me nervous.

After we finish eating, we leave the shopping mall and head out to Rylee's car. I take the front seat while Jaycee and Candie slide into the back. Rylee is quick to put on a pop playlist with all of her favorite songs, turning up the volume to the point my teeth are rattling in my head and my bones are bouncing in my body.

I roll the window down and close my eyes, relishing in the

feel of the wind sliding against my skin and through my hair, trying to ease my mind from the chaos running through it.

God, I just need to fucking relax.

When we get home, I linger behind Candie and Rylee to walk with Jaycee. I've been wanting to ask her about the mystery guy from *Black Rose* but didn't want to bring it up in front of the other girls since Jaycee seems to want to keep any information about this guy close to her chest.

"There's been something I've been meaning to ask you," I say slowly as we climb the porch stairs, the wooden creaking underneath our feet.

Jaycee turns to look at me. "What's up?"

I hesitate for a moment, not wanting to bombard her with questions. I stop at the top of the stairs, Jaycee still facing me. Her eyes roam over my features, almost nervously by the way they jump. "I just... Who is the mystery guy who got us into *Black Rose*? I'm just curious about him, especially since we know nothing about him."

"Oh." Jaycee breathes a sigh of relief, shaking her head. "I had no idea where you were going with that. You can't be so serious all the time, Ev."

I smile, blowing out a short breath. "Sorry. But seriously, who is he?"

Jaycee shrugs, looking down at her shoes. "He's just a guy I met in one of my classes. He's charming and sweet. We're only seeing each other casually, so I don't want to give out too much information just in case whatever we have fizzles out."

Okay, so it doesn't seem like she knows this guy is a vampire. That is a relief.

"I get that," I say with a reassuring smile. "What's his name? You don't have to give me his full name if you don't want to. And I promise I won't mention it to the girls."

If this guy is a vampire, I need to know who he is so I can make sure my best friend is safe.

Jaycee looks hesitant, unable to meet my eye. She must really like this guy if she's so desperate to keep his identity a secret. She fiddles with the hem of her white shirt, chewing on her bottom lip.

"You promise?"

"I promise."

She sighs. "Fine. His name is Ethan."

My eyes widen. There are probably a hundred Ethans' on campus, but I can't help but wonder if the Ethan she is talking about is the same one that plays on the WSU soccer team with Miles and Jaylen. It would make sense considering Jaylen was quick to defend the guy she had been with that night, almost as if he knew him personally.

I smile. "Your secret is safe with me, Jay."

My heart is pounding in my chest as I walk up the small pathway to the front door and realize that all the lights are off in the house, which is unusual since my parents should be home making dinner after getting back from work.

On Wednesdays, I typically get home late because I go to after-school dance practice with Rylee. Her mom is kind enough to give me a lift home each week to save either of my parents from having to swing by the school, which is out of their way from where they work, to pick me up. Miles gets home even later than me because he, too, has after-school practice for soccer, so Jaylen's mom drops him home.

Each week, I look forward to stepping through the front

door and being hit with the smell of Mom's delicious cooking wafting through the house from the kitchen and hearing the voices of news reporters coming from the TV while Dad catches up on the news.

Except, neither of those things happens when I walk through the front door.

With my hand on the doorknob, I look down the long hallway that opens into the kitchen. To my right, the living room is quiet with the TV switched off, and there are no delicious smells coming from the kitchen nor can I hear the sound of banging pots and pans or my mom's voice as she hums along to the tune of whatever is playing on the record player. Usually, it's Fleetwood Mac.

"Mom?" I call out as I close the front door behind me, my tennis shoes squeaking on the hardwood floor as I walk down the hallway. "Dad?"

When I reach the kitchen, I see two plates of half-eaten sandwiches on the dining table and two full glasses of water untouched. I frown as I take in the sight of the moonlight shining through the kitchen onto the table. I remember Mom saying she and Dad were going to take the day off from work to run some errands together, but it doesn't explain why their lunch is still on the table. The house is in complete darkness beside the moonlight shining in through the windows, and they don't seem to be home.

"Mom?" I try again, walking through the kitchen, and around the corner to the staircase. Maybe they're just in their bedroom and didn't hear me come in.

When I turn the corner, my heart leaps into my throat, twisting the air from my lungs as I struggle to breathe. The moonlight shining on the staircase illuminates the river of blood pouring down the steps, the droplets landing on the floor at the bottom into a large pool.

I try to stammer out words, but all that comes out are strangled breaths as I drop my backpack on the floor beside me and sink to my knees. I can see their bodies lying at the top of the staircase, their blood sliding down each step, and it takes everything in my body not to look at my mom's soulless eyes.

But I do. Even unblinking, I can see the hurt behind her green eyes, which makes me wonder what the hell happened before I walked through the door. Who did this to them and why?

Why?

As tears begin to fall down my cheeks, my heart shattering in my chest, I catch a glimpse of a shadowy figure at the top of the staircase. My eyes widen when I realize it's someone standing over my parents. I can't tell if they're looking at me or their bodies, but it's enough for me to freeze where I am, unable to move as fear holds me hostage.

For a moment, the shadowy figure and I stare at each other, neither of us moving. I blink several times to make sure I'm not imagining the figure, but each time I open my eyes it's still there, watching me, waiting. I thought I heard it say something, but all I could hear was the static ringing in my ears and my heart thrumming nervously.

The wind outside slams against the windows in the kitchen, rattling the glass. This must be enough to scare the figure because it turns and jumps through the upstairs window between my room and Miles's, disappearing into the depths of the storm raging outside.

After a moment, I gather enough strength to jump to my feet, my heart pounding in my chest, and rush to the landline in the kitchen, knowing I need to call 911 and not think about who that figure was and why it jumped through the window to escape.

As the call goes through to 911, a woman picks up the

phone, tears streaming down my cheeks and my body numb. I didn't register when the police arrived at the house or when Miles got dropped home. I don't remember being taken to the hospital for a check-up or even sitting in the waiting room at the police station with Miles's arm wrapped around my shoulders as I cried into his side, my Aunt Jas watching on with tear-filled eyes.

All I could think about was who that shadowy figure was and if it was the reason my parents were dead.

Evie.

With a start, I throw myself into a seated position. I clutch at my chest as I struggle to force air into my lungs, the memories from that night coming to me clearer now. For years I suppressed that night and what I saw, not wanting to think about it ever again. But lately, I'm beginning to see more and more and it's freaking me the fuck out.

The alarm clock on Rylee's beside table reads 3:20 a.m. and I sigh, flopping back down on the mattress and pulling the comforter up to my chin.

Why now, twelve years later, is my subconscious forcing me to remember the details of that night?

And who the hell was that shadowy figure I saw that night?

My mind must be trying to tell me something. I just don't know what. But I'm willing to find out.

CHAPTER 8
EVIE

I'm not sure that this is a good idea, but I don't have much of a choice. I can't say no, even if I wanted to. But the thing is, I don't want to say no. Even a little bit. I'm in this tug-o-war with my sub-conscious about doing this because a part of me knows I should decline my brother's offer, but then there is the other side nudging me forward to the edge of the deep black hole lurking in front of me, blindly telling me to just go and get it over and done with, despite Jaylen being present.

It feels like I'm being torn in two. I know I have to keep my distance from Jaylen because he's my brother's best friend and needs women to satisfy his bloodlust (I looked it up online recently), but I can't help but feel a slight pull to him, like a rope has been wrapped around my wrist and it's slowly being tugged on, drawing me closer. It's been just over a week since I learned his secret, and to say I'm nervous to see him again would be an understatement. This is new territory for me.

Either way, I need to keep him at arm's length. Well, *try to*.

This past week, whenever I wasn't doing work for class, I was trying to research anything I could find on vampires. But all I could find was lore from *Dracula*, *Twilight*, and *Vampire*

Diaries, and those don't help me in this situation, not when I'm dealing with the real thing. I was hoping to find a secret Reddit thread detailing someone's experience with a real vampire, but I was shit out of luck. I kept coming up blank and it frustrated me to no end. But I'm determined to learn more, even if I have to get the information straight from the source.

When I got Miles's text message earlier today during one of my research sessions asking if I wanted to come over for pizza, beer, and a movie, my first question was: who else is going to be there? I know for a fact that Jaylen will be present since they live together, so that wasn't news to me, but I wanted Miles to think I wasn't too keen by agreeing without asking who was coming first.

Turns out, my plan worked.

Miles responded that Ethan and another friend of theirs, Preston, would be stopping by as well, meaning I'd be in an apartment with four men—one vampire and a potential second. I haven't yet figured out if the mystery man Jaycee is seeing is Ethan on the soccer team and one of my brother's friends. But I'm sure as hell going to find out.

Walking up the sidewalk to Miles's apartment, I look up at the dark brick building, my eyes landing on the third floor out of six and move across the windows until I reach the one on the right—his apartment. Flashes of light illuminate from behind the sheer white curtain, an indication that the guys are already watching something on TV. Glancing down at my phone in my hands, I see I'm right on time.

To my annoyance, there is an unread text message from Roman. Ever since he began texting me a week ago threatening me with nude photos in an attempt to get him back, I have received multiple messages from him. Some with photos I didn't know existed of me that were not PG 13, and others were just threats to get back together with him if I didn't want the images to get out. It was exhausting, to say the least. And I'm getting over it. Fucking big time. I tried to call his bluff, but he has been relentless.

At this point, I don't know what else to do.

Roman: Come on, Ev. How long are you going to hold out on me? I have more of these if you're wondering. And I'm willing to show everyone. Just say the magic words and I'll stop.

With a huff, I ignore the message and slip my phone into my pocket. I can't believe this fucking guy. It seems he's not going to stop, but I don't know what to do about it. I can't go to Miles for help because he'll lose his fucking mind, and I don't want him to do something he'll regret. Besides him, I have no one else to turn to for help, leaving me to deal with this on my own.

As I approach the front door of the building, I glance at the motorcycle in the parking lot beside the apartment building. A shiver runs down my spine. I know who that bike belongs to, and I know for a fact how sexy he looks when he's riding it.

Damn, you, Jaylen Black.

Inhaling slowly, I walk through the front door to the building and climb the rusted metal staircase until I reach apartment nine. It doesn't take long for me to hear loud voices and laughter alongside the volume of the TV as something plays. Whatever they're watching is making them all laugh hysterically, my brother's booming laughter the loudest of them all.

Rolling my eyes, I lift my hand to knock as hard as I can

against the flimsy wooden door. I just hope that it was loud enough for someone to he—

The door swings open and a pair of bright ocean eyes stare down at me, a cheeky smile touching his lips.

Did he hear me coming with his heightened vampire senses? I should've known he would.

My breath catches in my throat at the sight of him as his strong sandalwood cologne consumes my senses. It takes everything in me not to audibly gulp at the way his lip ring glints under the light in the hallway or the way his hair is messier than usual and slightly damp as if he's just gotten out of the shower and hasn't styled it yet.

I pinch the skin on the top of my hand to remind me that we're not the only two people in the apartment right now. Any second my brother is going to appear—

"Ev!" Miles calls from behind Jaylen. In a flash, he's standing beside his best friend with a smile on his face. "You're just in time. The pizza should be here any minute."

I clear my throat and nod, stepping past Jaylen who isn't wearing a shirt and smells of soft-scented soap. I was right, he did just get out of the shower. As I walk further into the room and wave at Ethan and Preston sitting on the couch, it takes every fiber of my being to not turn around and check out the sharp ridges of Jaylen's abdomen—achieved by years of soccer training and a vigorous workout routine—or the way his eyes roam over every inch of my body.

Instead, I walk to the kitchen to grab myself a glass of water to cool the fuck down.

"Jay, go put a shirt on," Miles scolds from the living room as I chug a glass of room-temperature tap water. "My sister is here, jeez."

I hear Jaylen chuckle as he walks down the hallway to his bedroom. I sag against the kitchen counter and breathe slowly through my nose. Ever since our night at the *Black Rose*, the tension between Jaylen and I has been palpable, almost to the point where I find it hard to breathe. As much as my body reacts to him and his presence, I know what'll happen if I cross that line, and it's not something I'm ready to face yet.

Putting the now empty glass on the drying rack beside the sink, I maneuver it around the dishes that are stacked there that have likely been clean for days, knowing Miles and Jaylen. I do my best to ignore the mess on the small dining table as I head to the fridge to collect a beer before walking into the living room where all four men are now sitting on the two black leather couches across from a large TV.

The apartment is small, with only enough space for two couches, a small stand for the TV, a wooden coffee table they found on the side of the road, and a bookcase to store all their random shit. The off-white walls have chips in the paint and cracks in the roof. I swear this building hasn't been renovated since the early 2000s when shag carpet was a big trend and funky tiles in the bathroom and kitchen were in.

Jaylen has put a black shirt on to match his black sweat-pants, and his hair is still damp and falling over his eyes. I can feel them on the side of my head as I walk to sit beside my brother who left a space for me at the end. He purposefully sat in the middle to keep me separated from Jaylen on his other side, no doubt.

"So, what are we watching?" I ask, looking around the room.

Preston shrugs, running a hand through his short blonde hair as his hazel eyes meet mine. "You're the woman of the house, so we'll let you decide."

"Me?" I snort, looking to Miles who shrugs in return. "You want me to decide on what movie we watch? I don't know what everyone is in the mood for."

"Maybe a thriller?" Ethan suggests, his green eyes looking around the room before landing on me. "We trust your judgment, Evie."

I sigh. If I had known I would be in charge of choosing the movie we watch, I would've come prepared. Taking in Ethan's boyish features and sweet smile, I can't see this man being a vampire. But then again, is one able to tell who is a vampire and who isn't just by their appearance? It's unlikely, but I still have my suspicions about him.

I say the first movie that comes to mind. "What about *The Invitation*? I saw a trailer for it recently and thought it looked good."

Miles nods in agreement. "I've heard about that movie too, and even thought about watching it. What does everyone think?"

Ethan and Preston nod in agreement with my choice of movie, but Jaylen just gives me a knowing smile before he nods in agreement. What the hell is that about?

"All right, it's settled then," Miles says and starts scrolling through his phone, likely trying to find it on one of the streaming services he pays for. Before he can put the movie on, there is a knock at the front door. "The pizza is here!"

As he jumps to his feet to go collect the pizza, Jaylen turns to look at me. That knowing smile has returned. "I see what you did there."

I frown, not understanding his cryptic words. "What did I do?"

He smiles but doesn't say another word as Miles closes the front door, sets the pizza down on the small wooden coffee table, and presses play on the movie.

Throughout the movie, I can feel Jaylen's eyes on the side of my head, making it hard for me to focus on what is happening on the screen when all I can think of is the way he is watching me intently, somehow without Miles noticing. Thank God.

There is just something about the way he makes my body feel as though it has ignited into bursts of flames that make my head spin and my core clench that is so addicting. Whenever I'm around him, I crave the sensation and wish I could get more from him—anything—but know I'm unable to. Especially with my brother around, keeping a watchful eye on me.

As the movie gets closer to the end, I realize what Jaylen meant when he said, "I see what you did there." I unknowingly chose a fucking vampire thriller movie. If I could facepalm myself without receiving curious reactions from those around me, I would.

Before the ending credits start to roll, I excuse myself, needing to go to the bathroom—mostly because it feels as though I can't breathe properly because of the tension between Jaylen and me. Or am I just imagining it? I just need to take a breather before I grab another drink.

When I finish up in the bathroom and throw some cold water on my face, hoping to calm my racing heart and cool my hot skin, I step out into the hallway, only to be met by a large mass and piercing blue eyes. His face is partially covered by the darkness around us, the only light coming from above the front door to our left.

I look up at Jaylen. "What do you think you're doing?"

"I could ask you the same thing."

"Oh, really?" I say, raising a brow at him.

He grins, chewing on his lip ring. That action alone has me biting back a moan.

What the fuck is wrong with me?

"You should probably take a step back if you don't want my brother catching us being within a foot of each other," I say, trying to not sound as breathless as I feel. "You know how he is."

"You're probably right," Jaylen says, his voice just above a whisper. "But I also don't give a fuck if he catches us."

My breath hitches in my throat as I take a step back, now flush with the door. Jaylen surprises me by lifting both of his arms to rest his hands on either side of my head on the door, caging me between his thick arms. Being this close to him, breathing in his intoxicating scent as he stares down at me, has my mind spinning. I want to reach up and run my finger over the cool metal in his lip or brush my fingers through his messy hair, tugging gently on the roots. I want to touch every inch of his body and have him explore my own, but I know I can't, even if I want it so fucking badly.

I don't know what switch was flipped between us that took our friendship from friendly hellos to I want you, but it's driving me insane. I'm on a rollercoaster I can't seem to get off.

"We can't," I breathe, his lips inches away as he leans in. His breath is minty with a hint of whiskey, a scent I wouldn't think would work so well together but is now one of my favorites. "You need to step back."

"I know you want to, little angel," he says, his lips barely brushing mine. Flecks of red reflect in his irises, making me gulp. "I know you want me."

"I-I," I stammer, unable to form words. My mind is blank with nothing but the image of his eyes boring into mine, holding me hostage where I stand.

"Just admit it," Jaylen presses. "Your body is giving you away."

My thighs clench together on their own accord as my core tingles, and before I can utter a response, a cheeky grin covers his lips and he steps back, his arms dropping to his sides, allowing me to breathe in some fresh air. I'm all but spluttering for air as Jaylen leans against the wall across from me and smiles, knowing exactly what he's doing.

He's playing with me.

I should've fucking known.

"Was that really necessary?" I huff, folding my arms over my chest. "You're an asshole."

Jaylen shrugs. "I like watching you squirm and listening to the way the rhythm of your heartbeat changes when I'm near. Your scent is fucking delectable, too."

My cheeks burn at his words. I forgot about his heightened senses and the fact that he could read me like a book because of it. He may not be able to read my mind, but he can sure as hell read my body. I'm not sure which one is worse for me. Maybe it's good that he can't hear the thoughts I have about him. I'm glad no one can hear them.

"Miles could've walked down the hallway and caught us," I point out, and on cue, the three men in the living room laugh at whatever they're watching on TV.

Jaylen chuckles dryly, shaking his head. "I think he's a little too preoccupied to realize that we're both missing."

He's right, but it doesn't make the fact that Miles could've caught us any less real. I know he's only teasing me—at least, I think he is—but had Miles walked down the hallway and caught me pressed against the bathroom door with Jaylen inches away from my lips, we would've both been fucked, and he knows that.

My lips still tingle from the feel of Jaylen's breath fanning across them, and I can slightly taste mint and whiskey on my tongue.

"Besides, you have nothing to worry about," Jaylen says at my silence. "I would've heard him coming, just like I heard your heart racing when you arrived earlier."

I exhale slowly, knowing he's right, once again. Despite

this, I wish Jaylen had not stopped. I wish he had pressed his lips to mine, allowing me to fully taste the mint and whiskey lingering on them, or admit out loud that, yes, I do want him. More than he could possibly know.

But that didn't happen, and I don't know whether to be grateful or disappointed.

Jaylen Black is a danger to me and my heart. Not because he's a vampire that feeds on human blood to survive, but because I know he's capable of breaking my heart if I were to give it to him, and that fucking terrifies me.

"What are we doing, Jaylen?" I finally ask, my heart pounding in my chest. I know he can hear it, but I don't care. The question needed to be asked while I still have the nerve.

He cocks his head to the side, dragging his tongue over his bottom lip. "You tell me, Ev."

Before I can respond, footsteps pounding on the carpet in the living room, approaching us, brings me back to reality. Miles steps into the hallway, his eyes flicking between me and Jaylen as we stand opposite each other in the partially lit hallway. I wrap my arms around my waist and attempt to slow my breathing.

"What are you two doing?" Miles asks, approaching us slowly. I catch the suspicious look in his eyes.

"Nothing," I answer, pushing off the bathroom door. "I ran into Jaylen on my way out of the bathroom."

Miles's eyes flick to Jaylen who looks indifferent as he watches us, his eyes giving away nothing about what just happened. But I can sense that Miles doesn't believe that we innocently ran into each other. He can smell that something is going on, which isn't good.

"Okay," he says slowly, his eyes landing on me. "Come on, Ev. We're about to start the second movie. Preston wants to watch a comedy after the crazy movie you chose. I still can't believe what happened at the end. I was not expecting that."

I roll my eyes as I follow Miles down the hallway. When I reach the end, something in me makes my feet stop in my tracks, forcing me to look back at Jaylen. My heart lodges in my throat when I see his eyes glowing red in the darkness of the hallway, watching me carefully.

If there is one thing I learned about vampires through my research, it's the meaning behind their eyes turning red. It can be one of two things—anger or lust. And as Jaylen stares at me, his gaze intense, it's obvious it's the latter, and that has my skin prickling with excitement and fear.

CHAPTER 9
JAYLEN

S weat pours off my forehead and my breathing is ragged as I dribble the ball across the green grass and in one fluid movement, I kick the ball as hard as I can. I watch as it slips past Cain's hands to land in the top left corner of the net.

I smile and walk over to Cain to pat him on the back. "That was a good effort."

He inhales sharply, trying to get his breath back. "I'm so glad I don't have to defend against you in games, Jay. You put me on my ass every time."

He's not wrong about that. I would hate to go up against me in a soccer game knowing the strength and speed I'm capable of. Of course, I dial it back a tad to avoid suspicion. The last thing I want is for Coach and the rest of the management team to think I'm on steroids or something.

"Well, you're lucky you only have to defend against me during practice." I clap a hand over his shoulder. "Keep up the great work for tonight."

He smiles. "You too, Cap."

I jog back to where the rest of the team is standing, waiting for their turn to try and get the ball past Cain. He is one of our level's best goalkeepers across the country, so he is the perfect person to train with. If we can get the ball past him, then we can do the same with every other keeper we play against.

Preston steps forward to take his turn as I move to stand next to Miles and Ethan. They have already had their turn with Ethan failing to sink the ball into the back of the net while Miles succeeded.

Miles claps me on the back. "That was a solid shot. I swear Cain can never save one of your shots."

"You never fail against him," Ethan adds with a smile. "And that's why you're our captain."

I shrug and fold my sweaty arms over my training shirt. "Maybe one day he'll get lucky."

As Preston fails to get the ball past Cain, my heightened senses pick up on the conversation Roman is having with his two friends while they wait for the remaining players in line to take their turn. I have always hated the guy, not just because of what he did to Evie when they were dating, but because he's so fucking annoying and entitled. He thinks he should have everything handed to him on a silver platter, whether it's Evie or wanting the title of captain.

He joined the team the same year as me, Ethan, Preston, and Miles, and from the first day of training, I knew we weren't going to get along. It was clear he wanted to be captain so badly that when Coach gave the title to me, I heard Roman talking shit about me in the locker room when he thought I couldn't hear. But I hear everything.

He has made it clear he doesn't like me, and the feeling is mutual.

When he started dating Evie, I can't say I was angry because I was fucking livid. I knew what kind of guy he was because I had seen it firsthand playing alongside him for a couple of years. So, I wanted to warn her about him, but I didn't want to overstep my boundaries, especially the one Miles had put in place when we were in high school. He strictly told me I could never date Evie. I hated the idea, but I respected his wishes as my best friend. But fuck was it hard to sit back and watch that fucker Roman be with her. To kiss her. Be the reason she smiled. And know that he fucked her. It made my blood boil, but there was nothing I could do about it.

I heard the news about their break-up from Miles, and to say I was elated would be an understatement. I was fucking thrilled. It didn't take long for the school to find out he had cheated on her, but Miles didn't want her to know that, so he did everything he could to protect her from the truth as he had been doing her entire life since the death of their parents. I don't know how he managed to keep the truth from her, but it must've worked because as far as I know, she doesn't know the entire school is aware of what happened.

Ethan and Miles are talking about the game tonight, but all I can focus on is what Roman is saying to his friends.

"Are you sure it's going to work?" his friend Dale asks.

Roman has a smug smirk on his lips as he shrugs. "Who knows? But there is only one way to find out. I think once I up the anty on the photos, she'll come crawling back to me in no time."

My arms fall to my side, my fists clenching at his words. He's not talking about Evie, right?

"What if she tells Miles about it?" Jim, his other friend, asks, lowering his voice. "That wouldn't be so—"

"She won't tell Miles shit," Roman interrupts, running a hand over his shaved head. "After dating her for a year, I know she won't go to her brother for anything that involves her personal life because of how overprotective he is, no matter how much she threatens to do so. I know she'll try to handle this on her own and when she realizes she has no choice but to get back together with me, it will be too late for Miles to do anything about it."

What the fuck is he talking about? What is he doing to Evie that would make her take him back? The thought of her 'crawling back' to him makes me see red, my palms stinging from how deep my nails are embedded into my skin.

"If she is resisting now or even calling your bluff, how do you plan to make this work?" Dale asks, his brown eyes searching Roman's face.

"I will admit that the first few photos didn't work, but I have no doubt that the last one will be the cherry on top if she continues to ignore my warnings." The evil laugh that escapes his lips has me ready to go over there and put his head through the ground, but I reign in my anger. It won't do me any good to beat his ass until I know exactly what the hell is going on.

"Jaylen?"

My head snaps to the side at the sound of my name. Miles and Ethan are looking at me questionably.

"You all good?" Miles asks and looks past me to where Roman is standing a few feet away, laughing with his friends. His eyes darken at the sight of his sister's ex-boyfriend. "God, I fucking hate that guy."

"Me too," I say and clear my throat. "Anyway, what's up?"

"Coach said we're done with training for now. He wants us to go home to rest and have a big meal before the game tonight," Ethan says. "Mind if I hang out at yours before we head back?" The hunger in his eyes tells me he's starving for some blood, and so am I. As much as I would love to rip Roman apart and drink him dry, I know I can't, so I will have to settle for the hidden blood stash in my room that I share with Ethan.

"Sure," I answer and turn to Miles. "You coming too?"

He shakes his head. "Nah, I have something I need to go do."

"Let me guess, Cindy?" I raise a brow at him. He's been dating this mystery girl for a few weeks now and we have yet to meet her. All I know is that she is a student here and they met at a frat party, but that's it. But if he's not going to be at the apartment, it means we can eat in peace without fear of being caught by him.

Miles chuckles. "Maybe. Maybe not. It's none of your business."

Ethan playfully rolls his eyes. "Okay, sure. Well, I guess we'll see you back here tonight then?"

Miles nods as we leave the pitch and head toward the locker room. "Of course."

When we enter the cool locker room, I'm thankful to be out of the sun. I head straight to my locker, pull the black and red training jersey over my head, and replace it with a plain black T-shirt. I need to shower, but that can wait until I get back to the apartment. I sit down on the bench across from my locker and scroll through my phone while Ethan and Miles get changed out of their dirty training clothes.

At the sound of Roman's voice, I glance to the left to see him standing in front of his locker typing on his phone. Is he texting Evie? Not knowing exactly what he's doing to her makes my muscles tense with anger. Even though I know I should let this go because it has nothing to do with me, I just can't. I care too much about her to at least not make sure she's safe.

Roman turns his phone off and shuts it in his locker, making sure to enclose a small padlock through the handle before heading toward the shower room with his belongings.

"Okay, we're heading out now," Ethan says from behind me.

I turn to face him. "Just give me a minute and I'll meet you outside."

He nods as Miles claps me on the back. "I'll see you tonight."

I nod. "Have fun with Cindy."

He smirks in return before the two turn to leave, along with the rest of the team who aren't in the shower room.

With no one around, my curiosity gets the best of me. I have to know what the fuck Roman is texting Evie. As I stand and walk over to Roman's locker, my heightened senses tell me that there are still guys in the shower and no one has turned off the water yet.

Inspecting the lock holding the door shut, I decide that I don't have time to try and crack the password, so I just reach up, grip the small black lock, and rip it off. The snapping of metal can't be heard over the sound of rushing water from the shower room, so I continue what I'm doing.

I find Roman's phone lying next to his car keys and wallet. Without thinking, I pick up the device and the screen comes to life, asking for a passcode to be entered. Shit, I didn't think this far ahead. Surely, this idiot wouldn't have 1, 2, 3—

The home screen comes to life when I tap on the number 4. Of course, he's that much of a fucking idiot that his passcode would be the easiest number to guess. I'm not surprised.

I don't waste any time and head straight to his recent messages. Evie's name is at the top of the list and I see he texted her in the last five minutes, which is what he was doing before he left to go shower. Opening up the conversation, my eyes widen at the text messages between the two of them. It makes my blood boil seeing the way he talks to her. He's lucky that I'm refraining myself from marching into the shower room and ripping his fucking head clean off his body.

But Evie is strong. I can tell by her responses. She always has been strong-willed and ready to stand up for herself. But it doesn't mean she should have to deal with her ex-boyfriend threatening to expose her nudes if she doesn't get back with him. The image of her naked back in the shower is now burned into my mind, and not for a good reason. It makes my blood boil with rage that he is doing this to her. No man should treat a woman like this.

Roman is a sick human being. I know that fucking much.

The sound of a shower switching off reminds me I don't have time to stand here and read their entire conversation. I click back to the home screen, put the phone down where I found it, and close the locker door, making sure to shove the broken lock into my pocket. Walking back over to my gym bag, I sling it over my shoulder and close my locker.

As I leave the locker room, my vision red with hot anger, I hear Roman say, "Why the fuck is my locker broken?"

"Pass me a bag," I say to Ethan when I sit down on the edge of my bed, my curls still soaked with water. After getting out of the shower, I was too thirsty to take a couple of extra minutes to dry my hair. The hunger gnawing at my insides was too much to ignore.

Ethan scoots my desk chair across the shaggy brown carpet with his hand outstretched to me. "Someone is thirsty."

I snatch the full blood bag from his hand. "No shit, Sherlock. I'm fucking starving." I bring the small opening at the top of the plastic bag to my lips and suck the blood into my mouth. As soon as the cool liquid touches my tongue, the tension in my shoulders ceases and my mind clears. The satisfied feeling of quenching my thirst spreads across my body as I suck the bag dry.

The first drop of blood I had when I transitioned drove me into a fucking frenzy. My parents also drank from blood bags and gave one to me the night of my eighteenth birthday. But the hunger deep in my stomach was so strong that I lost control of myself. It took my dad restraining me with thick chains in the basement before I calmed the fuck down. They were afraid I was going to run out into the street and rip innocent people apart just to get to their blood.

And truthfully, I thought the same. I almost didn't recognize myself in that moment. In the blink of an eye, I was a whole new person. Human me was long gone, and that scared me more than I thought it would.

The next night, my parents died in what I was told was a car accident by the police, but I knew that wasn't possible. Not when vampires can only die by being staked through the heart or decapitated. They were killed and the scene was staged to appear as an accident. But why? To this day, I don't know. At first, I was adamant that I would find whoever did this, but I quickly came to the realization that they were either killed by a hunter or another vampire. Either option wouldn't be beneficial for me to look into because it could bring me more harm than good. But I haven't forgotten about them, and I never will.

After that night, I was alone in the new life I had just started. Lost and confused. And I needed to find the light at the end of the tunnel. Thankfully, that light was Ethan and his family.

"Slow down, cowboy," Ethan says, biting back a smile. "You're going to give yourself a tummy ache."

I roll my eyes and toss the empty bag beside me. Running both of my hands through my wet hair, the curls gliding against my skin, I release a deep sigh. The fresh blood flowing through my veins is what I needed after today.

"Penny for your thoughts," Ethan says.

I lift my eyes to meet his. "You don't want to know."

He shuffles on the seat and folds his hands in his lap. "Try me."

With a sigh, I sit up straighter. Ethan may get on my nerves at times with his witty remarks and joking personality, but he is a great listener. Even when I don't want to talk, he somehow finds a way to force whatever thoughts I have been keeping locked away out of my mouth. With Ethan being a vampire, he has been the only person I can turn to whenever I have issues that Miles cannot know about.

I remember the first time I met Ethan during the first day of practice in my freshman week. His scent stood out among the rest of the team when he walked into the locker room. Vampires can sense other vampires. It's hard to explain, but there is a difference between vampires and humans. Let's just say vampire scents smell like what a decomposing body would smell like. It took me a little while to get used to the specific scent of vampires, but soon enough, it just became another scent on the long list of things I could smell. And no matter how much cologne a vampire uses, we can always sniff out our kind. Now, I hardly notice it.

But from that day on, Ethan took me under his wing. His family helped me through a time in my new life that was meant to be my parent's job, and I couldn't thank them enough. They didn't have to do it because I was their son's new friend and barely knew me, but when they learned of what happened to my parents, they made sure to teach me everything I know now about vampirism. If it wasn't for them, who knows what my life would be like now?

"Okay," I say slowly. "I have a problem."

"What's the problem?"

The images of my little angel on that motherfucker's phone

flash before my eyes again. I screw them shut, hoping it'll erase them from my mind, but that's wishful thinking.

"Roman is blackmailing Evie with some not appropriate photos, and I'm trying so hard not to rip his fucking head off his shoulders."

Ethan's eyes go wide at my words. He leans back in the chair and releases a long breath, nodding slowly. "Okay, yeah. That is a problem. Does Miles know what's going on?"

I shake my head. "I don't want him to find out. I know what he's like with his sister, and I know he'll blow his fucking top if he learns about what's happening. He's overprotective to the point that I think Evie doesn't tell him certain things because she's afraid of what he might do." She has never told me this directly, but I would like to think I know her well enough to make the assumption, especially if her wanting to keep Roman cheating on her a secret is anything to go by.

Ethan chews on his bottom lip and nods slowly. "Okay, yeah, that's fair. But don't do anything stupid, Jay. What Roman is doing is terrible, but you need to control whatever it is you're feeling toward the situation. I know you want to protect Evie, you always have, but you need to keep a level head."

I understand what he's saying, but I can't ignore the rage building deep in my chest the more I think about what Roman is doing to her. No one fucks with the people I care about, especially not that piece of shit. He's a waste of fucking space on this earth.

"Just don't do anything rash until you know more, okay?" Ethan continues, holding eye contact. His relaxed posture and kind eyes remind me that I do need to think logically about the situation. I can't go in guns blazing until I know more.

You can bet your fucking ass I'm going to be keeping a close eye on him from now on.

I close my eyes and exhale slowly. The rage in my chest simmers to a dull ache, allowing me to think more clearly. "You're right."

Ethan grins and waves me off with his hand. "Oh, you're too kind. But you're absolutely correct." He stands from the chair and closes the lid on the cooler where we store our blood bags. "We're getting low on our supply."

I nod, thankful for the change in conversation. "We'll plan a trip to the hospital soon. I'm sure if we take it easy, we can draw out the last few bags."

I watch Ethan as he walks into my closet and gets to his knees with the cooler box in hand. He lifts the loose floorboard in the center of my closet and lowers the box into the small space. Oddly enough, the carved-out space was already here before we moved in freshman year. I don't want to know why or when it was made, but all I can say is I'm glad I picked this room over the one Miles ended up with.

Ethan gets to his feet and turns to me. "Whenever you feel the anger building again in your chest, just remember the breathing exercises my dad taught you, okay?"

I nod. "Okay," I lie.

I don't think breathing exercises are going to erase the deep desire I have to make Roman hurt as much as he's hurting Evie. No one fucks with my little angel. And if he doesn't stop harassing her, he's going to find that out the hard way.

CHAPTER 10
JAYLEN

The roar of the crowd from inside the stadium makes my eardrums ring, and I can't help but smile. I'll never get used to hearing the loud cheers and excited claps from the fans in the seats, waiting impatiently for the game to start. The feeling of seeing thousands of our black and red jerseys scattered around the stadium provides a rush of adrenaline that I crave, always wanting—needing—more of.

"Damn, they're fucking loud tonight," Ethan says from beside me as he slides his socks over his shin guards. "It's probably our biggest home game to date."

I nod, slipping my foot into my cleats, making sure to readjust my socks over my shin guards. "They're mental, and I love it."

"The Dolphins haven't lost a game all season, so we have our work cut out for us," Preston says from behind us, slipping his jersey over his head.

"Good thing we have a great captain that'll hopefully get us the win tonight." Ethan winks, nudging my shoulder. He was perkier than usual after our afternoon feed when we got back to my apartment after practice. We needed it to keep our energy up for the game.

I roll my eyes and lean my elbows on my knees for support. "You know I'll do my best. I always do."

In my freshman year of college, Miles and I decided to try out for the Raiders after doing so well for our high school team. Miles had gotten a sports scholarship that helped get him into the engineering degree we both wanted to do, but I didn't have the grades in school to quite make the cut, so I had to try out just like everyone else, while Miles was more than likely guaranteed a spot on the team.

Being who I am, I had to pull back on my abilities to make me appear just like everyone else. I couldn't allow myself to show my full strength and potential for fear of people growing suspicious. It's been that way my whole life. Over time, I've settled into a rhythm whenever I play soccer, knowing how much power to use and when. The last thing I need is for someone to realize that I'm not like others. I'm different.

"That's why you're the captain and not any of us." Preston laughs as he walks around to stand in front of us. After a moment, his eyes scan the locker room where the rest of the team is getting ready for the game. "Where is Miles?"

I pause, sitting up straight to glance around the room in search of my best friend. When I don't spot him, I shrug. "Who knows? I know he went to see the girl he's hooking up with after practice."

"What was her name again?" Ethan rubs his chin as if hoping that'll make him remember her name. "Oh, right. Cindy. But why would he go see her right before the game?"

"That's his business," I say, getting to my feet.

"He better not be fucking her so good that he misses the start of the game. We need him."

I understand Preston's concerns, but I know Miles and I know he'll wrap up whatever he's doing to be here on time. He knows how important this home game is to the club; it's not something he would miss on purpose.

"There is nothing to worry about. We just have to—"

A loud bang from the door swinging open and colliding with the wall behind it sounds through the room. Miles rushes in, all eyes on him, with his black gym bag slung over his shoulder. His green eyes are wild, and his hair is disheveled as he makes his way to his locker, unable to make eye contact with anyone as he passes.

Preston walks over to him and claps him on the back, about to open his mouth to say something when Miles jumps at the touch, whirling around to face him. His chest is heaving as he fights to catch his breath. I can hear the stutter in the rhythm of his heartbeat and feel the nervousness radiating from him.

I frown at his reaction. What the fuck is going on?

Preston takes a step back. "Jeez, man, chill out. Is everything okay?"

Miles inhales a long breath and nods, his shoulders slumping forward. "Y-Yeah, I'm all good."

"Where were you?" I ask, curious to know what could've set him on edge to be jumping like a scared cat. If he just came back from seeing his girl, he shouldn't be this on edge. Unless he's just nervous about the game tonight.

Miles spins around to open his locker, retrieving his jersey. "I was with Cindy. You know how it is."

I nod, though I don't believe him. His reaction doesn't make sense. But I'm not one to judge, especially not about what he does in his spare time. He's here now, so that's all that matters.

"How was she?" Preston asks with a wink.

I roll my eyes. "Enough about who Miles was fucking. We have a game to prepare for so get ready and be at the tunnel in five."

The team scrambles around the locker room, making sure their gear is on, shin guards ready, and fucking game faces on. The Raiders are a great team—we have only lost one game this season—but the Dolphins are just as good, so we need to make sure we're prepared for a tough ninety minutes.

With the team in formation in the tunnel, standing alongside the Dolphins, we walk out onto the pitch. My ears are ringing from the loud cheers, although my heightened senses make it seem louder inside my head. I do my best to block out the noise, glancing around the stadium as I take in all the occupied seats.

As we stand in a line, the team side by side ready to sing the national anthem, I glance up to see doe eyes looking back at me, and a warm smile touching her lips. My body ignites at the sight of her, in desperate need to be cooled down despite my already cold skin. This isn't a new sensation to me—I've always reacted this way around her, especially as she got older and I started to *really* take notice of her—but ever since she learned my secret, it's like a flip has been switched within me, out of my control.

And now, I just can't get enough of her, which is driving me insane.

Evie smiles in my direction before waving at Miles, who waves back from beside me as the national anthem starts. It amazes me that even though she has to deal with that fucker Roman harassing her by threatening her with nude photos, she still manages to smile and be her usual self. It makes me want to rip Roman's head off even more for hurting her the way he is.

All I can do is watch her. I focus on the way her brown hair falls over her shoulder like a cascading waterfall with the icy blonde section of hair shining under the harsh lights of the stadium or the way her mouth moves to form the syllables of the lyrics as she sings them proudly.

I can't help but wonder how that pretty little mouth of hers and those plump lips would look wrapped around my—

The song ends, and my team begins moving into formation. I hear words of encouragement from our coach, but they sound like static in my ears as I walk to the center line on the pitch.

I can't allow myself to be distracted by Evie for the next ninety minutes.

Focus, Jaylen.

The starting whistle kicks off the game and I look to my left at Miles, who nods in my direction. Oh, we're ready to kick some ass.

Sweat is pouring down the side of my face as I run across the field, the ball bouncing off the inside of my foot as I inch it toward the opposite goal. I can hear the opposing goalkeeper's racing heart as I get closer, the rhythmic beat growing more staggered as the defenders struggle to keep me away.

It's the exact same scenario as this morning with Cain. This keeper is almost as good as him, so if I stick to the same old tactic I use against Cain, I'll have this in the bag. So long as no one gets in my way and messes up the shot.

With one quick glance at the scoreboard, I know I only have twenty seconds left on the clock before the final whistle to sink this ball into the back of the net. It would give the Raiders the win. I can't fail. Not now.

I can sense the defenders hot on my heels, their

breathing heavy as they try to close in on me. But it's no use. Not when I can apply a little more of my power to keep out of reach. The keeper is staring me dead in the eye as I approach. He is standing in the middle of the goal box, so I slow down my pace, reel my right foot back, and kick the ball.

I stop dead in my tracks when I see the ball slide past the keeper's hands as he tries to save it, but he's not close enough as it flies into the back of the net.

An eruption of cheers from the crowd nearly blows the roof of the stadium off as I run toward my teammates and am instantly swept into a massive group hug as we celebrate the 3-2 win over the Dolphins. Miles is the first to clap my back and pull me into a tight hug, followed by the rest of the team as they form a tight circle.

As the Raiders celebrate, I look toward the crowd where I know Evie is and catch the wide smile on her lips as she watches me, her hands clapping along with everyone else in the stadium. All I can focus on is her and the way her amazonite eyes are lit up with joy as she watches me.

She has no idea how enamored I am by her. But she will soon.

"Well done, Jaylen," Coach Jones says, coming up beside me as I slide a fresh black T-shirt over my head. He claps me on the back, a huge smile on his face. He's an older man in his 50s with a goatee and gray hair. "You really were the star of the game."

I smile and turn to face him. "I appreciate that, but I

couldn't have done it without the rest of the team. I just hope I can continue to make you proud."

Coach grins, his fake teeth too bright in the dim locker room. "Just keep doing what you're doing."

I nod, watching as he walks away to talk to Ethan and Preston. It's been almost an hour since the game had finished, and I've spent most of that time in the locker room getting out of my sweaty uniform and celebrating with the team. My teammates have been congratulating me nonstop for the winning goal since walking off the pitch, but I've long since forgotten about it. The only thing on my mind is Evie. At this point, she lives in there rent-free, and I fucking love it.

I was hoping she would stay behind to see Miles after the game, which would allow me to see her too, but her friends dragged her away. It just means I'll have to find another way to get close to her. Admittedly, it has been a challenge to get close to her when Miles is as protective over her as he is. He's always been that way, I know this, but lately, he's been extra overprotective over Evie and I'm unsure why. He doesn't know what happened between us at *Black Rose*, so it couldn't be because of that.

Either way, I'm not letting it get in the way of what I want, and that's *her*. I want all of her, and I will stop at nothing to get what I want.

"Earth to Jaylen." Miles's voice snaps me out of my thoughts.

I look up from my open locker at Miles standing beside me, his brows furrowed slightly.

"You're deep in thought," he comments. "Is everything all good?"

I nod and turn back to my locker to finish grabbing everything I need to take home and shove it into my gym bag. "All is good, man. You?"

Miles nods. I can feel his eyes burning a hole in the side of my face as he watches me. "Yeah. I just wanted to let you know that I'll be home late tonight. I'm going to see Cindy."

"Again?" I quirk a brow as I sling my gym bag over my shoulder and shove my helmet under my other arm.

He chuckles. "I can't say no to good pussy when it's served on a silver platter. You know that better than anyone."

I do. Being who I am, I'm always looking for a woman to satisfy my cravings and bloodlust. I've been with too many women to count, but at some point, they all just blur together, and I can never remember their names or faces. They no longer fill the void deep within my chest. This doesn't bother me in the slightest because there has only ever been one woman I've truly wanted, who I know will satisfy the needs burning deep inside of me. But she's my best friend's little sister, who is off-limits.

Do I care? Not in the slightest. Never fucking have.

Ever since Evie was sixteen and she walked in on me hooking up with a girl at a high school party she knew she wasn't supposed to be at, I knew I would make her mine. Her soft doe eyes, wide with embarrassment, her plump lips pulled tight between her teeth, and her body vibrating with desire was enough for me to truly see her beauty. I don't know what it was about that moment, but it was like a lightbulb switched on above my head and I saw the *real* her. I no longer saw the little girl who liked to choreograph silly dances and ask annoying questions. I saw a woman who took my breath away and made my heart beat erratically by simply looking at me through her long lashes. It was enough for me to push the eager girl trying to hook up with me away without a second thought and take Evie home before her brother saw her at the party.

From that moment on, I swore I would protect her, and

make her mine. And I don't plan on going back on that promise anytime soon.

"Yeah, I get it," I finally respond to Miles. "Do what you have to do."

He nods, leaning down to collect his gym bag off the ground beside his feet. "If I don't see you in the kitchen tomorrow morning, you'll know why."

I clap him on the back as we turn to walk out of the locker room. Most of the guys have already left, leaving us and a few stragglers behind. Luckily for Roman, he didn't stick around, otherwise, I would have had to resist slamming his head into his locker.

We walk down the long corridor to the back entrance of the stadium. The humid air is warm against my cool skin when we step outside. I wave to Miles as he turns to walk toward his car in the parking lot. I parked on the other side of the lot, so I made my way toward my sleek black motorcycle parked alone. All the other vehicles had left.

I listen to the crickets chirping in the bushes beside my bike as I take my leather jacket out of my gym bag and slide it over my arms. With Miles being out of the apartment for the night, I'll be able to indulge in some much-needed blood to refuel all the energy I exerted during the game. With how long our stock is, I have to be mindful of how much I have. I may have only fed a couple of hours ago, but I need to keep my energy up when I can. Rooming with Miles makes feeding a lot more difficult because I have to hide my stash and drink whenever he's not home.

When the *Black Rose* opened in Pullman a few months ago, I could not have been happier. I heard about it through Ethan, who heard it through some other connections he had in town. We don't know much about the owner, other than he's a vampire, because he wants to keep his identity a secret. He opened the bar as a way for vampires in the area to feed safely on willing humans, and then compel them to forget that we exist. Many vampires were being discovered by hunters due to their recklessness when feeding on humans without consent, and it was becoming a problem in the vampire community. Creating a safe space for vampires to feed has allowed many of them to remain hidden and safe.

I would never make such a mistake because the last thing I want is for my kind to be exposed to the world.

Up until the past few weeks, the vampires in the community were staying well hidden because of the *Black Rose*. But somehow, a new hunter in town is managing to track down vampires and kill them. Almost as if they know who they're looking for. Whoever it is, they are smart for staging the murders as some kind of satanic ritual and not the work of a vampire hunter.

But I'm not stupid. I know it's a hunter coming after us. I just don't know who.

"Jaylen," a soft voice says from behind me.

I whirl around to see Amara standing with her hands clasped behind her back, pushing out her tits in the tiny white top covering her chest. She reaches up to flick her white-blonde hair over her shoulder as her eyes bore into mine.

I bite back a groan of annoyance. When I slept with Amara at a frat party a few weeks back, I should've seen the signs and stayed the fuck away from her. She has been obsessed with me ever since, and it's getting on my fucking nerves. I'm always getting calls and texts from her at random times throughout the night, asking if I want to come over. I never answer because I don't want to fuck her again. She wasn't a bad lay—her big tits are phenomenal—but I don't go back for seconds. At least, not in this case.

But it seems she doesn't know how to take a fucking hint.

"What do you want, Amara?"

She shifts on her feet. "I wanted to congratulate you on the game tonight. You did great." When I don't say anything, she continues, "And I wanted to check that you've been getting my calls and texts."

"I have."

"Oh," she says, her shoulders sagging slightly. "Well, I'm glad I was able to catch you before you left. Do you want to come over tonight?"

"No," I say, turning my back to her. "I'm not interested."

"Are you sure? I'll make it worth your time."

I snort, shaking my head as I slide my leg over the seat of my motorcycle, the cool leather sliding against the back of my thighs. "I doubt it." She may have been a decent fuck, but she's shit at giving head, so going back for seconds wouldn't be worth my time.

"You're such an asshole, Jaylen," Amara huffs before storming away, heading toward the main road.

Before I can slip my helmet over my damp hair, I smell the all-too-consuming scent of lavender and lotus that drives me fucking wild.

"Trouble in paradise, I see," Evie says as she steps under one of the street lamps, having walked into the parking lot from the entrance on the main road, passing Amara. "I never thought I would see *the* Jaylen Black having girl trouble."

My eyes rake over her delicious curves and slim waist in the black denim shorts and black cropped top she's wearing. I don't miss the large cocktail glass in her right hand that is half-empty or the way she slightly stumbles over her feet as she approaches me.

"That was nothing," I say, watching her carefully. "Why are you here, little angel? Came to see me?"

Evie rolls her eyes and flicks her long hair over her shoulder. "In your dreams. I wouldn't want to inflate your already large ego." Her words are slurred, but I can still make out what she is saying.

Did she leave whatever bar she was at to come back to the stadium? Why?

"I came to see Miles," she continues as she walks past me, not even stopping for a second. "You seen him around?"

I bite back an amused smile. "You just missed him. He left to go see his girlfriend."

Evie stops in her tracks and slowly turns to face me, her doe eyes slightly blurred. "Well, that's a shame. I might just text him."

She moves to walk past me, but my hand darts out to wrap around her wrist, halting her in place. Her breathing hitches and the rhythm of her heart stutters as she turns to look at me.

"Are you okay?" I ask.

The crease in her forehead makes me realize that the question may have come out of left field. But after what I learned today about Roman and the texts he's been sending her, I want to make sure she's okay. As much as I want her to know that I would do anything for her, even if it meant burning this entire fucking planet to the ground if she asked, I need to take this slow. If I have to watch from the sideline, keeping a safe distance to ensure her safety, then I will. But at this moment, as I'm looking into her soft eyes and seeing the pain hidden behind them, I can't help but let my guard drop.

Evie huffs and snatches her hand out of my grip as if she were on fire. "I'm fine. You should do something about that cold skin of yours. I wouldn't want you catching a cold."

I chuckle at her words. Even drunk off her ass with a cocktail glass in one hand and a scowl on her face, she's still the same witty Evie I have always known.

"When you admit you're attracted to me, I'll look at getting some hand warmers."

She rolls her eyes and walks past me toward the main road, chugging the remainder of the liquid in the large glass. "I guess neither of us will get what we want."

I tug my lip ring between my teeth and watch as she stumbles through the parking lot, hopefully heading back to the bar she came from. Before Evie leaves my sight, she slows her pace and pulls out her phone from her bag, reading whatever is on the screen before disappearing around the corner.

"Don't worry, little angel. I always get what I want."

CHAPTER II

EVIE

I can still feel the ghost of his fingers wrapped around my wrist, holding me firmly in place. It had spread a fire across my skin, one that I couldn't put out no matter how many more fruity cocktails I drank when I got back to the bar last night. All I could feel was the tingling sensation across my skin, reminding me how bad Jaylen is for me, but also, how insanely attracted I am to him.

Although, that's not something I'll ever admit to him.

My mind is screaming at me to stay clear of him and run as fast as I can in the opposite direction, but my heart seems to want to steer me in another direction, straight toward him. I know he's bad for me, but it seems my body doesn't give a fuck.

It's fucking with my head, and I don't know what to do.

After the game, Rylee, Jaycee, and Candie dragged me to the Tipsy Tiki down the road from the stadium to celebrate the Raider's win over the Dolphins. I had one too many cocktails and decided to go rogue and leave the bar. Drunk me wanted to see Miles even though I hadn't texted him before to see if he was still at the stadium. I don't know how the security guard let me leave the bar with my cocktail, but he was a legend for doing so.

When I arrived at the staff parking lot the team uses, I caught the back end of Jaylen and Amara's conversation despite how tipsy I was at the time. I didn't even know they knew each other, but I did hear her ask him to spend the night with her, which didn't shock me. Of course, he would've slept with Amara. I'm not saying she gets around, but I know *Jaylen* does, so it makes sense they would've crossed paths. I want to know more about their history, but it seems there isn't much given how dismissive he was of her.

I don't remember much of my interaction with Jaylen thanks to the alcohol I had consumed, but I didn't forget the way his cool palm felt against my flushed skin. With how intensely the memory is embedded into my skin, I don't think I'll forget his touch.

I sigh, and close the book on my lap, having given up on reading the same paragraph mindlessly. I look around the living room, noticing that the girls who were in here earlier had left without my knowing. Good, I welcome the silence.

It's Sunday, so most of the girls in the house are recovering from a wild Saturday night of drinking or doing the walk of shame as they walk up the staircase to their bedroom. But me? I'm sitting on the couch with a hot mug of tea and the current book I'm reading, violently hungover but with no desire to be in bed all day. I have found it doesn't help cure it but makes me feel even more like shit.

Dragging myself off the couch, I collect my book and half-drunk tea and head toward the kitchen. It's almost midday and the house is mostly quiet because everyone is in bed recovering. This means I have the kitchen all to myself to make a nice lunch and enjoy some time alone—

Well, I spoke too soon.

I stop just inside the doorway to the kitchen and watch as Amara turns to face me, her pale blue eyes piercing straight into mine. Her arms are folded over her chest and her white-blonde hair is in a messy bun on top of her head. I can tell by the way her shoulders are squared and her flaring nose that she's pissed.

Just fucking great.

"Evie." The tone of her voice makes it seem like it was painful to say my name. I clench my empty fist at my side. "I need to talk to you."

"Not interested," I say. Leaving my book on the island, I walk toward the kitchen sink to place my mug inside. I can see Amara leaning against the counter in my peripheral, her eyes trained on me. "There is nothing for us to talk about."

"You know very well there is. I saw you with him."

"With whom?" I play dumb, turning fully toward her. I know exactly what she's talking about, but I don't want to make this easy for her.

Amara rolls her eyes. "I saw you with Jaylen after the game. Are you looking to have my sloppy seconds?"

I snort, shaking my head. This bitch can't be serious, right? Her sloppy seconds? I fold my arms over my chest, matching her stance. If she wants to play games, I can play better than her.

"Sloppy seconds? Please. From what I overheard, he wasn't too keen on having you again, so I don't think you're in a position to be possessive over him, don't you think?"

Amara's jaw drops slightly at my words, and I bite back a snicker. Check and fucking mate.

"You need to stay away from him," she says, her voice lowering as if to intimate me. Unfortunately for her, it doesn't work.

I laugh, shaking my head. "You want me to stay away from

Jaylen? For what reason? So you can have him to yourself? I think you're dreaming, Amara."

She slams her fist on the countertop, the noise echoing throughout the room. "You listen here, bitch. Jaylen is mine, so it would be in your best interest to stay away from him or else."

I raise a brow at her. "Or what?"

"I will ruin your life," she says through gritted teeth.

I roll my eyes. "I'd like to see you try."

Not wanting to stick around to hear any more of her useless threats, I push off the counter and walk toward the door, making sure to collect my book off the island along the way. It's amusing to me that Amara, someone who may have slept with Jaylen once, is trying to warn me away from him. It's comical, really.

If I didn't listen to my brother's warning, then there is no way in hell I'm listening to hers.

When I reach the top of the staircase, my phone vibrates in my hand. I look down to see an unread message from Roman. I swallow hard. This nonsense has been going on for way too long now. When I was walking back to the bar last night, he texted me a fully nude photo of me in my closet that I didn't know he had taken. My face was clear and so was every inch of my body.

All the text said was: *You have one last chance or this photo will be online forever. I'm not fucking around anymore, Evie. Last chance.*

Let's just say, the text rattled me enough that now I refuse to open his recent message for fear of what I might find.

Amara's warning to stay away from Jaylen is still lingering in the back of my mind as I sit in my lecture this warm Monday morning. I'm not worried that she's going to 'ruin my life' as she so kindly put it. I just want to know what happened between the two of them for her to act this possessively over him that she thinks it's okay to go around threatening anyone who might get close to him.

She's batshit crazy.

I'm pulled from my thoughts when the professor announces the end of the lecture. Thank, God. All I've been able to think about for the past hour is going to Bluebird Co. to grab a bite to eat and a coffee. As I leave the building, I feel the warm, humid air on my skin, instantly making it feel clammy. I can't wait for the weather to start getting cooler.

Slipping my sunglasses over my eyes, I make my way to the coffee shop. I notice students splayed out on the grass areas eating lunch together or enjoying some time alone while reading a book or listening to music. It's a stunning day with not a cloud in the sky, so I understand the appeal. The campus is decorated with many trees and manicured gardens that make it appealing to sit outside instead of in the library. I might just have to do the same.

"The victim count is up to eight now," a girl says to her friend as they pass me.

The guy standing next to her gasps, his hand on his chest. "You're fucking kidding me. What the hell is going on in this town?"

The two of them walk in the opposite direction, taking their conversation with them. It doesn't take a brain surgeon to know what they're talking about. It's all anyone can talk about in Pullman.

Eight victims. Eight vampires have been killed in the past few weeks by a hunter.

Who the fuck is this person? They're clearly on a war path to take down all the vampires in Pullman. I should find it alarming that there are more vampires in Pullman than I thought, but each passing day reminds me that anything is possible in this fucking town.

As I round the corner to the street where Bluebird Co. is located, I run into something hard, forcing me backward. "What the fuck—" The words die in my throat when I see Roman's face, his eyes staring down at me.

Oh, for fuck's sake.

"Evie," Roman drawls, shifting the backpack further up his shoulder. He's dressed in a pair of blue denim jorts and a white T-shirt. "What a lovely surprise."

"For you maybe," I grumble. I'm not the least bit thrilled to see this motherfucker, once again. Are his threatening messages not enough that now he has to show me his face to remind me that he is still lurking in the dark corners of my life? "I'm getting really tired of having to constantly ask what the hell is it that you want."

"Then don't," he counters with a smirk. "Just enjoy my presence and call this a happy accident that we ran into each other."

I look past him at the coffee shop entrance that is only feet away, and huff. "It wasn't an accident, though, was it? You know my schedule for the week."

"You told me not to follow you, but not that I couldn't accidentally run into you."

I roll my eyes. Of course, he would say something like that. He must think I'm an idiot. "Okay, Roman. Whatever helps you sleep better at night." I step to the side, the coffee shop now in my direct line of sight. "Now, if you'll excuse me—"

Roman steps in front of me, blocking my view once again. I look up to see his eyes have darkened as they watch me. It sends a shiver down my spine. "I didn't say I was finished with the conversation, Evie."

I swallow hard and square my shoulders. I refuse to let this fucker intimidate me. "Get out of my way. *I'm* done talking to you. In fact, I never want to see your fucking face ever again."

His hand snaps out to wrap around my wrist and he uses his strength to pull me flush against his chest. Being this close to him used to make my skin flush and my heart race with excitement. But now, my heart is racing for a different reason —fear. I try to claw at his meaty hand to release his grip, but he doesn't let up. He only tightens his grip, making me whimper.

Oh, fuck.

"Let go of me," I whisper, unable to look him in the eye.

"You're mine, Evie," Roman says, his voice dark and dangerous. "Do you hear me? Mine! I don't care what you say or feel, you are mine. You always have and always will be. I told you that you had one chance to come to your senses and get back together with me. I didn't want to use the photos against you, but you left me with no choice."

My heart is pounding harshly against my ribcage at his words. *He's a fucking psycho.*

"I made a mistake, okay, Evie," he continues, his eyes hard. His breath fanning against my face at his proximity makes my stomach spin with nausea. "It'll never happen again, I promise you that. You're the only girl for me, and I know that now. Please, Evie, just give me one more chance to show you why we're perfect for each other, and why you're *my* girl."

I look around to see a few eyes of students passing by are on us but none of them stop to intervene. They just keep walking, acting like they don't see me being manhandled by Roman. It makes me angry that no one is stepping in when they can clearly tell by my wide, frantic eyes that something is seriously wrong here. Why won't someone help me?

What the fuck is he going to do to me? If his threatening texts are anything to go by, this man could be capable of anything, and that thought alone makes a nervous shiver race down my spine. *He's fucking unhinged.*

"I'll never be yours," I spit, anger building in my chest. I refuse to be a helpless damsel in distress that needs saving. I've been through enough shit to know how to take care of myself, even against Roman. "You're fucking delusional."

An evil grin spreads across his face, his grip tightening around my wrist. I claw at his wrist again and feel a thin layer of his skin give way beneath my nails. But it doesn't seem to affect him in the slightest. "No one is here to save you, Evie. Not your brother. Not your little friends. No one."

"You forgot about me."

My body stills at the sound of *his* deep voice. I can feel him standing behind me, his overwhelming scent of sandalwood consuming me. Roman's wide eyes as he stares behind me confirm my suspicions.

"If you don't let go of her, I'm going to tear your fucking hand clean off your arm so you're unable to touch her ever again. Only *I* can touch her."

CHAPTER 12
JAYLEN

Roman looks like he's just seen the devil, his eyes wide and unblinking. Good, because I can be the devil if I want to be. And if he keeps touching my little angel like that, he's going to find out really fucking soon just how far I'm willing to go for her.

"I'm not going to repeat myself," I warn, tilting my head to the side.

That does the trick. Roman snatches his hand to his chest, allowing Evie to rub the skin on her wrist where he had been gripping her. I bite back a growl at how red and raw her skin is. That motherfucker...

I take a step forward, closing the distance between me and Roman, but the coward steps back, not wanting to be in reach of me. That's probably a smart choice on his behalf because if I could get my hands on him, I'd wring his neck and show him who Evie belongs to. It sure as hell isn't him.

Evie turns to look at me, relief washing over her features. The pounding of her heart rings in my ears—loud like a siren. My nails digging into the palms of my hands as I fist them at my sides is the only thing stopping me from rushing forward and teaching this asshole a lesson.

It was bad enough that he was threatening Evie via text messages with photos of herself, but it's another to lay his fucking hands on her.

Roman holds up his hands in defense. "I-I'm sorry, man. I didn't mean to—"

"Shut up," I snap, not wanting to hear his sorry ass excuses. "If you want to live to see tomorrow then you better get the fuck out of my sight."

He nods, spinning on his heels to leave without a word.

But I stop him by calling his name. And like an obedient dog, he turns to face me, his body stiffening under my gaze.

"If you ever think about touching *my* girl again," I say, stepping forward to wrap a comforting arm around Evie's shoulders, pulling her close to my side, "just know it'll be the last thing you ever do because I'll track you down and fucking kill you. Understood?"

His eyes widen, nodding frantically. Roman doesn't speak as he turns and sprints down the street. I wait until he's out of sight before looking down at Evie. Her arm is wrapped tightly around my waist, her eyes staring up at me. I can't quite read the emotions swirling in the pool of blue and green, but it doesn't matter because I hear her heartbeat return to a normal pace as she relaxes into my side.

"Thank you," she breathes.

"What the hell was that all about?" I ask, running my knuckle up and down the smooth skin on her arm. I know the truth, but I want to see if she'll tell me herself.

She sighs, stepping away from my side to stand in front of me. I almost reach out and return her to my side, not wanting to feel the emptiness she left behind, but refrain from doing so because now is not the time.

"I don't know," she says, shaking her head. "Ever since we broke up he's been stalking me—"

"Stalking you?" I snap, clenching my fists at my side. I didn't know that.

"Nothing crazy, just hanging around my building after class or near my favorite coffee shop. It's nothing I couldn't handle," Evie explains, her words putting me slightly at ease. I know Evie is more than capable of looking after herself, but it still doesn't sit right with me knowing he's been stalking her. "He wants me to take him back, but after he—"

"Cheated on you," I finish, and her eyes snap up to me.

"You know about that?"

"Everyone knows about it."

She folds her arms over her chest. "Even Miles?"

I nod. "Even Miles."

"Shit," she curses. "Well, yeah, after he cheated on me, there was no way in hell I was ever going to take him back, but he didn't seem to understand that. He even went as far as... threatening me over text."

Not quite the full truth, but I'll take it. I don't want to push her too hard.

"Was that the first time he's ever laid a hand on you?" My jaw clenches, waiting for her response. If this isn't the first time he's touched her like that, I'm going to fucking ki—

"This was the first time, yes," she supplies, eyeing my face as she speaks. "I just..." She pauses, her tongue darting out to lick her bottom lip. "I was never scared of what he might do until just now. I knew I could handle myself, but it's clear he is unhinged so anything could've happened, and that's what I was worried about."

"Well, you have nothing to worry about because I won't ever let him hurt you."

The words fall effortlessly from my lips because it's true. There is not a chance in hell I'd let another person hurt her. They would never get close enough to even try because they would have to go through me, and that's just like asking for a death sentence. I want her to know that as long as I'm around, she'll be safe. And that's a fucking promise.

She smiles, chewing on her bottom lip. I bite back a groan at the sight.

"Well, thank you for stepping in when no one would. I knew I could handle myself, but I'm sure there would've come a point in time when I no longer could."

"Any time, little angel."

My eyes look over her frame, taking in her messy ponytail that I would love to have wrapped around my fist, her denim shorts and a cropped T-shirt, the material hanging slightly off her right shoulder, and the black tote bag on the other shoulder. She is so effortlessly beautiful, and she doesn't even know it.

"I've got to get going," Evie says, looking over her shoulder. "I wanted to grab a coffee, but after what just happened, I think I'm just going to go home and skip my afternoon class."

I shove my hands into the pocket of my black jeans. "Do you want a lift home?"

She pauses, her eyes roaming over my face as she considers my offer. "But...you drive a motorcycle."

"And?"

"And I don't want to die."

"You won't die," I say. "I'm a very safe driver."

Evie snorts, raising a brow at me. "Safe? There is nothing safe about a motorcycle. They're basically a death trap."

I smirk. "Not when you're with me. I promise I'll keep you safe. You have my word."

She considers me for a moment, her eyes locked with mine as she weighs her options. Ever since I bought my motorcycle in my freshman year, all I've dreamed about is getting Evie on the back of it, feeling her small arms wrapped tightly around my waist, and her thighs hugging mine. The thought alone has my cock stirring in my pants but now is not the time. *Soon.*

"What if my brother sees us?" Evie counters, her hand on her hip.

I smile. "You and I both know he won't see us. He's at practice."

"Where you should be," she points out with a raised brow.

I nod. She's got me there. "Yes. I was on my way when I sensed you were near. I can spot the rhythm of your heartbeat in any crowd at any time. It was the change in rhythm that told me I had to find you. And it was a good thing I did."

Her heartbeat is a sound I have grown to love because it allows me to read her like a book. I can tell when she is happy, sad, excited, and nervous just by the way her heart beats. It's intimate, really. I don't know why, but it makes me feel closer to her in a way. It's something I can't explain.

Evie sighs, shaking her head. "Okay, fine. You can take me home."

I grin, turn to my right, and extend my hand in the direction of the parking lot where my motorcycle is parked. "In that case, right this way, little angel."

When we reach my motorcycle, Evie stops short to give it a once over, taking in the sleek, black paint job and red-rimmed wheels. It's a Yamaha YZF R6, but I'm not going to disclose that information to her because I know she won't understand what I'm saying. She only sees this as a death trap.

On the way here, we stopped by the training facility so I could grab my helmet and let Coach know I'd need to miss training this afternoon. He didn't seem to mind if I missed this one session because he knew I'd make up for it later in the week with a double session. I was in and out in a flash, and thankfully, the team was already out on the pitch, so I didn't run the risk of running into Miles, Preston, or Ethan. That motherfucker Roman is lucky I didn't see him again. I'm using all the restraint in my body not to tear him limb for limb.

"How are we both going to fit onto that?" Evie asks, her eyes lifting to meet mine.

I step toward her and lift the helmet above her head. She stands still as I slip the black helmet over her head, securing it to her head—which is much smaller than mine—by tightening the straps under her chin.

Fuck me she looks hot.

"You're going to sit on the smaller seat behind me. But you must hold onto me tightly, okay?"

She nods, her eyes twinkling as they look at me through the slit in the helmet. "Okay."

I walk her over to the motorcycle and slip on my leather riding jacket. Hooking one leg over the seat, I pat the smaller seat behind me, indicating she can hop on. But she just stares at me.

"What?"

"You don't have a helmet."

"I know."

"But what if we get into an accident? I don't want you to get hurt."

I chuckle, tilting my head to the side. "I'm a vampire, little angel. Nothing can kill me. Unless it's a stake through the heart or I'm decapitated. I think I'll be fine driving you down the road."

Evie looks down at her feet as she walks toward me. If she wasn't wearing a helmet, she would be blushing like hell right now. She gingerly hooks her leg over the seat and slides into place behind me. I have to focus on starting the engine and not the fact that I can feel the firmness of her perky tits pressing into my back, the heat from her skin warming mine, or how strong her thighs are wrapped around me.

This is what I had been fucking dreaming of.

"Hold on tight," I remind her as I kick the stand off the ground and walk the motorcycle forward. Evie nods against my back, her cheek pressed to it as she looks to the side.

Gripping the handles, I rev the throttle, throwing the motorcycle forward. Evie squeals at the sudden speed when I turn out of the parking lot and join the traffic. Her grip around my waist tightens as I weave in and out of the cars. The wind against my face doesn't annoy me as much as I thought it would, but it's worth it if it means Evie is safe.

The closer I get to the sorority house, the more I never want this moment to end. But if I got her on this time, maybe I can do it again.

Turning the corner onto the street where Evie lives, the motorcycle crawls to a stop out the front of the house. Almost instantly I see a few sets of eyes peek through the front curtains, likely wanting to know where the loud engine is coming from.

Kicking the stand down with my boot, I tilt the bike to the side, securing it in place. Evie's hands loosen around my waist before she slides off the seat, my back now empty and cold without her presence. I slide off on the opposite side and turn to face her, watching as she slips the helmet off her head. Her hair is a mess, but it looks perfectly disheveled.

"How was that?" I ask, accepting the helmet from her outstretched hands.

"That was... exhilarating." Her bright eyes meet mine, the excitement reflecting in her irises.

I grin. "I knew you would like it."

"It was a lot more fun than I thought it would be," Evie admits with a small smile. "Thank you for driving me home, and thank you for... earlier."

"No need to thank me. I would do anything for you."

She bites her lip, looking down at her shoes.

"What did I say about biting your lip," I warn, my cock twitching at the sight.

Her eyes snap up to meet mine, a hue of red splashed across her freckled cheeks. "Right. Are you going back to practice?"

I shake my head. "No. I have something I need to take care of." Something I should've done earlier, but now seems like the perfect time. I've been trying to stay level-headed and think the situation through as Ethan had suggested, but I'm in the mood to release the rage building in my chest. "Are you okay?" I ask, licking my lips. "I want a serious answer, little angel."

A blush spreads across her freckled cheek and she nods. "I'm okay, I promise."

Her answer quietens part of the storm raging throughout my body, but I'm still vibrating with anger. "That's all that matters. You're safe now, and I want you to know that you'll always be safe with me."

Evie smiles and nods. Taking a couple of steps back, she clutches her tote bag tightly to her chest. "Okay, well, I guess I better get going."

"Wait," I call out before she can turn and leave. Her doe eyes meet mine, I find myself getting lost in them for a moment. "Um... is there anything new with you?"

Normally, I'm great at making small talk with the people in my life. But right now I'm finding it hard to converse because all I can think about is that motherfucker Roman. The anger in my veins is fucking with my head. But I don't want her to leave. I just want to hear her talk and be in my presence. I crave it.

Evie raises a brow at me. "You want to know what's new with me?"

I nod and lick my lips. I want to know every fucking thing

about my little angel, but I'll let her come to me with the information she wants to share.

She hums and taps her chin with her forefinger. I bite back a smile at the small action. It was simple and cute, but God does it remind me of just how innocent she is.

"Well, my classes are getting harder with lots of assessments coming up, so that's annoying." She hums and licks her lips. "I've been having lots of... dreams in the past couple of weeks about the night my parents died."

My brows shoot up in surprise. Out of all the things I thought she could say, this was not one of them. "Dreams?"

She shrugs. "Well, nightmares. They've been revealing snippets of information from the night I found them. It seems my mind has kept these small details hidden from me for twelve years."

Well, this is news to me. I thought Evie had shared everything she could remember with the police, but it seems there is still more lurking in the depths of her brain, waiting to rear its head. I want to know more about these dreams, but it's not something I want to push from her. If it's something she wants to share with me, then I will gladly listen.

"Have you learned anything useful from them?"

Evie shakes her head. "Not yet. Being forced to remember the dark details from that night has me wanting to talk to Miles and see if he knows something I don't."

I want to tell her that he does. Well, I think he does, but I can't be sure. "It wouldn't hurt to ask," I offer with a shrug. "What's the worst that could happen?"

"There any many things, I'm sure. But I don't want him shutting down on me, you know? He's been like that since we were kids."

I know exactly what she's talking about. Miles has a tendency to shut down emotionally when he no longer wants to face a tough conversation or deal with something in his life that needs to be taken care of. For months after his parent's death, it was hard to get more than ten words out of him because of how deep in his mind he was, likely thinking about the incident. Once he has retreated into his mind, it's hard to get him out. Believe me, I've experienced it firsthand.

"I get that," I say with a nod. "But just give it some thought, okay? Don't be afraid to speak up and seek the answers you're looking for."

Evie smiles and bites her lip. Her eyes widen as if realizing her mistake and takes a step back. She jabs a thumb over her shoulder. "I should go, but thanks for the ride. And for what you did today."

I grin. "I accept payment in the form of a kiss."

She rolls her eyes when I turn my head to the side and tap my cheek. "You're an idiot. I'll see you around."

"Don't worry, little angel, you haven't seen the last of me."

Without saying a word, she waves goodbye and turns toward the house. The eyes peeking through the curtains disappear when I meet them, and I bite back a smile. I lean against my bike, watching Evie as she opens the front door and disappears inside.

After what happened today, I need to keep a better eye on her. She is the most precious person in my life and I need to make sure she stays safe.

Before I have the chance to leave, my phone vibrates in my pocket. I pull it out to see Evie's name written across it.

Evie: We can't keep doing this.

I smirk, my arm resting on top of my helmet on the seat, her scent lingering around me.

I twirl the pocketknife around on the top of my index finger, the beam from the streetlamps outside illuminating half the room, glinting off the blade every time it spins. My eyes stay focused on the blade as I wait patiently. Being a creature of the night, this is my playtime, and I fucking love it. I don't mind having to sit and wait because I have eternity under my belt, so time means nothing to me.

Muffled voices in the hallway indicate I no longer have to wait. It's fucking showtime.

"Yeah, man, I'll see you in class tomorrow. I'll grab the coffee this time, okay?" the voice says on the other side of the door.

I continue to spin the knife, my eyes now focused on the door as it swings open, the light from the hallway illuminating the other side of the room before it is closed again, plunging the space into darkness. The person shuffles by the door, cursing as they kick their shoes off before they finally switch the main light on.

They don't notice me at first sitting in the corner of the room, watching them. He walks to his bed, drops a gym bag onto the mattress, and looks down at his phone. With his eyes on the device, he turns in my direction, and this is when he finally notices my presence. When his eyes meet mine, they

131

widen to the point it's probably painful, the phone slipping from his hands, thudding against the brown-stained carpet.

"W-What are you doing here? How the hell did you even get in?"

I snatch the pocketknife to the palm of my hand and use it to point to the open window, the glass now smashed into pieces on the carpet below. "Anyone can break through a glass window, Roman."

"But I live ten stories up," he murmurs, stumbling over his words as he takes a step back. "How the fuck—"

"It doesn't matter how I got into your dorm room," I interject, dropping my leg from where my ankle rested on my bent knee. "What does matter is why I'm here."

Roman's eyes snap between me and the bedroom door. His accelerated heartbeat tells me exactly what he's thinking.

"Don't even try to run. It'll just make this more painful for you."

He swallows hard, walking backward until his knees hit the mattress. "What do you want? If this is about what happened earlier with Evie, I-I promise I'll stay away from her."

I stand, looking down at the pocketknife with my initials engraved into the side. A gift from my father when I turned eighteen. I slip it into my pocket. "See, I'm hearing the words come from your mouth, but I don't believe you." When my eyes meet his, I know he can see that they are red by the way his face pales to almost the same color as his hair. "You thought you could use explicit images to get what you wanted, hmm? You thought you could put your hands on *my* girl? Well, you're about to see what happens to someone who touches something of mine that doesn't belong to them."

In the blink of an eye, I lunge forward, pulling him toward me. His scream is cut off by my hand over his mouth as I bring his back to my chest, my arm around his neck holding him in place. Roman thrashes against my grip, trying to scratch at my skin with his chewed-down nails, but he's no match for my strength.

"Now, do you want to do this the easy way or the hard way?"

He continues to thrash against me, which tells me his answer.

Tightening my grip around his neck, his body begins to slacken as I cut off some of his airway. This is a lot easier when he's not trying to struggle in my grip. I don't want this to be messier than it needs to be.

"Listen here," I whisper in his ear. "You're going to repeat after me. Got it?"

He nods, his grip around my forearms loosening.

"Good. Repeat after me: Evie is not my girl. She never was."

I drop my hand from Roman's mouth to allow him to speak. He swallows hard against my arm wrapped around his neck.

"E-Evie is not my girl. S-she never was."

I nod. "Good. Now say, I'm sorry for using those images to get what I wanted. I'm a sick bastard."

When Roman's breath hitches in his throat and he doesn't speak, I tighten my grip to the point I'm sure his vision is beginning to blur as his limbs grow heavy.

"I-I'm sorry for u-using those images to get w-what I wanted."

I grin, using my free hand to reach into my pocket and pull out my knife. The sound the metal makes when I flip it open is like music to my ears. Loosening my grip around his neck, I press the blade against his throat as he gasps for air. But he stills when he feels the cool metal, his eyes filled with fear.

Unfortunately for him, I enjoy seeing fear in people's eyes.

"I told you today that I would track you down and kill you

if you ever laid a hand on my little angel again." I lick my lips. I'm enjoying this way too much. This is a once-in-a-blue-moon thing for me. "I was going to let it go, but I realized that you're too much of a threat to Evie. You're a fucking psychopath who can't seem to listen. And because of that, I'm going to have to put an end to you."

"N-No, please—"

The blade slicing across Roman's throat forces whatever he was going to say to die in his throat, blood splattering across the walls of his room. His body instantly goes limp as the life is drained from him, and he falls with a thud to the floor.

My fangs lengthen as I bring the blade to my lips, running the flat side of it down my tongue, his blood hot and delicious as it slides down my throat. Oh, this is going to be good. Feasting on the blood of my enemy. What could be better? The cleanup is going to be a pain in my fucking ass though. Ethan is going to be so pissed when I call him to help.

But as I said, I will do anything to ensure Evie's safety, even if it means killing her piece of shit ex-boyfriend. After what he did to her, he deserved it. His actions were escalating, so I had to put a stop to it. I would go to the ends of the earth to protect my little angel. Even if it means burning it to the fucking ground.

CHAPTER 13

EVIE

Darkness. Nothing but darkness consumes my sight, making it hard for me to breathe. Almost like a heavy weight is being pressed down on my chest, forcing the air out of my lungs, and leaving me gasping.

But there is something else in the mix. Something... metallic. *Blood.*

The scent is so strong that I feel as though I'm drowning in it as it swallows me whole, sucking me deep into the depths of darkness. My body feels frozen in time while everything around me moves in slow motion. My fingers are numb, and I can't tell if I'm sitting or standing. I can't make much sense of anything as the metallic scent of blood settles deep within my senses.

My eyes feel heavy as they drag up the staircase, locking with the man at the top as he stands over the bodies of my parents. A shiver races down my spine at the intensity of his eyes. Blue like a sapphire gemstone, twinkling under the dim light of the streetlamps shining through the upstairs window.

But that's all I can see as they stare back at me, unblinking. For a split second, I catch an emotion behind them that takes me by surprise—*sadness*. So much sadness that it reflects in his irises, leaving me confused.

If he's the one standing over my parents—murdered—then why is *he* the one who's sad?

But just as quickly as the emotion presents itself, it's gone in the blink of an eye. Instead, it's the words I hear fall from his lips that still my beating heart in my chest, turning my blood to ice.

"*No! My sweet Rose...no. I was too late.*"

My eyes snap open, my heart beating so hard it feels as though it's going to slam through my rib cage. As I look around my bedroom, my vision is blurry, but I can make out Rylee's sleeping form in bed, her back to me as she faces the wall.

Once reality sets in and I know that it was just a dream, or rather, a *memory*, I fall back against my pillows, blowing out a puff of air.

What the *actual fuck* was that?

The words are still ringing in my head as I repeat them, trying to understand them.

My sweet Rose... no.

I was too late.

What does that even mean? And who the hell was that man I saw standing over my parents that night? And why was he so upset that my mom had been killed? Was he a friend of hers? If so, how did they know each other? My mom and I were close, so I met a lot of her friends, but I never heard her mention a man before.

But I remember the sadness in his eyes and the pain he was feeling. If they knew each other, they must've been close for him to have a reaction like that.

The more vivid these dreams become, the more I'm starting to realize that I must've suppressed a lot of memories from that night, hiding them away in the deepest part of my mind, never to see the light of day again.

But why now? Why after all these years am I starting to remember the details of what I saw? It just doesn't make sense. *None* of this makes sense.

I sigh, running a hand down my face as my heart begins to settle. The more I think about the dreams, the more confused I become. I desperately want to find out who the mystery man is, but there is no way for me to know because I didn't see his face, just his piercing blue eyes. That's all I know about him, and possibly all I'll ever know.

At my parent's funeral, I remember seeing all their close friends and our aunties and uncles. I remember each of their faces and the pity in their eyes as they shared their condolences with Miles and me, saying they loved us and that our parents would be proud of how strong we were. But out of the people there, I never once saw a man with piercing blue eyes. Believe me, I looked, hoping that maybe—just maybe—he would show his face. But he never did.

Now, he's just a faceless man I'll never know. And it haunts me. Clearly.

I think it was after the funeral that my memory of the man with blue eyes slipped into the vault, hiding from me for years. It happened without my knowing. It would explain why I'm only remembering the detail twelve years after the fact.

I may have been close with my parents—more so with my mom than my dad—but I can't shake the feeling that there is still so much more I need to learn about them. I have always felt that Miles knew more than me because he was the oldest and very perceptive when it came to our family. He may not have been there when I found them, but I have always gotten the sense that he knows more about what happened than he's letting on.

When the investigation started, Miles made sure he spoke with my Aunt Jas about any new details that the detectives could tell them. He was invested in what happened to them, wanting to make sure our parents got justice. He wanted to see their killer captured—something I was grateful for because I was too young to truly understand the magnitude of the situation. But now that I'm older, I want to know more of the details, but Miles still sees me as that young girl who needs to be protected. So, getting information out of him has been challenging, to say the least.

To this day, the police don't know who murdered them, and Miles is like a vault, keeping the details he knows tightly sealed.

But I'm tired of not knowing. I'm tired of being left in the dark as it swallows me whole. I want to know what happened that night, and Miles is the only person besides my aunt who can disclose that information to me.

As I grab my phone from the bedside table, I wonder if I told the police about the man I saw. Unfortunately, I don't remember much of what I said to the police that night. If I had shared that information with them, it would have likely been mentioned in the years since, but it hasn't.

Whatever the case, I need to talk to Miles about this before I start to go loopy from the memories coming back to me in full force in my nightmares.

Evie: You free today? I wanna chat.

A moment later, a response comes through.

Miles: Of course, lil sis. I can be ready in an hour.

I arrive at the coffee house down the road from Miles's apartment ten minutes early to grab myself a coffee. It's much needed after the nightmare I had last night. It's been a week since the Raiders and Dolphins game, and I have yet to see Miles. With how busy he is with soccer, school, and his new girlfriend, it makes sense that it would be hard to squeeze in some time with him. But I'm glad he was able to today.

With my iced coffee in hand, I step outside to sit at one of the vacant tables against the large windows that overlook the park across the road. The early morning sun is warm, but not as hot as in recent weeks, thankfully. As I watch the children climb all over the playground, chasing each other, their joyful squeals filling the air, I sigh with relief. I made the right choice meeting Miles here instead of going to his apartment. I wouldn't be able to think straight if I arrived and Jaylen was home.

Pounding footsteps down the cement sidewalk draw my attention away from the gleeful yelling of children and to my brother walking toward me. He's dressed in a pair of black chino shorts and a plain white T-shirt, his dark hair styled neatly.

When he spots me, a grin spreads across his face as he waves. "Evie! I'm not late, am I?"

I shake my head as he sits across from me. "Not at all. I arrived early to grab a coffee."

He nods, eyeing the cold drink in my hand before lifting his eyes to meet mine. "Okay, so what do you want to talk about? I have to be somewhere soon, so..."

I want to ask him where he needs to be, but I refrain because if I ask, I don't think he will tell me. It could be practice for all I know, despite it being a Saturday. While Miles and I have a great relationship, he tends to keep a lot of details about his personal life close to his chest, only sharing enough to keep me from asking questions. But after the nightmare or memory, rather, I had last night, I know I need to push him for answers about our parents because there is this nagging feeling in my stomach that he knows more than he's letting on.

"It won't take long," I answer, shifting in my seat. "I want to ask you about our parents."

Miles stiffens. "What about them?"

"Well, I want to know more about what happened to them the night they were killed. I know I was the one to find them, but I've blocked out a lot of those details. I'm aware that you and Aunt Jas were working with the police as we got older, but I was kept in the dark about most of the details." I shrug, looking down at my coffee cup. The fresh coat of black polish I got on my fingernails is already beginning to chip. "And I don't know... a part of me wants to know more about what happened to them because I'm ready to face the truth of what I saw that night."

I lift my eyes to see Miles staring intently at me, unblinking like he's stuck in time while the rest of the world moves around him. Frowning, I reach out to wave my hand in front of his face, and he blinks himself back to reality.

"Ev, I'm not sure that's such a great idea."

"Why not?" I ask, my brows furrowing.

He sighs, running a hand through his hair. His eyes shift to look across the road. "Because you went through a lot that night and I know you still struggle with nightmares about what you saw. I just... I want to protect you from the ugly truth as long as I can. And I don't think right now is the time to get into the details."

My mouth falls open. "How do you know about the nightmares?"

He turns to me with a deadpan look. "I'm your brother, and I like to think I know you well enough by now. You used to have them when you were younger, remember? For months after the murders you used to wake up crying in the middle of the night saying you missed Mom and Dad. I was always there to comfort you and vowed to protect you, which is what I'm doing." Miles licks his lips and casts his eyes down to where his hands rest on the table, folded over each other. "I promise I will tell you what I know about that night, but not right now. It's still an open investigation and the police are doing all they can to find Mom and Dad's killer."

The piercing blue eyes of the man I saw that night standing over their bodies appear in my mind. Would it be such a bad idea to tell Miles what I remembered? I want to tell him in the hopes that it'll help the police find the monster who took our parents away from us, but there is something deep within my soul telling me that he wasn't the person who took their lives. Maybe it was the pain in his voice as he said my mom's name or the sadness in his eyes when he looked at me, I don't know.

Then why was he there that night?

Nothing about the man adds up in my mind, but then again, I don't know much at all about the investigation, so that must be why I can't make sense of the mysterious man and his presence that night.

As much as I want to pressure Miles into giving me more information, I know he's not going to budge on his stance of keeping me in the dark to protect me. I want to tell him that I don't need protection anymore because I'm an adult, but that isn't going to change his mind, and I know that.

All of this is giving me a fucking headache.

I sigh. "I want to know who killed them, Miles," I whisper, shaking my head.

"It kills me that I don't remember more from that night or who hurt them."

I can feel tears forming in the corner of my eyes as my emotions get the best of me.

Miles reaches across the table and places his hand on my shoulder. The gentle squeeze he gives is comforting. "I know, Ev, and I'm sorry you feel this burden. But I promise you that once we know more, I will fill you in on the details, okay? Until then, you'll just have to be patient and trust me."

I blink back the tears and nod. Although I don't know if I can be patient. There is an itch inside my chest that is telling me to keep pushing, that the nightmares I've been having mean something. But what that something is, I don't know. But I'm going to make damn sure that I scratch that itch, whether Miles helps me or not.

CHAPTER 14

JAYLEN

"All right team, form a single line," Coach calls across the pitch.

I turn from the small circle I formed with Ethan, Preston, and Miles to look at where Coach stands in the middle of the pitch. Without saying a word, the team walks toward him and forms a line, side by side. His eyes move down the line, holding our attention for a beat before moving to the next person. He clasps his hands behind his back and rocks back and forth on his feet.

"Listen up. We may not have a game this week, but it doesn't mean that we can slack off in practice, okay?" he says, his eyes looking up and down the line. "The Panthers aren't going to be an easy team to beat next week, so we need to keep our heads in the game."

"Yes, Coach," we say in unison.

The Raiders and Panthers have a long-standing rivalry that dates back close to fifty years ago. We don't necessarily have beef with the players, but more so the team and club name as a whole. Although, I don't like a lot of the players. For as long as I can remember, the Panthers like to play dirty by performing late tackles that don't get called by the ref and pretending to be hurt when they're not to try and get us fouled or receive a penalty. I find myself frustrated each time we come head to head, but I try not to let it get to me.

Each time we have played the Panthers in the past couple of years, the Raiders have come out on top, but there were a few games where we got our asses handed to us. So, I understand why Coach is reminding us to take the game seriously, especially the closer we get to the finals. We want to be sitting at the top of the leaderboard, so we can't slack off now.

"Now, get back to it," he says, waving us away with his hand. "Jaylen and Miles, I want you to focus on goal shooting for the rest of the afternoon, got it? And if anyone needs anything, you know where to find me."

We watch Coach walk to the side of the field to stand in the technical area. When he turns to face us, we leave the line and go back to training. Miles falls in step beside me as we walk to the goal box on the other side of the field. Sweat glistens on his temples, and I know I mirror him. The sun is relentless today, but thankfully, my cold skin helps to regulate my body temperature.

When I transitioned at eighteen and my skin turned as cold as an ice cube, I was looking forward to not sweating anymore because why would a vampire sweat? We're technically dead.

Turns out that if I do enough physical activity, I'm able to sweat because my body is too slow in trying to keep me cool. Again, it comes back to the whole being dead thing. It's an odd thing to go through when you know you're no longer a human, but you can still sweat in some circumstances like one.

"Practice on a Saturday afternoon sucks," Miles says from beside me, tossing a soccer ball in the air. He catches it with ease and repeats the movement.

I slow to a stop when we reach the goal box. Cain is already warming up in front of it, his eyes hard and focused as if we were in an actual game. I turn to Miles. "Why? Do you have something better you could be doing?"

He smirks. "Oh, you know I do." He drops the ball at his feet. "I met up with my sister this morning. She wanted to ask me questions about our parent's death."

My ears perk up at the mention of Evie. I clear my throat and fold my arms over my chest. "Oh, yeah? Is everything all right?"

I watch as Miles lines his foot up with the ball, takes a few steps back, and then runs at it with as much force as he can. The sharp sound of his boot making contact with it echoes in my ears, and I watch as it slides into the top right corner of the net, just barely grazing past Cain's fingers.

"Shit, man," Cain curses, and punches the ground.

Miles exhales and turns to me. "Yeah, everything is fine. I just feel bad that I can't share more with her."

"I'm sure she'll understand," I say. Cain kicks the ball toward me, and I catch it with the inside of my right foot.

"I'm just trying to protect her, Jay. You know that," Miles says with a sigh.

I position the ball where I want it. I'm hoping to go low and sink it in the bottom left corner. I'm used to going high, but I need to brush up on my other goal-scoring options, and it also helps to keep Cain on his toes as well.

Once my shot is lined up, I take a couple of steps back and then run forward as quickly as I can. My foot connecting with the ball sounds across the pitch. I can feel the eyes of my team-mates watching as the ball flies past Cain and into the back of the net. Unfortunately, he dove to the right instead of going left.

Low whistles sound in my ear, and I smile. Turning back to Miles, I say, "Okay, but what are you protecting her from exactly? Evie is a smart girl who is strong and resilient. We've both seen that over the years. So, what makes you think she can't handle whatever it is you're keeping from her?"

Despite Miles and I being best friends, he doesn't confide in me much when it comes to information about the murder of his parents. I was there the day they were found by Evie and know that what happened to them was awful. But during high school, I know Miles was digging deeper into what happened. Whenever I would ask him if he had found something new, he would say that he couldn't share anything yet. It was clear he wanted to keep whatever he knew close to his chest, maybe for fear of it not being what he needed to get to the bottom of what happened.

As his friend, I respected his decision to keep quiet about it. But I know that whatever he's keeping from Evie, she can handle it. If anything, she has a right to know because they were her parents too, and she was the one to find them.

Miles sighs and turns to catch the ball from Cain. He drops it at his feet and places his hands on his hips, his eyes trained on the ball. "I know she can handle it. But... it's just not the right time. I don't want her to lose focus on her classes because she is digging for information on our parents. What happened that night was traumatic for her, and I fear that it may open old wounds if I reveal what I know." He drops his hands and runs one of them through his hair. The sweat coating the strands makes them stand on end. "It's just better if she doesn't know. Not yet, at least."

I nod and watch as he lines the ball up to take a shot. This time, Cain dives to the right, saving it from going in. A smile splits across his face as he hugs the ball close to his chest, pleased with the save.

"I understand." I want to tell him that he should trust that Evie can handle whatever information she is looking for, but it's not my place to tell him what he should do. "Evie mentioned recently that she has been curious about what happened to your parents because of the murders occurring around Pullman. I guess she's just trying to draw similarities."

Miles pauses and turns to me. His brows are drawn down into a frown. "When did you speak with Evie?"

Shit.

"Um." I hear the ball coming my way before I see it. Turning my body toward the goal box, I catch the ball before it collides with my head and drop it at my feet. "We ran into each other on campus on Monday."

The day I killed her asshole ex-boyfriend for putting his hands on her, I want to say but don't, for obvious reasons.

Miles hums as his eyes search my face. Is he looking for a sign that I'm lying? Well, he's shit out of luck because I'm the best damn liar in Pullman.

"I didn't know that you two talk," he comments, folding his arms over his chest. "What do you talk about with her?"

To avoid his intense eye contact, I focus on positioning the ball to go in the direction of the bottom left corner again. I want to see if Cain will guess that I'll take the same shot as last time.

"Just whatever," I say vaguely as I walk backward. With as much force as I can use without appearing suspicious, I kick the ball toward the net. To my surprise, Cain guesses correctly and saves the ball. "It's nothing for you to be concerned about."

Miles's eyes are blazing with what I can only assume is annoyance. "You know how I feel about you talking with my sister. I made it clear back in high school that she is off limits."

I roll my eyes. "I haven't forgotten. You like to remind me

whenever you get the chance. So, just relax, okay? There is nothing wrong with just talking."

If he knew the lengths I would go for his sister, going as far as killing Roman, I have no doubt he would try to beat my ass. This is why he'll never know. At least, I'll try my best to make sure he doesn't find out. It could ruin everything I have been working toward with Evie. I'm so close to breaking through the wall she put between us, I can feel it.

"It better stay that way," Miles warns, pointing a finger in my direction. "She's my little sister, and I need to protect her from guys like you. No offense, but we both know you're a man whore."

I hold my hands up in defense, a smile tugging at my lips. He's not wrong. "None taken. I get it. But just know that I would never do anything to hurt her. Ever."

Miles licks his lips and stares at me for a long moment, taking in my words.

It's true. I would never hurt my little angel, and I certainly won't let anyone hurt her. I made that clear when I took care of Roman. I'm not one to willingly kill people, but if they're a threat to me or the people I care about, then I will not hesitate to make heads roll.

When it comes to Evie, I would gladly burn this fucking planet to nothing but smoke and ash if she asked me to.

After a moment, Miles sighs and claps me on the back. The warmth from his hands through my training jersey spreads across my skin. I'm not sure if he has noticed the change in temperature of my skin over the years, and if he has, he has never said anything.

"I know, and I appreciate the sentiment. You are the only guy I trust her with, Jay. Growing up, you were always there for her if I couldn't be, and that meant a lot to me. It still does." He smiles and uses the hand on my shoulder to shove me backward playfully. "But you're still a man whore."

I laugh and shake my head, thankful that the conversation stayed light. "Yeah, yeah. Just kick the fucking ball before Coach kicks our asses for not training."

We spend the next hour shooting goals at Cain until the three of us grow tired. The sun is beginning to set low on the horizon, indicating that practice is coming to an end. Despite the tense conversation earlier, we put in a good effort and closed out the day feeling good. The Panthers are going to be a hard team to beat, but I feel ready for a fight.

"God, I can't wait to fucking shower," Ethan whines as he falls in step beside us. Blades of grass litter his sweaty neck, and his face is slightly pale.

"Me, too," Preston says from beside Ethan. He runs a hand through his short blonde hair. "I'm so glad we're not playing this weekend. I could use the break." He looks between the three of us. "Also, has anyone heard or seen Roman this week? I noticed he hasn't been showing up to practice."

"I haven't," Ethan says, shaking his head.

His eyes flick to mine, and I know he's still pissed that I asked him to help me scrub Roman's apartment clean of his blood. It was no easy task, especially having to wipe blood from the roof. Ethan complained the entire time, and rightfully so. We spent hours cleaning that shit hole until our hands hurt and sweat coated our skin. Getting Roman's body into the back of Ethan's car and having to beat the sunrise and the early dog walkers in Pullman was stressful. But remembering the soulless look in his eyes as I loaded his blanket-wrapped body into the car made everything worth it.

Ethan was silent the entire drive out to one of the many secluded woods on the outskirts of town. He wouldn't even look at me as we dug a six-foot deep hole and tossed the body in. I felt bad for involving him in the situation, but as a fellow vampire, it should be expected of him. I know I would drop everything to rush to his side if he were in a similar situation.

Nonetheless, I was grateful for his help.

"Neither," Miles comments with a shrug. "Maybe he left town for a few days. I'm sure he'll be back next week."

I don't say a word, and toss the ball in the air, hoping no one notices my silence. But thankfully, Preston moves on from the topic quickly.

"What is everyone doing tonight?"

"Nothing," Miles says as we walk across the pitch toward the tunnel that leads to the locker rm. "I might go see Cindy, but I haven't decided yet."

"I would ask how your girl is, but I doubt you'll tell me," Preston jokes and nudges his elbow into Ethan's side.

I roll my eyes. "I might go to the *Black Rose*."

"We haven't gone in a while," Ethan says, shooting me a knowing look from around Miles and Preston. "Maybe I'll join you."

"Same," Preston chimes in. "Although, I may have to meet you there. I think some of my friends from class want to go, too."

"What about you?" I ask Miles, bumping my shoulder against his.

"I might make an appearance if I don't go see Cindy," he says with a shrug. "See what all the fuss is about." He quirks a knowing brow at me. "Do you plan to meet up with a girl from your roster?"

The 'roster' he's talking about is the handful of women I would see on a regular basis. They only served one purpose— to fuck and feed on. But I put an end to the roster when I decided that it was time to pursue Evie and make her mine after she learned my secret. I've waited years for this moment, so there was no way I was going to fuck it up by continuing to see the girls on the roster.

The only girl I have my eyes set on is my little angel.

"I guess you could say that."

CHAPTER 15
EVIE

"**E**vie, do you want to go to *Black Rose* tonight?"

I look up from the book in my lap to where Jaycee, Candie, and Rylee stand in the doorway of my bedroom. Their eyes are resting on me intently, waiting for my answer. They had gone shopping this afternoon and asked if I wanted to go with them, but I declined because I wasn't in the mood to walk around a crowded mall for hours while they tried on clothes. Instead, I opted to stay in and read more of the book I had been trying to get into for a few weeks.

After my conversation with Miles earlier today, I needed some alone time to not think about the thoughts circling my mind. Ever since I had gotten home, all I could think about was the man with piercing blue eyes, who he was, where he was now, and what connection he had to my mom. When I came up with nothing, I needed to get out of my head for the afternoon and get lost in another world. And it worked, thankfully. Spending a couple of hours reading this afternoon has helped boost my mood immensely, so the thought of going to *Black Rose* tonight doesn't sound too bad.

I close the book and sit up straighter on my bed, crossing

my legs beneath me. "You know what? Fuck it, I'm in. Did your connection get us on the list again?" I ask Jaycee.

She shakes her head, a hint of redness coating her cheeks. "Not yet, but I can ask him. I'm sure he would be more than happy to help us out."

I nod. This 'connection' of Jaycee's is another mystery plaguing my mind. All I know is that his name is Ethan, and he goes to WSU. Besides that, I know nothing else. I have a sneaking suspicion it's the same Ethan on the soccer team who is friends with Miles and Jaylen, but I have no way of confirming it unless I ask him directly or Jaycee spills the beans to me. Sadly, I don't see either of those options happening any time soon.

Speaking of Jaylen... I wonder if he's going to be present at *Black Rose* tonight. From what I know about the bar and the *activities* that happen upstairs, it seems like the perfect place for him to frequent to get his *fix*, so to speak. But the thought of him being there with another woman has my stomach churning uncomfortably.

I shouldn't care what he does or rather *who*, but I can't ignore the way my chest tightens when I think about him with someone else. He's my brother's best friend, and nothing more. So, why can't I stop thinking about him, and the way his presence makes my pulse quicken and my core tight, thrumming for him? All I can think about is his fingers digging into my hips as he holds me close, running his sharp fangs along the base of my neck where my pulse throbs under his touch, waiting for the moment he sinks his—

"Evie," Rylee says, interrupting my thoughts. *Thank God.* "Did you hear what I said?" When I stare at her and give no response, she continues, "We're going to leave at eight, so be ready. I have just the outfit for you to wear."

I swallow hard, nervous to see what she has in mind. All I

can manage is a nod, and the girls squeal in excitement. Candie says something about going to get ready now even though it's four in the afternoon. But I don't pay attention to them. Not when I have a certain someone on my mind, wondering—hell, *hoping*—if he'll be at *Black Rose* tonight.

After what has been hours of getting ready for the night and taking a few shots of Tequilla in the kitchen, we're finally in the taxi en route to *Black Rose*. As the girls talk to each other over the sweet melody of *Dreams* by Fleetwood Mac blasting through the speakers—a request made by Rylee—I can't help but smile as I stare out the window.

The song reminds me of my mom and how it was her favorite song growing up. She used to tell me stories of her hitchhiking home from parties and bars with her Walkman, listening to Fleetwood Mac. I don't remember a time in my childhood when Fleetwood Mac wasn't playing through the record player she kept in the kitchen. It was what I looked forward to most days returning from school—watching her sway to the beat of the song as she stood at the stove, her long brown hair floating down her back in soft waves.

My mom was so stunning, and it pains me that I didn't tell her often enough.

I vividly remember her telling me the story of when she got picked up by a stranger one night after leaving a bar when she was my age, listening to *Dreams*, only to find out that the stranger was actually her new neighbor once he had dropped her home. I can remember the sparkle in her eye when she recounted the memory like it was a fond one that had more to it, but she never went further than that small detail, and I didn't think to ask.

God, I wish I would have just asked. My mom was always so carefree and loved life, and that's how I will remember her. I will remember the special moments we shared together and never lose hope that one day I will know the truth about what happened to her, and my father, because she deserves justice.

"Evie!"

My head snaps to the side at the sound of Rylee's voice. She and Candie are sitting beside me, their eyes focused on my face.

"Is everything okay?" Candie asks. "What were you thinking about?"

I clear my throat, shift in my seat, and tug the fabric of the dress further down my thighs. Why did I allow Rylee to talk me into wearing a black leather dress and heeled boots that sit around my calves? I should've fought harder to wear a simple pair of black jeans and a crop top. "Uh, nothing. It was nothing."

The look in Rylee's gray eyes tells me she wants to question me further, but she doesn't get the chance because Candie squeals in excitement. I look out the window to see the taxi pulling up to the curb outside of *Black Rose*. Much like last time, there is a line of people waiting outside that wraps around the building.

I follow Candie and Rylee as they slide out of the backseat and we're greeted by Jaycee as she gets out of the passenger seat, thanking the driver before he pulls away from the curb. We all link arms and walk toward the front door. Once our names are ticked off the list, we enter the bar and are immediately engulfed by strobe lights and techno music blasting from the DJ set up in the back of the room.

Just like the last time we were here, the tables are packed with people my age drinking, talking, and dancing. Nothing has changed. *Except for the fact that I know the truth behind this place.* As we walk toward the bar to order a drink, I try not to look around the room for a certain someone with messy curls and a lip ring. And I certainly won't let my gaze look behind me at the staircase that leads to the top floor. Nope. Not happening.

Inhaling slowly, I nod in response to Rylee when she asks if I want the same fruity cocktail as her. I'm not fussed about what I drink tonight, just as long as it has a lot of alcohol in it. I want to make sure I drink enough to forget about Jaylen, even if it's just for the night.

With our drinks in hand, we walk across the floor until we find an empty table. Thankfully, it's close to the bathroom and away from the staircase. The further away I am from it, the less tempted I will be to look in that direction.

"So, is this mystery man of yours here tonight?" Candie asks Jaycee as we sit down, wiggling her brows. "I want to know who he is!"

Jaycee blushes, chewing on her bottom lip. "He said he might show up, but that's not a promise for you all to meet him. Besides, it's still too soon in our relationship for me to show him off. I want to make sure that we're a solid couple before you meet him."

Candie pouts, her brown curly hair tied into a ponytail on top of her head. "Boo, you're no fun. I need some juicy goss before I explode." She turns to me, her eyes twinkling with mischief. "What about you, Ev?"

"What about me?"

She playfully rolls her eyes. "Don't think we don't know what's going on between you and Jaylen. We all know you went to see him after the game the other night."

My eyes widen. "I didn't go to see him. I went looking for Miles."

"Oh, please. Don't lie to us. We know all about the little crush you've had on him since you were kids," Jaycee says, biting back a smile. "And we all saw the look you two shared before the game. He's into you."

"So now the question is what happened between you two when you went to see him," Candie says with a smile.

"There is nothing to tell," I say slowly, sipping on my drink. The fruity flavors mask the shot of Vodka, but I can still feel the effects of the alcohol coursing through my veins. "But I do have something juicy to share." I gesture for them to lean forward, and they do. "Jaylen slept with Amara at some point recently."

They all gasped at my words. I knew they would have this reaction. Hopefully, this piece of information draws them away from asking for details about what happened between Jaylen and me. Although, there really is nothing to tell.

"Seriously?" Rylee asks, her eyes wide. "How do you know?"

"When I went to find Miles, I overheard his conversation with Amara in the parking lot and it seemed like she was asking him to come over again, but he said he wasn't interested."

"I wonder why," Candie smirks, nudging my arm with her elbow.

I roll my eyes. "Anyway, it seems that Amara also overheard my conversation with Jaylen after she left and went as far as threatening me to stay away from him."

"When did this happen?" Jaycee asks, her perfectly shaped eyebrows drawn into a frown.

I shrug. "The other day. But again, it's nothing crazy. I can handle Amara."

"I can't believe she would threaten you like that," Rylee

comments from beside me. "If you need us to say something—"

"I can handle her, I promise," I interject, waving off their concerns with my hand. "There is nothing for you guys to worry about. She can think what she wants about me, but I don't want to create tension between you all and her as well."

"Just know that we have your back," Jaycee says from across the table, a smile on her red-painted lips. "And I know for a fact that you could fuck her up in a fistfight."

I burst out laughing, shaking my head. This is why I love my friends. I know that no matter what, they will always have my back, and it's comforting.

Thankfully, the topic of conversation steers away from me and Jaylen to other random things going on in our lives. I try to focus as they talk about their classes or the shit assessment they had to do, but my mind grows foggier with each fruity cocktail I consume.

Perfect. That's what I wanted.

When there is a lull in conversation, I raise my glass. "Does anyone want another drink?"

Candie says yes but Rylee and Jaycee decline since they're only halfway through theirs. When I step off the stool, my legs wobble a little, but I manage to keep myself upright and walk through the throng of people to the bar. The scent of BO and cheap perfume assaults my nostrils, and I fight back a gag. Squeezing between the people mingling near the bar, I reach the front and order two more drinks, ignoring the sleazy smile the older man bartending gives me.

A soft tap on my shoulder forces me to spin on my heels, ready to fend off whoever it is that wants to talk to me, but I'm met with a familiar face.

"Evie," he says with a smile. "Fancy seeing you here."

"I could say the same to you, Preston."

His short blonde hair is spiked up with some type of hair product and he's dressed in a button-up shirt and chinos, every bit the typical preppy rich guy. I haven't seen him since the night I hung out with him at my brother's apartment a week ago. It's not often that I see him without Miles.

Wait, Miles—

"Don't worry, your brother isn't with me," Preston says as if he had read my mind. "I came with some friends from class and happened to see you walk past." I breathe a sigh of relief. "Well, it's good to see you. How have you been?"

"Good," he says with a nod, shoving the hand not holding his drink into his pant pocket. "Actually, I did approach you for a reason."

"Is everything okay?"

"Yeah, yeah, all good," he says, nodding slowly. His eyes dart from side to side as if he's looking for something—or someone—before they settle on my face. "I just wanted to ask if you've seen Roman this past week."

I pause, blinking up at him. "Roman?"

"Yeah. Have you seen him recently? He hasn't shown up to practice since Monday and he won't answer any calls or texts. It's like he's dropped off the face of the earth."

That doesn't sound like Roman. For as long as I've known him, he's always been attached to his phone, making sure to answer any texts or calls he's received, even at the worst of times. It was something that used to annoy the hell out of me. But hearing that no one has been able to get a hold of him for days is a little out of the ordinary for him. Not that I care what he's doing after the way he's been treating me, but it is a little weird. It must concern Preston enough that he thought to ask me—the ex-girlfriend—if I've seen him around.

I shake my head. "Not since a few days ago. It wasn't the... most pleasant of interactions, but he was okay when he left."

I'm not going to mention the details of Jaylen threatening him. It's not something Preston needs to know.

Preston pulls his hand out of his pant pocket to scratch his head, a confused look overtaking his sharp features. "Hm. Okay. That's weird but thank you for trying to help. I'm sure he's just gone back home for a few days and hasn't gotten around to checking his phone."

He doesn't sound confident with his words because even I know there is no possibility of that being an option. We both know Roman answers his phone even when he's at home.

"If you see him around, let him know I'm looking for him, yeah?"

I nod, even though there isn't a chance of me running into Roman again after what happened the other day, but I won't tell Preston that. He wants reassurance, so that's what I'm going to give him.

Wherever he is, I'm just glad that he has finally stopped texting me.

"Of course," I lie and put on the best fake smile I can muster when my face feels slightly numb from the alcohol.

The sound of glass tapping against wood draws my attention to the drinks behind me that the bartender has placed down. He makes sure to give me another creepy smile before I turn back to Preston, but as I do, I catch a flash of brown messy curls over his shoulder. My eyes follow the head through the crowd of people, watching as he ascends the staircase with a petite blonde girl hot on his heels, a smug grin turning her mouth upward.

I fucking knew it.

I had a feeling Jaylen would be here tonight, but it seems he's not alone.

My fingers curl around the base of the glasses in my hands. The condensation is cool against my burning skin as I follow their figures down the dark hallway, disappearing into one of the rooms on the right.

I shouldn't be surprised that he's still seeing other women even after what happened between—No, nothing happened between us, and I need to remind myself of that.

Yes, there is certainly some... tension between us, but it doesn't mean anything. At least, that's what I've been trying to tell myself. But seeing him with another woman makes my stomach churn uncomfortably and my body tightens with annoyance.

It makes me see *red*.

"Evie? Is everything okay?"

I look away from the staircase to meet Preston's eyes as they search my face. He looks a little confused by my change in mood, and I don't blame him. I also have no idea what the fuck is going on with me and my body.

Without thinking, I shove both of the glasses into his hand, making him fumble the glass he's already holding to accommodate two more and point behind him. "Take those to my table for me, please. I'll be right back."

I don't wait for his response before I slide through the throng of partygoers happily sipping on their cocktails and laughing among themselves. It's as if my feet are on autopilot as I climb the staircase, my mind and body numb—mostly from the alcohol but also the anger coursing through my veins.

Once I reach the top, my eyes scan each room through the open windows. I barely notice the threesome happening in the first room, a busty woman being taken by two other men, or the blood on the bed in the room next to it as a dark-haired woman sucks the blood from a male she is riding like a horse. Nothing seems to faze me as I continue to look for the one person who will capture my attention, something deep within me guiding my steps. An invisible force, maybe. I don't know what it is, but I don't seem to have any control over it.

Thankfully, I spot him a few rooms down through the open window.

Jaylen is sitting on the bed with the blonde woman on her knees between his parted legs. He's fully clothed while she doesn't have a top on, her bare back to me. His eyes are on her as she runs her fingers down his toned chest and abs before landing on his belt buckle.

That's when I burst into the room, my hand firmly gripping the door handle.

Jaylen is smirking before his eyes even meet mine. *That bastard sensed me coming.*

The blonde woman turns to look at me, her hand still hovering over his belt buckle. A deep scowl creases her brows as her eyes look me up and down. "Who the fuck are you? Can't you see that we're a little busy here?"

I don't look at her as she speaks, my eyes focused firmly on a grinning Jaylen. Oh, how I wish I could slap that shit-eating grin off his face.

"Evie," he drawls, his voice smooth like whiskey. "What a pleasure it is to see you."

I don't say anything as I stare him down, my blood boiling with anger knowing that bitch still has her hands on him. I don't know why I'm acting this way, but I won't stop either. I know I should walk away and forget this ever happened, but I *can't*, and that's the problem.

I don't know what the fuck is going on right now.

"Get the fuck outta here," the woman hisses, standing to her full height. She folds her arms over her bare chest as she shoots daggers at me.

Jaylen leans back on his hands, his abs flexing with the movement. "You should leave."

I swallow hard, shifting on my feet. Now that I'm here, I can't leave. If I leave, I know what'll happen in this room, and for whatever reason I don't understand, my heart isn't okay with that. Now that I'm slowly starting to get a taste of Jaylen Black, all I want is more.

I *crave* it. I *need* it. I *want* it.

But he's bad for me, I know this.

"You heard him," the blonde sneers, popping her hip. She uses a hand to shoo me out of the room like I'm a bad smell hanging around.

"Not her," Jaylen says, his tongue poking the side of his mouth in that cocky way that nearly has my knees buckling beneath me. "You. Get the fuck out and close the door behind you. It seems my little angel has something she wants to say."

CHAPTER 16
EVIE

My body shivers after hearing Jaylen call me his little angel again. He has made a habit of saying it more recently, and it's doing things to my body that I don't recognize. Even just being here has me confused, like why the fuck did I race up here like a bat out of hell?

I have zero control over my body and that worries me because I like being in control, but whenever Jaylen is involved, all that control goes out the fucking window. There is something deep burning within my chest like a fireball of emotion I can't quite put my finger on.

Anger?

Jealousy?

Whatever it is, it's making me act like an idiot.

I shift on my feet as we continue to stare at each other. The blonde woman is still standing beside Jaylen, her eyes laser-focused on me, her chest heaving with annoyance. But I couldn't care less about her. If she were smart, she would listen to him.

"This is fucking ridiculous," she scoffs, leaning down to collect her shirt, the material almost see-through it is that thin. "You told me we could—"

"Get the fuck out," Jaylen repeats, not looking at her but at me. "I won't repeat myself."

The woman huffs as she slips the shirt over her head, finally covering her bare skin, and collects her heels by the foot of the bed before storming out of the room, mumbling something incoherent under her breath.

To be fair, I would be pissed too if I were her, knowing she was about to suck the captain of the soccer team's—and arguably most popular guy on campus—cock but was interrupted.

Speaking of which... I glance down to see Jaylen sporting a massive hard-on, but with the way he's looking at me, his eyes full of mischief, I don't think he gives a fuck if I notice it or not.

I blush, realizing now that I may have overreacted coming up here after them when I had no right to. There is nothing going on between me and Jaylen, so why did my body feel the need to interfere in their plans? I don't know, but my mind is a cluster fuck of confusion and alcohol-induced haziness, so I'm not thinking straight.

"I, uh," I start, clearing my throat. "I'm sorry I barged in like that."

Jaylen tilts his head to the side, his icy eyes still focused on me. "It's fine. I'm more than happy to stop whatever I'm doing to talk with you since that's why you're here, or are you here for another reason?"

The playful tone in his voice tells me he knows my true intentions and why I'm here.

Shit.

"I, um... I just—"

My words die in my throat when Jaylen leans forward and stands to his full height. I watch intently as he walks across the room, standing directly in front of me, peering through the curls falling over his eyes. I close my eyes as his scent of sandalwood washes over me like a fucking tsunami.

"Were you jealous, little angel?" he asks, lowering his head to meet my eyes. "I can smell it all over you."

I swallow hard. Shit, I forgot about his super senses. It would make sense why he didn't seem surprised to see me when I barged into the room.

"You knew I was coming," I state as if he didn't already know that, ignoring his question.

"Yes." He smiles wide. "And I also knew you would be here tonight."

My eyes widen. "How did you—"

"I have my ways," he cuts me off, leaning back to stand to his full height, looking down at me. "I wanted to get you alone, and this was the only way I knew how."

My mouth falls open at his words. This whole thing was a setup. He fucking set me up.

"So that girl..." I trail off, unable to finish the sentence as shock continues to course through my veins.

"Was part of the plan," Jaylen supplies, that shit-eating grin still spread across his face. "And I caught you hook, line, and sinker. Just like I knew I would because you can't resist me, can you?"

I want to be mad at him for tricking me like this, making a fool out of myself. I want to slap him across the face and call him an asshole for what he did. But I don't do either of those things.

Instead, I channel all the pent-up energy in my chest and do the only thing I know will help release it. I wrap my arms around Jaylen's neck and pull him down to meet my eager lips, kissing him deeply.

When our lips touch, it's like a fire ignites between us, despite the coolness of his skin. I barely register when Jaylen leans into the kiss, wraps his arms around my waist, and pulls me flush against his chest. His skin is cool, but the muscles there are just as hard as they look.

Jaylen's tongue pushes against my lips, begging for entrance. I would be an idiot not to grant it. When our tongues slide across the other, a feverish moan escapes my mouth as my body burns with the power of lust and desire. My mind grows foggy as I grip him tightly, afraid of what'll happen if I let go.

"Fuck, Evie," Jaylen groans against my lips as his fingers dig into the skin around my hips. He pulls away long enough to look down at me, his icy eyes now a solid red. "Who said you could wear that dress?"

I'm breathless as I stare up at him, unable to form any words.

"Good thing I'll be taking it off you soon."

Oh, fuck *yes*.

Jaylen's cool fingers drag up the side of my right thigh as he attaches his lips to mine. He groans, and it sends a lightning bolt straight to my pussy. It's throbbing and wet for him, making my mind fuzzy with lust. I have always wanted to know what Jaylen tastes like, and it's safe to say he tastes like Fall—all cinnamon, whiskey, and sandalwood. And it's fucking addicting.

I bite back a moan as Jaylen's hand slips under the dress, toying with the edge of my panties, and he smiles against my lips, knowing exactly what he's doing. He presses his body into mine, his hard cock rigid against my thigh. The subtle ghosting of his fingertips over the skin on my hips is driving me insane.

"Jaylen, please," I moan, and throw my head back, allowing him better access to attach his lips to my neck. The thought of his fangs shooting out from his gums and sinking into my skin to drink my blood lingers in the back of my mind, but I push it down, not wanting to think about that side of him.

All I care about is what's happening now, and that's him dangerously close to grazing my wet core. One flick from his finger under my panties and he'll strike gold.

"I can smell how wet you are for me, little angel." Jaylen's voice is dark and low as he speaks the words against my skin. He pulls back to look at me, his once baby blue eyes now a piercing crimson staring back at me. "And I can't wait to fucking devour you."

I swallow hard. What have I just gotten myself into?

Jaylen spins me around and walks me backward toward the bed. I land on the plush black duvet with a soft thud, and my eyes graze up Jaylen's toned body. As if watching a fucking magic show, feeling hypnotized, I focus on the way he slips the long-sleeved button-up off his shoulders after slowly undoing the buttons. When the material hits the floor, I take in his bare chest, and the hard ridges of muscles, before looking down at the ink etched into the skin of his right arm.

This is the first time I've properly looked at the tattoos in detail. The large dragon on his forearm has its wings spread wide, and what appears to be a Pegasus is being ridden by a ghoul on his upper arm. The gaps between each design are filled in with various types of flowers. Lilies and roses stick out to me the most. The detail in the designs is mind-blowing, leaving me distracted while Jaylen pulls out the black leather belt from around his jeans, drops it to the floor beside him, and shoves the black jeans to the floor along with his briefs, leaving him fully exposed in front of me.

My eyes widen at the size of his cock standing at attention in my line of sight. The veins racing up the side are throbbing with anticipation and the crown is swollen, precum already leaking from the tip. He's fucking *huge*. But that's not what has my breath hitching in my throat. It's the fucking silver barbell pierced through the head, staring me right in the eye.

What the actual fuck?

Jaylen grins. "Have you ever fucked a man with a pierced cock?"

It's as if something clicks in my mind. A wire is replaced and I can see clearly now.

What the fuck am I doing? I can't do this with my brother's best friend. Who also happens to be a fucking vampire.

I don't know what the hell I was thinking when I followed him up here, but I sure as hell know I need to get the fuck out of here. My alcohol-induced fog is starting to clear and I can see the path in front of me, leading me away from this fucking room in this vampire club.

"I-I have to go," I murmur and get off the bed, slightly unsteady on my feet.

A frown creases Jaylen's forehead. "What? Evie, what are you—"

I don't wait for him to finish before I push past him and race out of the room. My chest is tight and my breathing is ragged as I run down the wooden staircase. I have a flashback of when I did the exact same thing after finding out that Jaylen is a vampire. But now, I'm running away because it's all too much. Him. My brother. My life. Everything. It's all too much that the only thing I can think to do is run.

I don't bother texting my friends that I'm leaving because I don't have time. Jaylen may have been naked, but he also has speed on his side whereas I can only run as fast as my legs will allow.

The humid air settles on my skin as I race down the darkened streets with only the streetlamps illuminating the way back to the sorority house. My limbs are heavy and I can't breathe properly, but I'll deal with it. I made the choice to run, so I must deal with the consequences of not being fit enough to run a distance like this.

Seeing Jaylen naked—and that goddamn sexy piercing—reminded me that I can't keep doing this with him. I can't continue this back-and-forth we have going on because I just know it's not going to end well. If my brother finds out, it's game over. He'll make sure I go nowhere near Jaylen, so I would prefer to just keep him at arm's length because I don't want him out of my life forever. I just need to steer clear enough to protect my heart.

I don't know if it's going to work, but I'm willing to put it to the test.

I round the corner and see the driveway to the sorority house in sight. Only I find the person I'm running from sitting on the front steps, anger blazing in those baby blues.

When I see Jaylen, I slow to a stop, put my hands on my knees, and double over, trying to catch my breath. "Oh, fuck me."

"I was trying to before you ran away," Jaylen says, tilting his head as he watches me. He's dressed in his clothes from earlier, the buttons at the top of his shirt unbuttoned to reveal the smooth skin of his chest. "Why did you run, Evie?"

Breathless, all I can do is watch as he stands from the steps and walks toward me. It's clear I didn't think this plan through, but I don't think anything through when Jaylen is concerned, so what's new?

"You left me alone in that room with my cock rock hard and my skin tingling knowing I was finally going to get to touch you," he says, and I can't help but drop my eyes to the obvious bulge in his pants. I swallow, remembering the barbell. "But instead, you ran away. Why?"

He stops in front of me, his height towering over me as I glance up at him. His features are hard and it's clear he's hot and bothered after what happened—or almost happened—but I don't have an answer for him. Not one that I want to explain anyway.

"We can't do this," is all I say, gesturing between us. "We can't."

"I don't give a fuck about what Miles thinks."

"Well, I do," I retort. "I'm me and you're... *you*. We couldn't be more different."

Jaylen's eyes darken. "That's where you're wrong, little angel. We're more alike than you think. I'm not going to stop, I hope you know that."

I sigh. I want to fight back, to tell him that he's dreaming if he thinks we can work out, but I don't. The exhaustion racing through my veins after the day I've had drains all the fight from my body. Instead, I decided to change the subject because, at this point, it's the only thing I have the energy for.

"So," I say slowly, licking my lips. "How did you become... *this*? Were you like this when we were kids?"

He stares at me for a moment as if deciding whether to drop the previous topic or not. When he sees I'm making no move to acknowledge what he said, he sighs and runs a hand down the side of his face.

"Yes and no. My parents were both vampires, so I was born with the gene."

I raise a brow at him. "They were? Woah. I didn't know that. So, when did you find out what you really are?"

"When I was twelve, I saw a kid on the soccer team get hit in the face with the ball because he wasn't paying attention. At that moment, as his nose gushed with blood, all I could think about was drinking it like it was water. I told my parents that night when I got home about what happened and they filled me in on everything."

"Was that when your parents told you that you're a vampire?"

Jaylen nods, shoving his hands into the pockets of his jeans. "They told me as much as I could handle. The rest I learned as I got older."

"Which was?" I ask, hoping he'll continue to tell me more.

His eyes meet mine. "We continue to age as any human would, but very slowly. We go through the transition phase at eighteen, but it isn't until we reach the age of forty-five that the aging slows down and that's our appearance for the rest of our long lives. I look my age now but when everyone around me reaches middle age and I still look like I'm in my 20s, that's when I'll have a problem."

I eye his face carefully, taking in his sharp features and smooth skin. So, vampires age at the same rate as humans, years-wise, but it's their appearance that ages slowly, keeping them youthful for longer. That's an interesting concept. It's certainly much different from every vampire movie or TV show I've watched.

"How old will you be when you reach forty-five in vampire years?"

Jaylen shrugs. "It could take a hundred years or more. I'm not sure. My parents were still youthful in appearance when they died, and I don't even know how old they were in human years. I never got the chance to ask."

I want to ask more about his parents because I know they died when he was eighteen from a car accident but knowing what I do about him and his family, I can't help but wonder if there is more to the story. Knowing that vampires can only be killed a certain way—at least, that's what I've read in books and Jaylen has mentioned in passing—I wonder if maybe the car accident story was a cover for something more sinister.

"This is all so fascinating," I say slowly, my tongue darting out to lick my bottom lip. "Thank you for sharing."

"Now it's time for you to share why you ran away earlier," Jaylen counters, folding his arms over his chest.

I sigh and shake my head. "We can't keep doing this, Jaylen. We have to stop."

I sound like a fucking broken-down record.

He takes a step forward. "I've told you already that I'm not going to."

"But you need to." My eyes meet his, and I can see the determination behind them, stronger than ever. "Because this has to stop."

I move to walk past him, but he grabs my wrist, holding me in place. He turns his head slightly to meet my eyes, his breathing slow and controlled. My heart lodges into my throat at how menacing he looks. "You may want this to stop, little angel, but there is no way in hell I'm ever going to. Over my fucking dead body."

And with that, he is gone, disappearing into the night. My breathing is heavy and my wrist is cold where his fingers grazed against my skin.

His words sound like a promise Jaylen plans on keeping, and it has me both nervous and excited.

CHAPTER 17
JAYLEN

The hunger deep within my core pulses, begging to be satiated, and relieved. It's a pulsing that vibrates through my entire body, almost bursting at the seams. It's a sensation I'm familiar with, which means I know what needs to be done tonight.

"Is it just me, or are you fucking *starving* too?" Ethan says from beside me, his feet kicked up on the coffee table, a gaming controller in his hand. His eyes are focused on the TV as he plays some sort of race car game. Maybe Formula 1? I don't know. I'm not into that shit, but he, Miles, and Preston are. "Do you have any of your stash left?"

I shake my head. "I'm almost out. You?"

"Same. I used the last of my supply a couple of days ago."

This means we have no choice but to go out and replenish our stash. Thankfully, Miles isn't home at the moment—he said something about going to see Cindy—so we'll be able to fly under the radar and away from his suspicious eyes. We only ever do this when I know he won't be around, and now is the perfect time, especially with him being at his mysterious girl-friend's place whom we have yet to meet.

We keep our stash here because Ethan lives in a fraternity house on campus, and it's too risky to keep a cooler full of blood bags in an environment like that. Who knows who could potentially stumble upon it in his room? Only if they're looking hard enough, but still. Which is why we keep our stash in my room.

Ethan curses when he doesn't come first in the race, coming second by a fraction of a second, and places the controller down on the coffee table, sitting up straight. "Well, I guess we're going hunting tonight."

I roll my eyes. "I would hardly call stealing blood bags from the hospital *hunting*."

"Tomato, tomato." Ethan stands, looking down at me expectantly. "Come one. We better go now before Miles gets home. Who knows how long he'll be fucking his girl for, and I want to eat tonight."

I stand, follow him to the front door, and collect my house keys on the stand nearby. "Why not go to *Black Rose* and take the girl you're fucking? You'll be satisfied in both ways."

Ethan waves me off as he opens the door, gesturing for me to walk past. "She's having a girl's night in with her sorority friends, Evie included. So, this is my only option."

As we walk down the hallway to the staircase, the mention of Evie has my spine tingling. I want to know what her blood would taste like as I sink my fangs into her smooth skin, indulging in what I could only hope would be the sweetest fucking thing I've ever tasted. If I ever get the chance to taste her, I know I'll become addicted, only wanting her blood to feed on. And I welcome the addiction.

"How are things going with Evie?" Ethan asks as he follows me down the stairs, grimacing at the state of the carpet. Yeah, it looks like someone died there.

"Good." I don't want to give him more information than that.

After what happened a couple of nights ago, her trying to keep me at arm's length, I don't want to let Ethan in on the fact that my girl is trying to push me away because I know he'll try to tell me to respect her wishes and yada yada. Well, unfortunately for her, I'm not one who can be easily pushed away.

"Just good?" he questions. "I saw you with her at *Black Rose* on Saturday night. That seems like more than good to me."

I reach the foyer and charge for the front door. "I don't want to talk about it."

Ethan follows me, hot on my heels as I step out onto the street of Pullman, taking our usual route to the local hospital. We've learned over time that the best way to get around this town at night is by foot to draw less attention to us. Driving a motorcycle isn't very discreet, so we walk whenever we need to go to the hospital.

I shove my hands into the pockets of my chinos as Ethan falls into step with me, the warm air settling on my frigid skin. Thankfully, the warm weather doesn't bother me since my skin always feels as though I've been standing in a freezer for far too long. As a kid, I always hated the hot weather, wishing it could be winter all year round. When I turned eighteen and completed my transition, that dream became a reality. But in return, I became... *this*.

"Okay, you don't want to talk about Evie, fine," Ethan says. "But what about Roman?"

"What about him?"

"You shouldn't have killed him, Jay."

I shrug. "He deserved it."

"Oh, really? You think slitting his throat and burying him in the woods was the right thing to do? I told you to fucking breathe through the anger, man."

Ethan's scolding tone does nothing to make me feel guilty for what I did to Roman. He has tried this tone with me too many times to count, and it never worked then, so it's not going to work now.

I'm not the type of vampire who enjoys hunting humans and draining them of their blood for fun. It has never appealed to me because it's messy and there is a lot more to do to cover your tracks afterward. Since turning eighteen, I have only killed five humans, including Roman now. Some were by choice and some were by accident because I couldn't control my bloodlust.

Controlling bloodlust as a vampire is no easy task. When I first transitioned, I couldn't control my need to fuck and feed on as many women as I could get my hands on. Until I met Ethan in my first week of classes at WSU. He helped me control my thirst and channel the energy inside that I needed to keep me level-headed. I eased into feeding from blood bags and not on humans, the same way he had learned from his parents when he transitioned. I was envious at first because I wanted that bonding experience with my parents, but I am thankful for his help because who knows what my actions would've escalated to.

But killing Roman was a no-brainer. He was a fucking asshole who got what was coming to him.

"Again, he deserved it." I look at Ethan from the corner of my eyes to see he's watching me. "He touched my girl, so he needed to be dealt with."

Ethan sighs, shaking his head. "You can't be going around killing anyone who is a threat to Evie. That's not how this works. *You* know that."

"I know I need to protect her," I counter, my jaw clenched. "She's special, Eth. I've told you this. She's... *different*."

"Different or not, you can't kill someone like that. Too

many people are starting to realize he hasn't been seen for over a week now, especially everyone on the team."

"Roman was a threat," I snap, getting annoyed with his badgering. "And now he's no longer one because I dealt with him. No one is going to hurt my girl."

I can feel the eyes of strangers on us as we walk through the streets, getting closer to the hospital. It's approaching midnight, so there aren't too many people out, but the people who are walking the streets make no attempt to hide the fact that they're watching us.

I've been told that vampires have this aura around them that draws people's attention, unable to look elsewhere as you pass by. I never fully understood the words of my parents until I completed my transition and started my freshman year at WSU. As soon as I got out of my car—before I bought my motorcycle—all eyes were on me. At first, it was unnerving to have that many people staring at me, but over time, the stares grew on me, slowly fading into the background of my mind to the point I no longer noticed it.

But every now and then, like tonight, I notice the stares.

"Jaylen..."

"I don't want to talk about it anymore," I interrupt. "I know what I'm doing."

"Okay then," Ethan says slowly and holds his hands up in surrender. "Do you want to talk about who we think the vampire hunter might be?"

I shake my head. "We could have all the theories in the world but it won't lead us any closer to finding out who this asshole is, so it's best that you drop it."

Ethan doesn't say anything to that, so we fall into a tense silence for the rest of the walk to the hospital, which I'm thankful for. I don't need him to criticize my choices when it comes to Evie. I know what I'm doing, and what I'm doing is eliminating all the dangers in her life, which included her piece-of-shit ex-boyfriend. After the way he has treated her, he deserved everything he got. If I hadn't stopped him, who knows what lengths he would've gone to trying to claim my little angel as his.

Not a chance in hell was I going to let that happen. And I let him know that before showing him who the devil truly is.

When the hospital came into view, we silently fell into our roles—Ethan is the one who collects the blood bags, and I keep watch. Walking around the side of the building, keeping to the shadows and away from the eyes of the night shift workers, we walk to the ground floor window that we know is where they keep the blood bags for donations. At first, I felt somewhat guilty for taking the bags that were meant for others, but in a way, those donors are also helping us, even if they don't know it.

It makes the process easier to have that mindset.

Ethan uses his strength to push up the sliding glass window and remove the flyscreen before slipping inside. I follow suit and make my way to the closed door to stand guard in case anyone enters unexpectedly. Worst case scenario, I compel the person to forget and leave without a word. This doesn't sound like such a bad thing, but one wrong move in a hospital could be our demise, so it's best that I'm standing by ready to de-escalate if it reaches that point.

In the few years we've been doing this, no one has ever walked in on us. Touch wood. But it still doesn't mean it won't happen at some point.

I'm sure the hospital has noticed the missing blood bags, but every time we stop by to replenish our stash, the window is still easily accessible, and we aren't met with the nasty surprise of someone waiting for us, wanting to catch us in the act. I'm not sure what they think happened to the missing bags, but I'm glad they haven't moved to do anything about it. Lucky us. *For now.*

Ethan moves effortlessly around the room, having done this plenty of times before. He takes a few bags from different blood types—he likes to have options—and slips them into the foldable bag he keeps in his pocket. He is prepared for anything at any time.

"You done yet?" I ask over my shoulder, straining my senses to listen through the door. I can hear the whirring of machines and multiple voices, but no footsteps heading in our direction. The smell of blood and death is strong in my nostrils, making my hunger growl in need.

"Almost," Ethan replies, moving around the room. "I'm grabbing a few extra bags because fuck it, why not?"

"Don't get greedy," I warn. The last thing we need is to draw more suspicion to the missing blood bags.

"Got it."

After a moment, Ethan tells me he's ready to go and I follow him out the window, through the shadows, and onto the sidewalk, walking away from the hospital. With this stash, we won't have to come back for a couple of weeks—if we can make it last that long. With my hunger growing, needy, and desperate, I don't know how long I can keep it at bay. I know what it wants, but I need more time.

With the stash replenished, Ethan and I indulge in a bag each when we return to the apartment, making sure to hide them away in the secret spot in my bedroom—under a loose floorboard in my closet. Even with the fresh blood coursing through my veins, relaxing my insides, the hunger is still growling, vibrating my bones.

Fucking hell.

Is this how it's going to be until I can get a taste of my little angel? I fucking hope not. It'll drive me insane.

It's almost two in the morning when Miles walks through the front door, his eyes landing on Ethan and me on the couch. We finished our bags earlier, so they've been disposed of already. Not knowing when Miles is going to be home is the reason why I hold back on feeding, but tonight, I couldn't keep the thirst at bay any longer.

"What are you two still doing up?" Miles asks, dropping his gym bag by the front door. As he walks further into the apartment, I notice a few twigs and pieces of bark in the strands of his messy hair, and he smells of soil.

If he was with Cindy, then why does he smell like he's been rolling around on the ground in the nearby woods?

"We should be asking you the same thing," Ethan counters, stealing a quick glance in my direction as Miles sits on the other couch beside us.

"Yeah, I decided to come home tonight," Miles says, leaning back and lifting his legs to rest on the coffee table. "You know how it is."

"Do we?" Ethan smirks. "You look like you just got done wrestling a grizzly bear."

Miles ignores Ethan's comment and looks between us. "What did you two get up to tonight?"

"Not much," I answer. "We stayed in."

He raises a brow at me. "Didn't stop by *Black Rose* again? You two seem to enjoy going there quite often."

I frown. "What are you getting at?"

He shakes his head. "Nothing, just an observation."

I can tell he wants to say more, his features and sharp eyes make that clear, but he doesn't. Miles stretches his arms above his head and leans further into the couch. "After going there the other night, I was reminded why I'm not a fan of the place."

I had forgotten that I ran into him the night I chased after Evie when she left me naked, hard, and frustrated upstairs. Before I could leave, I found Miles with Ethan and Preston at a table near where Evie's friends were sitting. When they spotted me, they asked if I had seen Evie, and I had to lie and say no because Miles was sitting close by watching me. It was a fucking nightmare to leave without getting sucked into a conversation with the guys, but I managed to slip away and beat Evie to the house.

"Oh yeah?" I question. "Why?"

"It just gives me a weird vibe," is all he says. His eyes land on me, hard and intense. "I thought I saw my sister there. Did you happen to see her before I arrived?"

My body stiffens but I show no other reaction. Did he see Evie before she ran out of the club? Is that why he's been acting a little strange since that night? No more than usual, but he just seems a little... off. I can't explain it. It feels like he's keeping something from me.

"No. I must've missed her."

"Hm," he hums. "I could've sworn I saw her, but maybe it was my imagination. She knows how I feel about the place, so I hope she listened to my warnings."

I want to ask what his warnings were, but I don't. If he knows what the *Black Rose* really is, that could be bad, because, in turn, he would know what *we* are, and that's the last thing I want. If my best friend found out I'm a vampire, I would be fucked. Ever since he was a kid, Miles has always been on the right side of the law, especially when it came to wanting to get justice for what happened to his parents. If he found out I drink human blood to survive, I don't even want to know what he would think or do.

My friendship with Ethan is easy because we know about each other—we figured it out as soon as we first met. Other vampires can sniff out other vampires. But my friendship with

Miles is a lot more complicated than that. If he finds out about me... it'll ruin everything.

I'll make damn sure he never finds out.

"She's a smart girl," I say after a moment.

Miles nods. "She is. Which is why she needs to be careful. I can't protect her all the time."

But I can, I want to say, but keep the words lodged in my throat. I can protect her, even if he doesn't know that.

Her scent fills my nostrils within seconds of me climbing the tree outside of her bedroom window. So fucking sweet that it feels like I'm a kid again running high with a sugar rush. As I perch on the branch that has become like a second home to me the past few weeks, it creaks under my weight but holds steady as I inhale deeply, wanting to fill as much of her scent into my lungs as possible.

The room is dark aside from the moonlight shining in through the open window. I would like to think Evie keeps her curtains open for me when I visit but I know that's wishful thinking.

Since the night she learned my secret at *Black Rose*, I have been keeping watch of her from my spot in the tree whenever I get the chance. I tell myself it's to keep her safe because she's special, but I don't know from what danger I'm keeping her safe from. Or maybe it's my sick way of always wanting to be close, her presence calming the storm raging inside of me.

Whatever the reason, sitting here, watching her sleep peacefully through the window, has become the best part of my day. I would rather sit here all through the night, making sure she's safe, than get sleep of my own. Not that I need much.

There is this nagging feeling deep within me that tells me that although everything is calm now, a storm will be rolling in to wreak havoc soon. I need to keep her sheltered and safe from any dangers lurking in the dark.

She is special, a voice within reminds me. *Protect her.*

CHAPTER 18

EVIE

"When will you be home?" Rylee asks on the other end of the line. "Some of the girls want to have a movie night and make popcorn that sounds like it could potentially give us diabetes with the amount of candy they want to add to it."

"Woah, you're really selling me on the popcorn." I laugh and shake my head. "And I should be home soon. I'm sitting outside my brother's apartment to see if he still has the book I left here a few months ago. I never got around to finishing it, so I thought I would drop by on my way home from class."

Rylee snorts. "That sounds really convenient, Ev. Are you sure you're not stopping by to see Jaylen?"

I roll my eyes. "Of course not. I do need the book back, and it's a good excuse to catch up with Miles."

She chuckles, and I just know that she is rolling her eyes at my response.

After what happened at the *Black Rose* four nights ago with Jaylen, I've realized I'm in way over my head. I shouldn't be as attracted as I am to him. Not just because he's a vampire, but because he's also Miles's best friend, and I can't do that to my brother. He made it clear I can't date any of his friends, especially Jaylen, so I need to respect that. No matter how fucking difficult it is to stay away.

At least, that's what I keep telling myself.

"Okay, whatever you say," Rylee responds. "Just let me know when you're on your way home so I can let the girls know."

"Don't wait for me," I say, eyeing the front of the building. I don't see Jaylen's motorcycle on the street, so that's a good sign. There is a chance that it could be parked in the parking lot beside the apartment building, but I like my chances of him not being home. "If you need to start the movie without me then I'm okay with that."

"Okay, if you're sure," she says, and then yawns. "I'll see you soon."

I smile. "Bye, Ry."

As I hang up the call, I slump in the seat of my car. The sun is setting low on the horizon, casting hues of red, orange, and yellow across the sky over Pullman. The swirls of colors behind the clouds make the sky look like it's a marble painting, taking my breath away. I swear the sunsets in Pullman are next level.

Before I switch off the engine, a man's voice comes over the radio. The way his words crack as he speaks shows that despite the need to be professional as a journalist, the topic is like a painful dagger to the heart.

"Sorry to interrupt the broadcast, Joe, but I have some sad news for the listeners of The Wave. I come to you with exclusive information about The Slayer serial killer lurking in the shadows of Pullman. A young couple from WSU was found deceased in the early hours of this morning behind the Tipsy Tiki. The wounds on their bodies match the MO of the other eight victims that have been discovered in recent weeks. Investigators say they are doing everything they can to catch this killer, but the residents of Pullman don't believe them. Until then, the local Sheriff urges everyone to stay safe and stick to groups of three or more because it seems that whoever this person is isn't afraid to take on two people at once. Thanks, Joe. Back to you."

Two more victims found? Whoever this fucker is isn't slowing down in their killings. In fact, they seem to be escalating with the rate of new bodies turning up dead in town. I want to know who this vampire couple is and if I have seen them around campus before, but it's not important. What's important is that this hunter is taken the fuck out because I'm afraid they will discover that Jaylen is a vampire. The thought of him being hunted down by a crazed vampire hunter doesn't sit right with me. I don't want him to be in danger, and he certainly is just by existing in the same town as the fucker hunting down vamps.

With a sigh, I unclip my seat belt and get out of the car. My heart is thumping nervously in my ears with each step I take into the foyer and up the rusted staircase. The dirt-stained carpet under my feet shows its age, matching the rest of the building.

Why Miles decided to move into the apartment, I'll never know.

I climb until I reach the third floor, my eyes instantly darting over to apartment nine. Rock music blasting through the hallway captures my attention. It sounds like it's coming from Miles's apartment, but I can't be sure.

I ignore the pounding of my heart in my chest and walk toward the door. Three raps of my knuckle on the splinted door can barely be heard over the music blaring inside the apartment. But somehow, the music stops and the front door swings open to reveal two baby blue eyes.

"Fuck," I curse. My fifty-fifty chances didn't go in my favor.

Jaylen frowns down at me. "That is no way to greet me, little angel."

My eyes roll to the back of my head as I fold my arms over my chest. "I was hoping Miles would be home."

He leans against the door frame and folds his arms over his chest. I can't ignore the way the thin black material of his shirt stretches over his biceps. The tattoos on his arm are calling for me to inspect them, but I force my eyes to meet his. I can't get sucked into his beauty like I normally do.

"Is there anything I can help you with?"

I look past his body into the apartment to see the book I need sitting on the small shelf by the front door. "Yeah, I just need a book I left behind a few months back."

Jaylen follows my line of sight to the shelf and then turns back to me, a smirk playing on his lips. "Well, if you want it, little angel, you have to come in and get it."

Does he think I'm that same eight-year-old girl who used to play silly games with him like we used to? "Can't you just give it to me?"

He shakes his head. The damp curls around his face swish over his eyes with the movement. "No can do."

With a huff, I push past him into the apartment. If he wants to play games then I will happily play, but on my terms.

The place smells of citrus and men's cologne. A mop and bucket catch my eye in the kitchen, and I spot cleaning products on the bench. It seems Jaylen was in the middle of cleaning the apartment before I knocked on the door. With how large and intimidating he is, I can't picture him performing domestic chores like mopping the floor and cleaning the kitchen.

I spin on my heels to face Jaylen, not realizing he is right behind me. My heart jumps in my throat at the closeness, and I take a step back. "I see you've been doing some cleaning."

Jaylen shoves his hands into the pockets of his black sweatpants. "With Miles at his girlfriends, I thought I would tidy the place up a little."

"Aren't you a good housewife," I comment, and turn back to the bookshelf. I'm painfully aware of Jaylen's sandalwood scent wafting over me and the coolness of his body. I'm reminded of when I ran away after staring down his hard cock, and he chased me back to the sorority house. At that moment, I was so consumed by him that I wasn't thinking straight. But I'm not going to let that happen again.

Snatching the book off the shelf, I turn toward the front door. "Okay, I best be going now—"

A sharp gasp leaves my lips when I feel Jaylen's hand wrap around my throat. In a split second, he has me pinned against the front door, his crimson eyes boring into mine. My eyes widen at the sight, and my body vibrates with fear and excitement.

"Jaylen," I say, my voice barely above a whisper. "Wh-what are you doing?"

"You're not going anywhere, little angel," he breathes against my lips, his scent intoxicating. "Not after how you left me the other night."

Shit. I should've known leaving him hot and bothered like that would come back to bite me in the ass.

"I've already told you that this can't happen." The words leave my lips but even I know they don't sound convincing. They sounded breathless and excited. That could be because I like the feeling of his large hand wrapped around my throat, squeezing just enough that I can still breathe but am painfully aware that he could restrict my airway with his strength in the blink of an eye. "Miles would kill us both."

Jaylen licks his lips, pulling his lip ring between his teeth before releasing it. "We both know I can handle Miles. But what I can't handle is you."

My eyes widen. "Me?"

"Yes, you. You drive me fucking insane, Evie. I never know what you're thinking, and I hate that. You're not easy to read like others. You never have been. I can only get a read on what you're feeling based on the rhythm of your heartbeat. But other than that, I'm fucking clueless, and I don't like the feeling."

I know he's talking about other women. He has to be. With how much of a playboy Jaylen is, it doesn't surprise me that he can easily read women. I'm sure his vampire abilities help with that. How? I'm not sure, but it must be true.

"I don't want you to read me well," I counter, swallowing hard despite the restriction around my throat. "This, what we're doing, is wrong and you know that. Why do you keep pursuing me?"

"Because you're mine," Jaylen says, pressing his body into mine. My heart stutters at the feel of his hard length pushing against my thigh through the fabric of his sweatpants. "And I'm not going to let you forget that, little angel. No matter how hard you try to push me away, I'm not going anywhere. Your words say you don't want this, but your body is telling me something different."

His words crash over me like a tidal wave. In all the years I have known Jaylen, I never once expected we would be in this situation. We have always been close, but when did the flip switch? How did we go from being friends to craving each other? It just doesn't make sense.

I hate that my pussy is throbbing. I hate that his words affect my body more than they should. And I hate that I like it.

"I would do anything for you," Jaylen continues, his cock pulsing against the apex of my thigh. I bite back a moan, and squeeze my thighs together, which doesn't go unnoticed by him because he smirks. "Little angel, I would go as far as to kill for you if that's what I needed to do to keep you safe."

My heart stills in my chest. "K-kill?"

Jaylen smirks and his tongue darts out to lick his bottom lip. "Yes, kill. Have you noticed that your piece of shit ex-boyfriend is no longer harassing you?"

My mind goes back to my conversation with Preston at the *Black Rose*. He asked me if I had seen Roman because he hadn't been seen by anyone all week and wasn't showing up to practice. I thought he had simply left town to visit his parents, and that was it. The thought of something more sinister being the case never once crossed my mind.

Until now, that is.

"Did you... kill him?" My voice is tight, and my heart is nervously slamming against my rib cage.

The sinister look that crosses Jaylen's crimson eyes gives me the answer I'm looking for.

He *did* kill Roman and for some odd reason... I'm not scared of him. If anything, I'm insanely turned on that he would go to such lengths to protect me.

Yes, killing people is bad, I know this. But Roman was threatening me and trying to blackmail me using photos. If Jaylen hadn't stopped him, who knows what lengths he would've gone to next to try and get me back? I do not doubt that Roman was unhinged and would have potentially tried to hurt me. How? I'm not sure, but I know it was possible considering the escalation of his actions.

So, if anything, I'm grateful that Jaylen put an end to any potential harm that may have come my way.

Do I feel bad that Roman is dead? Not really, but I know I should. It's fucked up that it doesn't faze me, but I can't bring myself to care when he was trying to hurt me. In my head, it only seems fair that his bad karma is coming back to bite him in the ass. I don't condone murder, but just this once I'm willing to look the other way.

"Does that scare you, little angel?" Jaylen's lips are barely brushing mine. I want to reach forward and attach mine to his, but his hand around my throat restricts any movements from me. "That I would kill for you?"

I shake my head the best I can. "No."

"No?" he parrots and then smiles. I gasp for air when he releases his hold on my throat, his hand sliding down the front of my shirt until it reaches my waist. His fingertips are ice cold, but I welcome it because my skin feels as though it's on fire. "Good, because I would gladly burn this fucking town to the ground if it meant protecting you."

Before I can open my mouth, Jaylen has his hand over it. He spins me around so my back is flat against his chest, his eyes focused on the front door.

"It seems we have a problem."

I want to ask what he's talking about, but I can't get a word out. All he can hear is muffled words falling from my lips, but he doesn't seem to care. He pulls me down the hallway until we reach his bedroom. He kicks the door open with his foot and drags me inside.

"Stay here," he commands, placing me on the edge of his king-sized mattress. "If you don't want your brother to know you're here, then you better not make a fucking sound."

My eyes widen. "What! Miles is here?"

"He will be in a minute," Jaylen says, looking over his shoulder. "I heard his car pull into the parking lot."

"Right, I forgot about your super hearing," I mutter under my breath. "Wouldn't it be easier if I just left now and waited down the hallway until he got inside?" I can't let Miles find me in his apartment with Jaylen, *alone.*

He shakes his head. "I'm not done with you yet."

His words only make my pussy throb harder, and I want to punch myself. *Get a fucking grip, Evie,* I scold myself. I need to remind myself that although Jaylen handled Roman for me, and I'm grateful for that, whatever is happening between us can't happen. Unaware of my presence, hiding in his bedroom with my brother in the living room, is proof enough.

Keys jingling at the front door put me on high alert. Jaylen shoots me a knowing look before walking out of the room and closing the door behind him. As I listen to him greet my brother casually as if I'm not hiding in his bedroom, I glance around the large room. For an old apartment, the bedrooms sure are large.

I quickly realize I have never stepped foot in Jaylen's bedroom. Why would I? The style of the room certainly fits his personality, that's for sure. The sheets under me are black satin and the bed frame is black wood. Across from the bed is a black desk with a computer monitor on top and a black leather chair. It doesn't surprise me that every piece of furniture is black, even the bookshelf to my left. The only color in the room is the spines of the books on the shelf.

It's a room fit for a vampire.

My right leg bounces under me as I nervously rub my hands together in my lap. Miles's voice grows louder as his footsteps echo down the hallway. I hold my breath as I listen to him enter his bedroom next door and then walk back into the living room. Their voices are too muffled to hear exactly what they're saying. Instead, I focus on the blood rushing in my ears.

God, I hope my brother doesn't walk in here. I'll be fucked if he does.

Instead of sitting around waiting for Jaylen to come back, I quietly stand and walk around the bed to the bookshelf. My eyes scan the bright colors on the spine. Who would have thought that *the* Jaylen Black would have *The Great Gatsby, To Kill a Mockingbird*, and *Frankenstein* on his shelf? Not me. I roll my eyes when I see the tattered spine of *Dracula*. Of course, a vampire would have read that book.

It never crossed my mind that Jaylen might be an avid reader. Based on the number of books on his shelf, I would guess he likes to read in his spare time. I don't know why the thought surprises me so much. I guess I always pictured him spending his downtime when he's not in class or at practice at the *Black Rose* or with other women. It's a pleasant surprise.

I squat to look at the stack of vinyl records next to a record player that has seen better days. If I had to guess, it looks to be as old as the one my mom had. The wooden base is worn, likely due to sun damage, and it has that musty old smell like when you walk into an antique store emitting from it.

I run my fingers over the top of the vinyl records and smile to myself. I like seeing this side of Jaylen. The one he doesn't let others see.

The bedroom door swings open behind me, and for a split second, I consider dropping to my stomach in case it's my brother. But when I smell sandalwood, I breathe a sigh of relief. Standing to my full height, I turn around to see Jaylen in front of the closed door, his baby-blue eyes watching me with amusement.

"Snooping around, I see," he comments, tilting his head to the side.

I walk to stand by the edge of the mattress and shrug. "I got bored. You didn't expect me to just sit here in silence, did you?"

He smiles and shakes his head. "Not at all, little angel. I know you too well. Did you find anything of interest?"

I bite back the smile threatening to turn up the corner of my mouth, and instead fold my arms over my chest. "Yeah, that you like to read books. I never would've guessed that." I smile to myself and jab a finger over my shoulder. "That's a nice record player. Where did you get it from?"

Jaylen folds his arms over his chest and looks at the bookshelf. For a moment, his blue eyes almost appear hazy with an emotion I can't put my finger on. "It was my mom's. She gave it to me a week before she died. Much like your mom, she would play that damn thing every time she cooked dinner. It was her most prized possession."

I smile. Jaylen doesn't talk about his parents much, especially in the years following their deaths. Even when they were alive, I only met them a handful of times because they were very private people. Miles knew them a lot better than me, but that was because Jaylen's mom would take them to and from practice most weeks. My mom tried her best to befriend Jaylen's parents, but they preferred to keep to themselves, only having to interact with my parents if they had to. I now know their reasoning for doing so, being vampires and all.

From what I knew about them, they were lovely people and even better parents to Jaylen. It was tragic when they died. I could tell their deaths hit Jaylen hard, but he was good at putting on a brave face and eventually resorted to just not speaking about them at all. I guess it was easier to ignore the pain he was feeling than to acknowledge it.

"It's beautiful," I say, remembering my mom's record player. My aunt has it now, but once I finish college and move into my own place, it'll be the first thing I take with me. I smack my lips together and roll on the balls of my feet. I don't want to push Jaylen by talking about his parents, so changing the subject is easier. "Okay, so what do we do now?"

"Well, as much as I would love for you to stick around, you have to go. Miles wants to invite the guys over for drinks and a movie, so you won't be able to leave through the front door."

I frown. "So, how do you expect me to leave?"

The grin on his lips tells me I'm not going to like his answer. My suspicions are correct when Jaylen marches across the room, scoops me up in his arms in one fluid motion and walks toward the large window beside his bookshelf.

"What the hell are you doing?" I whisper-shout, holding onto his shoulders for dear life. The hardness of his body is lethal. "You're not going to—"

"Jump out the window," he finishes for me as he slides the window up with one hand, the other splayed firmly across my ass for support. "Sorry, little angel. It's the only option."

Before I can protest, Jaylen swings his legs over the ledge and jumps off the side of the building with the force of a fucking kangaroo. A squeal leaves my lips as I wrap my arms around his neck. Wind rushes past me, filling my ears and drowning out the fear racing through my veins.

In the blink of an eye, Jaylen lands swiftly on the ground. Blood rushes in my ears as I pull back to stare into the depths of his eyes. I want to slap him across the face for doing that, but I'm frozen in his arms, unable to do anything but breathe heavily. Adrenaline is coursing through my veins, and I hate to admit it... but that was the most thrilling thing I've done in a long time.

"See how easy that was," Jaylen says as he lowers me onto the patch of grass beside the building. My legs are wobbly, but I manage to gather my bearings quickly enough.

"You're an asshole," I huff and run my hands down the front of my shirt—anything to avoid looking into his eyes.

"Come on, you enjoyed it." The amusement in his voice doesn't go unnoticed by me.

Inhaling a deep breath, I lift my eyes to meet his. "Thanks for getting me out of there without Miles seeing me. That could have been disastrous."

"I still don't care if he finds out," Jaylen comments, referring to whatever is happening between us.

I fold my arms over my chest. "Well, I do. We can't keep doing this."

Jaylen bites his lip and takes a step back. "Let's see how long you continue to lie to yourself, little angel."

Before I can respond, Jaylen wraps his hand around my wrist and pulls me toward his chest. A gasp slips past my lips, but he catches it when his lips connect with mine. Heat explodes in my chest at the contact, and I melt into his touch. His lips are ice cold, but I enjoy the way my lips tingle against them, and the chills that spread across my skin.

The kiss is short and sweet, but filled with passion and lust, making my head dizzy.

Jaylen pulls away, leaving me wanting more, and pushes off the ground, shooting into the air. I stand stunned and watch as he grips the ledge outside of the window and pulls himself in with ease. He pops his head out, curls in his eyes, and waves before disappearing.

I sigh and spin on my heels to walk back to the car. When I reach the driver's door, I close my eyes and inhale a deep, calming breath.

I left the fucking book I came for in the apartment.

CHAPTER 19
EVIE

I bounce on the balls of my feet, watching the barista as she makes my coffee. Caffeine is much needed after class today. I can feel myself slowing down and caring less about my classes and more about the strange murders occurring in town. Not to mention I have an attractive vampire always lurking nearby, appearing when I least expect him.

It's safe to say that my mind is elsewhere, so I need this coffee to liven me up enough to go to the library and work on an assignment that is due next week. If I go back to the sorority house, I know I'll get distracted by my friends or whatever themed night is planned for dinner by the sisters in charge. They say that getting the girls in the house together will strengthen our bond, but I disagree. Not all the sisters can be friends—I think the tension between Amara and me is proof enough. And I'm sure some of the other girls have their issues too, which is why I need to steer clear from the house and stay in the library for guaranteed peace and quiet.

The hiss of the milk frother fills my ears as I look down at my phone, checking for any new messages. I see I have two— one from Miles, and the other from Rylee.

> Rylee: Hey! I didn't catch you before you left but wanted to ask if you're going to be back in time for Taco Thursday.
>
> Amy is making sure everyone attends...

God, these girls sure do love their themed nights. That's two this week already.

> Evie: As appealing as it is to spend the night with the entire house eating tacos, I'm going to have to pass. I have a big assignment due next week that I need to start. But I'll see you later when I get home. Enjoy those tacos! Hopefully, Jenny isn't on the meat tonight... LOL.

Next, Miles's message.

> Miles: Sis! Just wanted to check in on you. We'll have to catch up for lunch sometime soon whenever you're free. But I'll be seeing you at the game this weekend, right?

"A large vanilla iced latte to go!"

My head snaps up at the sound of the barista's voice calling out my drink order. Slipping my phone into the back pocket of my jean shorts, I walk around a tall man standing in front of me, and head to the counter where I see my drink sitting. As I reach for the drink, smiling at the worker, I can already feel the cool condensation on my fingertips. The weather is starting to cool down as the warm summer heat shifts to a cooler fall, bringing with it spooky season and pumpkins.

As I wrap my fingers around the base of the plastic cup, so does another hand, one much larger than mine. Confused, I lift my eyes to the tall man beside me, the one I had stepped around to reach the counter. His deep chocolate eyes look back at me with a hint of amusement twinkling within them.

"Well, this is awkward," he jokes, not letting go of the cup.

I laugh softly, tightening my grip on the cup. "It's only awkward if you say it is. But I do believe this is my coffee."

He raises a sharp brow at me, biting back a smile. "Are you sure about that?"

My eyes roam the stranger's face, taking in his soft features and tousled blonde hair that looks dyed because of the brown regrowth peeking through. He looks like the classic boy next door type of guy you would see in romcoms or read about in romance novels with his blue jeans and letterman jacket even though it's still slightly humid outside. And dare I admit it, but he's very attractive.

"Sorry, but you don't seem like the type to drink iced vanilla lattes," I point out with a smile.

He gasps, his free hand lifting to rest on his chest. "I take offense to that. Iced vanilla lattes are my go-to. Who says a man can't enjoy a sweet coffee?"

He's right. Most guys think it's uncool to drink sweet coffees, opting instead to drink Americanos because it's 'manlier'. But I disagree. Sweet coffee should be enjoyed by all.

I laugh at his words, shaking my head softly. "Okay, fine. You win. Truce?"

The man lets go of the cup to extend his hand between us, a

soft smile touching his lips. "No, I concede. The drink is all yours. You're lucky you are cute, otherwise, I would have fought harder for the drink."

My cheeks warm at his flirty words as I shake his hand, his skin warm in my palm. At least, I think he's flirting with me. I'm terrible at picking up on this kind of stuff. I can only really tell when Jaylen is flirting with me because he's so blatantly obvious about it. But this guy is more subtle, making it hard for me to read him and his motives.

"That's a shame because I would've quite enjoyed a stand-off." I grab the coffee just as the barista brings over another one, having seen our little exchange. "Anyway, I'm going to enjoy this coffee after a hard-fought battle."

I turn to walk away, already sipping on the goodness of the drink. There is nothing better than the taste of victory.

"Wait," the man calls after me, falling in step beside me as I walk toward the exit. When I feel him beside me, I stop and face him. He's looking down at me with kind eyes and a fresh drink in his hand. "I didn't catch your name."

"That's because I didn't say it."

His tongue darts out to lick his lips as a smile curves up his mouth. "Is there any chance you'd tell me now?"

I consider his question. As much as I'd like to tell him no so I can leave to go to the library and just be alone, I must admit that I do like the boyish charm and calm vibe he gives off. After everything that happened with Roman, I'm a little nervous about inviting any new guys into my life in a romantic sense for fear of getting hurt again. But maybe it wouldn't hurt to just see what happens with this man. Who knows what could happen? Past me would've been terrified of that saying, but new me isn't as worried.

Although I don't know what the hell is going on with Jaylen, I'm still free to do whatever I like with whomever I want, so fuck it. I'm going to take a chance on this guy and see where it lands me.

This could end in happiness or total fucking chaos.

"Evie," I finally say. "You?"

"Kale," he smiles. "It's a pleasure to meet you."

"Likewise. Do you go to school at WSU?"

Kale shakes his head. "I attend UC Berkeley."

I shift on my feet, moving to the side and out of the way of the people coming in and out of the shop. "Then what are you doing all the way out in Pullman?"

"My dad is the coach for the soccer team at Berkeley, and I happen to be on the team also." I want to laugh at the irony of this piece of information. *Of course, he is a fucking soccer player.* "We're here checking out the stadium for the game on Saturday night. Dad wanted to see the facilities and location before the team arrived in town tomorrow."

"Well, WSU does have an amazing stadium," I say. "My brother is on the team, so I've seen it all firsthand."

Kale grins. "Your brother, you say. Well, I'm going to apologize now if we kick their asses. But don't hold that against me, okay?"

I laugh, shaking my head. I'm enjoying Kale's charm and his ability to make me laugh without trying. It's been a long time since I've met anyone like him.

"Be careful, I don't want you choking on those words too early."

Kale runs a hand through the blonde mess atop his head, his smile bright and warm. "Look, maybe you're right about that. But a guy can hope, right?"

"There's nothing wrong with that," I say. "But I will be in the crowd, so no pressure or anything."

"Well, in that case," he says, pulling his phone out of his back pocket, "would I be able to grab your number? If you're going to be at the game, I'd like to take you out for a drink afterward. Are you an expresso martini girl? You seem like the type."

I chuckle at his joke, my eyes locked on his phone that is outstretched between us. Instead of listening to the negative voice in my head telling me to decline and be on my way, I'm going to, for once, listen to the positive side telling me to take this attractive man up on his offer and see where things go.

What is the worst that could happen?

I take his phone from him and begin typing my number into a new contact. "Sadly, I'm not. But I will allow you to buy me a drink to see what type of girl I am.

Kale grins, taking back the device when I hold it out for him. "I want to guess the fruity cocktail type, but I want to be surprised." He turns to hold open the door for me, following me out into the warm midday air.

The hair on the back of my neck stands on edge, letting me know that *he* is waiting nearby, watching. I can feel his eyes boring into my skin as I turn to face Kale, ignoring his presence. "Good luck on Saturday, but don't be too sad if you lose, the Raiders do have that effect on most teams."

Kale blows out a breath and licks his lips. "I guess we'll see who will be eating their words after the game. The losing team buys the first round of drinks?"

"Deal," I say, chewing on my bottom lip. "I'll see you around, yeah?"

He nods, smiling. "Of course. See you soon, Evie."

"No, you won't."

I groan, running a hand down my face at the sound of his voice. It's taking everything within my soul not to walk over to where he sits on his motorcycle and push him off. Instead, I wave goodbye to Kale as he walks away. When he walks past Jaylen, I get the sense there is more to be said.

"Lose her number," Jaylen calls out after Kale as he continues to walk away, his brows furrowed as he grips his helmet tightly under his right arm.

With a huff, I march over to Jaylen. I can feel his eyes on me as I approach, stopping beside him. Seeing the shit-eating grin on his plump lips makes me want to slap it off his face but also kiss him. Whenever I'm this close to him, my mind tends to go blank and I can't think properly. It drives me insane.

"What was that?" I demand, folding my arms over my chest.

Jaylen shrugs and rests the helmet on his jean-clad thigh, his eyes roaming over my body until they land on my face. "I should be asking you the same thing, little angel."

I wave my hand in the space between us. "This, us, is not anything, okay? If I want to get a guy's number, I can. We're not a thing, Jaylen."

"That's where you're wrong, Evie. You're mine."

I scoff, shaking my head. "You're delusional. And stop listening in on my private conversations with your super hearing."

Jaylen doesn't say anything. Instead, he gets off his motorcycle and steps toward me, his eyes boring into mine from his towering height. He takes my coffee, places it on the ground beside us, and slips his helmet over my head with a devilish look in his eyes.

"Let me show you why you're *my* girl, little angel. No other man can ever touch you but me."

Jaylen pulls the bike to a stop near the edge of a cliff that looks over vast land just outside of Pullman. The leaves on the trees as far as the eye can see are beginning to turn brown as fall approaches. The air is fresh as I breathe in deeply, eyeing the largely uninhabited area. There is not a house in sight, just barns, cows, sheep, and lots of trees. Just in the distance, I can make out a running river getting lost on the horizon.

Wherever we are... there is not a fucking soul in sight.

I swing off the seat behind him and pull the helmet, resting it under my arm. "Why did you bring me here?" I want to punch him in the arm for leaving my coffee behind, but I don't.

"Because," he says casually as he too gets off the bike, turning to face me. I must admit that he does look sexy in that leather riding jacket and combat boots. His hair is messy over his eyes from the wind gliding through it. *Get it together, Evie.* "I wanted to show you where I come when I need alone time."

I eye him suspiciously as he slowly walks around the bike to stand a few feet away. "Do you... kill people out here?"

Jaylen chuckles and shakes his head. "No, Evie, I don't kill people out here. The quietness helps me clear my head."

I blow out a sharp breath and nod. After his confession last night about killing Roman, I'm not sure what he gets up to in his spare time. He could have killed way more people that I just don't know about. The thought is unnerving, to say the least. So Jaylen coming out to a place like this on his motorcycle to clear his head is not something I would have thought he would do—

In the blink of an eye, Jaylen is standing in front of me, his ocean eyes staring down at me. The intensity in them is enough to send a nervous shiver racing down my spine.

"What are you doing?" I ask, unable to look away.

"I want to know why you got his number."

I square my shoulders. Okay, so it seems we're doing this right now.

"Because I can, Jaylen."

He shakes his head, soft curls brushing across his forehead. "No, you can't."

"You can't tell me what I can and can't do," I argue with a frown, not backing down from the stare-off. Who is he to tell me what I can and can't do? "I don't belong to you."

Jaylen grins and tugs his lip ring between his teeth before releasing it. "See, little angel, that's where you're wrong. You *are* mine, and you always will be."

He leans down and presses his lips against mine, and I can feel the urgency by the way his hands come up to grip the side of my face as he pushes his tongue into my mouth, claiming me. I'm helpless as he consumes me. The only thing I'm capable of doing is groaning into his mouth and pressing my body against his to help ease the need throbbing from my pussy.

I hate that as soon as he touches me, I lose all the self-control I had been holding onto for dear life. How is it that he can just swoop in and throw me for a loop with just one touch? It's unfair.

Jaylen's hands lower to rest on my hips, knocking the helmet out from under my arm. It crashes to the dirt-covered ground beside us. He rocks into me, his hard cock rubbing against the apex of my thigh. All I can picture is the barbell through the crown and what that would feel like inside of me.

Am I going to find out?

A strangled cry leaves my lips when Jaylen pulls away, his crimson eyes filled with lust and desire.

"Turn around and bend over the seat."

My eyes widen at his request. "I don't—"

"Just do it, Evie," he demands, his tongue darting out to lick his lips.

Excitement and curiosity bubbles within my chest at the thought of what could happen next. We're out here alone with not a single car or person in sight. Just the two of us.

Anything could fucking happen, and that's the thrilling part. I can just give in to the attraction I feel for him. At this point, it's bursting at the seams, no longer wanting to be kept hidden.

Doing as I'm told, I turn and bend over the seat, resting my stomach on the warm leather. I fold my arms against my chest and expose my ass to Jaylen. With my back to him, I'm unable to see what he's doing, but the audible groan from his lips doesn't go unnoticed by me.

"That's my good girl," he praises. I jump when I feel his cold fingertips running up the length of my thighs before stopping at the hem of my denim shorts. "You won't be needing these." In one swift movement, he pulls them down my thighs, exposing the black lace panties I chose this morning.

I clench my slick thighs together, the pressure building in my core almost unbearable. "Jay-len."

I hold my breath when he runs a finger down the cleft of my cheeks, tracing the thin material acting as a barrier between him and my soaked pussy. I try to wriggle my hips to ease the pressure, but it does nothing.

"So eager," Jaylen comments. He pushes the material to the side and runs his finger along my slick folds, aching for him to touch it. To relieve the pressure. "This cunt is mine. Do you hear me? Mine."

Without warning, he plunges his finger into my pussy, eliciting an almost animalistic cry from my lips. I bite back another cry as he pushes his finger deeper, hitting the spot that drives me crazy before pulling back at a painstakingly slow pace.

"You're so tight and wet," Jaylen comments, running his left hand over the curve of my ass before slapping it so hard the sound echoes across the clearing along with the cry from my lips. "You take me so well, little angel. Almost as if you were made just for me."

I screw my eyes shut and focus on the sensation already building in my core, threatening to throw me over the edge. I haven't been touched like this since I broke up with Roman, so my body has been craving this feeling for a long time. *Too fucking long.*

Before I can dive off the edge, Jaylen removes his finger with a pop, and I groan in frustration. If he's just going to play with me, I'm going to lose my goddamn mind.

"Not yet," he says as he runs his hand over the ass cheek that I'm sure now has his handprint in red. "I want to taste you as you come on my tongue."

His dirty words are something I'll never get used to because Roman never spoke like that during sex, but oh God is it the sexiest thing ever. Hearing Jaylen speak like that has my mind spinning and my core tightening.

The shuffling behind me has me confused as to what he's doing, but when my ass cheeks are spread and something wet plunges into me, I realize Jaylen is on his knees with his tongue tracing my pussy.

Oh, my fucking God.

I moan as his skillful tongue plunges deep inside me, licking and sucking to the point that my mouth goes dry and I forget where I am. I forget that I'm bent over Jaylen's motorcycle with his handprint on my ass cheek and his tongue deep inside my cunt.

"Jay-len," I groan, biting my lip so hard the taste of metallic coats my tongue.

He simply grunts against my slick core, vibrating my entire body. He grips my ass painfully hard that I'm sure it'll leave a bruise, but I don't care. At this point, I would let him do anything, and that worries me.

"You taste so fucking sweet, little angel," he says against my dripping pussy. His fingers move to my front to flick the sensitive nub pulsing with anticipation. "And it's all for me."

All I can focus on is the steady build in my core and my cries of pleasure as they echo across the clearing. It's when Jaylen uses his finger to stroke my clit that my vision goes white and a loud cry escapes my lips, screaming his name, and forcing me over the edge. My legs shake against the side of the bike, barely holding me up. If it wasn't for Jaylen's strong hand on my ass, I would've fallen against him.

Jaylen keeps licking and sucking me as I come down from my high, my muscles spasming with the aftereffects. With one last lick, he stands to his feet, and leans over me, pressing what I'm sure is his painfully hard cock against my ass as his lips find my ear. White spots dance in front of my eyes as I turn my head just enough to peer into the side mirror on the bike and see Jaylen's crimson eyes staring at the side of my face, his fangs extended, his tongue moving across them.

The sight alone has my pussy aching for him again.

What the fuck is wrong with me?

I just let this man—my brother's fucking best friend— bend me over his motorcycle and bring me to an earth-shattering orgasm, and I still want more?

"Are you really going to tell me that the loser you met today will make you come like me, little angel?" he whispers in my ear. His crimson eyes meet mine in the small mirror, and he smiles. "Next time, it'll be my cum dripping out of you. As my girl, I expect you to wear me with pride as I am with your cum all over my tongue and face. And I'll never let you forget it."

All I can do is stare at him, unable to say a word because *fuck me*. What the hell do I say to that? I want to tell him, for what feels like the hundredth time, that we can't do this. But it's clear my body fucking thinks otherwise.

When I don't say anything, Jaylen stands and takes a step back, allowing me room to breathe. It feels like a heavy weight is pressing down on my chest, making me dizzy. It could also be the aftereffects of the orgasm, but I know it has to do with Jaylen and his ever-consuming presence.

Inhaling sharply, I push myself off the seat and turn to face Jaylen. His eyes are partially red and blue as he stares at me. Under the light of the afternoon sun, they almost appear purple.

"Let me help you." He walks forward and grabs the jean shorts pooled around my ankles. I had almost forgotten that I was pantless. I stand in silence as he pulls the material up my legs and fastens the button. He lingers for a moment with his hands on my hips and the promise of touching me again, but something pulls him away, forcing him to take a step back. Jaylen runs a hand through his messy hair. "I should get you home."

I eye his hard cock hidden behind the confines of his jeans. The way it strains against the material almost looks painful, and if it is, he doesn't say anything.

"I have time," I find myself saying. My eyes scan the vast area in front of us. I had no idea Pullman could be this beautiful. "Unless you have somewhere to be."

Jaylen looks surprised by my response, but I don't know why. Despite the push and pull between us, I do enjoy spending time with him. I always have. He is so interesting to talk to, even if we are talking about nothing important. When we were kids, I could listen to him talk all day because of his smooth, deep voice, and I still could.

Finally, he shakes his head. "Nope. We can stay as long as you like."

I smile and walk toward the cliff edge. The dirt is rough under my hands as I sit down, my legs swinging over the edge. Being this close to the edge of a cliff, my life balancing in its hands should make me afraid. I could easily fall and hurt myself, or worse. But with Jaylen sitting beside me, his overwhelming scent of sandalwood mixed with earth puts my mind at ease.

I'm never afraid when I'm with him.

Jaylen turns to me, his shoulder gently brushing mine. I can see questions brimming behind those curious eyes of his. There is so much he wants to ask me or say, but nothing is being said. It's not very often we spend time like this together —alone. There is always the fear that my brother could be lurking, ready to catch us in a compromising position. But out here, it's just the two of us. No Miles. No friends. And no distractions.

It's just us.

"So, what's new with you?" The question is so simple, yet it allows him to take the conversation in whatever direction he likes.

Jaylen visibly relaxes at my words and leans into me. His frigid skin sends a shiver across my body as he wraps a strong arm around my waist, pulling me into his side. "You really want to know what's new with me?"

I turn to look up at his side profile. At this angle, I can see just how sharp his jawline is. "Of course, I do. There was a time when we would spend most of our time together, or have you forgotten about that?"

When Jaylen and Miles went to high school, we didn't

hang out together as much as we did when we went to the same school. I guess Miles realized that it wasn't 'cool' to be seen with his little sister all the time. From then on, he put more distance between the three of us, and we no longer spent every afternoon talking and doing random activities together. It was an odd feeling going from being so close with my brother and Jaylen to only talking to them when it was necessary. Miles and I were still close, don't get me wrong, but I grew further apart from Jaylen in the process, especially when I went to high school and Miles came up with his stupid no-dating rule.

At the time, it did hurt to see us all growing apart, and no longer the close trio we once were. But as time went on, I realized that it was the natural progression of life. Sooner or later, Miles would've put some space between us as he grew older, I knew that. I just didn't want to believe it.

Jaylen looks down at me, his eyes filled with an emotion I can't quite read. "How could I possibly forget that, little angel? I used to love spending time with you and getting to see more of your dorky side. But it seems you haven't changed a bit."

I playfully roll my eyes and lean my cheek against his arm. "Okay, no need to come at me like that."

The chuckle that rumbles in his chest makes me smile. "All right. What's new with me? Well, nothing, really."

"Nothing?" I ask, turning to look at him. "You're a goddamn vampire, surely there has to be something."

He shakes his head. "Nope. Nothing."

"Woah, I didn't realize you were so boring," I tease, unable to hold back the smile tugging at the corner of my lips.

He bites his lip ring and squeezes my hip playfully, eliciting a sharp squeal of surprise from my lips. "Watch what you say, little angel. I wouldn't want to have to shove something in there to keep you quiet."

My cheeks flame at his words. He means his cock. *Oh, my fucking God.*

As much as I would love for that to happen, I'm enjoying this moment between us. I haven't laughed like this with him in a long time, and I don't want it to end because of my big mouth. Instead, I change the course of the conversation to something that has been on my mind.

"So, what are you planning to do after you graduate this year?"

Jaylen stays silent for a moment, so I trace my finger over the black and white rose inked on the top of his hand. The lines are so delicate for such a rugged man.

"I don't know," he answers quietly. "I have the rest of eternity to figure it out, don't I."

"I mean, you're right, but you don't plan to do anything else? Like travel or get an engineering job?"

He shrugs. "Like I said, I have the rest of eternity to do all that. At some point, life is going to feel meaningless, you know? Doing the same old mundane things day in and day out. I'll eventually see the entire world, so there will be nothing new for me to explore. I could get every single degree possible because all I have is time to study and learn new things. But at what point will my life ever have meaning to it?"

His words settle heavily on my shoulders. I have never thought about it like that before. Being a vampire means you will likely live to see Earth crumble from global warming over the next however many hundreds or thousands of years or whatever else may come after it. All you have is time to do the things you want before it no longer becomes interesting or exciting. You're just... existing.

Knowing that is what Jaylen's future looks like saddens me more than I thought it would.

I slip my fingers through his, wanting to bring him some

sort of comfort. "Let's not think about the future, okay? All that matters is the present."

Jaylen's unblinking eyes are focused on our intertwined hands resting on my thigh. I want to know what he's thinking about, but I don't get the chance to ask before he speaks.

"You're all I need in life, little angel. Nothing else matters."

I chew on my bottom lip as guilt gnaws at my stomach. As much as I enjoy being like this with Jaylen—carefree and relaxed—I know this is as far as it can go. How can we possibly be together when he has time on his side and I don't?

Even though this feels right, I know it's wrong. In what world can a vampire and a human be together? It just can't happen, and I know that. But Jaylen doesn't, and that's the problem.

CHAPTER 20
EVIE

"You what!"

I cringe at the pitch of Candie's voice, her eyes wide as she stares at me from across the kitchen island. When the girls asked to have a girl's night in and make homemade pizzas, I should've known I would get this reaction when telling them about Kale. I was contemplating keeping the details to myself, but since we're meant to go out for drinks after the game tomorrow night, I figured I would have to spill the beans eventually since I would have to leave them.

It's better to get it out into the open now instead of telling them at the game. This way, they can get all their questions out in one go.

"Yeah," I say, spreading barbeque sauce across the base of my pizza. I made the dough into a heart shape.

"Okay, so let me get this straight," Jaycee says, holding up her hand. "You're going on a date with a player from the opposite team?"

"It's not a date," I clarify. "But... yeah."

"When did this happen?" Rylee asks from beside me. She is sprinkling cheese over her square-shaped base.

"Yesterday. I met him at Bluebird Co. on campus. He and

his dad are in town checking out the facilities before the game."

"Is he cute?" Candie asks, her eyes big and bright as she awaits my answer.

I smile. "He's very boy next door cute, and funny, too." The girls sigh happily, swooning over Kale. I totally understand their reaction. I'm sure that's the effect he has on most women he crosses paths with. "I'll point him out at the game."

"But what about Jaylen?" Jaycee asks, reaching over to grab a handful of pepperoni. She's dressed in a baggy T-shirt and pajama bottoms. We all decided to wear matching pajamas for the occasion, so we all look the same as we stand around the kitchen island.

I frown, looking up at her. "What about Jaylen?"

She shrugs. "Aren't you guys like..."

I scoff, shaking my head. "We're not anything, Jay. I don't know what the hell is going on with him, with us, but we're certainly not *anything* as far as I know."

"Look, I think it's great that you're putting yourself out there," Rylee interjects with a smile. I eye the smear of flour across her cheek. "Just keep being yourself and living your life, and I'm sure everything will fall into place, whether that's with Jaylen or Kale."

I have to agree with Rylee. After Jaylen took me out to his favorite spot in Pullman and ravished me on his motorcycle yesterday, I thought that maybe going out with Kale might be a bad idea. But after thinking about it some more once Jaylen dropped me home, I realized that I can't wait around to see what is going to happen with him because realistically, I'm not sure if anything can happen at all.

Yes, I'm attracted to him, but knowing that Miles is always going to be there keeping a close eye on me makes it harder for us.

Jaylen says I'm his girl, but am I really? And what does that mean to him?

"You're right," I say as I sprinkle some ground beef onto my pizza. "I'm just going to let the universe guide me through this, and what will happen will happen. There is no point in fighting it."

Jaycee sips on her wine before nodding in my direction. "Does Jaylen know that you're going out for drinks with Kale?"

"He does."

"Girl, you're playing with fire here," she says, licking her lips. "But I trust you. Just... be careful, okay?"

I give her a reassuring smile. "I always am. I can handle Jaylen, don't worry. I won't get myself into something that I can't get myself out of."

Candie stiffens, her eyes looking behind me as she stops putting toppings on her pizza. Glancing over my shoulder, I see Amara standing by the refrigerator watching us. Her brows are furrowed as she observes the scene before her eyes move to me.

"I couldn't help but overhear your conversation," she says, fiddling with the messy bun on top of her head. "Who is this Kale guy you speak of?"

"It's none of your business," I say through gritted teeth, turning to face her fully.

"If you're dating someone else, that means Jaylen is free game," she smirks, folding her arms over her chest that is covered by a worn oversized T-shirt.

Her words leave an odd taste in my mouth. I know she has a history with Jaylen, but it seems he doesn't care for her the way she does for him. That was evident from what I overheard after the game a few weeks ago. I wish she would get the hint, but it's not my place to say since nothing ia going on between me and Jaylen. But still, her words rub me the wrong way.

"If I were you, I'd get the fuck out of my face before you regret it," I say as calmly as I can. "If you want to go for Jaylen, be my guest. Just don't drag me into your shit."

Amara stares at me for a moment, her eyes hard, before she huffs and leaves the kitchen, her feet slapping against the floorboards. When she is out of sight, I sigh and turn to face the girls. I can feel their eyes on me, wanting to say something but all that fills the space around us is silence.

"That was... woah." Candie is the first to break the silence. "What the hell happened there?"

I shake my head. "She just gets on my fucking nerves, that's all."

"I feel that," Rylee says, offering a comforting smile. "But don't worry about her, okay? Let's enjoy some homemade pizza, a glass of wine, and a fun and flirty romcom."

I smile, grateful for the support of my friends. My head may be a fucking mess because of Jaylen and now Kale being thrown into the mix, but I'm glad I can switch off when I'm with my friends and not think about what's going on outside of being with them.

It's not something I realize I enjoy so much until this very moment.

"You're right," I say, picking up my glass to sip on the crisp white wine. "I'm going to switch off and forget about everything that's going on in my life and focus on the present."

The girls smile as we lift our glasses in the air to cheer to my words, and I can't help but giggle and lean into my best friend as we continue to decorate our pizzas.

With our stomachs full of delicious pizza and wine coursing through our veins, we make our way into the living room to watch a movie. There are two other girls on the couch sitting quietly as they read a book, so we join them and switch on the TV.

The screen flickers to life, revealing a news reporter looking very sombre as they deliver a piece of news. That seems to be a common occurrence these days in Pullman. Our laughter dies down when we read the 'breaking news' headline.

'Another victim discovered in Pullman that has been linked to the string of murders.'

"Oh, shit," Jaycee breathes as she leans back on the couch beside me, her eyes glued to the screen. "This is getting crazy now."

Candie turns the sound up, capturing the attention of the other two girls in the room as we listen in to the news reporter.

"There has been another murder victim discovered this afternoon, bringing the death count to eleven. A lady was walking her dog through Conservation Park when she made the grizzly discovery," the woman reports. "Investigators were quick to announce that this murder shares many similarities to that of the serial killer's MO who is running loose in Pullman. We were told that this victim, a woman in her 20s, was drained of her blood, and a new detail that is now being shared by investigators is that all the victims share the same mark—an upside-down cross carved into their forehead. Investigators believe that this could be the result of a satanic ritual—"

"Whoever this person is that's killing people is so fucking messed up," Rylee comments, holding her wine glass close to her chest. The fear in her eyes doesn't go unnoticed by me. "Like, seriously."

"I know," Jaycee says, shaking her head. "I'm afraid to be alone outside once the sun sets. Who knows who this crazed killer is and who their next target might be? I don't want to be next."

As the girls talk among themselves, I ponder the details shared by the reporter, especially the new detail about the upside-down cross carved into their forehead.

A memory from when I was eight comes to mind. My mom told me about something similar that was happening in the late '70s when she was my age. It might seem morbid that she shared such disturbing details with me at that age, but I was always into that kind of thing growing up that it got to the point where I would ask my mom to tell me about mythical creatures, cults, and true crime stories. After many hours of nagging, she finally caved and sat me down for a long discussion, and one of the things she mentioned was a series of murders in the late '70s in Pullman where the victims were drained of their blood and made to look like it was part of a satanic ritual. They never did catch the killer.

But there was one detail that has always stuck with me—those victims also had an upside-down cross carved into their foreheads.

Could it be that the murders that are happening now are being done by the killer from all those years ago? Or is it someone new? A copycat killer...

But who would do such a thing, and why now? None of this makes sense to me.

Knowing what I know now from Jaylen, it would make sense for someone who knows about vampires to want to carve upside-down crosses into their foreheads because of their immortality. But why make it look like a satanic ritual if it's just a vampire hunter wanting to eliminate vampires? If it was the same thing that happened in the 70s, then surely the current killer would know about the past MO to be able to recreate it, especially if they are both hunters.

Trying to wrap my head around all these details is hurting my head. It's hard to make sense of the situation when I don't know all the details or who is behind the murders.

I tune back into the conversation happening around me and decide to keep this piece of information to myself. What I know won't help the investigation in any way. But this piece of information has reignited my need to find out who is behind my parent's murder. I only know so much, but I'm hoping the memories my subconscious has locked away will be able to help me.

"Do you think it is actually some weird ass cult that is doing this?" Candie asks, looking between us. "Because if it is, that's messed up."

"Who knows what is truly happening," I say, clearing my throat. "But what I do know is that we need to be careful, okay? Try to go out in pairs or small groups just to be safe."

"Agreed," Jaycee said with a sharp nod. "Who knows who this psycho fuck is, so just stay safe and vigilant."

The conversation shifts from the murders in Pullman to what movie we're going to watch, the girls wanting to watch something light after hearing about the tragedy on the news. But all I can focus on is the connecting detail from the murders in the '70s to the current ones. My mom's voice rings as clear as day in my mind, recounting the details from the '70s and how hot the topic was on the news at the time.

So, my question is: who the hell is this hunter? And why are they recreating the murders from the '70s?

My eyelids are heavy as I stare down at the book resting in my lap. The words are a blurred mess, and I can barely make sense of what is going on in the story so I start to reread paragraphs in the hope my mind will catch up. But it's no use.

With a sigh, I admit defeat and close the book. I rub my eyes with my knuckles, and it feels like scratching an annoying itch. The time on my phone reads just after midnight. Glancing over at Rylee's sleeping form, I realize that now might be a good time to call it quits for the night and attempt to get a good night's sleep.

After the movie earlier tonight, I came upstairs to be alone and gather my thoughts. I couldn't focus on a single scene of that movie because my mind was racing with all the new details about the murders in Pullman and the hopeful connections I made to the case back in the '70s.

Not wanting it to consume me fully, I decided to pick up the book I started recently, but I found my mind wandering to possible suspects and motives instead of reading the words on the page. I couldn't come up with any noteworthy suspects or motives before Rylee walked into the room and announced she was going to sleep. I could tell she wanted to ask if I was okay because of how abruptly I left after the movie ended, but she kept the question to herself and slipped under the sheets.

I've been trying to read for the past three hours, but have retained absolutely nothing.

Yeah, it's time to hit the hay.

Ping!

Frowning, I look down at my phone on the bedside table, its screen illuminated. Who the hell is messaging me this late?

When I see Jaylen's name on the screen, my heart skips a nervous beat.

What does he want?

I sit up straighter in bed and stare at his words. I want to tell
him that I can do whatever the hell I want because he doesn't
own me, but I don't. Instead, I say the one thing that I know
will piss him off. Why? I don't know. Maybe I'm just delirious
from the lack of sleep I've been getting with my constantly
racing mind, or maybe it's because my mind knows that if he is
willing to bend me over his motorcycle just for getting another
guys number, then who knows what he might do if I go on a
date with said guy.

It's a fucked up thought to have, I know. Jaylen literally
killed Roman for what he did to me, so I should be treading
lightly in that regard. But I still want to test the bounds and
maybe even just fuck with him a little because why not?

I just know this is going to come back and bite me in the
fucking ass.

What sounds like a twig snapping outside my window
captures my attention. The sky is inking black with not a single
star twinkling. Even the moon is hidden, not wanting to make
an appearance tonight.

My heart rate spikes at the sharp sound. I close my eyes
and take a deep breath. "It's probably just a squirrel."

Ping!

227

. . .

> Evie: How?

I hold my breath as I wait for his response. It's probably not wise of me to be egging him on like this, but I must admit that I enjoy it. I'm not used to seeing this possessive side of Jaylen, and while most would tell me to run because it's a red flag, I tell myself that red is my goddamn favorite color.

It's almost as if I enjoy walking on fire, waiting for the moment the flames consume every inch of me.

Ping!

> Jaylen: Wait and see, little angel. It'll be a reminder to any fucker who thinks they can claim you. The pain I cause will remind you of what I'm capable of.

I swallow hard and try to ignore the pulsing in my core. Oh, *fuck.* What the hell have I just gotten myself into?

CHAPTER 21
JAYLEN

I f it were possible for my ice-cold veins to be filled with fire, then I would go up in flames like a fucking matchstick. I haven't known anger like this before, so I don't know what to do with myself. All I can do is sit and stare at my locker, my right leg bouncing rapidly.

The chatter in the locker room is muffled in my ears like I'm underwater. If I wanted to, I could tune in to the conversation with my enhanced hearing, but all I can hear is that motherfucker saying, "I'll see you soon," to my girl. My fucking girl. How dare he think he can even go anywhere near her? And don't even get me started on her agreeing to go out with him in the first place like she doesn't know any better.

I made sure to show her why she is my girl and no one else's. I can still taste Evie's cum on my tongue and feel how tight her pussy was wrapped around my finger while I had her bent over my motorcycle screaming my name.

Yeah, I'd like to see the fucker try and take my girl away from me. In fact, I fucking dare him.

My fists involuntarily clench on my thighs as I stare ahead, trying to get my anger in check. Knowing that this Kale guy plays on the opposing team tonight has me wanting to go out there and kick his ass, but that would land me in a pool of deep shit with Coach, so I need to reign in some of the anger to get through the game. I can save the ass-kicking for afterward if I have to.

A hard hand comes down on my shoulder. I snap my head up to see Miles looking down at me, dressed in his jersey. "Everything okay, Jay? You look a little tense."

I roll my shoulders back to try and ease some of the tension building within them. "I'm all good. Just getting in the zone for the game."

"Yeah, this is going to be a tough one. The Panthers are a great side, so we'll have our work cut out for us tonight."

I nod. "Is it time to go out there already?"

Miles takes a step back, allowing me to look around the locker room. Everyone is dressed in their uniforms ready to go. Some are even making their way out of the room behind Coach, cheering and hollering as a way to hype themselves up. Preston and Ethan eye me from the entrance to the locker room, waiting for my next move. Being the captain of the team, I'm sure it's just them looking for some guidance, or they think something is up because I've been sitting on this bench shirtless with no cleats on for the past thirty minutes.

"Let's go," I say and push myself to stand. Miles smiles at me as I slip my feet into my cleats and pull my jersey over my head.

Even as we're walking out onto the pitch, the cheers from the crowd are almost deafening, all I can focus on is Evie's heartbeat in the stands and how annoyed I am that she agreed to go out with that fucker after the game. The thought alone has the fire in my veins roaring to life, taking control of the anger building deep within my chest.

Shit. This isn't going to end well. I can feel it.

Before I knew it, the starting whistle had blown and the

game was underway. I don't feel like I am in control over my body. Like something deep within my soul is moving my limbs and controlling which direction I run in.

Every time I see Kale's stupid head of blonde hair, my vision blurs, and all I can see is red as the sound of Evie's heartbeat drowns out all the other noises around me. It's a feeling I have never felt before and I don't know what the hell is going on, but I have no choice but to lean into it.

"Jay, heads up!" Ethan shouts and I turn to see the ball flying through the air.

I headbutt it toward their goal, but a Panther player snatches the ball and kicks it to the other side to where Cain is standing in the goal box.

"Get your head in the game, cap," Miles says as he races past me.

With a huff, I follow him, trying to get in a good position to steal the ball, but it doesn't happen because a Panther player kicks for a goal. Thankfully, Cain saves it. I'm watching from the halfway line as Cain kicks the ball to Preston.

Although it feels like everyone around me is moving in slow motion, I'm running faster than I probably should for a normal human, but I'm no longer in control of my movements or limiting my abilities as I race toward their goal, hoping Preston can get it to me, but that fucker Kale steals it from him. It's almost as if I'm having an out-of-body experience, watching my body from feet away. Whatever is driving this anger deep within me is fucking pissed, which only makes the redness around my vision worsen.

When I see Kale with the ball running toward me, it's like something snaps in my chest, a taut string of a bow and arrow pulled too tightly, and now my entire vision is red as I rush toward him, faster than normal.

All I see is his eyes widen before I drop into a slide tackle, my leg out straight as I make contact with his ankle, nowhere near touching the ball. The sound of his ankle snapping and his sharp cries of pain are like music to my ears. At the same time as the referee rushes over to issue me with an instant red card, I hear Evie's sweet voice from the crowd.

"What the fuck, Jaylen!"

With my blurred vision, I barely register Miles coming to my defense to the referee, my coach yelling at me from the sideline, likely asking what the hell I was thinking, or the voices from the crowd in a mixture of cheers and boos. All I register is walking off the field with one of the staff members chasing after me. I vaguely remember telling him to not follow me because I wanted to be alone before I rush down the tunnel, and into the locker room.

My skin feels hot, burning me from the inside out as if whatever just possessed me is trying to crawl through my skin. With a huff, I pull my jersey over my head, shove my shorts and underwear down my legs until I'm naked, and walk into one of the open shower stalls. The cold water that gushes out of the shower head isn't nearly enough to put out the fire raging around me. The snapping of bone echoes in my head, drowning out the other noises consuming me.

"Fuck," I grunt, pounding a closed fist against the white tiles, desperately wanting the pain to ease the fire burning within me, but it does little to help.

I rest my forehead against the cold tiles as the cold water washes over my head and down my chest and back. My eyes flutter close at the sound of footsteps approaching. Specifically, Evie's footsteps. Her heart is racing, the rhythm all over the place.

Oh, she's fucking pissed.

"Jaylen!" she shouts when she enters the locker room. When I don't answer her, she follows the sound of running water. I can feel her behind me, every bit as angry as I had anticipated. "What the *fuck* was that out there!"

I exhale sharply when her floral scent fills my nostrils, making my already foggy brain worse. Whenever she's around, I lose all the self-restraint I have, and it drives me fucking insane.

"Me?" I say, turning my head to look over my shoulder. Her eyes are focused on me but I know she's trying hard to not look at the rest of my naked body. "What the fuck are *you* doing?"

Her jaw drops. "*Me?*" Evie marches forward until she's standing beside me, the cold water bouncing off my skin and splashing onto her black T-shirt. The material begins to go see-through, showing what appears to be a black lacy bra beneath. "Don't you dare try to turn this around on me, Jaylen. You fucking snapped Kale's ankle and got yourself a red card. What the hell were you thinking?"

"I wasn't thinking," I snapped, turning my body to face her. I'm aware that she is so close, and I'm naked with my cock as hard as a rock, but I don't care. Evie does her best to keep her hard amazonite eyes on my face, but I can tell she wants to take a peek, and I don't blame her. "I wasn't thinking, Evie. Do you know why? Because you're the one who decided to take that loser up on his offer to take you out when you know you're *my* girl." She jumps when I plant both of my hands on the wall beside her head, cold water cascading down my arms and onto her body, further wetting her clothes. "I proved that to you the other day."

"Why do you keep saying that?" she retorts, her voice shaking slightly.

"Because you are," I answer, lowering my face so that we're at eye level. "You're my girl, little angel. No one else's, and certainly not that fucker whose ankle I snapped. You're *mine*."

"I'm not your property, Jaylen. You can't just claim me as

yours and expect me to go along with it. That's not how this works."

The fire in her voice and the arousal I can smell coming off her in waves only make me harder.

Fucking hell.

"Your body says otherwise," I point out, tilting my head to the side. "Tell me, if you went out for drinks with Kale, would you let him touch you like I have?"

Evie's eyes widen at my words, her throat moving as she swallows hard. "That's none of your business."

The wavering in her voice tells me all I need to know.

She wouldn't have let him touch her, because she knows that I'm the only person who can make her reach the highest point on a mountain and freefall into bliss.

"I may not be able to compel you, but I know when you're lying."

"You don't know shit," Evie retorts, her chest heaving with each breath she takes.

I smirk, enjoying this reaction from her way too much.

"I know that your pussy is dripping wet for me. I can fucking smell it, Evie."

She gasps, pushing her head back into the wall. Her clothes are soaked all the way through, the blonde and brown strands of hair sticking to the side of her face as water continues to rush over her, showing every curve of her sweet body.

"You will be the death of me," she breathes as I run the back of my finger down the side of her cheek, pushing away the wet strands of hair. I'd have to be blind to not see the lust burning within her irises and the way her body shifts forward, brushing against my hard cock. I bite back a groan at the touch as all the restraint I had been trying to hold onto these past few weeks completely slips through my fingers, sending me over the edge.

"Oh, you fucking know it, little angel."

Wrapping my hand around the back of Evie's neck, I drag her forward until our lips clash in a heated kiss. Within seconds, her hands are all over my body, touching every wet inch they can as if she's afraid this will be the last time. My skin is feverish wherever she touches, despite the cold water rushing over us. I press my body against hers, pinning her against the wall as my tongue devours her mouth.

A strangled moan leaves her lips when I move my hand to wrap around her throat to hold her in place. The wet material of her shirt brushing against my hard cock forces a moan from my lips, but her mouth is quick to catch it, swallowing it greedily as she runs her fingernails down my chest.

My eyes nearly pop out of my head when she grabs the base of my cock, stroking it fast and hard. I pull away from her mouth, gasping for air as I lean my forehead against hers. Evie's breath is warm against my lips as she continues to pump me, her hand soft and warm wrapped around me.

"As much as I would love to shove my cock into that pretty mouth of yours, I would rather have your pussy wrapped around me."

The shudder that runs through her body makes me smile. Using my quick speed, I pull the wet T-shirt over Evie's head and push down her jean shorts until she's standing in just her black lacy underwear, her skin smooth and delicate. I want to admire her beauty, but right now, all I can think about is plunging myself inside of her and feeling how tight she is around me.

I pull down the thin material covering her perky tits, admiring the roundness of them and how smooth her skin is. I could worship my little angel's body until the end of time if given a chance. She is the most beautiful woman I have ever seen—the softness of her skin, the little freckles that decorate her curves and stomach, and the way we fit together perfectly.

I fucking can't get enough of her.

I bend and take one of her rosy nipples into my mouth, sucking and licking. Evie groans and runs her hand through my hair, tugging softly on the roots. A few curse words spill past her lips and I can't help but smile. I love that those sounds are only for me.

I flick my tongue against the sensitive area before pulling away. My hand slaps the side of her breast, the sound echoing across the room. Evie's eyes widen and her breathing quickens.

Oh, she likes that.

"Face the wall."

Evie bites her lip and turns to face the wall silently like the good girl I know she is. Running my fingertips down the base of her spine until I reach the lacy panties, I waste no time ripping them away from her skin, tossing the material to the side. She gasps loudly when I grab her waist and bend her forward, pressing her chest and right cheek against the cold tiled wall.

"Jaylen," she groans, wriggling against me, trying to push her perky ass against my cock.

I slap the smooth skin, hard, earning a sharp yelp from her. "Patience, my good girl."

Evie's heavy breathing as she anticipates my next move brings me more joy than I thought it would. I run my index finger through her slick folds, her arousal strong as it fills the shower space. Ready for me to just slip right in.

"Jaylen, please," Evie pleads, her eyes finding mine over her shoulder.

I grip her thin waist a little tighter with my left hand and use my right to grip the base of my cock to bring the head to her wet pussy, dragging it through her wet folds. Her body shudders when my piercing brushes against her sensitive skin, making me smile. I knew she would love it.

"I'm not going to go easy on you, little angel," I warn, meeting her eyes once again. "The bruises I'm going to leave on your hips and the hand prints on your ass will be a reminder of who you belong to. I warned you last night, and I'm always a man of my word."

Before she can utter a response, I grab her ass cheeks, spread them, and push my cock through her folds. A cry leaves Evie's lips at the same time I groan when I bottom out, her pussy hugging me tightly. So fucking warm. I've waited way too long for this moment, and now that it's finally here, I feel complete.

"Fuck, you're so tight," I say through clenched teeth, dragging my dick back just to slam it into her again. My hand connecting with her ass echoes across the room.

Evie can barely form words as I move my hips against her, my fingers digging into the soft skin around her hips for support. The water is still rushing over us as our bodies move together. I find myself looking toward the front of the locker room at the closed door as the wet sound of skin slapping together echoes throughout the shower. I know it's not the end of the first half yet, but I would hate for someone to walk in right now, especially Miles.

Another cry is forced from Evie's lips when I reach forward and wrap my hand around her neck, squeezing tight enough that it's pleasurable and not completely constricting her airways. The soft sounds that fall from her lips are all for me, driving me absolutely insane.

"That's it, Ev," I praise, slamming my hips against her harder. "You take my cock like the good girl that you are."

I can feel my fangs lengthening as the hunger for blood— her blood—stirs deep within my stomach, but I fight back the feeling. As much as I would love to give into my bloodlust and sink my fangs into her neck, now is not the right time. I continue to drive into her, my pace quickening as the seconds tick by. I reach down with my free hand to grab one of Evie's arms, pulling it behind her back while I let go of her throat with the other to reach around and grab one of her breasts. It fits perfectly in my hands. I squeeze it roughly, earning a moan from my little angel.

"Are you on birth control?" I ask through gritted teeth, driving my cock deep inside of her.

All she can manage is a sharp nod. She groans as I palm her with one hand, pulling her off the wall until her back is flush against my chest, my cock still pounding into her soft pussy. The new position is almost too much for me as my vision begins to blur and my stomach tightens.

"Jay-len," she cries, her breathing rapid.

"Fuck," I grunt, my hips slamming into hers. "I'm going to fucking co—"

Evie cries out as she falls over the edge, and I'm not too far behind her, unloading into her wet core. My fangs brush against my lips as I grunt and slam my hips into her one last time, shooting my seed deep inside of her before pulling out.

My limbs feel heavy, but I manage to hold Evie up in my arms as her body comes down from the orgasm. The water is now freezing as it runs over the both of us; Evie's clothes are a forgotten pile in the corner. Her hair is sticking to the side of her face and her breathing is heavy as she tries to catch her breath.

"Holy fuck," she whispers, dropping her head back to rest against my shoulder.

I wrap an arm around her waist, holding her close to me. "Do you believe that you're my girl now?"

Evie spins on her heels to face me, her eyes heavy with

desire, and her cheeks stained pink. She opens her mouth to speak, but in the distance, I hear a whistle blow, signaling the end of the first half.

"Shit," I curse, letting go of Evie to grab her wet clothes from the floor.

"What?" she asks, confused.

"The first half is over. You've got to get out of her before the team comes down."

Her eyes widen as she realizes the gravity of the situation. "Fuck."

While she busies herself with straightening her bra and attempting to find her ruined panties, I switch off the shower and walk over to my locker. Pulling out a clean T-shirt, I turn to give it to her. "Here, wear this."

Evie eyes the graphic T-shirt for a second before she takes it and slides it over her head. The material falls around her shoulders, the hem reaching the middle of her thigh like a dress. God, she looks so cute in my clothes. I slip on a pair of gym shorts to cover up before the team walks in.

"When you go home wearing my shirt with no underwear, just remember whose cum is dripping down your thighs."

She bites her lip and it takes everything in me not to drag her into the shower and bend her over again, but I can hear the team getting closer, so I take her by the shoulders and guide her to the back door that opens into a hallway, leading out to the parking lot.

As Evie steps out into the hallway, she turns to face me, her cheeks flushed. She shoves at my bare shoulder with her hand. "I'm still mad at you for what you did tonight."

I grin, leaning against the door. "I know." I want to lean down and press my lips against hers, but there is a good chance she might slap me across the face, so I stay where I am.

Without saying a word, she huffs, spins on her heels, and

rushes down the hallway as the team walks into the locker room, their voices filling my ears as Evie's heartbeat moves further away.

"Jaylen!"

I close my eyes at the sound of Coach's voice. I'm so fucked.

CHAPTER 22
EVIE

I wake to the violent vibrating of my phone on the bedside table. With sleep in my eyes, I fumble for the annoying fucking device. Once in my grip, I rip it from the charging cord and answer the call, not bothering to check the caller's ID.

"What the hell do you want?"

"Woah, someone is awfully chipper this morning."

I roll my eyes at the sound of my brother's voice. Throwing my arm over my eyes to protect them from the assault of the morning sun, I say, "Miles, I don't want to repeat myself."

"Fine, fine," he says, but I can still hear the amusement in his voice. "I'm calling to see if you want to grab lunch together today. It feels like I haven't seen you much recently."

"It's probably because you've been spending a lot of time with this Cindy I've heard very little about," I counter. "Was this not something you could've texted me instead of calling at the ass crack of dawn?"

"Oh, I didn't even realize the time," he says. "Time seems to be getting away from me lately."

I throw my arm off my eyes, squinting under the harsh morning sunlight. "Okay, lunch, got it. Can I go back to sleep now?"

He laughs. "Yes, sorry. Meet me at your Bluebird Co. at midday. My treat."

"Wonderful." I roll my eyes. "I'll see you then."

I don't wait for his response before I hang up the call, toss the phone beside me on the bunched-up duvet around my waist, and fall right back to sleep.

I breathe in the cool air, thankful that the weather is finally starting to cool down. Gone is the humidity, now replaced with a fresh breeze that feels cold against the exposed skin of my arms. I didn't think about bringing a light jacket with me just in case the weather is cool, but I don't mind. I'm quite enjoying the fresh air as I walk across campus to meet Miles for brunch. My core still aches from how hard Jaylen fucked me two days ago.

He really meant it when he said the pain he would cause me would remind me of him.

Miles is such a nuisance for calling me at 6 a.m., probably on his way home from seeing Cindy. He's been dating her for a few months now, but I am yet to meet her or even see a damn photo. For all I know, she could be fake, but I doubt that. Miles is popular with the ladies, so she's more than likely real, but he just doesn't want to show her off yet.

Moving around a couple my age walking a large fully black German Shepherd along the sidewalk, I pull out my phone and tap on Kale's number. After what happened at the game on Saturday, I've been meaning to send him a text to see if he's doing okay. Well, as good as one can with a broken ankle. I've been a little distracted by the events that unfolded in the locker room with Jaylen but now seems like a good time to send a quick message while I have the chance.

> Evie: Hey! I'm sorry it has taken me this long to message, but I hope you're doing okay. It's terrible what happened, so I hope you recover quickly.

It doesn't take long for Kale to respond once I hit send. I guess being on bed rest with a broken ankle will do that to you.

> Kale: Hey, you. I'm happy to hear from you!
>
> I apologize I couldn't take you out after the game. I don't know when I'll be back in Pullman since I'll be out of action for the next few months, but I hope to see you in the future if you're down.

I smile. Kale is a sweet guy, but after the way Jaylen reacted to him wanting to take me out for drinks, going so far as to snap his fucking ankle, maybe it's for the best that I don't see him. But I could see myself being friends with him because he seems nice and genuine, which is something I look for in my friends.

> Evie: I would love that. Get well soon!

When the coffee shop comes into view, I hoist my tote bag up higher on my shoulder and walk inside. The cold air blasting from the air conditioner above the door makes me shiver. It doesn't take me long to find Miles in the busy shop sitting at a table in the back corner by the front windows. He's looking outside, his mind clearly elsewhere. I can tell when he's got a faraway look in his eyes because they glaze over and twitch slightly.

Walking through the crowd of people lingering by the front counter, I make my way to the table and sit across from Miles in the empty seat. There is an iced vanilla latte alongside a plate of avocado toast—my favorite.

"Hey," I say to break Miles out of his trance.

He blinks, turning to meet my eyes. For a split second, he still looks like he's somewhere far away from here, but that is quickly replaced with happiness as he smiles at me. "Ev! I'm so glad you could make it." He points to the coffee in my hand, halfway to my mouth. "I see you've already found the coffee."

"What, do you expect me to just let it sit there and go to waste?"

He chuckles, shaking his head. "I've already eaten, so go right ahead."

I don't need him to tell me twice. I'm quick to dig into the toast, my stomach growling, reminding me that I didn't eat a quick snack before I left. After Miles woke me up, I fell back to sleep until nearly 11:30 a.m., so I was scrambling to get dressed and leave on time.

"So, what do you want to talk about?" I ask after swallowing a bite of toast.

Miles shrugs and leans back in his seat. "What's new with you?"

Oh, God. Where to fucking start? So much has happened to me since we last spoke, but I can't tell him about any of it. Not about Jaylen in the locker room or the shit that had been going on with Roman. So, instead, I say, "Oh, nothing. Just school."

"I didn't get a chance to catch you after the game on Saturday," he says, folding his hands together in his lap.

I pause, my tongue darting out to lick my lips. "Uh, yeah. I had to head home early."

Miles nods before his eyes light up with excitement. "Wait, did you leave before or after that kid on the Panthers got his ankle snapped?"

I can still hear the sound of Kale's ankle snapping in half from the force of Jaylen's slide tackle. I think everyone in the fucking nosebleed section heard it. I'm still annoyed at Jaylen for what he did, but I can't deny that my anger and his jealousy led to the most mind-blowing sex I've ever had. I'm still confused about my situation with him, so I push it to the back of my mind for now.

"Um... after."

Miles slaps his knee as a laugh bursts from his mouth. "I can't believe that happened. The poor guy never saw it coming. I didn't even know Jaylen was that strong that he could do something like that. The red card will be a blow to the team for the next three weeks because of the severity of the injury, sadly."

"I was meant to go out for drinks with that guy after the game," I say, knowing full well that Miles is going to go into overprotective big brother mode, but it just slipped out.

He pauses, his eyes searching my face. His hair is styled back from his face with a little bit of gel and he's wearing a white T-shirt. It's his go-to style these days.

"You were going to go out with that guy?" he asks, voice slow. "How do you know him?"

I set my knife and fork down beside the plate of half-eaten avocado toast. "I don't really know him, actually. We met last week in this coffee shop after accidentally reaching for the same drink. After talking some, he asked if I wanted to grab a drink with him after the game, and I said yes."

Miles stares at me for a beat too long, his emerald eyes boring into mine. Maybe telling him about Kale was a mistake. I've been down this road with Miles many times, so it's nothing new. It still doesn't make it any easier, though.

"When were you going to tell me about him?"

I snort, shaking my head. "Miles, I met the guy one time. I'm not going to tell you every time a guy fucking talks to me. You need to relax, okay? I'm a big girl who can take care of herself. I don't need you screening every guy in my life."

"But what if they're an asshole like Roman?" he retorts. "I know things didn't end well between you two and you were left hurt. I never want to see you that upset again."

"And I won't be," I counter. "I'm not dating anyone right now, so you can relax. You'll know if I am."

Miles folds his arms over his chest, a skeptical look on his face as he regards me. "Okay, fine. But what a random coincidence that Jaylen destroyed him. It's almost like he knew he needed to sort him out for me."

I almost choked on the air in my lungs. *Yeah, what a fucking coincidence*, I want to say, but keep the words lodged in my throat. Jaylen knew exactly what he was doing when he slide-tackled Kale, and that's what annoys me the most. He did it on purpose instead of just talking to me about it.

"Yeah, what a coincidence."

Thankfully, after that, Miles switched the conversation to one that wasn't bordering on Jaylen territory and instead asked me about classes, and I asked him about Cindy. He didn't say much about her, just that she was a nice girl and he liked her a lot. He said his classes are going well, and the Raiders are playing great, so he couldn't be happier.

We continue talking until Miles gets a call from Cindy asking if they can meet up.

"Sorry, I've gotta go," he says, standing from his chair. I follow suit. "But I'll see you around, okay? Stay safe, little sis."

I smile, walking around to give him a hug goodbye. "You too. Have fun with your girlfriend."

Miles shoots me a wink before rushing through the now-quiet coffee shop. Checking my phone, I see it's nearly 3 p.m. Damn, I didn't realize we had been sitting around talking for three hours. It has been a while since I have really gotten the chance to sit down and have a deep conversation with my brother. It was nice. Thankfully, he didn't bring up anything to do with the murders or our parent's murder investigation, so I was able to switch off from thinking about that for a little while. A nice reprieve from the constant rollercoaster of thoughts racing through my mind.

Swooping my tote bag off the floor next to my chair, I swing it over my shoulder and head for the exit. When I step outside into the cool afternoon air, I slip my earbuds in and begin the walk back to the sorority house. The music blasting in my ears is a good distraction, but not enough to stop me from seeing Amara walking in my direction through the crowd of students.

With a heavy sigh, I slow to a stop and pull my earbuds out, slipping them into the pocket of my jean shorts. I can practically see the steam coming out of Amara's ears as she approaches me, the tight black dress she's wearing riding up her thighs.

"What is it now, Amara?" I say, my voice flat and unimpressed. "I thought we had said everything that we needed to."

"I thought you were dating someone else," she sneers, stopping in front of me with her arms folded over her chest.

I frown. "I never said that, and even if I was, it's none of your business."

"It is my fucking business when you told me Jaylen is free game but here you are not leaving him alone."

I inhale slowly and ball my fists at my sides, my nails digging into the skin of my palm. I don't know what it is about Amara, but whenever she is near me, I'm filled with anger that I have never felt before.

"What the fuck are you talking about?"

With her brows furrowed, she drops her arms and pushes at my shoulders. I stumble backward, a fire building in my chest. "Don't play fucking coy with me. My friends told me they saw you go down to the locker room at the game on Saturday when Jaylen got the red card. Now, why would you go down there when you were supposed to be going out with someone else?"

"That's none of your business," I say through gritted teeth. I'm very aware that there are people around, watching us with hawk eyes, but I'm seconds away from jumping over the edge and losing my fucking shit on this girl.

"You're just a whore who likes to get around." Amara shoves at my shoulders again, her voice growing louder. "Did you spread your legs for him, huh?" She smirks, popping out her hip. "In that case, I hope you enjoyed my sloppy seconds, bitch."

All it took was for the last ounce of self-restraint that I was holding onto for dear life to snap. That's all it took for me to rear back my arm, clench my fist, and slam it against Amara's big nose. I saw the blood splurt from it and heard her cries of pain, but all I could focus on was the satisfaction that washed over me from having shut her the fuck up. The dull ache spreading across my hand doesn't faze me in the slightest.

She fucking deserved that.

Hearing her talk about Jaylen like that rubbed me the wrong way. A need to protect what I have with Jaylen—whatever it is—came over me like a tidal wave. After what happened with Kale and the way Jaylen possessed my very being in the locker room, claiming me as his, the thought of another woman touching him makes me see red. That includes Amara and her persistent attempts at seducing him.

I don't know what the fuck is going on between us, but I'm willing to find out. He makes my body burn like it never has before and that has to mean something. The attraction between us is tense and wild, that's undeniable. It's enough to make my head spin, and clearly, punch someone in the face.

Once my eyes refocus to see her lying on the ground clutching her bloody nose with horrified onlookers looming by, I kneel by her side with a smile and my head tilts to the side as I take in her pathetic frame.

"Remember this moment and the pain you're feeling the next time you want to run your mouth," I say calmly over Amara's loud cries of pain, her eyes, filled with tears, unable to meet mine. "This is your sign to stay the fuck away from Jaylen, because next time, it'll be more than just a punch to the nose."

"You did *what!*"

I turn away from the window beside my bed to face Rylee. She is cross-legged on her bed, her eyes as wide as a saucer. When I returned from brunch with Miles, I was still on edge from the interaction with Amara that I had no choice but to tell her. Not before I paced the entirety of the small bedroom too many times to count, needing to blow off some steam.

"I just kind of... happened," I say with a shrug. Her eyes follow me as I walk to the edge of my bed and plop down, the springs in the mattress squeaking under my weight. "I don't regret it, though."

Rylee shakes her head, but I can see the corners of her mouth twitching into a smile. "Woah, I can't believe it. You punched Amara in the face and likely broke her nose. That has to be the best thing to happen all year."

I raise a brow at her, fighting my own smile. "You're glad I punched her?"

"Of course!" Her voice goes up an octave. "I mean, she deserved it, right? Especially after the way she has been acting toward you in recent weeks. She can't expect to poke a lion with a stick and it not fight back at some point."

She is absolutely right. Amara backed me into a corner each time she confronted me about Jaylen. I could feel the restraint beginning to fray each time she gave me a dirty look or told me to stay away from him. Finally, the string snapped, which resulted in me busting her nose. I can still hear the sound of her bone-crunching beneath my fists, and I must admit, it's a satisfying sound.

"I just hope she doesn't press charges." The thought hadn't occurred to me until after the fact. There were a lot of witnesses who saw what happened, so if Amara wanted to get me done for assault, she would have a lot of people who could back up her story.

Rylee waves away my concern. "I don't know if she would go that far. If anything, she knows what you're capable of now, so this might have been what she needed to back off and leave you alone."

I sigh. "Yeah, maybe you're right. But I wouldn't be surprised if she went to the police."

"Just wait and see what happens, Ev," she says, offering me a smile. "But I'm proud of you for sticking up for yourself and not taking her shit. It's not cool that she would come at you like that all because of Jaylen."

"She's a psycho," I say, rolling my eyes to the back of my head. "She can talk shit about me behind my back for all I care, but for her to say those things to my face was uncalled for. And, of course, I wanted to stand up for Jaylen, too. He doesn't deserve that kind of treatment either." Rylee bites her lip to hold back a smile. I roll my eyes playfully when she wriggles her brows at me. "No, none of that, Ry. I don't want to hear a single word about it."

She covers her mouth and nods, although I know she's grinning like a fucking Chesire cat. "Okay, okay. Not a single word, I promise."

Inhaling a deep breath, I flop backward onto the bed and stare at the ceiling. After spending time with Miles this afternoon, I realized that I need to pay a visit to my Aunt Jas. We didn't talk about our parents specifically, but we did talk about random childhood memories that triggered a thought. It wasn't something I had considered until that moment that now seems like a great idea.

Why hadn't I thought to do it until now?

If I want to know more about my parents—what they were like before they died and any other useful pieces of information—then my aunt is the best person to go to. She knew them like the back of her hand, so if I'm going to take a step forward in finding out what happened to them, then I need to pay her a visit.

CHAPTER 23
EVIE

This house holds many memories for me—mostly good—but also reminds me of all I have lost in the past ten years. When I see the rose gardens by the front door and the large oak in the front yard with the rickety wooden swing hanging from its sturdy branches, I'm reminded of why I moved here in the first place. And why I had to spend the rest of my adolescence living with my aunt.

Gripping the steering wheel a little tighter, I inhale slowly through my nose and exhale through my mouth. I shouldn't be nervous to see my Aunt Jas, but I am. She is the reason why Miles and I had a roof over our heads after our parent's murder and why I'm able to afford to live in the sorority house with everything I could possibly need. If it wasn't for her generosity and willingness to be there for us when we needed someone the most, we would've ended up in the system and possibly separated. She kept us together, and I couldn't be more grateful.

We keep in contact whenever we can, but what I want to talk to her about can't be a conversation through text messages. I need to ask her in person, to see her reactions and hear her answers, instead of trying to understand her words through a screen. If anyone knew my mom better than my dad, it was Aunt Jas.

After hearing the details on the news of the upside-down crosses being carved into the foreheads of the murder victims last week, I knew I had to pay a visit to my aunt to see if my mom had disclosed any further information to her about the murders in the '70s. I'm hoping it somehow has a connection to the current murders happening in Pullman. I want to try and draw a connection to my parent's murder, but they weren't vampires so that wouldn't make sense. But still, I want to learn something—anything—that might help all of this make any fucking sense. While I'm here, I may as well ask her if she knew of Mom having a friend with piercing blue eyes.

Learning more about who my parents were might help me figure this whole thing out and bring me one step closer to figuring out who killed them.

Aunt Jas is only a short drive down to Lewiston, reminding me of the years I grew up here with my brother. We had a lot of fun living with our aunt despite the dark storm cloud that constantly followed us after the murders. Jaylen's parents lived a few streets away from us, which is why the three of us were always together growing up.

I smile as I get out of my car and walk toward the front door. Not much has changed about the house since moving to WSU two years ago. The rose bushes have gotten bigger, and the blue slates on the exterior have begun to weather as the elements get to it. I'm sure the upkeep is a lot for Aunt Jas to maintain. Before she took us in, she had a husband, but he died of an incurable illness. She doesn't talk about him, and I respect her wishes to keep the ordeal private. But it does mean she has to take care of the house herself, and I do worry about her at times.

My closed fist collides with the front door and I take a step back, clasping my hands behind my back. I can hear Anut Jas's footsteps approach from inside the house, the floorboards having grown squeakier over the years. When the door swings open, I'm met with a pair of pale blue eyes staring back at me, surprise crossing them first before it morphs into happiness.

"Evie!" Aunt Jas squeals, rushing forward to wrap me in a big hug. "If I had known you would be dropping by, I would've made my world-famous chocolate chip cookies that you and Miles love so much."

I smile against her shoulder as the cool scent of lavender and rose washes over me. Another thing to add to the growing list of nostalgia. "I wanted to surprise you." I pull away but still keep my hands planted firmly on her slim shoulders. "And it seems it worked."

Aunt Jas still dresses like she did when she was my age in the '70s, wearing black flared pants and a bright green top that shows off her slim arms. I remember when she would show Miles and me photos of her and my mom when they were my age hitting the bars in their stylish outfits and crazy big hair. Looking at her now, I swear this woman hasn't aged a day in her life.

"Come on in," she says as she loops her arm through mine and pulls me into the house. I manage to close the door behind me before we walk too far away. With what's happening in Pullman, I don't want to take any chances. "I just put the kettle on for some tea. Care for a cup?"

"Please," I say with a smile and slide into my seat at the dining table. Growing up, the three of us had our favorite seats at the table. Mine faced the backyard, overlooking the apple and lemon trees. "I'm sorry to just drop in on you like this. I hope you're not too busy."

"Nonsense," Aunt Jas says, waving me off with her hand as she walks to the cupboard above the stove and pulls out two tea cups with floral patterns. "You know me, I don't have much else going on besides going to my book club twice a week and meeting up with some of my friends for coffee in town. Besides that, I stay home to cook and clean. I enjoy it."

"I know," I say softly, watching her as she moves around the kitchen. She recently had it renovated. Gone was the pale green cabinetry that is now replaced by off-white cupboards and a brand-new stove.

Growing up, Aunt Jas and I would sit down every Sunday morning with a pot of tea and cookies to catch each other up on our weeks. It was a nice way for us to fill each other in on what was new, especially as I was going through high school and dealing with friend or boy drama. But sitting here now like this with her makes me smile, reminding me of all the times that we laughed and cried together.

Aunt Jas sets a cup of hot water down in front of me, making sure to slip the teabag in before taking the seat across from me. I wrap my hands around the warm mug and look out at the backyard through the backdoors that open onto the deck, taking in the apple and lemon trees that have only grown bigger over the years.

"So, to what do I owe this lovely visit from you?" Aunt Jas says, breaking the silence. "Is everything okay with school? And Miles?"

"Yes and yes," I say, taking a sip of the tea. "School is good, and Miles is doing well. I don't know how often he calls to check in with you, but he's doing good, I promise."

She smiles. "That's all that I can ask for." Shifting in her seat, she tilts her head to the side. "Okay, so what's going on?"

I exhale slowly, my leg bouncing underneath the table as I try to find the right words to start the conversation with. "I've been having... nightmares recently."

"The same ones you've been having since the incident?"

I nod, swallowing the lump in my throat after hearing her call my parent's murders an 'incident' but it's her way of sugarcoating the situation. "Yes, those ones. When I finished high school, they stopped for a couple of years until recently. As in the past few weeks. At first, they were vague, not showing me much more than when I found... them."

"Have they gotten more detailed?" Aunt Jas asks, her eyes focused on me.

I nod. She has always been so perceptive when reading me. It's like I'm an open book to her, and I am in so many ways. She has seen me at my lowest and my best, so there is nothing this woman doesn't know about me.

"There has been one detail of the dreams that have been sticking out to me," I say slowly, the glowing blue eyes flashing behind my eyelids. When I blink, they're permanently printed there.

"Which is?"

"I keep seeing a man standing over my parent's bodies, and he has these... piercing blue eyes that stare right through my soul."

Aunt Jas blows out a sharp breath as she leans back in her seat. I can see the wheels turning behind her eyes as she takes in the new information. Ever since that night, I haven't once recalled seeing a man standing over their bodies like my mind was trying to protect me from such detail. Until now.

But why now? Why is the vault my mind locked away these memories in suddenly opening now, revealing new details I once didn't remember?

"A man..." she says, chewing on her bottom lip. "That's odd."

"I agree." I nod. "Any idea who it could've been?"

She shakes her head, leaning forward slightly to cup her

steamy mug. "That is a mystery, sadly. Maybe you walked in on the man after he had... you know."

After he had finished killing my parents, I want to finish for her, but I don't. I understand what she is trying to say, but I can't get the man's words out of my head. Of him calling out for my mom as if he were in physical pain. Would a man who had just killed her, and my dad, be that distraught?

None of this is adding up.

"I understand what you're saying, but yeah, maybe that's what it was." I keep the details of what the man said in my nightmares to myself because I don't know enough to come to a conclusion about what it means, and I don't think my aunt will be much help with the limited information I have.

"Investigators are still looking into their case," she says after sipping on her tea. "I know it's moving slowly, and I wish we knew more about what happened, but we just have to be patient. If you learn anything in your dreams that might be of help then let me know and we can go to the station together, okay?"

I nod. "Of course."

"Are you being safe in Pullman?" Aunt Jas asks, her blues searching my face. "Especially with all those murders."

"I am. I remember Mom telling me about satanic murders that occurred in the late '70s that were similar to the current ones. Did she ever talk to you about those?"

She shakes her head. "When I was your age, I was very into true crime and staying safe. I had to tell your mom multiple times to be careful when hitchhiking a ride home at night, but she didn't fear anything, or care much about the dangers of it. But it was when she started dating a guy at the time that she got more into true crime, especially the satanic murders that were happening. I already knew my fair share of the details, but she never discussed them with me. She did say that she was really into it. Curious, if anything."

I pause, my brows furrowing. "Wait, she dated someone before Dad?"

Aunt Jas's eyes widened as if she realized that was something she wasn't supposed to share with me. *Well, too late.* "Um... yes. Well, kind of. She was seeing this guy and your father at the same time."

My eyes nearly bulged out of my head. "She was *what?*"

Aunt Jas rubs the back of her neck, unable to look me in the eye as she laughs nervously and flips her blonde hair over her shoulder. "Um, yeah. It's not something she wanted you kids to know, but I guess the cat is out of the bag now, huh?"

"Some bloody bag," I murmur, trying to wrap my head around the bombshell that my mom was dating my dad and another man at the same time. My mom was a beautiful woman, so I didn't doubt that she had men falling at her feet all the time, but I didn't expect to unearth this detail. "Wait, so who was the guy?"

Aunt Jas shrugs. "No idea."

I frown. "You don't know who he was? Like, not even a name?"

She shakes her head. "Nothing. Your mom was very secretive about him. No matter how hard I tried to get her to at least tell me his first name, she wouldn't budge. I had a feeling that she really liked him, otherwise, she would've been more open about sharing him with me."

So, Mom liked this man enough to keep him a secret, but was open about telling Aunt Jas about Dad? This piece of information confuses me more than ever because now I want to know who this man is, why it didn't work out between them, and how she ended up with my dad.

I was never really close with my dad, no matter how hard I

tried. Miles was close with him, mainly because they bonded over sports and other boy things. But we could never get to that point in our relationship, no matter what I did. I always felt like something was... missing. He wouldn't look at me with love the same way he did with Miles and I never understood why. Don't get me wrong, he loved me, I know that, but I could tell he didn't give me enough of himself like he did with Miles as if he were holding back for some reason. And to this day, I never learned why our relationship was like that.

"So, how did she end up with Dad?"

"All I know is that the mystery man she was dating had to leave Pullman abruptly, and from then on she grew closer to your dad. They started dating, got married, and had you and Miles. The rest is history."

I lean back in my seat, my mind racing with so many questions and not enough answers.

Aunt Jas sits up straighter, her eyes brightening as if she has just remembered something. "Actually, there was one thing your mom told me about the mystery man."

"What was it?"

"She said that when she met him, she instantly fell for his kind smile and how safe she felt with him."

I smile, my heart warming at her words. I can picture my mom smiling from ear to ear while telling Aunt Jas about this man. But I don't understand why she would keep this man a secret right up to her death, essentially taking his name to the grave with her. Learning who this guy is will feel like an impossible task if I attempt to look into him.

Where the fuck would I even start?

"I thought I knew my mom, but it seems there was so much about her I didn't know."

Aunt Jas must hear the sadness in my voice because she reaches across the table to hold my hand, squeezing gently.

"Evie, don't dwell on that fact. Your mom wanted to be the best version of herself for you and Miles and that's what you got. What happened in her past before she had you both doesn't matter anymore. Whoever that guy was is no longer important in the grand scheme of things, okay?"

I nod, although I can't shake the feeling that he is important to the narrative. Was he the man standing over their bodies in my nightmares? I don't know many details about his features, but it is a possibility, right? Unless my brain is just telling me what I want to hear so I can finally gain some closure.

"We need to let the investigators handle the case, okay?" Aunt Jas says, breaking through my thoughts. "They say they're close to finding an answer as to what happened, so we just have to trust the process." She lets go of my hand and stands, peering down at me through her long lashes. "Now, how about I whip you up something for lunch, hmm? I'm sure you're hungry."

I watch as she walks toward the refrigerator and looks inside for the ingredients to make sandwiches. As I watch the back of her head, all I can think about is the mystery man my mom dated and how, or if, he plays some type of role in what happened to her.

I have so many questions and not enough fucking answers.

CHAPTER 24
EVIE

I haven't had one of my nightmares for a little while, and it's starting to put me on edge not knowing when I'll have the next one. There was a pattern being formed where I would have one every few days, so I knew when to expect it. But now, I haven't had one in just over a week and it's starting to make me nervous.

Is that it? Is that everything my subconscious has to show me? A man with piercing blue eyes standing over my parent's bodies? Surely, there has to be more than that, but my mind isn't allowing anything new to slip past the seals of the vault which has the memories hidden away.

It's frustrating, to say the least. I feel closer than ever to learning more about what happened to my parents but my mind is stopping me from taking any more steps closer, leaving me confused and annoyed. I so badly want to know who did this to them so I can bring some justice down on their asses, but that result feels far out of my reach.

Who is the man my mom dated before Dad? And what other details about their deaths can't I remember? The visit with Aunt Jas two days ago helped, but not enough.

The murders in Pullman now and the ones from the '70s

are giving me motivation to figure this thing out. I wish I could say my parent's murders are connected, but they weren't vampires, so that wouldn't make any sense. It's just wishful thinking.

Unless... the copycat killer is taking inspiration from the serial killer in the '70s by using their exact MO to draw suspicion elsewhere. It's certainly a plausible idea, but still doesn't help answer the question of who killed my parents.

I sigh, flopping down onto my bed, my eyes trained on the ceiling. My mind has been a jumbled mess the past few weeks —always running and never slowing down. Between digging up information on my parents, school, my friends, and navigating whatever the hell is going on between me and Jaylen, I haven't had a chance to sit down and just fucking breathe for a minute. It's exhausting.

The vibration of my phone on my chest makes me groan. Who the hell is that now? I was looking forward to lying in my bed today and doing nothing since it's a Friday night. Thankfully, I have no plans, so I can just lounge around in my pajamas and eat as much junk food as I want.

Jaylen: Can I see you tonight?

I read his message at least ten times before I type a response. I haven't seen Jaylen since the game last weekend. I'm not sure what he's been doing, but my heart skipped a little beat when I saw his name on my screen.

Evie: It depends.

Jaylen: On what?

Evie: What we're doing.

I sit up and press my back into the mound of pillows behind me, waiting for his response. I know I just said I don't want to do anything tonight besides eat junk food and rot away in bed, but the giddy and excited feeling in my chest is telling me to go out with Jaylen.

For the past few weeks, I have been trying to fight the attraction between us, not wanting to get involved with him for fear of getting hurt. But something tells me that he's not going to hurt me. Maybe it's the possessiveness or constantly referring to me as his girl, but I don't think he's out to hurt me. In fact, I think the opposite, and it has me jittery with excitement.

I never thought I'd see the day when Jaylen Black was chasing one girl, let alone that girl being me. He's used to having all the girls in his life falling at his feet, not the other way around. I don't want to get my hopes up or think too much about it. I'm just going to go with the flow and see where it takes me because I could be looking at this all wrong.

Jaylen: Black Rose.

My heart skips a beat reading his text. He wants to go to the *Black Rose* with me. Alone? The thought has my stomach twisting with anticipation.

Evie: Okay. We need to be discreet, though. I don't want my brother to find out.

Jaylen: Of course, little angel. I'm great at being discreet. I'll see you at 8 p.m., and make sure you're wearing a dress for me.

I swallow hard, re-reading his last message over and over. *Make sure you're wearing a dress for me.* What the hell are you up to, Jaylen Black?

I leave the sorority house at ten to eight to avoid too many questions from the girls. When I told them I was going out tonight, I lied and said it was to go visit Miles. There were looks of suspicion from all three of them, but eventually, they let it go and told me to have a good night.

I feel bad about lying to them, but if I told them what I was really doing and who I was seeing, they would bombard with me a magnitude of questions, and that's not something I feel like doing tonight. It's best if they think I'm going to see Miles instead of Jaylen.

The black dress I plucked out of my closet is flowy around my thighs with little sleeves to cover my shoulders. Now that fall is upon us, the evening air has grown chilly, making me realize that I should've grabbed a light coat before I left the house.

Oh, well. Too late now.

Peering up the road, I don't see Jaylen anywhere. I rock on the heels of my Vans while I wait. I still can't believe Jaylen got me into a dress just by asking. I could say lust talked me into it, so I'm going to stick with that answer. I'm doing this because I like the way I feel when I'm with Jaylen, and not because I want to please him.

A single headlight approaching from down the street comes into view. I watch as Jaylen pulls his motorcycle to a stop on the curb beside me, his face covered by a black helmet. One I've had the pleasure of wearing a couple of times. At first, I hated riding on his bike, but now, it's a thrill I have grown to enjoy, especially if it means I get to wrap my arms around his waist, feeling the hard muscles under his shirt.

Jaylen slides the helmet off his head, his tousled curls falling around his face. He smiles at me, resting the helmet on his black jean-clad thigh. "My little angel, you look stunning."

I blush. "Thanks. You too."

He swings his leg over the seat and steps toward me. I watch silently as he slips the helmet over my head, careful to push my loose hair over my shoulder, cascading down my spine. His fingers linger on my neck, a reminder of when he choked me in the locker room shower last week. I try to clench my thighs subtly at the memory, but I know Jaylen can smell my arousal when he smirks.

"Okay, let's go." Taking my hand, he leads me to the motorcycle, helping me onto the little seat behind his. When he's seated in front of me, I wrap my arms around his waist and rest my cheek on his back. His earthy sandalwood scent assaults my nose, and I inhale deeply. "Hold on tight, little angel."

I do as he says, holding on for dear life. Jaylen revs the engine and pulls out onto the street. The wind blowing through my hair is a welcome bliss I have come to enjoy whenever I ride with Jaylen. I never thought I would feel so... free being on the back of a motorcycle. Only a few weeks ago I was scared shitless to get on one. Now, I fucking love it.

The ride to the *Black Rose* doesn't take long. As Jaylen parked in the parking lot next to the building, I found myself wishing we could have driven for longer. Maybe drive somewhere out of Pullman just so I could continue to feel that blissful feeling as if I'm walking on air. But sadly, that is just wishful thinking on my part. I can't just ride away into the sunset with Jaylen.

Jaylen silently grabs his hand around mine and guides me to the entrance of *Black Rose*. As usual, there is a line wrapped around the building of partygoers wanting to get inside. While Jaylen is getting our names checked off the guest list, I can't help but wonder how many of these people actually make it inside if their names aren't on the list. I would hate waiting outside in this weather on the off chance that you're maybe let in.

"Come on," Jaylen says, tugging on my hand.

I tear my eyes away from the line and follow him inside. As we walk into the room, music is bouncing off the walls and the voices of people yelling over the music sounds in my ears, making me cringe. I'll never get used to the sudden overload of noises whenever I step into this room. With it being a bar on the smaller side, the noise is only intensified. But with Jaylen's super hearing, I'm sure he'll hear me just fine.

"Take a seat and I'll grab us a drink," Jaylen says, turning to face me. "What do you want?"

"Whatever you're having."

He raises a brow at me as an amused smile tugs at his lips. "Really? Are you sure?"

Not really. "Yes," I say with a nod. I want a fruity cocktail, but being here with him, alone, I know I'm going to need something stronger.

"Okay," he says and turns to walk to the bar.

Walking around the room, I managed to find a tall table with two stools at the back. It feels a little quieter down here away from all the people dancing around the DJ deck on the opposite side of the room.

Settling onto the seat, I watch the back of Jaylen's head as he stands at the bar, waiting for our drinks. It doesn't take me long to notice the number of eyes looking in his direction from all around the room. Mostly women with their friends, giggling as they point at him, no doubt expressing how hot he is. As if I don't already know that. But he seems oblivious to the attention as he collects our drinks and walks toward the table.

All the women watching him follow his movements across the room, and I can't help but chuckle when they find me sitting at the table he's walking to, a scowl spreading across most of their faces. This is a reminder of how much attention Jaylen draws his way. No matter where he goes, women are always watching him.

"One whiskey on the rocks," Jaylen says as he places the glass of brown liquor down in front of me and slides onto the empty stool, oblivious to the eyes trained on the back of his head.

I eye the mystery drink, wondering what the hell is in it. "What kind of whiskey is this?"

He shrugs, bringing the glass to his lips. "They're all the

same to me." I watch his throat as he swallows the drink, his lip ring resting against the rim of the glass.

I did ask for a strong drink, so I can't back down now, no matter how badly I want a fruity cocktail. *Don't be a little bitch, Evie.* Bringing the cool glass to my lips, I take a small sip of the brown liquor. It instantly burns my throat going down, but it warms my stomach as soon as it settles.

Huh, maybe whiskey isn't so bad after all. The taste is horrendous, but I like the feeling I'm left with afterward.

Jaylen bites back an amused smile as he looks around the room, unaware of all the eyes watching him still. I take in his sharp jawline and soft, smooth skin. He drags his lip ring between his teeth, releasing it a moment later.

I swear to God, that is single-handedly one of the most attractive things he does. It drives me wild.

Calm down, Evie.

"So, do you enjoy boxing these days?" Jaylen asks, turning to look at me again. I catch a glimmer of amusement in his eye that makes me frown. *What the hell is he talking about?* He chuckles. "I heard about what happened with Amara the other day."

My cheeks go up in flames. Shit. How did he find out?

"She deserved it," I mutter and take another sip of the crisp whiskey.

"I know," he says, leaning forward to rest his elbows on the table with his eyes focused on me. I'm instantly swept away in his ocean eyes, pulling down some of my defenses. "But why did you really do it?"

"Because she was pushing my buttons," I admit, the alcohol already going straight to my head. Fucking hell whiskey is some strong shit. "And I had to put her in her place."

"So I heard." He grins, his tongue darting out to lick his

bottom lip. "It didn't have anything to do with the fact that you were defending my honor, right?"

My eyes snap open at his words. "Um, no." I can't let him know that I punched Amara in the face because the thought of her seducing him made me see red. So, instead, I'm going to play this cool. I don't need to inflate his ego more than it already is. "Don't flatter yourself, Jaylen. I did it because she was pushing my buttons and I snapped. End of story."

The shit-eating grin on his face tells me he doesn't believe a fucking word that I'm saying.

To change the subject, I grab the cool glass and bring it to my lips, downing the rest of the liquid. If I'm going to get through this night, I'm going to need more liquid courage. The whiskey works fast spreading through my veins, making my fingertips slightly numb and my limbs a little heavier.

Oh, yeah. Now we're talking.

Jaylen points to the empty glass. "Impressive, little angel. Would you like another one?"

I nod. "Keep 'em coming."

"Aye, aye, captain."

With Jaylen at the bar, I feel like I can breathe properly again. It's hard to keep my thoughts straight whenever he's around. The alcohol is making my head fuzzier than it already is, and I'm slowly letting go of the reigns I had been holding on so tightly to.

To my surprise, the DJ switches up the music to play a new popular country music song that has been blowing up online. It happens to be my fucking jam, too. How can I not dance to "Dicked Down in Dallas"?

As soon as the music starts, I'm on my feet and moving toward the crowd of people dancing in the middle room, having forgotten about sending Jaylen to the bar for another drink. I have no control over my limbs as I begin to do the dorkiest dances that would make most people cringe, but it feels appropriate for the song.

Halfway through the song, I'm doing the shopping cart dance when I spot Jaylen in my peripheral. He's sitting on the stool with his legs spread and his elbow resting on the table, his eyes focused on me. There is a hint of a smile ghosting his lips, but I can't tell if he's amused or embarrassed for me. It could be both, honestly.

I twirl my pretend lasso in the air and throw it toward Jaylen, catching him around the waist, and then pull him to me. When he doesn't go along with my move, instead choosing to raise an eyebrow at me, I release the rope and wave him off. That's on him for being a Debbie Downer and not dancing with me.

As the song comes to an end, I turn on my heel to walk further into the crowd, now in the mood to dance, when I run into what feels like a hard wall, knocking the breath out of my lungs. Stumbling backward, I manage to stay balanced on my feet and look at what I ran into. It wasn't a wall. I ran into a person. A very tall and burly man. When he turns to face me, I'm struck by how pretty his eyes are despite his rugged exterior. Is he from somewhere north in Europe?

"I'm so sorry," he says and helps me to stand upright, his hand under my elbow.

"I should be the one apologizing," I say, looking up at him, getting lost in the depths of his bright eyes.

The man smiles down at me, warm and comforting. He runs a hand through his brown hair which is short on the sides but long on top. His beard is rather impressive—well-groomed for its length. "You have very pretty eyes." The corner of his mouth turns up into a half smile, almost as if he's remembering a distant memory.

"You too," I say without thinking.

In a flash, I'm standing behind Jaylen, his sandalwood scent wafting off him in waves. "You keep your hands off her," he warns, his voice low and menacing.

I look past him to see the man laugh, not at all threatened by Jaylen. "I was just making sure she was okay."

"I can do that," he growls, and I roll my eyes.

Always so possessive.

The kind man chuckles and shoves his hands into the pockets of his long pants, his muscles flexing under the thin white shirt he's wearing. His skin is a little more weathered like he's seen a lot of sun, but he can't be much older than forty.

"Ah, young love." He smiles to himself and shakes his head as if remembering another past memory. "I used to have a love like this many moons ago. Cherish it because you never know how long it'll last."

"Love?" I squeak, stepping out from behind Jaylen.

"Who are you?" Jaylen quizzes, ignoring his statement about love which has me sweating.

"Fenrir," he says and gestures around the room with his hands. "I own the *Black Rose*."

I blanch at his words. He's the owner? Trust me to fucking walk headfirst into the back of the owner. I'm such an idiot.

"And you're Jaylen," Fenrir comments, pointing at Jaylen. "I've seen you in here a lot these past few months." He then turns his attention to me. "And you are?"

I swallow hard. "Evie."

Fenrir smiles. It's bright and warm, like the sun is shining down on me despite it being nighttime and I'm standing in the middle of a crowded bar. "It's a pleasure to meet you, Evie."

I smile. My mind is fuzzy from the whiskey consuming my senses, so I have zero control over the words that leave my mouth next. "Random question, but what made you name the bar *Black Rose*?"

"Oh, I named it after the love of my life."

The words make my insides melt. "That is so cute. I bet she's a very lucky girl."

A sad smile crosses over Fenrir's lip but it's soon replaced by a happy one. "She is. Now, I'm going to stop talking and let you get back to your night. It was a pleasure to meet you both, and if you ever need me, I'll be around." "Dreams" by Fleetwood Mac begins to play, and Fenrir smiles, shaking his head. "I love this song." He turns and walks away, heading toward the bar.

I wave goodbye while Jaylen continues to stare daggers into the back of Fenrir's head. I slap his arm to grab his attention. When he looks at me, I point at his chest, jabbing my finger into his hard muscles. "You need to be nice. It was my fault I ran into him, so chill out."

Jaylen huffs and guides me back to our table with a cool hand on my lower back. "I didn't like the way he was looking at you."

"And what way was that?"

He shrugs as he slides onto the stool. "I don't know, but I didn't like it."

I roll my eyes and grab the glass of whiskey in front of me, needing a sip after all that dancing. "Did you not like my lassoing?"

Jaylen grins. "It was very cute. But you do have two left feet."

I gasp, feigning hurt by throwing my hand over my heart. "I'll have you know that I'm a great dancer."

"With those moves? Yeah, right. You've been a terrible dancer, even when we were kids."

I remember when I would put on a 'performance' for my

brother and Jaylen in our backyard, pretending I was on Broadway or something. As Jaylen so nicely put it, I was a terrible dancer and couldn't sing for shit, but it was the fun I had doing those performances that counted. And tonight is no different.

I roll my eyes. "You're just a hater."

The conversation soon turns to us talking about things we did together as children and how much life has changed in the last ten years. We keep the topics light, only discussing classes, our interests, and how soccer is going for Jaylen. With his red card, he's not allowed to play the next three games, but he did ask if I'm going to the home game next week, and of course, my answer was yes. Even if I can't watch him play, I still need to support my brother.

After a couple more drinks, I began to feel lightheaded and very sleepy. Jaylen takes this as our sign to leave. With one arm wrapped around my shoulders, he guides me out to his motorcycle in the parking lot.

I frown, turning to look at him. "You can't drive home."

"Yes, I can."

"But you've been drinking."

Jaylen chuckles as he slips the helmet over my head, tightening the strap under my chin. "I'm a vampire, little angel. Or did you forget that? Alcohol doesn't affect me like it does humans. I would need to drink a lot to even feel tipsy."

"Woah," is all my alcohol-induced brain is capable of saying before I'm being hoisted onto the motorcycle and told to hold on as Jaylen gets on too.

With the wind in my hair and my mind blank, I close my eyes and enjoy the feel of Jaylen's cold skin through his leather jacket and how light my body feels. I wish I could stay in the moment forever, feeling weightless like a feather floating through the sky.

But sadly, it comes to an end all too soon when Jaylen stops out the front of the sorority house, killing the engine. With wobbly legs, I slide off the motorcycle and take off the helmet, my hair likely a frizzball after being trapped inside.

Jaylen comes around and takes the helmet from me, resting it on the seat behind him. He looks down at me, his eyes sharp with flecks of red peeking through the blue. My core tightens at the sight, already knowing what he's thinking. He wraps his arms around my waist and pulls me flush against him, my hands immediately going up to rest against his hard chest.

"I like seeing you in a dress," he says against my lips, his breath warm despite how cold his skin is.

"Why did you ask me to wear a dress?" The question has been at the back of my mind since receiving his text earlier. Drunk Evie wants to know why he wanted me to wear a dress for him.

His hands slide up the side of my thighs, his touch cool against my hot skin. I hold my breath as he drags them up and under the material of the dress, using both hands to grip my ass checks. I gasp when he pulls me closer to him, feeling his hard cock through his pants. A shiver races down my spine when I think of his piercing and how it drove me absolutely wild.

"I wanted to be able to touch you," Jaylen says, his eyes roaming my face. "But it seems those multiple whiskeys on the rocks were too much for you, so I'm going to refrain from doing what I wanted."

With my heart in my throat and no air in my lungs, I ask, "And what was that?"

He grins. "You'll have to wait to find out. But I'll settle for a kiss."

The man doesn't need to tell me twice. A fire has been lit in my chest and all I can think about is attaching my lips to his, hoping his cold skin will cool me down. It must be the alcohol making these choices for me, but I do have to applaud her for them because the pull between us is only getting stronger the more time we spend together.

When Jaylen's lips brush against mine, an involuntary moan escapes my mouth at the contact. He smiles against my lips. "Always such a good girl for me, little angel."

"Less talking, more kissing," I murmur and press my lips against his, needing to feel the heat and passion.

Wrapping my arms around his neck, I pull him closer, allowing him to deepen the kiss. My body feels hot, and my mind is a whirlwind of emotions as I push Jaylen to sit on his motorcycle while I half-straddle his lap, not giving a fuck if anyone sees us. The groan that bubbles from within his chest only adds to the fire between us as I thread my fingers through the curls at the nape of his neck, wanting to swallow more of his sounds that make my thighs slick with need.

We're making out like two horny teenagers that have never kissed before.

God, what the hell is Jaylen Black doing to me?

CHAPTER 25
EVIE

hat does one dress up as when invited to a Halloween party at a frat house? The obvious answer would be a sexy maid or nurse outfit because it's the easiest option. But me... well, I like to dress a little more... *covered*.

Jaycee heard about the party from one of the residents of Alpha Delta Phi last minute while in class this afternoon. She rushed home and demanded that we all go, despite us not having any costumes planned, and it being a Monday night. Luckily for me, I had the perfect pieces of clothing to create the look of the character I had in mind.

Descending the staircase, I can feel multiple pairs of eyes watching me. I lift my eyes to see Jaycee, Candie, and Rylee standing in the foyer with amused looks on their faces.

"I should've expected this from you," Rylee says, biting back a smile.

I pause on the last step and look down at the long black dress hanging from my frame. "What?"

"Of course, you would dress as fucking Wednesday Addams for Halloween," Jaycee snorts. She's dressed as a cowgirl in short denim jeans and a flannel that she has tied into a knot above her belly button. Of course, a cowboy hat is a must.

"You should've gone as Cruella de Vil," Candie says, dressed in a sexy devil costume.

My hand touches the blonde streak I have pulled back into the braid hanging over my shoulder. "I didn't have the clothes to recreate that outfit. Besides, everything in my closet is black, so dressing as Wednesday was the easiest option."

"Well, I think you look great," Rylee comments, putting a hand on her hip. With her long blonde hair and grey eyes, she makes the perfect Barbie. She turns to look at Jaycee and Candie. "We all look great."

"We need to take some photos before we go," Candie says, clapping her hands together. "I'll go ask Emily if she can take some for us since she isn't going." She rushes down the hallway to the lounge room where I can hear the TV playing a movie.

Most of the girls in the house are also attending the party, but the majority of them have already left. Candie said we shouldn't get there too early, so that's why it's nearly 10 p.m. and we have yet to leave.

Candie rushes back to the foyer with a tired-looking Emily in tow. She's in her pajamas, and I envy her. Although I'm excited to go to the party, I know I'm going to regret it when I wake up with a hangover in the morning before my class. But that tiny detail isn't going to stop me from going. Halloween is one of my favorite holidays of the year, so I'm always down to attend a party if I can.

It's been a little over a week since Jaylen and I went to the *Black Rose* together. I haven't seen him since—I figured it was because he's been busy with practice. Still being suspended for the red card incident, he has been training extra hard for when he is allowed to return in two weeks—but we do text on occasion about random stuff. He likes to ask me how my day has been and if I got up to anything interesting. Although I haven't seen him with my eyes, I would often get the feeling that he is watching me from a distance, and I find that comforting, in a weird way. I want to ask him if he's going to the party tonight, but I know he's a busy man with a life, so I'm sure he's got plans already.

Just this week, three new victims have been found murdered around Pullman. When I wasn't studying, I was researching the current murders and the case from the '70s. I found podcasts that cover the cases in hopes that they know something I don't, and I even went to the local library to pull up old newspaper clippings from the '70s that covered the case. Unfortunately, I wasn't able to find anything noteworthy. But it does seem that the details of both cases are similar, which makes me think—however old they might be—is committing the crimes, or a copycat is behind them.

Whatever the case, I'm determined to get to the bottom of it.

Once we've taken what feels like a hundred group photos on the front porch, the four of us link arms and begin the short walk to the Alpha Delta Phi house. It's only a few streets away, so we arrive within minutes.

The house is old with the wooden panels on the side rotting away, leaving large gaps in the structure. How are people still allowed to live here? Fake spiders and cobwebs hang from the bushes in the front garden and there are numerous carved pumpkins stacked on each other on the rickety porch. The floorboards creak under our feet as we enter through the front door. We're immediately met with strobe lights and loud EDM music blasting from within the lounge room to the right.

I hold onto Rylee's arm a little tighter as we walk through

the house, past the mass of students, and enter the kitchen. It's not as loud in here, but it's just as packed with people trying to grab drinks from the large cooler in front of the island.

"Want a drink?" Rylee shouts over the music and loud voices.

I nod and watch as she and Jaycee walk toward the cooler, leaving me with Candie by the kitchen island. They return with four cans of beer. If I'm drinking beer tonight then I'm going to be in for one hell of a hangover tomorrow.

The four of us walk to the lounge room to join the mass of people on the makeshift dance floor. As we dance to the beat of the music, I take in the costumes around me. Every year, I tend to see the same costumes but executed in different ways— cowboys, sexy nurses and maids, Batman, and even Bob Ross. I spot another girl dressed as Wednesday Addams across the room, and we smile in acknowledgment of the other.

The music switches from EDM to remixes of popular pop songs. A chorus of screams floats through the air when a Brittney Spears song begins to play. Candie jumps up and down in excitement before swaying her hips to the beat. I can't help but smile.

Rylee grabs my hand and twirls me around. I giggle, following her lead. Jaycee joins in too and we form a little circle while Candie is swept away by an attractive man dressed as Jack Skellington. Her eyes meet mine and I wiggle my brows in response.

I don't know how long we stand in our small circle dancing to whatever song is played next, but I know my head is growing fuzzy from the beers I've consumed and my muscles are beginning to tire. Turning to Rylee, I tap her on the shoulder to get her attention. When she turns to me, I throw my thumb over my shoulder. "I'm going to head outside and get some fresh air. Do you want to join me?"

She shakes her head. "I'm good. I'll stay here with Jay. If you happen to see Candie around let me know. I want to make sure she's okay."

I nod. Candie left a few songs back with Jack Skellington. I can only imagine what the two are getting up to.

Leaving my friends on the dancefloor, I push my way through the throng of partygoers until I reach the back door that leads to the deck. The cool air that rushes across my skin the moment I step outside is refreshing. My skin was beginning to grow hot and sweaty with all the dancing. Wearing a long-sleeved dress doesn't help either.

There are only a handful of people sitting at the outdoor dining set—some smoking and laughing, and some playing on their phones. As I descend the small steps off the deck, I breathe in a lungful of air. The backyard is large and backs onto a small section of the surrounding woods. The trees sway softly in the wind, the leaves rusting together to create a symphony of sounds. The further I walk across the cropped grass, the quieter the music and voices get.

Stopping at the edge of the backyard, I lean against one of the trees, letting my head fall against the trunk, and close my eyes. The alcohol is making the blood in my veins warm and I can feel how loose my muscles are. This is the point of tipsy I like to be at because I still have control over my words and actions. If I were to drink more, I would lose all of that control.

A twig snapping behind me forces my eyes open. Spinning on my heels, I look out at the trees for any sign of movement. My heart races as my eyes scan the dark space.

What the hell was that?

Just when I'm about to head back to the house, I see the outline of a person standing among the trees. My heart just about leaps into my throat when they move toward me. I take a step back, stumbling a little on my jelly legs, but I manage to catch myself on the tree beside me.

"H-hello?" I call out to the person. When they hear my voice, they stop. "Who are you?"

The person takes a step forward. Half of their body is partially illuminated by the lights shining from the back of the house. My eyes widen when I see the person has no shirt on and is wearing a Ghostface mask.

"What the fuck..."

The person takes another step forward, their entire body now visible under the light. My eyes roam across the chiseled chest of the man and the sharp lines of his muscles. His hands are shoved into the pockets of the black chinos he's wearing. The tension in my shoulders evaporates at the sight of the tattoos littering their right arm.

My hand flies to my chest where my heart feels like it's going to burst through. "Fucking hell. You scared the shit out of me."

He doesn't say anything, just tilts his head to the side. I can't see his eyes through the mask, but I know they're watching me intently.

What the hell is he up to?

Without saying a word, Jaylen turns and walks further into the woods. Frowning, I look over my shoulder to see the people sitting on the deck have now gone back inside, leaving the two of us alone out here. Turning to his retreating back, I can only assume he wants me to follow him. Why? I have no fucking clue.

How did he know I was going to be at this party? It's possible he came to the party not knowing I would be here, which makes sense given his status at WSU. Everyone wants Jaylen Black at their parties.

With a sharp inhale, I force my legs to walk into the woods.

Twigs and leaves crunch under the weight of my combat boots. The further I walk, the less vision I have from the lights at the house. The loud music is nothing but a dull thud in the back of my mind. The only thing I can hear is my heavy breathing and the chirps of crickets.

"Jaylen, where are you?" I call out, having lost sight of him. "Whatever you're doing, this isn't funny."

I should be scared of being out in the woods alone with a vampire, but if anything, the thought has my pussy throbbing with anticipation. Jaylen not saying anything only intensifies the feeling because I don't know what he's up to.

With a huff, I stop next to a large tree and survey my surroundings. I can't hear a thing or see shit. I know that wherever he is, he can see me and that has the hair on the back of my neck standing on end.

I feel like his prey. A helpless animal he is hunting, ready to attack at any moment. But oddly enough, I'm enjoying it. My skin prickles with excitement as I spin around, looking in every direction.

A rush of wind moves past me as I'm pushed up against the tree behind me. My eyes widen when the soulless eyes of the Ghostface mask stare back at me. Jaylen has his hand around my throat, holding me firmly against the trunk. I can feel pieces of bark digging into my skin through the material of the dress, but I welcome the pain. Just as I welcome his fingers tightening around my neck, restricting some, but not all, of my airflow.

"Jaylen," I gasp. I clench my thighs as the throbbing between my legs continues.

Shit. Who would've thought I would be this turned on by Jaylen in a fucking Ghostface mask? Not me.

"What's the matter, little angel? You look like you've seen a ghost."

My breath hitches in my throat when I feel his fingers trailing down the front of my dress. His cold touch sends goosebumps across my skin and ignites the fire burning in my core.

I hold my breath when his fingers stop to rest on my hip. I'm unable to take my eyes off him when his hand slips beneath my dress, his fingers going straight to my soaked pussy. I'm not embarrassed by how turned on I am by this. In fact, I fucking love it.

"Hmm, so wet for me already," Jaylen coos. He tilts his head to the side as one of his fingers slips past my underwear and grazes across my core. "Do you like this, hmm? Do you like my hand around your throat while I play with you?"

I manage to nod because that's all I can do with his tight grip on my throat. I want to shout, *fuck yes*, but the words would come out as a squeak. Not seeing him for a week or feeling his hands on me has my body vibrating with excitement and anticipation.

He chuckles. It's deep and sexy and has my mind fucking spinning. I just want him to touch me, so I can relish in the cool feel of his fingers inside me. I want to feel him. All of him.

"Of course, you do, my sweet little angel."

Without warning, he plunges one of his fingers deep inside of me, forcing me to cry out. My walls clench around him as he thrusts in and out. My hands come up to grip Jaylen's wrist for support.

"You take me so well," he praises as he slips in another finger, quickening the pace. "My good girl."

"Mo-re," I manage to say, my voice barely above a whisper.

Jaylen pauses his movements, and I can't help but whimper. "You want more?"

I nod, and he loosens his grip on my throat, allowing me to suck in a lungful of air. Glancing down, I see the outline of

Jaylen's cock straining against the fabric of his pants. My fingers itch to touch him, but I refrain from doing so. I'm letting him take the lead here.

"On your knees," he commands, taking a step back. "Now."

My chest heaves as I stare at him, wishing I could see his baby-blue eyes. But I do as I'm told. I drop to my knees, ignoring the sting of twigs and leaves digging into my skin. Lifting my head, I look deep into the depths of the black holes in the mask through my lashes.

Jaylen steps forward, his fingers coming to rest under my chin. The muscles in his abdomen flex as he stares down at me. "If you want more, you're going to have to work for it, little angel."

My pussy throbs in anticipation as I watch Jaylen use his free hand to unzip his pants and pull out his hard cock. Being out here in the woods alone with nothing but the moon shining down on us feels... forbidden, but fuck do I love it.

A crack of thunder sounds overhead.

"Open your mouth."

I eye the piercing through the head, remembering how good it felt hitting the deepest part of my core. I never thought I would enjoy a piercing like this on a guy, but it has grown on me.

I open my mouth as wide as it'll go and Jaylen wastes no time slipping his hard length passed my lips. I gag around him when he hits the back of my throat, which elicits a deep groan from him. Jaylen moves one hand to the two braids on either side of my head and wraps them around his fist, allowing him to control my movements. The other hand lowers to wrap around my neck as he moves in and out of my mouth.

"Your mouth is so fucking warm, little angel." Jaylen squeezes my throat a little tighter, and I gag around him, the fullness almost too much. "I can feel myself fucking your mouth. Do you like that, hmm?"

Spit slides from the corners of my lips and down my chin as I nod. I don't know how I'm taking all of him considering his length. My head is fuzzy and white dots are beginning to form in front of my eyes, but I soldier on. I want to please him, and if that means he fucks my face until I pass out, then so be it.

Jaylen picks up the pace, his piercing slamming into the back of my throat with each thrust. He uses the grip in my air to hold me still while he shoves his hard cock in and out of my mouth, using me as he pleases. My thighs are slick with arousal and my pussy is pulsating so hard it's almost painful.

Another crack of thunder overhead makes Jaylen slow his pace. He releases his grip on my throat and runs his knuckles down my cheeks, smothering the drool across my skin. A raindrop lands on the tip of my nose.

"You're so beautiful, little angel," Jaylen says, his voice low as he looks down at me. He stills his hips and pulls out of my mouth. I gasp for air, my chest heaving with each breath. But I don't have time to recover before I'm hoisted to my feet. He wraps his hand around my waist and shoves me against the tree. "You ready to hold on tight?"

"Yes," I say breathlessly, still trying to recover from gagging on his cock.

In one swift movement, Jaylen lifts me off the ground, and instinctually, I wrap my legs around his waist and my arms cross over his shoulders. Being at his eye level, I can see his baby blue eyes through the holes in the mask and my core tightens. Except they're not blue anymore. They're bright red. I gasp when I feel his fingers brush against my soaked pussy and push the thin material of my underwear to the side.

"Your cunt is fucking ready for me," Jaylen says gruffly,

holding me tightly with one arm. "Who would've thought my little angel would be so turned on by a mask."

My cheeks flame at his words because he's right. I have never been one to enjoy having sex in public, let alone feet away from a frat party with Jaylen wearing a Ghostface mask. But there is just something that Jaylen does to my body that I can't explain. I crave him, and his touch. I'm always left wanting more and it's driving me crazy.

"Hurry up," I whine, my body vibrating with desire.

I feel a few more raindrops land on my face, but I ignore the impending rain.

Jaylen chuckles, and I just know he is wearing a shit-eating grin behind that damn mask. "You're so eager, little angel. But you did work for it with that sweet mouth of yours."

Before I can respond, I feel the tip of his cock pushing past my swollen lips. I throw my head back and groan into the darkness as he fills me completely. When his piercing brushes against the spot that drives me crazy, I drip my nails into Jaylen's exposed back.

"You're so fucking tight," Jaylen grunts. He lowers his head to my shoulder, his hands holding me up by my ass. The plastic of the mask is cold against my skin. "And you're all mine."

I'm unable to speak as he thrusts into me, each one sending a spark of light across my vision at the same time lightning shoots across the dark sky. I don't notice the sharp pieces of bark sticking into my back or the burn in my thighs as I keep them firmly wrapped around Jaylen's hips. All I can focus on is the feel of him moving inside of me, my walls clenching around his hard length, and the low grunts falling from his lips.

Raindrops begin to fall heavier now, soaking through my dress. I watch as they slide down the plastic of the Ghostface mask and land on Jaylen's bare chest. I want to reach out and touch him, but I don't want to lose my grip.

Jaylen removes one hand from my ass to wrap around my throat, constricting some of my airflow. Being choked was not something I was into when I dated Roman, but with Jaylen... I just can't get enough of it. There is just something about putting my ability to breathe in the palm of his hands that turns me on more than it should. I try to suck in a breath, but his grip on me is too tight. All I can do is stare into his crimson eyes as he drives into me relentlessly.

"That's it, little angel. I want you to come for me," Jaylen growls, slamming his hips into mine.

I cry out as the pressure begins to build in my core, tightening almost painfully. But I welcome the pain because if Jaylen wants me to come on his cock, then that's what I'm going to do.

"Jay-len," I gasp when he hits my G-spot with his piercing. I clench around him and he groans, likely just as close to the edge as I am. The sound of skin slapping against each other echoes through the trees, getting lost in the wind.

My wet hair sticks to the side of my face as the rain falls heavily around us. With what little breathing ability I have, I try to take in the fresh scent of leaves mixed with rainwater. It is one of my favorite scents.

Jaylen releases my throat to move the wet hair off my cheeks. His crimson eyes bore into mine and I get lost in them, mesmerized by their beauty. When I first saw his red eyes, I was scared shitless. But now they're a reminder of the way his body reacts to mine, and I fucking love it.

He slams into me again, forcing me to throw my head back and cry out. I'm so close to the fucking edge but I don't want this to stop. I don't want to lose his touch when it's all I'm craving. But I know I can't hold out for too much longer.

With one last thrust, Jaylen and I groan at the same time, falling over the edge of the cliff into total bliss. I can't see straight as I feel Jaylen empty himself inside of me. I just know he's going to have me go back to the party with his cum dripping between my thighs and if I'm being honest, I don't mind at all.

Jaylen sighs as he lowers me to the ground. I hold onto his biceps to steady my shaky legs, afraid I might fall on my ass. My hands move to roam across the hard panes of his chest, taking in the contoured lines of his muscles and the ink embedded into his skin.

This man truly is a work of art.

"You can take the mask off now," I say breathlessly, biting back a smile.

He tilts his head to the side. "Are you sure? I happen to enjoy wearing it if it means my little angel will react like that."

I blush and push at his shoulder, the coldness of his skin sending a shiver down my spine. "Jaylen, come on."

"Fine."

When he removes the mask, his messy curls fall over his crimson eyes. I'm quick to notice that his fangs have pierced through his gums, glinting under the moonlight. Curiosity gets the best of me, and I lift my fingers to run across one of them gently, feeling just how sharp they are.

Jaylen pulls away, his hand coming up to wrap around my wrist. "Careful. I wouldn't want to hurt you."

"How does it work?" I ask softly, lifting my eyes to his. They're a mixture of red and blue now.

He frowns. "What do you mean?"

"How do you... turn someone into a vampire?"

Jaylen licks his lips and releases my wrist. I watch as he stuffs himself back into his pants and leans forward to fix my dress that got pushed askew.

"It's a complicated process," he answers vaguely.

"Can you tell me?" I don't care that it's raining and my clothes and hair are soaked.

The thought that Jaylen could turn anyone he crosses paths with into a vampire hadn't entered my mind until now. It has me curious whether he could turn me into one right here, right now. Not that I want him to do it, but I'm curious to hear the process.

Jaylen stares at me long and hard for a moment, making me think he's not going to tell me. He sighs and runs a hand through his messy hair. "To keep it short and sweet, a vampire has to drain the blood of a human, leaving them with a small amount, but it won't be enough for them to survive. Once the human is dead, the vampire has to fill the body with their blood. At the same time, a small trace of venom will be produced by the glands in their mouths that will then mix with their blood and begin the transition of turning the human into a vampire."

I let his words circle in my mind for a moment before I speak. "So, basically, the venom mixed with the vampire blood is kind of like a potion for immortality."

Jaylen smiles. "Yeah, something like that. There is more to it than that, but that's the general idea."

I nod. "It sounds... painful."

He shrugs. "I guess it would be."

I raise a brow at him. "Have you never turned anyone before?"

"No. I haven't felt the need to. And as I said, it's a lengthy process. One that I don't want to deal with."

I nod. That makes sense. If you have to go through all the effort to drain a human's blood and replace it with your own, you would want to have a good reason for doing it.

"Can you heal humans with your blood?"

Jaylen nods and shoves his hands into the pockets of his pants. "I can."

When he doesn't elaborate further, I decide to change the topic. As much as I would like to ask him more questions, it seems he doesn't want to talk about it. I point to his bare chest and the Ghostface mask on the ground beside his feet. "Want to tell me why you scared the shit out of me tonight?"

He shrugs, biting back a smile. Water droplets fall from the curls hanging in front of his eyes. "It's Halloween, and I wanted to see my little angel."

"How did you know I was here?" I question, raising a brow at me.

Jaylen licks his lips and tugs his lip ring between his teeth. "I always know how to find my girl."

I want to ask him what he means by that but a cold shiver races down my spine, reminding me that I'm standing in the rain and it's fucking freezing. I turn toward the frat house, barely able to see it through the trees and wonder if the girls have noticed I've gone missing. I don't want them to worry about me, especially with a serial killer running around Pullman.

"I should probably go." When I turn back to Jaylen, his eyes are boring into mine.

He steps forward and lifts his hand to my cheek, cupping it gently. I unconsciously lean into his touch. "I like your costume. It suits you."

"My friends thought I should've been Cruella de Vil."

He chuckles and plays with one of the wet braids hanging over my shoulder. "I like this better."

"Evie!"

My heart stutters in my chest at the sound of Rylee's voice sounding through the air. I snap my head toward the house and spot her frame walking around the backyard through the trees.

Shit.

"I really should go—"

I'm cut off by Jaylen's lips slamming down on mine, swallowing my words. I groan into the kiss as it deepens. His cold tongue laps against mine, making my knees almost buckle beneath me. But just as quick as his lips attached to mine, they were gone. "I'll see you soon, little angel," he breathes against my lips.

Before I can respond, his body is no longer in front of me, leaving me cold and empty. I look around, unable to see where he went. Damn him and his vampire speed.

"Evie, are you out there?"

As I turn to walk back to the house, I spot the Ghostface mask on the ground and smile. I scoop it up into my hands and rush through the trees to where Rylee stands in the backyard, still calling my name.

When I emerge from the treeline, I make eye contact with her. Rylee's shoulders sag in relief, her once perfectly styled blonde hair now a sopping mess around her face. I feel guilty that she was so worried about me that she ruined her outfit just to look for me.

"Hey, I'm here," I say when I reach her, my breathing heavy.

"Where the hell were you?" she demands and looks past me at the dark woods. "I thought you were lost, or worse."

I know what she wanted to say but the word got caught in her throat.

Dead. She thought I could have been dead.

"I just went for a walk," I say, reaching up to push the wet hair out of my face. "Let's go back inside and get warm. Sorry you ruined your outfit looking for me."

Rylee sighs and steps forward to wrap me in a tight hug, not questioning my poor excuse. "I'm just glad you're okay." When we pull away, she points at the mask in my hand. "Where did you get that?"

I look down at it and smile. "Oh, I just found it."

We turn to walk to the deck steps, our arms linked. Rylee sighs. "Don't tell anyone this, but I had the biggest crush on Billy Loomis. He was so sexy in *Scream*."

I chew my bottom lip, remembering how my heart raced when I saw Jaylen in the mask. "Yeah, me too."

CHAPTER 26
EVIE

"Come on, Candie, we need to leave now or we're going to be late."

I watch as Candie races down the staircase, her hair flying behind her with the speed at which she is running while she clutches her handbag to her chest. Her eyes meet mine when she reaches me standing in the foyer by the front door, my hand on the doorknob ready to go.

"Sorry, I had a nap this afternoon so I was running late putting my make-up on," she says breathlessly.

I pat her on the shoulder and pull the door open, gesturing for her, Rylee, and Jaycee to walk ahead of me. "That's okay. We've all been there."

"Some more than others," Jaycee teases as she nudges Candie playfully. "And we're not going to be late. Evie is just paranoid about not being ten minutes early to the game."

"Hey," I protest as we walk toward the taxi waiting for us. We could walk, but the girls want to go for drinks after the game, so this is an easier option. "It's not a crime to want to be early to an event. The thought of being late gives me the shakes."

"It's okay," Rylee says, linking her arm through mine as we

walk down the steps to the driveway. "We love your little quirks."

I roll my eyes. "Okay, enough. Just get in the car you lot."

The four of us get into the taxi, making sure to greet the driver with a smile as we direct him to the stadium on campus. The last time I was at the stadium was when Jaylen slide tackled Kale so hard he snapped his ankle and also fucked me so hard in the locker room shower I swear I saw stars and forgot my name. It was an intense night, to say the least.

But tonight is different. Jaylen isn't playing because of his three-game match ban for the red card he got three weeks ago, so he will be on the sideline while he watches his team play. I'm sure it has been hard for him to take a step back, especially when the Raiders are doing so well this season. I hope the team doesn't feel too off-put by not having their captain on the field. I know they have won their last two games, so I hope they can keep that momentum heading into tonight's game.

"So, Evie," Candie says from beside me. "How are things with your brother?"

I turn to her, the blush on my cheeks obvious from thinking about Jaylen. "He's good. Why?"

She shakes her head, her bouncy brown curls swishing around her face. "No reason."

"Does it have anything to do with the fat crush you have on him?" Jaycee interjects from the front seat, turning around. She wiggles her brows suggestively, making Rylee and I laugh. But Candie isn't too impressed.

"Hey!" she whines, folding her arms over her chest. "That was meant to be a secret."

"We all knew," Rylee says from my other side, leaning forward to look past me at Candie. "It's so obvious."

I nod. "She's right, C. Everyone in the house knows."

Candie's face pales. "Y-You knew?"

From the first day I moved into the sorority house and Miles helped me move my stuff in, I could see in her eyes the moment she fell for my brother. Her eyes lit up and she had a dreamy look that was obvious to everyone in the room but went unnoticed by her like she didn't know she was doing it. Candie is a sweet girl, so I didn't want to bring it up and embarrass her. I know how some sisters are about their friends crushing on their older brothers, but it's not a problem for me. If anything, I find it sweet that she likes him so much. It seems the sentiment was lost on my brother.

I nod. "Yeah. I'm sorry I didn't tell you. I didn't want to embarrass you or anything. But trust me, I don't mind that you have a crush on my brother."

Her eyes widen as she shifts in her seat. "Really?"

"Of course. Maybe if things don't work out with Cindy, I can put in a good word for you."

A smile lights up Candie's face and she reaches over to wrap her arms around my shoulders, resting her cheek against my arm. "You're the best, Ev."

I smile and pat her arm just as the stadium comes into view. A mass crowd of fans is already gathering outside in front of the gates, so the taxi driver drives around to the other side of the stadium to avoid the traffic and queue of cars lining up to find a spot in the parking lot across the road. We thank him and make sure to tip extra for driving us in peak traffic.

The four of us make our way to the front gates to get our tickets scanned. Once inside, Rylee and I go find our seats while Jaycee and Candie grab drinks and something to eat. The game is scheduled to start in twenty minutes, which is why I wanted to get here earlier. I can't stand not being on time to make sure I'm prepared for when the game starts. Otherwise, everything around me feels chaotic and unorganized.

We walk to our section in the lower bowl and find our seats

in the fifth row. Being Miles's sister, he was able to hook me up with the best seats for each home game. We are sitting across from the technical area where the coach, other staff members, and players on the bench sit. And it provides a great view of the entire field.

This is why I love home games.

"I'm sorry about outing Candie earlier," Rylee says from beside me.

I shrug. "It's okay. It's better to have the secret out in the open now so she doesn't have to hide her feelings around me. I think it's cute that she has a crush on Miles."

"I'm convinced every other girl in the house does too," she jokes. "That or they have a crush on Jaylen. There is no in-between."

The mention of Jaylen has my stomach rolling with excite-ment. I have been trying my best to keep my distance from him, but somehow, he manages to draw me right back in without even trying. After what happened at the Halloween party on Monday when Jaylen fucked me senseless in the woods, something flipped between us that I don't know how to explain or fully understand yet. Something just feels... different. If anything, I'm not going to dwell on it because who knows what it could mean. It could be my imagination for all I know.

"That doesn't surprise me," I comment.

I look up to see Jaycee and Candie walking down the aisle to our row, their hands full of Vodka Redbull drinks and hotdogs. My mouth waters at the sight. When they sit down, we fall into small talk over our drinks and food, waiting for the game to start.

Soon enough, everyone in the crowd is on their feet as both teams walk out onto the pitch. I cheer as loud as I can when I see Miles leading the Raiders out as the next person to step in as captain.

My eyes land on Jaylen as he walks beside their coach, his hands shoved into the pockets of his black jeans. His signature black T-shirt hugs the muscles in his chest and arms perfectly, a delicious sight. My eyes roam over the tattoos on his right arm. Every time we've been together, I haven't taken a moment to inspect the ink etched into his skin, looking over the pieces of art attached to him forever. I would love to ask him about them, but we're always preoccupied doing other things, which I'm not complaining about.

He runs a hand through his messy hair as he walks to stand in front of one of the leather chairs in the technical area that looks like it should be in a race car, waiting for the national anthem to start. His eyebrows are drawn down as he looks at the ground. If I didn't know any better, I would say he's disappointed that he's not out there with his team.

I feel partially responsible considering he was so worked up because I agreed to go out with Kale. But then again, we're not dating and we're certainly not in a relationship. So Jaylen's actions are all on him. But it does warm my heart knowing he would go to such extremes for me, no matter how risky or stupid.

That sounds fucked up, my subconscious tells me.

I shake her out of my head and focus on the pitch as the national anthem comes to a close and the players get into position. I spot Miles on the right side of the field closest to where Jaylen is sitting. As if he can feel me watching him, Miles's eyes find mine and he waves. I smile and wave in return. He then waves at the girls before the whistle is blown and the game starts. Candie just about passed out next to me from that small interaction with my brother.

During the game, I get caught up in what's happening,

watching as the Raiders almost score a goal but the keeper manages to save it or vice versa. I'm on the edge of my seat in the second half that I don't notice Jaylen has left the field. It isn't until the final whistle is blown at the end of the second half, the Raiders only just winning 2-1 in the last five minutes, that I notice I have a text message from Jaylen.

> Jaylen: I want to see you.

> Evie: Now? Aren't you supposed to be celebrating with the team?

"Hey, let's go," Rylee says from beside me. She pulls on my elbow until I'm on my feet and drags me toward the aisle where everyone else is exiting. "Who are you texting anyway?"

"No one," I answer quickly.

Another message from Jaylen comes in.

> Jaylen: I should be, but I'd rather see you. I can give you a lift home if you like.

I bite my lip as I follow behind the girls into the concourse of the stadium. The buzz of the crowd around me rings in my ears, their voices being drowned out. When Rylee stops by the bathroom so Candie and Jaycee can go in, I turn to her.

"Are you still going out with the girls?"

"I am," Rylee says with a nod and leans her back against the wall by the entrance to the bathroom, giving me a suspicious look. "You're still coming too, right?"

I consider my options here. Should I go out with my friends, sink a few cocktails, and then get a taxi home at three in the morning drunk? Or do I allow Jaylen to drive me home to spend some time with him? Although I don't know what's going on between us, no matter how hard I try to fight my feelings, I always come back to him and want to be around him. My body is fighting hard against the logical part of my brain that tells me getting close to Jaylen is a bad idea, but the way my body reacts to him is unlike anything I've experienced.

What's the worst that could happen, right? All I'm doing is getting a ride home from him which means I can be in bed before 10 p.m. Which, in all honesty, sounds more appealing to me right now than going out. I could use some quiet time. At least until the girls come home drunk and need assistance getting to their rooms.

"I'm actually not feeling the best," I lie, rubbing my stomach. "Must've been the hotdogs."

"Oh," Rylee says, her brows furrowing as a splash of concern covers her features. "That's a shame because those hotdogs were delicious, but maybe you just got a bad one. Do you want me to come with you? I don't mind—"

"No," I interrupt a little too abruptly. "I'm fine to get home, really. I can call a taxi and I'll send you a message as soon as I get home."

Rylee nods, having bought my lie about not feeling well. I feel bad for lying, but I knew if I told her and the girls the truth about what I was really doing they would be on my ass about it, asking a million and one questions that I don't feel like answering right now.

There is nothing wrong with a little white lie, right?

Rylee leans forward to hug me, her sweet floral scent consuming me. "You get going now. I'll tell the girls what's happening."

I smile as I pull away. "You're the best. Have fun and I'll see you later, okay? If you need anything, just let me know."

"Of course, Ev."

I wave goodbye to Rylee and turn on my heels, walking to one of the many exits of the stadium. I look down at my phone, making sure to glance up every few steps to avoid running into someone as I type a response to Jaylen.

> Evie: Where should I meet you?

I stand on the sidewalk a block away from the stadium, watching as the crowd of fans move throughout the campus, heading into bars and restaurants to celebrate the win. Well, the Raiders fans are. I don't know about the losing team.

My eyes scan the road for Jaylen's motorcycle. He told me to meet him here away from the watchful eye of my brother. I was instructed to walk a block away and stand across the street from the local Mexican restaurant and wait for him. To distract myself, I wrap my arms around my waist and rock on my heels, watching as people walk in and out of the restaurant. I can hear music blasting from the building, mixing with the chatter of the fans walking past me. I notice the way they eye me as they pass by, likely wondering why I'm standing on the sidewalk by myself, but I ignore them.

Glancing down at my phone, I read two texts from Jaycee and Candie. They must've sent them after they got out of the bathroom and Rylee told them I went home.

Jaycee: I'm sorry you don't feel good! Get some rest, E.

Candie: I'll make sure to drink extra cocktails for you!

I laugh at Candie's message and shake my head, slipping the device back into my small black side bag. I'm glad I decided to wear black denim shorts tonight and not a dress or skirt. Although, not wearing pants around Jaylen does have its perks. Images from the night of the Halloween party weave their way into my mind. I can still feel the way Jaylen gripped my ass cheeks, spreading them as he pulled me flush against his hard cock.

Having sex out in the woods while it's raining would be some people's nightmare because of how dirty it can be and the possibility lingering in the back of their minds that they could be caught at any second. Not to mention there is a fucking serial killer on the loose. But me? I couldn't care less. I welcome the danger because I know that when I'm with Jaylen, I am not only safe but also because all logic goes out the goddamn window, no matter how hard I try to reign it in.

You only live once, right?

The roaring of an engine draws my attention to the road,

and I watch as Jaylen pulls his motorcycle up to the curb. I'll never get used to seeing this man on a motorcycle. He lowers his leg to the ground to stabilize the bike before he pulls the helmet off, his curls bouncing around his face.

"Hey," he says, gesturing for me to come closer. "You ready?"

I nod as I step up to the bike. Jaylen turns on the seat to face me, his ocean eyes locked on mine. He smiles, reaching his hand out to rest on my cheek. I hold my breath when his finger traces my bottom lip, the movement holding me captive as I watch his face, unable to do anything else.

"So pretty," he says softly before dropping his hand to slide the helmet over my head.

"You're such a tease," I huff as he tightens the strap under my chin.

He grins and lets his hands fall to his side as he inspects the helmet. "Only for my little angel." Jaylen pats the seat behind him. "Hop on."

I glance up and down the straight, not looking for anyone in particular but just hoping my brother doesn't appear out of nowhere before sliding on behind Jaylen. When I wrap my arms around his waist, his left hand drops to my calf before sliding up to my thigh, his skin cold against mine.

He hums in disappointment and pulls his hand away. "You're not wearing a dress."

I roll my eyes. "Maybe you should've requested it earlier."

"I'll know for next time."

"Only if you're lucky," I tease, pressing my chest into his back. I smile at the audible groan that leaves his throat.

If Jaylen only wants to drive me home to spend this short amount of time together, I'm not complaining. I don't know his intentions, but I'm sure I could guess.

Jaylen roars the motorcycle to life, flips on the indicator, and merges into the traffic effortlessly. I relish the feel of the cool air against my skin and the wind blowing through the ends of my hair as we leave campus and get onto the main roads of Pullman.

"I'm going to take the long way back," Jaylen calls over the roaring of the wind passing by us.

I simply nod, although I'm sure he could've heard me if I whispered a response. I'm enjoying the tranquillity of just being in the moment and not having to worry about anything but being engulfed by the night.

I turn my head to look up at the sky, noticing the lack of stars. Shit, is it supposed to rain tonight? I vaguely remember Jaycee mentioning it while we waited for Candie to get dressed, but it didn't stick with me.

My concerns are confirmed when a raindrop lands on my exposed arm.

Oh, *shit*. I'm fine being on the back of the bike so long as it's a clear and rain-free day. But the rain has made me nervous ever since the fateful night I found my parents. I don't know what it is, but I think my brain associates rain with danger after that night, so I have always been weary of it. I was fine the night of the Halloween party when it rained because I knew there was no chance of me being in danger while in the woods. But being on the back of a moving motorcycle... yeah, my heart rate is fucking spiking.

Panic begins to gnaw at my heart and I sit up straighter. "Jaylen, can we go back now? Rain makes me nervous."

The rain begins to fall heavier as we drive through the main streets of Pullman. There are people everywhere, lining the streets. With it being a Saturday night, all the college students are out in force.

"Of course," Jaylen says and flips on his indicator to turn right in the direction of the sorority house.

I hold on a little tighter as the rain begins to soak through my graphic T-shirt and shorts. The droplets slide off the leather of Jaylen's jacket, so to distract me, I watch as they slide down the material and fall onto my drenched thighs. The wind rushing by is no longer peaceful, but loud and annoying as it fills my ears. All I can focus on is the whooshing sound and the trees that are a blur as we drive past.

I hate how all it took was for it to rain to make me suddenly feel uncomfortable, the pleasures of riding with Jaylen no longer enjoyable.

When I was a child, my mom couldn't keep me out of the rain. As soon as the first drop would fall, I would have my gum boots and raincoat on, ready to play outside. Jaylen and Miles would stay inside to play video games, so I would go outside by myself. My go-to was finding ladybugs in the garden and making up a little story for them as they tried to hide from the heavy rain. My mom would sit on the back porch and watch with amusement and a wide smile. She used to call me her rain child.

But now... I fucking despise the rain, all because of that night.

"Hold on, little angel," Jaylen calls out to me as we near an intersection.

I do as he says and hold on even tighter. If he wasn't immortal, I'm sure I would be pushing all the air out of his lungs with my grip. The squealing of the tires in my ears roars to an all-time high, and I slam my eyes closed, my heart racing in my chest.

"Fuck!" Jaylen shouts, his body stiffening.

I turn my head to the right to see a car roaring through the intersection, running the stop sign. The headlights are blinding, momentarily creating spots of white light dancing across my eyes.

I'm so disorientated that I barely register when Jaylen swerves out of the way of the car, the tires locking up as they screech across the gravel. It feels like the bike fishtails before I can no longer feel the cool leather beneath me or the warmth from the engine racing up my legs.

"Jaylen!" I cry when I can no longer feel his body against mine. I can no longer feel anything. Just the way my stomach twists painfully as I freefall through the heavy drop of rain, my eyes screwed shut.

"Evie!" Jaylen calls out, but he sounds far away.

I open my eyes in time to see the wet asphalt come into view as I fly face-first toward it. Bracing for impact, my shoulder slams into the ground with a hard thud, my head bouncing off it. I cry out as the rough surface connects with my skin and I slide forward with no sense of direction. All I can see is the sidewalk in front of a house illuminated by the street lamps. I don't know where Jaylen or his bike went.

My skin is burning, and my head is pounding as I try to sit up, but my limbs feel heavy, and I slump back down on my scraped shoulder. *God that hurts like a motherfucker.*

I can feel a sense of darkness washing over me, forcing my eyelids to close. I try to fight the feeling as best as I can, but I'm powerless as it consumes me and my body. As my mind drifts to a peaceful place and my body grows limp, I can hear Jaylen shouting my name in the distance, his voice filled with panic.

Why is he panicking? I'm just going to shut my eyes for a moment and sleep. I'll see him when I wake up.

CHAPTER 27
EVIE

I'm drowning in the metallic scent of blood.

But not just anyone's blood—my parent's blood. And *lots* of it. It's running down the staircase and pooling at my feet as I stare up at them and the man standing over their bodies. I meet his eye, and for a moment, we stare at each other, neither of us moving. But in the blink of an eye, he's gone, and I'm being wrapped up in the arms of my Aunt Jas.

When did she get here? I don't remember calling her or the police. How did she get here so fast?

I let her walk me out of the house and onto the front porch, watching as multiple police officers rush inside the house with their guns drawn. I want to tell them about the man I saw, but the words get stuck in my throat and all I can do is cry on my aunt's shoulder as she hugs me close, running her hand down my hair in a soothing motion.

I don't know how long we stay like this on the bench under the front window. The tin roof above rattles as the heavy raindrops slam down on it, the sound filling my ears and drowning out the voices of the police officers nearby. It feels as though time is moving in slow motion as I watch them walk in and out of the house, carrying plastic bags filled with unknown items.

The men in white hazmat suits scare me a little, but Aunt Jas reassures me that they're just doing their job, but wouldn't tell me what that was.

Two detectives—a young woman with short brown hair and an older man with a gray beard—stopped by to talk to me and my aunt but I don't recall much of the conversation. Aunt Jas did most of the talking. I only answered a few questions.

When they walk away, for some reason, my brain tunes into their conversation. They're a few feet away, but somehow, I can hear what they're saying.

"So, she just walked in and found them?" the younger woman asks.

The older man nods, looking down at the notepad he had been writing on. "That's all she knows from my understanding. But she's in shock, so that's understandable. If any other details come to mind in the next few days, her aunt will bring her into the station."

The woman nods and glances in my direction, but doesn't see me watching them. "The upside-down crosses carved into their foreheads are a little odd, right? It reminds me of an old case that has gone unsolved since the late '70s."

"I was thinking the same thing too," he said, lowering his voice a little. "But for now, we'll keep that detail to ourselves, okay? I don't want to worry the family right now. Once we have more evidence to link it to the unsolved case file or find out if there is a copycat going around, then we can fill them in. But until then, we keep it on the down-low."

An upside-down cross? That sounds awfully familiar to what my mom had told—

"Evie!"

My eyes snap toward the pathway as the downfall of heavy footsteps against the wet pavement fills my ears, drowning out the conversation from the detectives. I spot Miles running up the pathway, his eyes wild. Behind him, Jaylen stands beside his mom's car, the rain soaking his messy curls. His blue eyes are filled with concern as he watches me, something I have never seen from him before.

"Evie! Are you okay?" Miles calls as he pounds up the front steps. "What happened?"

I open my mouth to speak, but the words get stuck in my throat. My tongue feels heavy and my mind grows foggier, my vision blurring at the edges.

"Evie? Can you hear me?"

His voice sounds distant like he's feet away and not standing right in front of me.

"Evie."

I open my mouth, but again, nothing comes out.

"*Evie!*"

My eyes snap open at the sound of my brother's voice. I find him standing over me, his eyes wild and frantic like they were that day. They search my face, but I don't understand why he's so worried. The last thing I remember before my vision went dark was leaving the soccer game, getting on the back of Jaylen's bike, and then it started raining, we turned at an intersection, and—oh. I understand why he's worried. It's all coming back to me.

The rain, the motorcycle, the car, the wet gravel, and Jaylen calling my name before I passed out.

Shit.

My eyes glance around the room, realizing I'm in a hospital bed when I spot the IV drip beside me and smell the disinfectant wafting throughout the room. The walls are white and the incessant beeping of machines behind me makes the pounding in my head worse.

Using both of my hands, I push into the thin mattress to try and get into an upright position, but the searing pain in my shoulder makes it difficult. Glancing to both sides, I notice that there are no other patients. I'm grateful for the private room.

"Evie, relax," Miles says with his hand on my shoulder. "Your right side is all cut up and bruised, so just take it easy, okay? The nurse has put you on an IV drip to get your fluids up after you passed out, and they are giving you morphine for the pain."

I nod and turn to him. As I do, I spot Jaylen standing in the corner of the room with his arms folded over his chest and his intense eyes locked on me. His features are hard, but I catch the glimpse of worry that passes through his eyes before he looks away to stare at the floor. There isn't a scratch on him.

Swallowing hard, I return my attention back to my brother. "What happened?" My voice is croaky and my throat is tight, so I clear it in the hope it'll help relieve the pain. "How long have I been out for?"

"A couple of hours. You had an accident. I don't know how you walked away with only minor injuries," he says, his voice a little hard, unlike his usual carefree tone. "Jaylen called to tell me what happened." Before I can say anything, Miles turns to Jaylen. "I don't know what the fuck you were doing with my sister, but now would be a good time to explain yourself."

Oh, *shit*. With my fuzzy brain, I hadn't considered the fact that Jaylen would've had to tell Miles that we were together since he was the one to bring me to the hospital, I'm assuming. That means I'm going to be in deep fucking shit, I just know it. Miles is overprotective, I know, but after his warning to stay away from Jaylen, I have a feeling this isn't going to end well.

"I gave her a lift home," Jaylen says quietly, staring at the ground, unable to meet Miles's eyes.

"Why?" Miles demands. I can feel the anger flowing off him in waves as he stares down his best friend from across the room.

I try to catch Jaylen's eye from around Miles's body, but my shoulder is in too much pain to do anything but sit up straight. A hospital gown covers my body, my soaked clothes from earlier no longer in sight. Looking out the window beside my bed tells me that it's still dark with the rain pouring just as hard outside, slamming into the window.

"I ran into her after the game and asked if she wanted a lift since she was heading home. Her friends were going out but she just wanted to go home, so I offered to be nice."

A lie, but it's one that lines up with what I told my friends, so I'm going to roll with it. Miles doesn't need to know the truth. It'll only make this situation worse.

"You should've asked me to take her home instead of letting her get on that death trap," he said through clenched teeth. "That bike is fucking dangerous."

"It was an honest mistake," Jaylen says, tearing his eyes away from the reflective floor. "It was raining, the ground was wet, and some asshole ran the stop sign. It was an accident. I was being careful, I promise. I would never willingly put Evie in danger."

"I don't fucking care," Miles snapped, his voice dripping with venom.

"Stop talking about me like I'm not here," I interject, tired of feeling invisible while my brother goes into asshole mode. "It was my choice to accept the ride, so I have to deal with the consequences. Besides, as Jaylen said, it was an accident, so just relax, okay? Neither of us is seriously hurt."

Miles doesn't turn to face me, instead continuing to stare down Jaylen who continues to stand against the wall, his shoulders tensed and a guilty expression on his face as he looks between the floor and my brother, but never at me.

"You don't have a scratch on you," Miles points out and my heart stutters in my chest. *Shit.* I know for a fact Jaylen heard that because his eyes quickly glanced in my direction before returning to my brother.

"My leather jacket and long pants protected me. Evie was wearing my helmet."

I can't see Miles's reaction to that but his shoulders are still tense, meaning he's not done with this conversation. The tension in the room is palpable and almost suffocating. This is exactly how I thought he would react if he were to ever learn of me and Jaylen spending time together alone. While I love that he wants to protect me, he can't do it for the rest of his life, especially since I'm an adult.

While I appreciate his efforts to look after me, it's also frustrating that he doesn't listen to me when I say I can look after myself. I'm no longer that little girl who he found broken on the front porch ten years ago on that fateful day. I'm stronger than that, and he knows it, but he's just too afraid to admit it because admitting it means he has to loosen his reigns on me. And I don't think he's capable of doing that. Or ready.

"Just let it go, Miles," I plead, and reach out to tug on the sleeve of his jacket.

He turns to face me, his brows set into a deep frown. "You're hurt because of him, Ev. What did I tell you about staying away from him?"

"I know what I'm doing," I say, looking into his eyes. "All I did was accept a ride home, that's it. There is nothing else going on." I can feel Jaylen's eyes on me as I say the words, but I stay focused on Miles. I don't blame Jaylen for what happened. He's made it clear that he would go to the ends of the earth to protect me, and I believe him. What happened tonight was simply an accident.

He sighs and runs a hand through his hair. He's dressed in a pair of blue jeans, a white T-shirt, and a black bomber jacket. There are dirt marks on the front of his shirt, but they're mostly hidden by his jacket. I wonder what he was doing before he raced to the hospital.

"You need to be careful, Ev," he says softly, lowering his voice so Jaylen can't hear, but I know he can. "I can't lose you too, okay?"

I soften at his words, my resolve slipping. Sometimes I forget that I wasn't the only one traumatized by our parent's death. My brother may not have found their bodies, but he was there for everything else—the police reports, the funeral, the media wanting a statement, and the knowledge that we have to live life without them. It's a hard pill to swallow, not just for me, but Miles, too. So, I understand his need to protect me, but sometimes, he needs to protect himself, too.

"I'm not going anywhere," I promise, reaching out to squeeze his hand resting on the bed rail, "You won't lose me, Miles. We're in this together."

He nods, unable to meet my eyes, instead choosing to stare at the mattress. "Just... if you need a ride home at any time, please text me first, okay? I don't want you on that death trap ever again."

I nod. Getting into an accident on Jaylen's bike is a reminder of why I was hesitant to get on it at first. But it isn't enough for me to swear off it all together. I enjoy the way I feel when I'm riding with him—weightless and carefree. It's something I haven't felt in a long time, and I want to hold onto that feeling for a little while longer.

Miles turns to his best friend who hasn't moved from his spot in the corner of the room. "You watch yourself, Black. I don't want to catch you with my sister ever again, you hear me? She's off limits, or did you forget about that?"

Jaylen's jaw ticks as his eyes meet Miles's hard stare. I can tell he wants to say more but ultimately decides to let it go. His features soften and he sighs, clearly not in the mood to argue with my brother.

"I hear you loud and clear," he says quietly, which is unusual for him. I've never seen him this... quiet, with a sad expression on his features that I can only interpret as guilt.

Miles doesn't say anything as he turns his back to him to face me. I can hear him speaking to me, but all I can focus on is Jaylen when he turns his ocean eyes to me, holding me in place. He mouths, 'I'm sorry,' before he shoves his hands into the pockets of his jeans and walks out the door.

My mind is a jumbled mess as I try to make sense of everything that has happened tonight—the accident and the tension between my brother and Jaylen. Miles continues to speak, but all I can focus on is the nightmare I had before I woke up, his voice fading into the background of my mind.

It was another warning, I know it. Why else would my subconscious reveal the detail that my parents also had upside-down crosses carved into their foreheads like the victims in the '70s and the ones in the present day? They're all connected, I know it now.

My parents were murdered by the same person, or at least a copycat killer. I don't know for sure that the victims in the '70s were vampires, but the ones happening currently were. So, now my question is: why were my parents murdered in the same way when they're not vampires? And who the hell is behind the killings?

I don't know the answer to either question, but I'm determined to find out. I'm closer than ever to finding out the truth about what happened, I can feel it.

CHAPTER 28

JAYLEN

Evie: Hey. I just wanted to check in again to
see if you're doing okay. I haven't heard from
you since the night of the accident. I just want
to know that you're okay.

I run a frustrated hand through my hair, re-reading her
words until my eyes start to sting.

Fucking hell. I hate that I've been ignoring her texts
for the past week, but I can't bring myself to respond. Images
of her lying on the wet asphalt with blood trickling down her
arms and legs from deep gashes have haunted my every
waking thought since the accident. All I can think about is
when I called her name and she didn't move a muscle. She
didn't even bat an eyelid.

For a split second, I had thought I lost my sweet angel. And
if that were the case, I don't know what I would've done with
myself. Well, I know what I would've done, but it's not something I want to think about.

I should've heard that fucking car coming toward us, but I
was too focused on getting her home and out of the rain.

When she didn't respond, it took everything in me to not

pick her up in my arms and use my vampire speed to rush to the hospital. But there were people walking on the street who saw the whole indecent. A lovely older couple rushed over to help. I could have easily compelled them to forget they saw us, but I forced my mind to slow down and take a second to think about what Evie would want. It didn't feel right running around town like a bat out of hell with her in my arms. If she was conscious at the time, I'm sure I know what she would've told me to do.

I'm not sure if I made the right call to inform Miles of what happened when Evie got taken away in the ambulance with the older couple watching on. I knew he would've been pissed that I was alone with his sister and got into an accident, but I know Evie would've wanted him there when she woke up. So, I put my feelings aside and did right by her.

And now I'm dealing with the consequences of that decision.

"How long are you going to wallow in guilt?" Ethan asks from where he sits at my desk, spinning on the chair with his eyes trained on the ceiling.

I drop my phone onto my chest and close my eyes. "For as long as I want to."

"You've got to forgive yourself at some point. It wasn't your fault."

My eyes snap open to look at Ethan who has now stopped spinning on the chair, his eyes on me. "It was my fault though. I'm the reason we crashed. I'm the reason she ended up in the fucking hospital."

"No, the car that blew through the stop sign is at fault. Not you," Ethan points out. He inhales a deep breath and releases it slowly. "Look, you need to do something to take your mind off Evie."

"Like what?" I raise a brow at him. "The last thing I want to do is go out."

"Not even to your favorite strip club?" He wiggles his brows at me, and all I can do is roll my eyes.

"I don't want to go there."

Ethan frowns. "Why not?"

"Just because I'm not talking to Evie doesn't mean I want to go to a strip club and have other women shove their tits in my face. Your girl may be okay with you doing that, but I don't want to do that to mine."

"Hey," he whines and shakes his head. "There is nothing wrong with just looking. I don't touch, of course. But to each their own." Ethan adjusts himself on the seat. "You've got to stop being a party pooper and get out of the apartment. You've been rotting away in your bed for the past week."

I sigh. He's not wrong. It's been a struggle to get out of bed this past week with the guilt weighing heavily on me. "What's the point in doing anything when my best friend is pissed at me for hurting his sister and I feel too guilty to text said sister back because I feel like an asshole for what happened."

Ethan waves me off with a hand. "Miles will come around, don't worry. He can't stay mad at you forever. But you can't stay in this room hoping something will change."

With a huff, I run both of my hands down my face and groan. "Fine, if I go out with you tonight will you get the fuck off my back?"

He grins. "I can't make any promises, but sure."

I wish I hadn't agreed to come out with Ethan. The strobe lights hitting my eyes are annoying me and the music blasting from the speakers above the stage is making my head pound. I haven't fed in a few days because it's been the last thing on my mind, so my senses are at an all-time high since my body is weaker than usual.

Every fucking thing is annoying me.

"Come on, Jay. Are you sure you don't want a lap dance? It'll be on the house," Preston says, turning his head to look at me. I don't acknowledge the woman grinding on his lap in what appears to be scraps of lingerie that barely covers anything.

When we arrived at the *Clubhouse*, I wasn't expecting to see Preston and Cain standing by the entrance waiting for us. I should've known Ethan would invite them, but I was hoping he would keep it low-key. I forgot that isn't his style. Whenever he does anything, he likes to go all out, even if it's as simple as going to a strip club. What was supposed to be an outing to get him off my back has now turned into a group activity. Not surprisingly, Miles couldn't join us because he went to Cindy's house. Although, I am thankful considering we're not on good terms at the moment. The apartment is... tense, to say the least. Very frosty, and that's coming from me.

He's never been this mad at me before, not even during all the years we spent growing up together. I'm sure if the anger was over anything else he would've gotten over it by now, but because Evie is involved it's taken his emotions to a whole other level. I have no idea how long he's going to stay mad at me or if he'll ever forgive me. I can only hope he does because despite all the shit we've been through he's still my best friend. I need him in my life.

It seems I've dug myself a grave at the tip of his shoes and I don't see myself getting out of it anytime soon.

I fold my arms over my chest and look toward the stage. A woman wearing a thin red thong has her large tits out as she twirls around the pole in the center by her legs while older men sitting at tables beside the stage throw multiple one-dollar bills at her.

"I'm good, but you enjoy."

Cain snorts from his seat beside Preston, looking at me past the woman on his lap. She is wearing a matching hot pink lingerie set, her nipples peeking through the thin material. "You're such a bore, Black. Come on and let loose for tonight. There are plenty of girls to go around."

"Look, it was hard enough to get him out of the house, so let's enjoy this small win," Ethan says. He too has a woman grinding on his lap with a seductive smile on her lips.

I roll my eyes and lean back further in the plush seat. The copious amounts of whiskey I have had tonight are doing nothing to dull the ache in my chest. All I can think about is Evie and if she's doing okay. Miles hasn't spoken about her this past week, which irritated me at first because I was waiting for any type of update on her but got nothing.

It would be easier to just text her back, I know that, but I can't bring myself to do it. I needed to take a step back and let her heal in peace. Miles being pissed about the situation and now knowing we have been hanging together has complicated things more than I would have liked. It was inevitable, really. There was no way we were going to be able to keep him in the dark forever, but I was hoping we would have a little more time without him knowing.

Every night since the accident, I have dropped by the sorority house to check in on her, using the shadows to hide and watch from afar. Seeing her sleeping peacefully has put some of my mind at ease, but it still doesn't change the fact that I hurt my little angel when I'm the one who is meant to protect her.

I grip the cool glass in front of me and bring it to my lips. The burn of the whiskey as it races down my throat is a welcome sensation. I just wish it would numb my mind for the rest of the night, but I would need a lot more than just a few glasses. I would need a whole goddamn bottle and more to get even remotely close to blacking out.

The thirst for blood gnaws at my stomach, but I fight back the urge. I can't focus on the need to feed right now, especially not in this setting. But I can't ignore the blood thrumming through the veins of the women at our table. It only intensifies the hunger building in my stomach, making my mind spin.

I close my eyes tightly and breathe through the ache, not wanting to accidentally reveal my red eyes to anyone at the table. That would be a fucking nightmare.

"Jay, you good?"

My eyes snap open at the sound of Ethan's voice. His brows are drawn down in a frown and his face is filled with worry. He can probably sense my struggle.

I nod and swallow thickly. "Yeah. I'm good." My voice is hoarse and my throat is tight.

"If you need anything, just let me know."

I know what Ethan is trying to say. *If you want any blood, just let me know.*

"I'm fine."

Ethan nods and goes back to focusing on the petite woman sitting on his lap. Preston and Cain are smiling like idiots as they look at the two women on their laps, no longer concerned over the fact I'm not interested in getting a lap dance.

When I first started college, I would frequent the *Clubhouse* many times a week because I was a horny fucking nineteen-year-old and a baby vampire. I would come by most nights and compel the dancers to give me a free lap dance. It never went as far as me feeding on them because I knew that could cause problems for me if I were to fuck things up and somehow reveal my true identity. Thankfully, the *Black Rose* opened in my sophomore year, so I had no reason to go to the *Clubhouse*. So, being back here after years of not coming is odd. Like a memory has been unlocked deep in my mind.

When we arrived earlier, a few of the dancers gave me knowing looks because they recognized me. But nothing really has changed here. The tables still have dents in the wood and most table legs are still wobbly with pieces of torn-up cupboard under the leg to stabilize it. The room still smells like cigarettes and whiskey, and the foam floor tiles on the stage still have scratches embedded in them from the heels of the dancers. Nothing has changed, besides the dancers that come and go.

"You look like you could use a dance."

I look up at the sound of a familiar voice and make eye contact with chocolate brown eyes. The amount of time I spent staring into them, wondering whether I should sink my fangs into her neck, was embarrassing. Being a baby vampire, I just wanted to feed and fuck all the time, but knew I couldn't. Not if I wanted to stay hidden from the hunters. Every time I stopped by the *Clubhouse*, I always found myself being drawn to her because her eyes were comforting, somehow talking me down off the edge. She always knew how to get me to talk, even if I didn't want to. At first, I found it annoying, but over time, I grew to enjoy talking with her about what was happening in my life.

"Amethyst, it's been a while," I say, watching as she turns to sit her half-naked body on the handrest of my chair. Her long blonde wig falls straight over her shoulders.

"Long time no see," she grins, her chocolate eyes meeting mine. "I see you have company tonight."

"Yeah, my friends dragged me out of my apartment, much to my displeasure."

Amethyst quirks a brow. "Is everything all right?"

I shrug and fold my arms over my chest like I'm a fucking child. "Yes and no."

"Girl troubles?"

With a sigh, I nod. "Yeah, I guess you could say that."

She adjusts in her spot and leans forward to rest her hand on the back of the chair, her eyes locking with mine. "I never thought I would see the day that Jaylen Black would have girl troubles. Who is it?"

"Evie."

Amethyst's eyes widen. "*The* Evie. The one you used to tell me about?"

I nod. "But I fucked up, so I'm wallowing in self-pity, as my friend likes to put it."

"Whatever you did, it doesn't matter," she says, her warm eyes on mine. "You just need to make it right."

I sigh. I understand what she and Ethan are saying, but I can't bring myself to do it. After what happened with Miles in the hospital room, and seeing my little angel lying in that bed, I knew I needed to take a step back and let the steam cool off. It doesn't seem like Evie is pissed at me, but I'm pissed at myself for putting her in danger like that.

"I don't know how," I admit. This is the first time I have ever felt lost in my life. My mind won't tell me what I should do next. When I think I might know, a voice in the back of my mind casts doubt over my decision, and I'm left feeling lost once again because what if that tiny voice is right and I make things worse?

I just want to do right by Evie.

Amethyst places a hand on my shoulder, her long nails digging into my skin through the material of my jacket. "You know what to do, Jay. You're a good man. I know that deep in my heart. You have a lot of love to give but not enough confidence to commit to it. Whatever you need to do to get back into Evie's good books, you just have to trust that it's the right decision and everything else will just fall into place." She pats me tenderly on the shoulder and pushes herself off the handrest. "I know how patient you were for this moment when you could finally get the girl, so don't fuck it up now. Don't let her slip through your fingers, okay?"

"But I don't—"

"You've got this, Jay," she interjects, a warm smile touching her lips. "You always have."

I nod, letting her words wash over me. Damn, I really did open myself to this woman when I first started WSU. I felt both reassured and called out in one breath. But I know she's right. She always is.

Amethyst claps her hands together, her eyes focused on mine. "Now, do you want to take me up on that offer for a dance? I know it'll make you feel better."

I can feel Ethan, Preston, and Cain's eyes on me as I look up at Amethyst. I shake my head. "Not tonight."

She smiles and pats my shoulder. "Well, you always know where to find me if you do. And I hope everything goes well with Evie. She's a lucky girl."

I roll my eyes when she winks at me and watch as she walks away to another table of men nearby, putting on her award-winning smile.

"What was that all about?" Preston asks. The dancer he was with before has now left. "How do you know her?"

"She's an old friend," I say, not wanting to elaborate.

Turning to my right, I see a busty woman walking by

wearing black lacy lingerie. She smiles at me when we make eye contact, and I wave her over. She happily walks over to the table. When she's closer enough, I wrap my fingers around her wrist and lock eyes with her. "You're going to take my friend here for a dance, okay?" I push the words into her mind, watching as her blue eyes glaze over for a split second before they return to normal.

The woman nods with a smile and walks over to Preston, holding out her hand. "Care for a dance?"

Preston frowns and looks over at me. "What the hell—"

"Take the dance," I urge, and lean back in my seat. "In fact, all of you should go for a dance."

"But what about you?" Cain asks as he stands to his feet. The dancer who was grinding on his lap earlier eagerly wraps her arms around his waist, batting her long lashes at him.

"I want to be alone."

Preston and Cain waste no time and hurry away to the private room with their girls. Ethan lingers with his, watching me carefully.

When I meet his eyes, I point to the dancer on his lap. "Remember, you can look but you can't touch."

Ethan chuckles. "Don't worry, my girl knows what I'm doing here. In fact, she's jealous she isn't here with me because she has always wanted to go to a strip club."

I raise a brow at him. "Well, aren't you two a match made in heaven?"

"Come on," the redhead on his lap says. She stands to her feet and holds out her hands for Ethan.

He gives me a last look before taking her hand and they walk away from the table. When I'm alone, I sigh. Reaching into my pocket, I pull out my phone and scroll through all the text messages Evie has sent this past week. My fingers itch to type a response, but I can't move them.

Fuck.

Amethyst's words circle around my mind. *You just need to make it right.*

God, I wish it were that easy. But maybe she is right. I just need to put some trust in myself and what I have with Evie. Once I forgive myself for what happened, we can move forward. But I can't wait too long, I know that.

But when will be the right time?

CHAPTER 29
EVIE

It has been nearly two weeks since the motorcycle accident and when I learned the truth about what happened to my parents. I hate that it took an accident like that for my subconscious to reveal such a pivotal piece of information that it chose to store away as a trauma response. I understand why it was kept hidden from me then, but I don't know why it was unveiled now.

Is it because I'm taking small steps toward learning the truth and I just need a nudge in the right direction?

But then what does it mean for the man I saw standing over their bodies that night? Was he a vampire hunter? Was he the one to kill them?

The one thing I can't wrap my head around is why my parents were targeted when they weren't vampires. If they were vampires, I'm sure I would know about it by now. Knowing what I know about these creatures now, if I were a vampire, I would be one by now having gone through the transition process at eighteen. But that didn't happen to me or Miles.

So, why them? It just doesn't make any sense.

Other than that nightmare, I haven't had one since. Is that

my subconscious telling me all I need to know? If there is nothing left for me to remember, where do I go from here?

I've made the connection between all three of the situations—the old '70s case, the current murders, and my parent's case—but I'm no step closer to finding out who is behind any of them.

I sigh and look out the window of my bedroom at the leaves starting to turn brown in the big tree beside the house. Leaning my head against the window sill, I watch the light breeze rustle through the branches as the sun begins to set on the horizon. Now that fall has finally arrived, this has been my favorite spot to sit in the afternoon. Essentially being on house arrest doesn't leave me much room for other activities.

House arrest is a little dramatic, but ever since the accident, Miles has been keeping a close eye on me to make sure I take it easy. The nurse let me go the next morning after it happened and told me to relax for a couple of days, but Miles has taken it to the next level, going as far as asking my friends to make sure I stay at home when I'm not going to class to ensure I heal correctly.

I only sustained some deep grazes and bruises from the fall, so there wasn't much to let heal. Thankfully, I walked away with only minor injuries, which is odd considering the intensity of the accident, but who am I to complain? My suspicion tells me that Miles wants to keep me home to make sure I don't see Jaylen, which is a little extreme, in my opinion. I didn't fight it at first, but I'm beginning to grow antsy being stuck inside all the time. I want to get out of the house. I can't take two steps out of my bedroom without someone asking what I'm doing.

It's exhausting, to say the least. I feel... trapped, and I don't like it.

My phone vibrates on my bedside table. Sighing, I step

away from the window to check it. My heart catches in my throat when I see Jaylen's name on the screen.

Jaylen: My little angel, what are you doing tonight?

I haven't seen or heard from Jaylen since the night he left the hospital. After the tense conversation between him and my brother, it seems he kept his word about staying away. I tried to reach out a few times through text, but I got no response. For some reason, it makes my heart feel heavy knowing that he would be so willing to stay away after how possessive he's been recently. But he's also my brother's best friend, so I understand he's been put between a rock and a hard place. It could also be because of the guilt he feels for the accident. He doesn't need to feel guilty because neither of us got seriously hurt.

After a week, I found myself missing him more than I thought I would.

So, why is he messaging me now after two weeks of no contact?

Evie: Miles essentially has me on house arrest while my wounds finish healing. So, I'll be in bed like most nights.

Jaylen: Can I see you tonight?

> I miss you.

My heart lurches reading his words. Swallowing hard, I type a response.

> Evie: I can't leave. My friends are also keeping a close eye on me.

> Jaylen: Don't worry, I've got you.
> Be ready in five.

My eyes widen as I stare at the screen. Five minutes? I'm in sweatpants and an old T-shirt I wore in high school. What the hell am I supposed to wear if I don't know where he's taking me?

Without thinking, I rush to my closet and pull out a flowy, plain black dress that rests halfway down my thighs. I don't know what possessed me to wear a dress, but I know Jaylen likes it when I do, so who am I to complain?

You're thinking with your pussy, my subconscious tells me.

I roll my eyes, wishing she would shut the hell up.

Throwing my hair into a high ponytail, I check my reflection in the mirror behind the bedroom door to make sure I look somewhat presentable. Five minutes doesn't leave me with a lot of time to do much else than make sure I look like I haven't been lounging in bed for two weeks.

Thankfully, my friends are downstairs watching a movie. I told them I wanted to be alone, which I'm now grateful for.

Tapping on the bedroom window forces my heart in my throat. My eyes look through the mirror to see Jaylen sitting in the tree outside of the window. His hair has gotten longer, the bouncy waves falling into his eyes and curling behind his ears. He smiles and waves, showing off his straight teeth and charming smile.

I inhale a deep breath and turn to walk across the room to the window. Sliding the window open, I fold my arms over my chest. "What the hell are you doing?"

"I've come to rescue you," he says matter-of-factly.

Leaning forward, I look past him at the tree, noticing he's balancing on a thick tree branch that reaches out toward the window, falling a foot short of touching it. Jaylen is dressed in black sweatpants and a matching hoodie, looking effortlessly stunning.

"I didn't realize I called for Prince Charming to come knocking at my window. What if someone sees you?"

Jaylen glances to his left at the street. "No one is going to see me, and if they do, I can just compel them."

I roll my eyes. "Right, I forgot that is one of the many tricks up your sleeve."

"Do you want to see another?"

"I don't know whether to say yes or no," I reply, and raise a brow at him.

He simply shrugs and leans forward until his head is in line with the window sill. "Well, too late. Your five minutes are up."

In the blink of an eye, Jaylen wraps his arms around my waist and pulls me through the open space, careful not to hit my head on the way out. I hold back a surprised squeal as we fly through the air before landing on the ground. I grunt on impact and turn to stare up at Jaylen who is wearing a shit-eating grin.

He releases his hold on me but keeps one arm wrapped around me as we walk to the front of the house. "That was one of the many tricks up my sleeves."

"What? You flying through the air like a fucking bird." I had forgotten he could do that. While it's terrifying in the moment, flying through the air, it fills me with a surge of adrenaline that makes my head spin.

Jaylen shrugs and stops at his motorcycle parked on the curb. "I wouldn't call it flying so much as freefalling and landing on the ground without a scratch."

I shake my head and turn to the death trap, staring it down nervously. The last time I was on this thing, I went skidding across wet asphalt and passed out. It's the reason I'm on unofficial house arrest and haven't seen Jaylen for two weeks.

Now, we have a love-hate relationship, because while I despise it for the accident that occurred, I love how my body feels when I ride it, my mind so relaxed and carefree. It's something I've been craving, but also nervous about since I woke up in the hospital.

"Are you okay?" Jaylen turns to face me, his sandalwood scent wafting over me. God, I've missed that smell.

I inhale slowly and nod, needing to take a couple of deep breaths to control my racing art. "I'll be okay."

He sighs and tugs his lip ring between his teeth. "I'm sorry... for what happened. It was all my fault. I should have protected you and I fucking failed."

I shake my head. "It wasn't your fault. It was that asshole who ran the stop sign. If it wasn't for your sharp senses, we would've been roadkill."

His baby blues hold mine as we look at each other, neither of us moving. I can see the pain and worry behind them. He still feels guilty about what happened, but I don't want him to be anymore because what happened is in the past, and everything is fine now. I'm fine.

"If something bad had happened to you... I don't think I would've been able to live with myself. I would have gone fucking mental. I wanted to message you earlier, but I just—"

I lift my hand to rest on his chest, his cool skin noticeable through the thickness of the sweatshirt. With his muscles tense and his eyes hard, he watches me, anticipating my next words.

"Forgive yourself for what happened, please. I don't blame you for the accident, so stop blaming yourself, okay? I don't want to dwell on it any longer."

Jaylen nods and inhales a deep breath before he rests his hand under my chin, forcing me to stare into his ocean eyes. I'm immediately captivated by them. "Do you trust me, little angel?"

Without thinking, I nod, because I do trust him, even when I probably shouldn't.

"I do."

He smiles and leans forward to press his mouth against mine in such a delicate kiss that I'm surprised he was capable of such tenderness. "Okay, let's go."

"Where are we going?" I ask as he slips the helmet over my head and fastens it under my chin.

Jaylen takes his lip ring between his bottom teeth, tugging on it for a moment before releasing it. God, I love when he does that.

"The *Black Rose*. I haven't seen my girl in two weeks, so I'm dying to get a fucking taste of you."

Black Rose is vibrating with music when we walk through the door. I have become all too familiar with this bar in the past few weeks that I recognize the same DJ on the decks in the back of the room and the same sleazy bartender working at the bar. I never pictured myself becoming a regular at a bar, let alone one that doubles as a feeding ground for vampires, but I enjoy coming here. The vibe of the dark lighting and furniture mixed with the atmosphere of laughter is enjoyable.

"Let's go," Jaylen says as he tugs on my hand, guiding me toward the staircase.

"Woah, someone is eager," I tease as I follow, taking the wooden steps quicker than usual because of his fast pace. "Slow down, tiger."

"We don't have time for that," he comments when we reach the top.

I blush as we walk down the hallway, stopping at the last door on the right. The room is dark when we enter, but Jaylen switches on the lamp beside the bed covered in a black sheets and comforter. The walls and carpet are plain and dark in shade. It doesn't do a great job of hiding the blood stains littered throughout the room, reminding me of just how many vampires and humans have come through this room.

God, I would hate to be the person who has to clean in here after a feeding session.

"Bed. Now," Jaylen commands, and wastes no time pulling his sweatshirt over his head, leaving him shirtless as he drops the material at his feet.

Instead of listening to his command, I take in his sculpted body and the way his abs flex when he breathes. I'm convinced this man is a work of art because who the hell looks like this? It blows me away every time.

"Evie," he warns, his baby blues darkening to the crimson color I have seen a handful of times.

"Okay, okay," I say, throwing my hands up and sitting on the bed. "Your wish is my command."

As I sit, I watch Jaylen move to stand in front of me, his crotch at eye level. I can see the outline of his hard cock through the material of his sweatpants. The sight alone has me clenching my thighs together as the pressure builds in my core.

Without saying a word, Jaylen grabs the hem of my dress and lifts it over my head. He eyes the red lacy lingerie set I'm wearing that matches his eyes and grins, pulling his lip ring between his teeth as he admires me.

"God, you're fucking beautiful."

I blush and chew on my bottom lip. But that only makes his eyes darken further. Oh, right. I forgot me doing that drives him crazy. Maybe if I keep doing it he'll—

"If you don't stop doing that, I'm going shove my cock between those pretty lips of yours."

Releasing my lip, I nod and watch as he shoves his sweatpants and briefs to the floor. He steps out of them and grips his throbbing length in his large hand, pumping it slowly as he looks me in the eye.

"You know what, I think I'm going to do just that anyway." He grins, stepping closer with his legs on either side of mine. "Open your mouth and show me how well you take my cock."

I eye the barbell through the crown of his cock as it glints under the dim lighting. Jaylen has my body brimming with fire, and I'm desperate for an escape.

Doing as I'm told, I open my mouth, breathing heavily through my nose as I look up at Jaylen through my lashes. He groans as he grips the base of his length and brings it to my lips. In one swift movement, he pushes himself inside. His skin is cool against my tongue as he slides in further, a deep groan slipping past his lips.

I'm glad I don't have a gag reflex.

"Fuck, your mouth is so warm."

Jaylen brings both of his hands up—one wraps itself around my hair while the other holds my throat tightly. He doesn't squeeze hard enough to restrict my airflow, but it is a thrilling sensation of limited air in my lunges that has me gasping for more, only to open my throat further for Jaylen to push himself deeper.

Saliva pools at the corner of my lips as he continues to fuck my mouth, a whimper bubbling in my throat. I'm so full of him that I don't know what to do. I know I need to focus on breathing through my nose to avoid choking on his cock, but all I can think of is the way his piercing feels when it touches the back of my throat and drags along my tongue with each movement.

All of these sensations combined have my pussy aching to be touched.

Jaylen pumps his hips faster as he swells inside my mouth, hitting the back of my throat in quick succession. Tears spring to my eyes as I fight back the urge to gasp for air. I want him to use me for his own pleasure because I fucking love the way he bites his lip ring as lust clouds his crimson eyes. Knowing that he looks that way because of *me* has me ready to jump over the edge without so much as being touched.

"That's it," he grunts as he continues to fuck my mouth. "I want you to take all of me. Every last fucking drop."

I nod, unable to do much else. I want to taste him. To feel his cum slide down my throat. To consume him like he consumes me.

With one last pump, hot liquid shoots down my throat as

Jaylen groans loudly, his head falling back to stare at the ceiling. A salty taste coats my tongue, but I fucking love it. I bring my hand up to wrap around the base of him, finally taking control back. Using my tongue, I lick every last drop off his skin before pulling him out with a soft pop.

Jaylen looks down at me with a grin. "Oh, you greedy girl."

Saliva dribbles down my chin and my lungs are gasping for air, but I don't care. All I can focus on is him and what's going to happen next.

He reaches between my thighs—my legs voluntarily parting for easier access—and runs his finger over my drenched folds, a wicked grin forming on his lips. "Oh, you're already fucking soaked for me." He pulls his hand back and points to the bed. "Lie down."

I do as he says and lie on my back. He crawls onto the bed, his body hovering over mine as he stares down at me with his crimson eyes. He reaches between us and hooks his finger around the material of my panties. In one swift flick, he shreds the thin material from my skin and throws the remnants to the side.

"There, that's much better," he says, voice thick with lust.

Jaylen leans down and captures my lips, his tongue filling my mouth as he dominates me. I'm just as greedy as him, wrapping my arms around his neck, bringing our bodies closer. I'm craving physical touch, and I hate that he's taking so long. I want to feel him inside of me already.

I part my legs to allow him to settle between them, his cock brushing against my sensitive core, and his hands on either side of my head to hold himself up. I groan into his mouth, which only makes him smile. As his tongue devours mine, he reaches between us and brings the head of his dick up to brush through my folds, making me see white spots as I try to focus on kissing him but also how he feels against me.

Jaylen pulls away to look down at me. "Are you ready?"

I can only nod because I'm afraid words will fail me. I spot two pointy edges peeking out from beneath his top lip and realize that this would be when he feeds while he's fucking. At first, the thought scared me shitless because what if he takes too much blood and kills the person he's feeding on. But the more I think about it, the more I realize just how much self-control Jaylen has to be able to feed on fresh blood and not take too much. It must be hard for him, but it shows he's trust-worthy in that department.

It has me curious. What would it feel like to have his teeth in my neck while he sucks my blood from my veins? It sounds like something out of a horror movie, but it has my pussy throbbing at the thought.

And, of course, Jaylen notices.

He runs the back of his fingers down my cheek. "What are you thinking about?"

"You," I admit softly. "And how you... feed on humans."

He raises a brow. "And why are you thinking about that?"

"Does it... hurt?"

"Being fed on?" he asks, licking his lips. When I nod, he continues, "Yes and no. From what I understand, it's very plea-surable, but it can be painful."

A mixture of pleasure and pain...

The smile that touches Jaylen's lips is soft. Too soft for his rough exterior. "Are you asking because you want me to feed on you, little angel?"

I blush and turn my head to the side. "Maybe. How do you normally feed?"

"Blood bags," he answers as his hand comes up to rest on my cheek, forcing me to look at him. "Ethan and I get them from the hospital."

I fucking knew it! My suspicions of Ethan being a vampire and the one dating Jaycee have now been confirmed.

I can only assume they don't get the blood bags willingly, but that's a conversation for another day.

"Evie," Jaylen says softly, his warm breath blowing across my lips. "Do you want me to feed on you?"

As I stare into the depths of his red eyes, feeling the passion and lust radiating from them, all I can do is nod because I do want him to feed on me. I'm curious about what it would feel like and if it truly is as pleasurable as he says.

I'm reminded of the night I walked in on Jaylen with a busty woman in this very club, and it was clear that the woman was in ecstasy as he fed on her. That's what I want. I want to feel that with Jaylen because I trust him. My body craves the way he touches me—so gentle yet dominating. I'm aware that he could so easily rip my throat out and drain me of my blood, but that fear lingering in the back of my mind doesn't change my decision.

Jaylen's eyes widen. He's surprised by my answer. "Are you sure? I don't want to hurt you."

"You won't hurt me," I point out. "You've shown me that."

His tongue darts out to lick his lips as he nods. He doesn't say anything as he attaches his lips to mine again, eliciting a soft moan from me. His touch is gentle and slow as he runs his fingers up the curves of my body to rest beside my head. With how wet I am, he slips right in. He groans in my ear as my walls hug him tightly, clenching as he pushes in and out.

"Fuck, I forgot how tight you are," Jaylen groans as his eyes meet mine.

With the curls falling over his red eyes and his lips slightly parted as he drags his cock in and out, I can't help but want more. I need to be closer to him. I need to feel more of him. I need *more*.

"Harder," I urge, digging my nails into the skin around his hips, wanting him to move faster. "Feed on me, Jaylen. Please."

His fangs lengthen at my words, their razor-sharp edges making me nervous. But I have nothing to fear. I just need to remind myself that Jaylen is going to keep me safe like he always does.

Jaylen reaches up with his right hand to turn my head to the side, exposing the right side to him. His fingertips leave a trail of goosebumps as he brushes them along the delicate skin.

"So fucking beautiful," he whispers. "I can hear the blood pumping in your veins."

"Take it then," I moan as he hits that sweet spot. "Fuck me and feed on me."

He groans and nuzzles his nose into the crook of my neck. "You don't have to tell me twice."

When the tips of his fangs pierce through my skin, a sharp cry is forced from my throat but it quickly turns to a moan as the pain begins to subside and I focus on the way he's moving inside of me—slow and gentle at first. The slurping sound in my ear is unsettling, but I push the worry to the back of my mind and enjoy the soft moans coming from Jaylen's throat as he feeds.

I close my eyes and get lost in the pleasure and subtle pain. It's a combination I would never have thought would work, but it fucking does and it's driving me insane, pushing me closer and closer to the edge—already.

Stars dance in front of my eyes as Jaylen's hips meet mine in slow, deliberate thrusts. It's not his usual pace, but I like it. It feels more... intimate. We feel connected—both physically and mentally. It's an odd sensation, to say the least, but I welcome it with open arms.

With Jaylen's chest against mine, I run my fingernails

down his back as the pressure begins to build in my core. "Jaylen, I think I'm going to—"

The words die in my throat as I fling myself over the edge, my legs shaking and my body fuzzy as I lose myself to the depths of the orgasm coursing through my muscles. *Woah, that was quick.* A few seconds later, Jaylen follows suit, groaning in my ear as he unloads inside of me, making my head dizzy as I come down from the high.

Tearing his lips away from my neck, Jaylen pulls back to look me in the eye. Blood—my blood—is smeared across his chin with small droplets forming at the corner of his mouth. His brows are slightly furrowed as his eyes search my face.

"Is everything okay?" I ask, lifting my hand to rest on his blood-covered cheek.

"Yeah," he says slowly, tilting his head to the side as he assesses me. "You taste fucking delicious, little angel. Unlike anything I've ever tasted."

I smile, my body sagging into the mattress, feeling spent. "That's the first time anyone has ever told me that."

He chuckles and leans down to kiss me, smearing my blood across my swollen lips. "And it better be the only time. Now, let's get you cleaned up."

We stare into each other's eyes for a beat, neither of us making an attempt to go get cleaned up. Without thinking, I run my hand through his curls, smiling at the way they feel moving through my fingers—so silky soft.

Jaylen smiles as his eyes search my face. He leans on his left elbow and uses his right hand to caress my cheek, the touch featherlight. A cold chill spreads across my feverish body. God, I needed that after the intensity of what just happened.

I let this man fucking feed on me. He drank my blood straight from the source. While it was painful at first, it soon morphed into the most pleasurable thing I have ever felt in my life. It was as if a million fireworks were exploding across every inch of my body. That might sound weird, but it's true.

It has me wanting to do it again, but maybe not tonight. I don't know how much blood Jaylen took, but I'm spent. All I want to do is lie here in his arms as his sandalwood scent wafts over me like a blanket. I feel safe in his arms, especially after what just happened.

I trust this man with my life, and it's the most scary realization because I never in a million years thought this would be happening with my brother's best friend, no less.

"What are you thinking about?" Jaylen asks softly. "I can see the wheels turning behind those pretty eyes of yours."

"You," I admit softly, unable to look away from the way his irises slowly switch from red to baby blue. It should be studied by a scientist. "And me. Us, I guess."

I close my eyes at the feel of his fingers tracing the base of my throat, and ghosting over the two puncture marks I know are in my skin. "We don't have to do this right now, little angel. I just want to hold you."

My heart melts at his words. He wants to... hold me? Damn, who am I to decline his offer? As much as I want to have this conversation with him, maybe it should be saved for a time when we're not naked in a vampire feeding room above a club.

"Okay," I whisper.

Jaylen maneuvers us so that we're under the black sheet with me pulled flush against his frigid chest and his strong arm wrapped firmly around my waist. I can feel his hard cock pressing into the curve of my ass, but he makes no move to act on it. His fingers brush through the strands of my hair, sending a chill down my spine. I'm sure the act had no thought behind it besides muscle memory, but this feels so intimate that my heart is ready to explode.

Us being here together like this shouldn't be happening.

But why does it feel so fucking right? I shouldn't want Jaylen to hold me so tight like he's afraid I'm going to slip from his grasp and disappear in the wind. I shouldn't enjoy the way the tips of his fingers as they trace over my hips. I shouldn't want him as badly as I do, yet here I am.

This feels right, so who am I to stop it?

I nuzzle into his arm and trace the curves of the ink etched into his skin. As his fingers caress my body, admiring it, I follow the lines of the designs, tracing them as if I were the one to permanently put the ink into his skin. Every design is purposely placed on his arm, allowing not a single inch of untouched skin.

I admire the detailed dragon on his forearm, tracing over its wings. "What's the story behind this tattoo?"

Jaylen's roaming hand stills on my hips, his fingers digging into the skin. I feel his cool breath on my neck as he says, "How much time do you have?"

I smile. "All fucking night."

The chuckle that rumbles in his chest is infectious, vibrating through his entire body. I want to make him laugh like that every chance I get.

"God, I fucking lo—" He stops abruptly and clears his throat. "If you have all night, then so do I, my sweet angel."

I chew on my bottom lip, biting back a smile. "All right, let's hear the story. And don't leave anything out."

CHAPTER 30

JAYLEN

"What are your plans for the evening?" Miles asks Ethan and me as he swings an overnight bag over his shoulder, heading toward the front door. "Anything interesting?"

Ethan and I turn to share a look from our spots on the couch in the living room before he turns to Miles. "Nothing. We're just going to watch a movie and order a pizza."

"You off to see Cindy?" I ask.

He nods, not looking in my direction. "Sure am."

Ever since the car accident, things have been... a little frosty between me and Miles, to say the least. Whenever we're in the same room together, whether it be the apartment or the locker room, he won't say more than a few words to me. I tried to keep it light between us for the first week, but I just grew tired of him ignoring me for what happened with Evie.

Yes, I'm at fault for what happened since I was the one driving, and it's been fucking eating me alive ever since, but it was an accident. That fucking asshole in the car came out of nowhere and ran the red light, clearly not having seen my bike. The dickhead in the car is so lucky I didn't have the chance to chase him down and snap his neck for what he did to my little angel.

After seeing her over the weekend, I all but confirmed that she is something special. Not only can't I compel her, but her blood... it doesn't taste *human*. I've drunk a lot of human blood, and have dappled in animal blood, so I can tell the difference. But hers... yeah, something is different about it, but I can't quite put my finger on why.

In saying that, she is fucking delicious. I knew she would be. After my transition when I was eighteen, I had been longing to get a taste of her sweet blood. I could smell it pumping through her veins, teasing me whenever she was around. But now that I've finally tasted her after all these years, I'm an addict. All I want is her fucking blood, but I have to settle for a random donor because I'm running low on my supple.

If I could bottle Evie's blood up and drink it every day, I would be the happiest fucking man on the planet.

"Have fun," Ethan says cheerfully, waving goodbye to Miles. "See you in the morning, yeah? We have that big game tomorrow night, so Coach wants us at the stadium early for a last-minute training session."

"Of course," Miles says as he collects his keys from the tray beside the door. "I'll be there." He silently leaves, not bothering to look at me.

Ethan blows out a long breath and turns to look at me. "Fuck me that was icy. I didn't believe you when you said there had been a lot of tension after the accident."

I sigh and run a hand through my hair, tugging on the roots. "Yeah, but he'll get over it."

"Will he? He still seems pissed."

"Yeah, I got that." I shake my head. "He better not let his feelings affect the game tomorrow. We can't fuck this up." It's the first game of the semi-finals, and with our team at the top of the leaderboard, we need to be at the top of our game to ensure our spot in the final.

"Just talk to him about it," Ethan suggests with a shrug.

"I tried that. It didn't work." With a huff, I stand to my feet. I don't want to talk about Miles and his inability to let this shit go. "Let's go. We need to get this over and done with."

He stands to his feet and stretches his arms above his head. "You're right. I'm fucking starving, too."

"You and me both."

I follow him to the front door and we walk into the hallway. The walk down the staircase to the foyer is silent, but the silence doesn't last long when we step out onto the street, taking our usual route to the hospital.

"So, what's new with you?"

I glance at Ethan as he falls into step beside me, shoving his hands into his pockets. His dirty blonde hair is already tousled by the slight fall breeze.

"Save the small chat," I say and look straight ahead. "You already know what's been going on."

"You're right, I do. You've been a busy man," he comments. "Okay, well, if you don't want to talk about how your friendship with Miles is in turmoil for going after his sister, shall we discuss the murders in Pullman?"

I raise a brow at him. "Again? We've already talked about this. We have no way of finding out who is behind this unless we become a target ourselves. And last time I checked, I don't want to be staked, drained of my blood, and left in a park for someone to find."

"Me neither, but aren't you the least bit curious as to who is committing the killings? I mean, what's to say they won't come after us, too?"

I sigh. There is no way to know whether we're safe or not.

Whoever is tracking down these vampires and killing them must be part of some vampire hunting guild that is being given names of vampires in the area. How they come to know that information is beyond me.

I'd like to think I live a discreet life when it comes to my lifestyle. I don't feed on humans—unless they're willing, of course. That's what the *Black Rose* is for—and I only take donor blood from the hospital when it's necessary. I'm not like other vampires who enjoy the thrill of chasing down a human and indulging to the point they almost kill them. I'd much rather get my fix from blood bags or at *Black Rose*. Using the rooms upstairs at the bar means I get to fuck and feed at the same time. The blood bags are the second option.

Ever since Evie learned my secret and my need to protect and be around her all the time has grown stronger, I haven't thought about sleeping with other women and feeding off them. All I want is my girl and her sweet but strange blood. It's not something I ever thought would happen.

I've known Evie for a long time, and for a while, I only saw her as Miles's little sister who would follow us around whenever we would hang out, almost like a shadow. But now... I'm obsessed with her. I found myself thinking about her whenever I was alone or thirsty. I want to consume her and claim her to make sure everyone knows she is fucking mine. It's an intense feeling I have never felt for a woman before, and while it should scare me, I instead embraced it. Told myself that no matter what, I needed to protect my girl from anyone or anything that might bring her harm.

The only thing standing in my way of fulfilling the promise I made is her fucking brother.

"We'll be fine," I tell Ethan after a moment of silence. "If we continue to keep a low profile, then we should be fine, okay?"

He exhales sharply and nods. "Yeah, you're right. How

could this hunter possibly know about us unless we somehow reveal ourselves? It would be stupid of us to risk something like that."

The hospital comes into view thanks to our quicker than normal pace. It's been a few weeks since we were last here, so I hope they haven't added more security guards around the perimeter to prevent break-ins. That would be a problem for us, but it's nothing our compelling skills can't handle. We're no strangers to it.

"How's your girl?" I ask as we walk into the forest behind the hospital. Ethan is always asking about my life, making me feel bad that I don't ask enough about what's going on with him.

He walks ahead of me as we form a single file through the thick brush. "She's good. We're going out for drinks after the game tomorrow night. She hasn't told her friends about me yet since we wanted to keep it on the down low, but I think she's ready to let me meet them."

"That's exciting," I say and look to my left to survey the perimeter for security guards. We got lucky tonight because there is not a soul around. My ears pick up voices from inside the building, but thankfully, there is no one walking around outside.

"I really like her," Ethan says and stops by a thick tree to glance over at the window to the supply room. "She's the *one*, man. I just know it."

I clap him on the back. "I'm happy for you."

Ethan turns to smile at me. "*The* Jaylen Black is happy for me? Woah, my life is complete now."

I roll my eyes. "Oh, shut up. We have a job to do, so get your head in the game."

He salutes me. "Aye, aye, captain."

We surveillance the area for a couple of minutes to make

sure no security guards were going to pop up randomly and catch us in the act. Once we're satisfied we're alone, Ethan props the window up, pulls off the flyscreen, slides in through the open hole, and I follow. We've done this so many times I could do this with my eyes closed.

While I stand guard at the door, Ethan moves around the dark room and collects blood bags, putting them into the foldable bag he brought with him. Our eyes allow us to adjust to the dark room easily, almost as if we have night vision. It means we can stay hidden in the room without the need to flip the light switch on.

Checking my watch, I see we've been in here for three minutes, so we need to get a move on. I prefer to not be in here for longer than five minutes in case a nurse needs to stop by for whatever reason. It's a risk I'm not willing to take, but thankfully, I haven't heard anyone walk by the room since we arrived.

"Are you nearly done?" I ask and look across the room to where Ethan is raiding the fridge where the blood bags are stored.

"Almost," he says, sliding two blood bags into the already-filled bag. "Okay, now we're good."

"Let's get out of here."

Standing by the open window, I keep watching the door while Ethan slips out. Once he tells me the coast is clear, I climb out the window and land on the ground with a small thud.

"Another successful raid," Ethan cheers as I put in the flyscreen and close the window quietly behind me. "This is becoming almost too easy."

I turn to face him. "I wouldn't get comfortable with—"

My words are caught in my throat when my eyes meet the black ones standing behind Ethan, a gun drawn to the back of his head. Ethan's eyes are filled with panic, sensing the stranger behind him. His body is rigid as he stares straight ahead at me, his eyes screaming, 'What the fuck do we do?

Fuck.

The person behind him is wearing a black mask with white cracks in it that cover their entire head with only holes cut out for their eyes. It looks sturdy, possibly made out of a tough material that is hard to break. They are dressed in black pants and a black long-sleeved shirt with leather gloves adorning their hands, not allowing me to get a sense of who they are. I can't even smell their scent, almost as if it has been masked in some way.

Who the fuck is this person?

"Put your hands up," the person demands, their voice distorted as if a special effect has been placed over it. The hesitation in their voice didn't go unnoticed by me. "Now."

"Okay," I say, doing as they say. "What do you want?"

The person is dressed like a robber, but why would they be here to rob the hospital?

"You," they say, and then point to Ethan. "Both of you. You're an abomination to society."

My stomach plummets to my toes as their words wash over me. Oh, *fuck.* Have we just encountered the hunter running around Pullman killing vampires? It would make sense as to why they are here cornering us after stealing blood bags. But how did they find out about us? We have been careful to mask our tracks and only take what we need.

How did they find us?

"You don't have to do this," Ethan says, his eyes never leaving mine. "We're good, I promise. We don't hurt humans."

"That doesn't matter," the stranger spits, their distorted voice filled with hate—for us. "Your kind shouldn't exist in this world. You bring nothing but pain and suffering to the innocent people you choose to hurt."

"We don't hurt anyone," I repeat Ethan's words. The person is still pointing the gun at Ethan, but I can feel their cold, dark eyes on me. They almost feel... soulless. "We were born humans before we transitioned. We still have our humanity and care for humans, not wanting to bring them any harm."

My eyes meet Ethan's and I try to communicate our next course of action to him through my eyes. He nods, understanding my silent words. We have known each other long enough to be able to communicate through our eyes. And thankfully, it's going to come in clutch with this situation.

The thought of dying had never occurred to me until this moment, staring into the void-like eyes across from me in the dead of night with nothing but the moonlight to illuminate part of their mask. It's a menacing sight, to say the least.

Is this what those vampires had to see before they met their fate?

I'm sure as hell not going to go down without a fight, so this person better be fucking ready.

"All your kind does is harm humans!" the masked person shouts, jabbing the barrel of the gun harder into Ethan's skull. "That is why I'm here to put an end to you, so you can no longer hurt another person. You will meet the same fate as all the others, and there is nothing you can—"

"Now!" I shout, rushing forward at the same time Ethan throws his head back, slamming the gun into the face of the masked person.

They cry out as Ethan spins on his heels and the two of us tackle the stranger to the ground, our super speed and strength working in our favor to subdue them. The person thrashes in our grip with me holding down one arm while

Ethan holds the other, our supply tossed to the side, forgotten about.

The masked person tries to use their legs to kick at us from behind, but it does nothing to help them get out of our grip. I turn to look at the gun lying beside us and reach for it, bringing the barrel up to rest on their forehead. They instantly stop moving as their dark eyes find mine, their breathing hard.

"If you don't want your neck snapped in half and left for dead, you'll answer my question," I warn, pressing the gun harder against the mask.

The masked person stares at me for a heartbeat as if deciding whether to fight back or give in and do what I say if they want to live. I have every intention of destroying this motherfucker, but they don't need to know that. All they need to know is I want my questions answered first.

When they don't say anything, I continue. "How did you discover us?"

"It's obvious when a hospital reports blood missing from their supply," they answer but don't supply any further details.

Okay, so it seems the hospital did know that blood was going missing, but why is the hunter only confronting us now after the operation has been going on for a couple of years? Unless our schedules never managed to sync up and tonight just happened to be when we both decided to be at the hospital.

I wonder how long they have been trying to track us down?

"Why didn't you kill us right away?" I demand. "You had the opportunity."

"I needed to see what I was dealing with first."

I grind my teeth together and look at Ethan. He's wearing a worried expression on his face as he looks between me and the masked person.

"What are we going to do?" he asks quietly.

I know what we need to do, but I want to get as much information from this fucker as I can about who they are and who they work for. I can't just kill them before I know what *I'm* dealing with first. It would be easier to kill them and get this over and done with, but I need to tread carefully and play my cards right first.

"Give me a second," I say to Ethan before turning my attention back to the masked person. Their eyes are still on me, unblinking as they stare up. "Who do you work for?" When they don't answer, I press the gun against the mask harder, the splintering of material sounding in my ears. "Who the fuck do you work for!"

"You should probably keep your voice down—"

A flash of light moves across the masked person's face. I snap my head to the side to see a security guard rushing toward us with their flashlight focused on us like a huge fucking spotlight.

"Hey! What is going on over here?"

Ethan grabs me by the shoulders and pulls me off the masked person, who is quick to get to their feet. They take one last look at me before they turn and sprint into the treeline, disappearing out of sight.

Motherfucker!

"Let's go!" Ethan shouts as he scoops up the bag of blood and drags me in the opposite direction of the security guard, who is still chasing after us, telling us to stop running. "Jay, come on!"

With a grunt, I shove the masked person's gun into the waistband of my jeans and take off running after Ethan, releasing my super speed enough to get me out of harm's way and out of sight of the security guard. I follow Ethan into the treeline until we come to a stop behind a large tree, hidden in the cover of darkness.

With my heart in my throat, I press my back against the trunk of the oak tree and stare up at the foliage, wondering what the fuck just happened.

"Holy fuck, man," Ethan breathes, shaking his head. "We just had an encounter with the fucking vampire hunter committing the murders. I don't know how we managed to walk away from that in one piece. That was insane!"

"Insane indeed," I say, remembering their dark eyes boring into my skin. Who the fuck was that? As if remembering the lethal weapon in the waistband of my pants, I make a mental note to destroy it before we return to the apartment. "But just because we walked away now doesn't mean we're safe, Ethan. If anything, we have a massive fucking target on our backs now.

CHAPTER 31
EVIE

Today is the first game of the semi-finals and the girls and I are going all out. We are wearing matching Raiders jerseys, our hair down and straight, and the team colors striped across our cheeks with face paint. With this game being as important as it is for the team, I want to show my support for Miles and Jaylen. The girls were more than happy to jump in on the matching outfits.

"Cheers to the Raiders," Jaycee says as she holds a shot glass in the air. We are standing around the kitchen island ready to go to the stadium, but Candie insists that we take a shot of Tequilla before we leave. Something about it being for good luck, but I think she just wanted a cheeky pre-game shot.

"Cheers," we say in unison and tap our glasses together before taking the shot.

The clear liquid burns on its way down my throat, but I welcome it. Besides the night at *Black Rose* with Jaylen a week ago, this will be my first proper outing since the accident. I'm looking forward to spending time with my friends as we watch a game of soccer. Fall is my favorite season, so I'm finally going to be able to enjoy the cool, fresh air without feeling guilty for sneaking out.

This past week I've been focusing on school and making sure I'm up to date on all tutorial work and any assignments I have coming up. I wanted to make sure I had nothing else to worry about other than this game.

Thankfully, none of my friends noticed when I left the other night. Not even Rylee, but that was because she had fallen asleep on the couch in the living room watching a movie with some of the other girls in the house. It worked out in my favor, so I'm not complaining.

"Okay, let's go," Rylee says and gestures for us to exit the kitchen. "The taxi is already waiting for us."

On the way out of the house, I grab my side bag and light cardigan from the back of the couch. I catch Amara's eye from her spot on the far side of the couch, her nose bandaged up after I broke it. She doesn't hold eye contact for long before she turns her attention to the television. The shudder that wracks her body doesn't go unnoticed by me, giving me more pleasure than I thought it would.

Now she knows not to fuck with me.

The four of us walk outside to the waiting taxi and pile in. Rylee and Candie slide in bedside me while Jaycee takes the front seat. We must look odd to the taxi driver, an older man with graying hair, as he pulls out of the driveway, or maybe he's not shocked at all since I'm sure as a driver he would get this a lot around campus.

My phone buzzes in my pocket. It's a message from Jaylen. As the girls engaged in a conversation about classes, I read his message.

Jaylen: Are you coming to the game tonight?

I smile as I hit send, my fingers instinctually touching my neck where Jaylen had sunk his teeth into me, feeding on my blood. It was the most erotic moment I had ever experienced. Who knew a vampire sucking your blood and fucking you at the same time could bring so much ecstasy? Thankfully, the bite wounds healed quickly, so the girls didn't notice them.

After that night together, something inside me flipped, pulling me closer to Jaylen now more than ever. It's almost as if my body has given up on fighting this string pulling us together. I fought it for so long that now I'm tired of fighting. Jaylen has proven to me that he's not going to break my heart. In fact, he's willing to go to the ends of the earth for me, and that means something to me. More than I thought it would from him.

I don't want to get ahead of myself, but I'm willing to see where fate wants to take us.

"So, Jay, what are your plans for the night?" Rylee asks, breaking through my thoughts. "I know Candie, Ev, and I are heading home after the game, but what are you doing?"

"Um, I'm going out for drinks afterward," Jaycee says from the front seat.

Candie squeals and claps her hands together excitedly. "Is it with your mystery man?"

I lean over Rylee to look at Jaycee through the side mirror, her cheeks a hot pink.

"Maybe, but I don't kiss and tell."

I playfully roll my eyes. "Are we ever going to meet him?"

Jaycee turns in her seat to face us, a smile touching her plump lips. "Soon. I promise."

"That's good enough for me," Rylee says with a smile. "As long as you're happy."

Jaycee grins, her cheeks somehow growing pinker. "I am."

"Oh, we're here!" Candie calls from beside me, her eyes focused on the stadium as it comes into view.

Our driver drops us around the other side of the stadium where there is less traffic, and the four of us walk to the front gates. Once inside, it's mine and Rylee's turn to grab the drinks and food while Jaycee and Candie find our seats.

Rylee turns to me in line. "How are you doing?"

"I'm fine," I answer with a shrug.

She gives me a deadpan look. "No, how are you *really* doing? Especially after the accident."

"Oh," I say, and chew on my bottom lip. "I'm fine. It was an accident, and neither of us got hurt."

"I'm sure it must've been hard for you," Rylee says as we take a step forward. "And I'm sorry for putting you on house arrest. Miles was very... convincing about it."

"It's not your fault. I know how he can be, but I appreciate you all looking after me."

It hasn't been an easy couple of weeks, to say the least, but I'm happy and healthy, which is all I can ever ask for. I'm just hoping that Miles will loosen the reign he has around me now that my wounds have healed and the girls are no longer keeping an eye on me.

I hate that I've created tension between my brother and Jaylen, but I'm also not responsible for Miles's feelings. If he has a problem with me getting close to Jaylen, then that's on him. I know what I'm doing and am more than capable of handling a guy like Jaylen. If our relationship keeps progressing the way it is, Miles is just going to have to get used to it. I'm not going to be his little sister forever.

"But still, I'm sorry about what happened," Rylee says as

she pats my shoulder gently. We're now two people away from the front of the line. "It seems things are going well with Jaylen."

I smile. "It's getting there. I enjoy spending time with him, so only time will tell what's going to happen next."

"Just be careful, okay?" she warns, throwing a knowing look my way. "I don't want to see you get hurt."

I wave off her concern. "I always am, Ry."

If she had said that to me a couple of months ago, I would be nodding my head and telling her that I promised to be careful because I was convinced that Jaylen would shatter my heart into tiny pieces if given the chance.

But not now. It's clear that Jaylen wants to cherish my heart and protect it with his life. And I'm more than willing to let him do so.

"Next!" the cashier calls out, and the two of us step forward to place our order.

Minutes later with our food and drinks in hand, we head down to our usual section across from the technical area, ready to watch the first semi-final game of the season.

JAYLEN

I smile at Evie's text before slipping my phone into my gym bag. As much as I would love to continue texting her, I need to get ready for the game. After what happened last night at the hospital, I'm a little wary about going out on the field because the hunter knows who Ethan and I are now, so we're going to be like sitting ducks in a sold-out stadium. The motherfucker could be hiding in plain sight and we wouldn't know it.

All I can hope is that the hunter isn't able to gain access to the stadium to hurt us. But it doesn't mean we're safe after the fact. From this point on, we're fucked. All it takes is a stake through the heart—for either of us—and we're toast. Literally. I have a good thing going for me with Evie, so I don't want to jeopardize that.

I know most vampires tend to move around a lot as they get older and it becomes obvious that they aren't aging like the rest of the people their age, or they're found out by a hunter and need to flee to save their life. Right now, I don't want to flee. I don't want to run away. I want to kill the fucker hunting and killing the vampires in Pullman. But I can't do it alone. I'm going to need Ethan's help, so we need to stick together and not get caught alone.

I sigh and run a hand down my face. The locker room is filled with chatter and music blasting from a speaker. Preston insisted on playing a hype-up playlist before the game to get everyone in the mood. But all it's doing is irritating my sensitive hearing. I can't focus on one thing at a time because of all the noise ringing in my ears.

"Has anyone fucking seen Roman?" Coach calls across the locker room, anger dripping from his words. "It seems he doesn't know how to answer his fucking phone when we need him! I haven't heard from him in weeks, so if anyone knows anything about his whereabouts, you tell me right away."

A hand on my shoulder makes me snap my head up. Ethan is standing over me with his jersey on and his hair styled back neatly with gel. He has a nervous look in his eye, one I'm too familiar with. We're both shaken after last night.

"You okay?" he asks as he sits down on the bench next to me, placing his cleats between us.

I nod. "As okay as I can be knowing a crazy fucker is hunting us down."

Ethan sucks in a sharp breath. "Yeah, that sounds about right." He looks over his shoulder before leaning in closer and lowering his voice. "I see things are still tense between you and Miles."

I look over my shoulder at where Miles is sitting across the room with Preston by his side. He's glaring in my direction, but it's nothing new since the accident. He has been giving me the cold shoulder for weeks, but this morning when he showed up for practice he seemed extra cold. Like hell had frozen over him or something.

"I don't know what is up his ass." I stand to my feet and grab my jersey out of my locker, sliding it over my head. I can't be fucked dealing with Miles when there are more pressing matters to deal with. Like fending off a fucking vampire hunter. Fastening the captain's armband around my right bicep, I turn to Ethan. "You need to be careful out there tonight, okay? We need to be vigilant for any threat because we don't know the identity of the hunter, so they could be hiding in plain sight waiting for their moment to strike."

Ethan inhales slowly and stands to his feet. "Gotcha. I've got your back and you have mine."

I half-heartedly smile and pat him on the shoulder. "All we have to do is get through the game and you can go have a drink with your girl."

That puts a smile on his face.

"You're right. We've got this. If we stick together, the hunter can't take us both down."

I nod. "You're exactly right."

"Okay, Raiders, it's show time!" Coach calls from his spot at the front of the room, and gestures for us to follow him out to the tunnel. The cheering from the crowd intensifies as the

MC for the night announces the game is minutes away from starting. "Let's go out there and put on a great game for the fans."

"Yes, Coach!" the team says in unison as they make their way out of the locker room.

I linger behind to tie the laces on my cleats before following the team out. As I pass by the single-line formation to join Coach at the front, I can feel Mile's eyes searing a hole into the side of my head. The hole gets bigger when I stand in front of him. I can feel him watching me like a hawk.

What crawled up his ass and died? I understand he's pissed about the accident, but he has to fucking get over it eventually. We're best friends for fuck's sake.

A moment later, we run out onto the field, and the crowd erupts in loud cheers and hollering. The atmosphere makes me smile. This is why I love soccer. This is why I enjoy coming out here each week to put on a show. It's all for the fans. The lights, the cheers, the smell of the fresh grass, and the adrenaline give me a high I've never felt before.

Both teams form a line and face the crowd, ready to sing the national anthem. My eyes scan the crowd until I find a pair of amazonite eyes staring back at me. Evie smiles and waves at me. Her sleek two-toned hair is straight over her shoulders, and she looks fucking stunning wearing a Raiders jersey with the number twelve on it, something I haven't seen on her yet. I might need to take that off her later tonight and remind her why she should be wearing my number—fifteen.

Before I can return her smile, her face falls as her eyes move to the right of me. Frowning, I lean forward to see Miles two players down from me looking between Evie and me, a murderous gleam in his eyes and his jaw clenched so hard I can hear his teeth grating together.

Oh, *fuck*.

CHAPTER 32
EVIE

I swallow hard at the sight of Miles glaring at Jaylen and me. His jaw is clenched, and his eyes are hard, the normal green color now dark, almost black. Jaylen must see the look he's giving us because he nods in my direction reassuringly as if to say, 'It's okay'.

Damn, I didn't know Miles is *still* pissed about the accident. Or is he angry for another reason? Oh, my God. He better not have found out that I snuck out last weekend to see Jaylen.

"What's up with Miles?" Rylee leans over to whisper in my ear.

I shrug and look away from the field to meet her eyes just as the national anthem finishes. "I guess he's still pissed about the accident. It's been ages since it happened, so I thought he would've gotten over it by now." I don't mention the potential for him to be angry over me sneaking out when I was supposed to be on house arrest because she too doesn't know.

"We both know how protective Miles is over you," she says as we sit down. "Have you talked to him much since you got out of the hospital?"

"Yeah, a little. He sends me a text message every day to

check in, but I haven't seen him in person for over a week. We haven't had a chance to properly talk about what happened."

All Miles knows about that night is that Jaylen offered me a ride home, and that was it. As far as he knows, it was an innocent act that he overreacted about. So, why is he shooting daggers at Jaylen from across the pitch as they move into their positions?

"Well, just talk to him after the game if you get the chance," Rylee suggests as the whistle blows for the start of the game, an eruption of cheers bellowing around us.

The Jets get to kick off, so I watch as Jaylen runs forward to try and steal the ball from the opposing team. Despite the tension between him and my brother, he plays as strongly and efficiently as he normally does every single game. Somehow, Preston gets the ball off a Jets player and passes it to Ethan who runs with it down the field to where Jaylen is standing in front of the goalkeeper, ready to strike if he gets the chance.

Unfortunately, the ball is stolen from him, now moving down to the other side. My eyes find Miles on the field, and I notice that he's watching Jaylen when he should be keeping an eye on where the ball is since he is an attacking midfielder. He's standing with his hands on his hips, not moving a single muscle. I can't tell if Jaylen can feel his eyes on him, but if he does, he doesn't show it.

As the first half continues, I can feel the intensity radiating off Miles in waves from where I'm sat in the crowd. I don't know why he's so focused on shooting Jaylen daggers when he needs to focus on getting the ball to him. He has already missed a few opportunities to score because he wasn't paying attention to where the ball was. They would've been on target thanks to Jaylen.

The whistle blows, signaling the end of the first half. Watching as the Raiders and Jets rush off the pitch to take a break, I exhale a sharp breath and slump in my seat. The score is 2-1 with the Jets in the lead. This is unheard of for the Raiders. They have never been down on points in the first half, so the fact that they are must be putting a lot of pressure on them.

Jaycee leans past Rylee and Candie to look at me. "Well... that was something."

"Yeah, what the hell was that all about?" Candie comments, looking between us. "Miles seems distracted."

"He better get over whatever is bothering him if he wants to help the Raiders get back on top." I sigh and run a hand through the ends of my hair. "I'll talk to him after the game to see if he's okay. Maybe he's having problems with Cindy and he's taking it out on Jaylen because he is already angry about the accident." Honestly, who knows what the fuck is going on with him, but it's putting the Raiders in jeopardy. If they lose, they're out of the finals.

I don't miss the way Candie smiles at the possible idea that Miles might be having girl trouble.

My attention is drawn to my phone vibrating in my pocket. When I pull it out, I see a message from Jaylen.

Jaylen: I'm going to talk to Miles after the game. It's clear he's still pissed about what happened.

Evie: Maybe I'll talk to him first since I haven't had a chance to discuss the situation yet.

Sorry for putting you in the middle of this.

> Jaylen: It's not your fault, little angel. I chose this. I chose you. I can handle your brother.

My heart swells reading his words. It still hasn't sunk in whatever is happening with Jaylen. I just want to take one step at a time and enjoy each moment because who knows what could happen tomorrow or the next day. I can't take anything for granted.

But I don't know what to do about my brother. I'm at a crossroads. I know I need to go comfort him and see if everything is okay, but deep down, I know he'll just continue to be his overprotective self until he feels that there is one hundred percent nothing going on between Jaylen and me. I hate that I have to keep something like this from him because all I want is for him to be happy for me, but he's not going to be happy when he learns that I've been hooking up with his best friend.

I'm going to keep it from him as long as I can because if he's acting like this over something so innocent as accepting a ride home, then he's going to lose his fucking mind when he learns the full truth. In a perfect world, I would make sure that doesn't happen, but this is real life, and reality likes to kick me in the ass whenever it can.

When I don't text back right away, another text from Jaylen pops up.

> Jaylen: Can I see you after the game?

> Evie: Where should we meet?

"Ev, do you want another drink?" Jaycee asks as she and Candie stand from their seats.

I nod but don't look up at them. "Yes, please."

They leave to grab more drinks, and Rylee joins them to go to the bathroom.

> Jaylen: By the exit to the hallway I sent you to with my cum dripping down your thighs.

My eyes widen at his words, and I slam the screen against my chest, thankful the girls aren't sitting beside me. If they had looked over my shoulder and read that... my cheeks burn feverishly as I type a response.

> Evie: Okay, enough with the dirty mouth. I'll see you after the game. Good luck!

As I slip my phone into my side bag, my skin is flushed despite the cool temperature. The sun has fully set, bringing out the twinkling stars overhead. It's a perfect fall night for a tense game of soccer. I can only hope that Miles pulls his head in before he steps back out onto the pitch.

Moments later, the girls return with more drinks just as the teams run out onto the pitch. We cheer along with the rest of the crowd as the whistle blows for the start of the second half.

The Raiders need to get their shit together if they want to make the finals. I would be sad if they were to fall now after the great season they've had.

I don't know what happened in the locker room during the halftime break, but Miles is no longer glaring at Jaylen and is actually keeping an eye on the ball, allowing Jaylen to score a goal with his assist not even five minutes into the second half.

A loud cheer escapes my lips as I jump up and down with the girls. The Raiders are making a comeback, thank God. With the score at 2-2, they need to get ahead to avoid extra time or even a penalty shoot-out if there is no outcome from that.

As the seconds and minutes tick by, I grab Rylee's hand, holding onto it for dear life. There are two minutes left in extra time and the score is still tied. I can tell both teams are frantic to get a goal to win the game. Jaylen hasn't been able to get another goal because the keeper has saved them or it wasn't quite on target. The same goes for the Jets.

It's been a tense half, to say the least.

When Preston gets the ball and kicks it down to Ethan, the crowd gets to their feet in anticipation of what is going to happen next. I hold my breath when Ethan passes the ball to Miles and he makes a run for the goal. Side-stepping a Jets player, he kicks the ball to Jaylen who headbutts the ball with such force that it glides past the keeper's hand to sink into the back of the net in the top left corner.

A chorus of cheers sounds through the stadium as the scorecard changes to 3-2 and the referee blows the whistle to end the game. I turn to Rylee and we squeal at the same time, jumping into each other's arms to celebrate the nail-biting win.

All the Raiders players circle Jaylen on the pitch and congratulate him on the goal. A warm smile spreads across his face as he hugs his team members. It's a heartwarming scene to witness. My eyes widen when I see Miles pat Jaylen on the shoulder and offer him a smile, which Jaylen returns.

Maybe they managed to sort out their differences in the locker room, which will make my conversation with Miles easier later on.

But first, I have to go see Jaylen. Maybe I'll give him a special surprise to congratulate him on the win.

"I'm going to see my brother before we leave," I tell the girls—a white lie—as we leave our seats and walk into the foyer. The throng of fans moves past us so quickly that it feels like they're moving at twice the speed.

"Where should we meet you then? Jay is going for drinks with her boy toy, so instead of going home, we should also hit the town. I fancy a fruity cocktail after that win," Candie says with a smile.

"That sounds great," I say and return her smile. I don't know how long I'm going to be with Jaylen and Miles, so I don't want the girls to be waiting for me for too long. "You decide on a bar and I'll meet you there."

They nod and hug me goodbye before heading toward the exit. After a moment of standing in the middle of the foyer, I make my way to a different exit that is closer to the back door that leads from the locker room out to the staff parking lot. I can still remember how fast my heart was racing when I left through that exit after Jaylen gave me his shirt to wear with no panties. The adrenaline coursing through my veins was exhilarating. Almost being caught by the team had my heart racing nervously, but the adrenaline outweighed it.

I had called a taxi to take me home and the driver was a little confused to see me slide into the back seat with dripping wet hair in an oversized T-shirt. If only he knew the real reason. When I got home, the girls weren't home since they stayed for the second half, so I made sure to clean up and put on my pajamas before they returned. I texted them to say that I had gone home because I wasn't feeling well—again. Yes, I know. It's a lame excuse, but one that worked in my favor.

And now weeks later I'm standing in the same spot I waited for the taxi driver to arrive, now waiting for Jaylen to walk through the door. I pace impatiently, eager to see him. He hasn't sent a text to let me know what he's doing, but it's been long enough since the end of the game that he should be here soon.

My head snaps up at the sound of the creaky metal door swinging open. Jaylen steps out in his uniform with his hair a sweaty mess, the curls hanging loosely around his face. Even covered in grass and sweat, he still looks delicious enough to devour.

Control yourself, Evie, my subconscious reminds me.

When Jaylen's baby-blue eyes meet mine, he smiles. "My little angel."

The words make my heart stutter in my chest.

I take a step forward, and so does he. "Good game. That winning goal was a sight to see."

He smiles and runs a hand through his messy hair. "I was a little worried for a moment there. I thought we were fucked."

"But as usual, you managed to bring the Raiders another victory. Maybe... you deserve a treat."

Jaylen's eyes widen at my words before a smirk forms on his lips. His eyes darken as he takes another step forward, his hands lifting to rest on my hips. He pulls my body flush against his chest, and a squeak of surprise slips past my lips.

"Well, if my girl is offering, who am I to say no?"

I don't know what it is about Jaylen, but whenever I'm around him, I turn into a different person. The primal need to rip his clothes off and devour him is strong, consuming every rational part of my brain. But I also want to explore every inch of his skin and kiss him tenderly. With the way he's looking at me, his eyes filled with lust and specks of red taking over his irises, I know he feels the same.

My hands drag down the front of his stained jersey feather-light, wanting to tease him. If he wants a treat, he's going to have to work for it. I can feel how hard he is for me already. My core tightens as my pussy throbs.

"Teasing me, are you?" he groans and drags his lip ring into his mouth. "You're going to be the death of me."

The sound of a gun cocking in the still air forces my eyes wide. Jaylen's face mirrors mine.

"No, I'm going to be the one to cause your death, bloodsucker."

With my heart in my throat, I look past Jaylen to see Miles standing behind him with a gun pointed directly at the back of his head. His eyes are hard and tense, no longer the vibrant green I'm used to seeing. Instead, they're almost... black. And soulless. He's dressed head to toe in black clothing as if he hadn't just been playing a game of soccer less than thirty minutes ago.

"Miles?" My voice is shaky. I'm finding it hard to comprehend what I'm looking at right now. Why the fuck is he holding a gun to Jaylen's head? And did he call him a bloodsucker?

"Get away from him, Evie," Miles demands, not looking at me. "He's dangerous."

"So, it was you," Jaylen says slowly, licking his lips. He's staring past the top of my head, our chests still touching as he grips my waist firmly. "You masked your scent well."

"What?" I ask, snapping my head up to look at Jaylen. "What do you mean by that? What happened?"

"I should've taken you out when I had the chance," Miles seethes, ignoring my question. "I'm not going to hesitate this time."

I step away from Jaylen and move around him to get a better look at Miles. I almost don't recognize him with the hateful look in his eyes.

"What the fuck is going on?" I demand, looking between him and the gun in his hand. "Put the gun down, Miles. This is a little dramatic, even for you. You need to move on from the accident. It's done now."

Miles finally flicks his eyes to me and a chill runs down my spine at the darkness swirling within them. "Evie, it's more than that. This motherfucker is a vampire who needs a stake through his heart. And I'm going to be the one to deliver it. Ironic, right?"

I stumble back a step as his words hit my chest. Did... he just say what I think he said? No. It can't be. I *refuse* to believe it.

My brother isn't a killer. The same brother who would patch me up when I would scrap my knees or would help me with my maths homework when I couldn't understand an equation. The same brother who has been by my side through thick and thin after our parent's murder. This isn't the same person I have known my whole life.

Whoever this is... I don't know him. He's a shell of the brother I know.

I swallow the sour taste in my mouth, my eyes locked on his. "Miles..."

"Save your words," he snaps. "You already know the answer."

"Evie, you need to leave. Now," Jaylen says, his eyes staring straight ahead.

Miles's face twists with anger as he slams the gun into the back of Jaylen's head. "You shut your fucking mouth, you abomination. I don't want to hear another word from you."

Jaylen grunts as he holds the back of his head, his face twisted in pain. Miles doesn't let up on his stance, keeping the gun close to Jaylen's head, his finger resting on the trigger.

My mind is moving in slow motion and I'm finding it hard to catch up on what the fuck is happening.

"You're... t-the hunter," I say, my words almost failing me.

Miles scoffs and shakes his head. "You knew about him, didn't you?" When I don't answer, a humorless laugh escapes his lips. "I should've known that the two of you were sneaking around behind my back. I was too busy to see the signs. The motorcycle accident should've been a dead giveaway, but I was too busy chasing the fuckers robbing the hospital of blood bags."

"Why are you doing this?" I plead as tears spring to my eyes. It feels like my whole world is spinning on its axis, ready to freefall at any second. "Why, Miles?"

"To avenge our parents," Miles simply replies, his eyes moving to look at where the gun is pointed at Jaylen. "It's too much for you to understand, Ev."

The connection I had made between all the murder cases is finally starting to make sense, although, some details of the puzzle aren't as clear yet. Like why our parents were targeted and the reason behind their connection to the other cases. A lot of the details don't make sense yet.

"How did you find out they were killed by a hunter?"

Miles frowns, flicking his eyes to meet mine. "They weren't."

"What do you mean?" Now it's my turn to frown.

"They were killed by a filthy bloodsucker," he explains. "After their deaths, a woman came to me after practice one day and told me the truth about what happened. She explained that vampires do exist and that they were the reason my parents were dead. She asked if I wanted to avenge their deaths, and it was a no-brainer."

"So, you became a vampire hunter?" I ask, trying to connect the dots. Surely, there has to be more to the story he isn't sharing with me. Which doesn't fucking surprise me. He's pretty damn good at keeping secrets.

Miles presses the gun against Jaylen's skull again. He hasn't moved an inch, his body rigid as he stares ahead. "I am yet to find the person who killed them, but I will. Until then, I plan to take out every fucking vampire I can."

My mind races through the memories of the past few months, trying to find a time when Miles would've been acting differently or not his usual self. The times when his clothes were a little dirty or he appeared tired spring to mind. Each time I had brushed them off, not paying any mind to it. But now...

"So, Cindy—"

"Is real," Miles interjects, his tone screaming boredom—of this conversation, no doubt. "Well, it's a fake name for a real person—the woman who helped me become who I am. I needed a cover for all the nights I went out hunting."

I wrap my arms around my waist for comfort as I realize my brother had been lying about the truth of our parent's death for years. Why wouldn't he have just told me? Why did he go at this alone? I had every right to know what happened considering I was the one who found them dead.

"Evie, you need to go," Jaylen says quietly, his hands reaching toward me. "I don't want you to get hurt."

Miles growls and holds the gun above his head, ready to bring it down on Jaylen's skull again. "Did you not hear when I said to shut the fu—"

Miles is on the ground in the blink of an eye, and the gun skitters across the ground. My eyes meet Ethan as he kicks the gun further across the parking lot. I lose it in the darkness as he moves to stand beside Jaylen.

"Miles?" Ethan cries, looking at his friend on the ground as he holds his hand over the wound on his head, blood pouring between his fingers. "You're the hunter?"

"I'm just as shocked as you are," Jaylen grunts as he rubs the back of his head. "There are wood bullets in that gun. I couldn't smell it the other night when he had his scent masked."

"So, that was Miles that tried to take us out at the hospital?"

The topic of the hospital reminds me that I am clueless as to what the fuck they're talking about. I know they go there to collect blood bags for their stash, but had Miles confronted them while they were there?

"Jaylen, what is going on?" I demand, walking to stand in front of him.

He places his cold hands on my shoulders, his eyes boring into mine. They're completely red now as I'm sure he's brimming with anger from almost having a bullet put into the back of his head.

"Evie, I wasn't kidding when I said to leave. This could get dangerous and I don't want you to—"

"He's my brother," I remind him sharply, staring into the crimson pools. "What are you going to do with him?"

Jaylen sighs and licks his lips. "I don't know yet."

I place my hands on his hard chest and lean into him. "Please don't hurt him. I'm sure he doesn't—"

"Look out!" Ethan shouts from beside us.

Looking past Jaylen, I see Miles back on his feet and running straight for Jaylen with a large wooden stake in his hand. *Where the fuck did he pull that from?* His eyes are wild and he's screaming as he charges forward. But in the blink of an, my view is blocked before I hear a squelch followed by a loud groan.

"Ethan!"

Jaylen catches Ethan's body as he goes limp, the stake sticking out of his heart. My hands fly to my mouth to catch the cry ready to explode from my chest as I take in the scene. Jaylen lowers Ethan's body to the ground and pulls the stake from his chest, tossing it to the side carelessly.

"Ethan, can you hear me?" Jaylen's voice is filled with panic as he searches his friend's face.

Ethan's already pale skin is now almost translucent, his breathing ragged and sharp. His eyes meet Jaylen's as he struggles to catch his breath. Jaylen covers the gaping wound in his chest, but it's no use. Even I know what a stake to the heart will do to a vampire.

"You're not dying on me," Jaylen shouts as blood smears across his jersey and up his arms as he covers the wound.

Ethan smiles sadly and places his hand on Jaylen's arm. "Tell Jaycee I love her, and I'm sorry." His skin is beginning to turn gray and the color in his eyes fades rapidly. "Ple-ase."

I blanch at his words. Jaycee? So, I was right about them dating, which means she is probably waiting for him to meet her for drinks...

A growl snaps my head up from Ethan and Jaylen to see Miles with the bloody stake in his hand, charging forward with it raised above his head. The wild look is back in his eyes and saliva is seeping from the side of his mouth like he's a wild animal.

I don't know what comes over me. Maybe it's adrenaline or fear, but I know I need to do something. Anything. I just watched Ethan take a fucking stake to the heart. I can't let the same thing happen to the man I—

It's like I'm moving in slow motion as I leap forward to stand in front of Ethan and Jaylen seconds before Miles brings the wooden stake down. A searing pain shoots throughout my chest and my fingers instantly go numb. A strangled gasp slips past my lips as I stare at my brother, my vision blurring at the edges. I have never felt immense pain like this before. It feels as if a fire is burning inside my veins, but my skin feels cold and tense.

"Evie!" Jaylen's voice cries from behind me.

All I can do is stare into my brother's eyes as they soften. He looks from my face to the wooden stake sticking out of my chest before they widen, and he steps away as if he had been electrocuted. Regret crosses his face; his features are no longer wild and hard, but filled with pain and regret.

"Ev," he whispers, his hands shaking as he holds them up in front of his chest. "I-I didn't mean to—" He reaches for me, his hands covered in Ethan's blood dripping from the stake, but the sound of Jaylen's booming voice makes him think otherwise.

"What the fuck have you done?" Jaylen shouts as his arms go around my waist and I fall limp against his chest. He lowers me to the ground, careful to place my head gently on the cement. Each rustle of my body sends another shot of fire scorching across my body. I groan in pain, biting back the tears. I look to my right straight into Miles's tear-filled eyes as he stares down at me, shaking his head slowly. Shock and confusion settle over his features.

"Mi-les," I croak, my voice hoarse and scratchy. My vision begins to blur at the edges like I'm underwater. "Please..."

"I-I'm sorry, Ev" Miles stammers, taking a step back. His hands tremble by his side and for a brief moment, I think he's going to reach out to me when they lift ever so slightly. His eyes are on the stake sticking out of my chest. Oddly enough, I can no longer feel it. My body is numb to everything besides the multiple emotions passing through my brother's emerald eyes. "I didn't—I can't." Without warning, he spins on his heels and sprints across the parking lot, disappearing around the corner as he blends in with the fans leaving the stadium, unaware of what is happening down here.

I want to feel disappointed and be pissed that my brother left me to fucking die in a parking lot with a wooden stake in my chest, but I'm unable to focus on anything other than the searing pain bursting across my body or the blood rushing in my ears.

He had his chance to put his beliefs aside to help his sister, but instead, he chose to run. His flight really took over at that moment, and I hate him for that. If that was truly my brother, he would've done anything to help me.

Whoever that fucking man is... he's not my brother.

"Evie, you're going to be okay." Jaylen brushes the hair away from my face. His eyes are frantic as they look over my body. "I can't believe that motherfucker stabbed you."

"I-It's okay," I wheeze, trying to suck more air into my lungs but they feel like they're on fire along with the rest of my body. The pain has returned in full force, the moment of reprieve a false sense of security. "I'm o-okay."

"No, you're not. You have a wooden stake through your chest for fuck's sake because you tried to save me."

And I would do it again, I want to say, but it hurts to speak.

As my vision blurs further, I can feel myself slipping away.

384

My head is heavy, and I can no longer move my limbs. Breathing is difficult and I can't think straight. All I want is to find peace away from the fire and burning. I just want—

"Keep your eyes open," Jaylen demands from above me, his eyes searching my face. "I'm not going to lose you, Ev. I will plunge a stake into my heart before I let you leave this earth. I only just got you, so I'm not going to lose you now."

Unable to speak, all I can do is smile up at him as a single tear slides down my cheek. Even if I were to die right now, I would be content knowing I got to spend the time I did with Jaylen. I didn't want to admit it for fear of having my heart broken, but I'm falling for this man. My brother's best friend. A vampire. The man makes me feel protected and safe, and that is all I have ever wanted—to feel safe.

I'm his girl without a doubt. His little angel. And that's something I'm happy to take to my grave.

"I'm not letting you die," he grunts as his fangs pierce through his gums, glinting under the streetlamps. "Over my fucking dead body."

The sound of skin ripping reaches my ears, but all I can focus on is the white light forming above me in the shape of a halo. If this is my time to go, I will gladly step into the light. I just know my parents will be waiting for me and that thought comforts me more than the peace I'm seeking from the pain splitting me in two.

Something hot and metallic fills my mouth, almost choking me, before my vision darkens and I feel my soul leave my body, floating in the open air above.

Is this what it feels like to die?

EPILOGUE

Darkness. That's all I can see.

I don't know which way is up or if anything is around me at all. It just feels like I'm floating, suspended in the air as I float away for all eternity. My fingers are numb, and my limbs feel heavy. Everything hurts.

Do I exist? Or is this just a nightmare I can't seem to get out of?

The darkness threatens to consume all my senses, forcing my eyes shut. The thought scares me, but my body hurts too much to care. If I just let go, will the ringing in my ears silence and the pain in my limbs cease?

Maybe that's what I need—peace and quiet.

If I close my eyes and let go, will I finally get that? The peace that I have been searching for since the death of my parents?

My head grows foggy as my body feels like it goes into freefall, the darkness pulling me under, under, under until the pain stops and my mind clears.

Is this what it feels like to be truly at peace? To just let everything... go?

I smile, the darkness no longer scaring me as it did before.

In fact, I welcome it. If I could lie in this position, pain-free, I would gladly accept my fate, because I no longer want to be in pain.

But just as quick as the peace came, a fire spread through my veins, forcing my eyes open. My limbs feel heavy, and my heart is squeezing in my chest painfully. I'm unable to get fresh air into my lungs as I stare at the darkness around me, gasping, painfully aware of the blood pumping in my veins.

In the distance, the darkness opens to reveal a bright white light shining down on me, blinding me momentarily. The pain increases, and once again, I feel as though I'm floating. Higher and higher I go until I reach the base of the light.

The searing pain inside my chest deepens as I stare at the beam of light. And within the blink of an eye, I've descended into darkness once again.

Thank you for reading Blood Sport! Sorry about the ending—I know that was rough and may leave a lot of you heartbroken. But just know I didn't want to do it. I had to do it for the plot. SORRY! In saying that, I appreciate you reaching the end of the book and (hopefully) loving Evie and Jaylen's relationship as much as I do. Their story will continue in Blood Night, Book 2 of the Blood Lover—coming soon, I promise!

ACKNOWLEDGMENTS

Woah, I can't believe I made it to this point after so many unfinished book ideas I just felt 'weren't good enough' to be my debut novel. But when Evie and Jaylen's idea popped into my head, I knew it was a match made in heaven. I wanted to write a story that incorporated all of my favorite tropes— brother's best friend, sports romance, and vampires—and just hoped it wouldn't be a huge mess, but thankfully, the story turned out the way I envisioned it.

The idea for this story just randomly popped into my mind after having a discussion with my friend, Haley, about there not being enough vampire stories available these days. I knew from then that I wanted to write a vampire story for her and anyone else who was still in their *Vampire Diaries*, *Twilight*, and *True Blood* era. I knew for Evie and Jaylen's relationship that I wanted it to be a lot of push and pull, so I hope I achieved that. It's always fun to write a character's internal conflict—namely Evie's—of walking that fine line of keeping a safe difference from someone they know they shouldn't be with but also the potential of one wrong step and falling in love, bringing with it drama, passion, and above all, intense desire and lust. It was certainly a fun process developing these characters!

If it weren't for the lovely people in my life who helped me get this book over the finish line, I would still be stuck in the 'is this good enough?' mindset.

I would like to thank my amazing beta-beta readers—Haley and Kellie. If it weren't for their good ideas and motivation, this book would be nothing. I can only thank you so much, but I'm going to do it again. THANK YOU!

Next, I want to thank my wonderful editor—Anisa. She is one of my closest friends and went out of her way to make sure this book was the best it could be. She hated the late-night editing sprints, but she did it for me and I couldn't be more grateful for her.

To my lovely beta readers who gave me the best advice—Lili, Rushanea, and Annastasia. Your feedback helped enhance the plot and storytelling of this book, so thank you for all of your hard work and willingness to help.

To my wonder partner for having to listen to me talk about ideas I had for this book and listening whenever I got excited by my beta readers' reactions to the ending of the book.

To Melissa for designing the most stunning book cover I have ever seen. It was an absolute pleasure to work with you!

To Emily for the AMAZING character art of Evie and Jaylen. You brought my vision of them to life, and I'm obsessed.

Lastly, I want to thank my readers who read my book. I appreciate the support you show me so generously. You're all amazing!

I can't wait to continue Evie and Jaylen's story in Book 2!

ABOUT THE AUTHOR

Chloe lives by the beach in New South Wales, Australia, with her two fluffy cats, partner, and twin sister. Ever since she was young, she has always loved to read and create stories in her mind whenever an idea presented itself and got into the romance genre in high school by reading *After* by Anna Todd on Wattpad. In recent years, her love for storytelling grew and she decided it was finally time to put pen to paper and share her ideas. She is always coming up with new ideas, so stay tuned for future projects.

Let's connect!

If you would like to keep up to date with me and learn about any future projects, please follow me on social media:

Instagram: @chloehigginsauthor

TikTok: @chloehigginsauthor

Goodreads: Chloe Higgins

If you would like to leave a review of Blood Sport and share your thoughts on the book, I would greatly appreciate it!